P9-EDJ-389

A LIFE ON THE LINE

Elizabeth ran breathlessly through the night streets. She no longer looked back over her shoulder. Her feet hurt. Her throat was scraped raw by her ragged breath. But she wasn't getting those messages. Her mind was too narrowly focused once she'd realized what might be about to happen.

She ran up the steps of the police station and slammed through the double doors. Behind a long counter stood a white-haired cop whose bored expression didn't change. A black phone stood silently at his elbow. Elizabeth put her hands on the counter inches from it.

"I have to use that phone," she said.

The desk cop pointed at the far wall. "Pay phone."

"I don't have any money. Someone's life is in danger." She saw immediately that that didn't impress him. She started over. "I have a crime to report. A very serious crime, but I'm not going to do it until you let me make a call."

"Calling your lawyer?"

She shook her head. "My husband. Please!"

Finally he sighed, reached into his pocket, put a dime on the desk between them. She snatched up the coin and ran.

The phone rang three times. Elizabeth pictured it ringing in the room where his body lay unmoving on the floor. Then he answered.

"John. Thank God. Listen," she said.

"Where are you? I thought you'd be—"

"John!" Her voice, slightly higher, stopped him. "Listen. You've got to get out of there right now. Now, John. Mr. Cook has been murdered."

"At the office? Elizabeth, get away from there! You don't know, they might—"

"I'm at the police station. Downtown." She gave him the address. "I'm all right. But the men who killed him are on their way to our house. *Please*, John! Get out of there now. Hurry!"

TRIPWIRE

Jay Brandon

BANTAM BOOKS
TORONTO • NEW YORK • LONDON • SYDNEY • AUCKLAND

This is for Mark Brandon and
Jo Ann Brandon.

TRIPWIRE

A Bantam Book / June 1987

All rights reserved.
Copyright © 1987 by Jay Brandon.
Cover art copyright © 1987 by Larry Lurin.
This book may not be reproduced in whole or in part, by
mimeograph or any other means, without permission.
For information address: Bantam Books, Inc.

ISBN 0-553-26279-3

Published simultaneously in the United States and Canada

Bantam Books are published by Bantam Books, Inc. Its trademark, consisting of the
words "Bantam Books" and the portrayal of a rooster, is registered in U.S. Patent
and Trademark Office and in other countries. Marca Registrada. Bantam Books,
Inc., 666 Fifth Avenue, New York, New York 10103.

PRINTED IN THE UNITED STATES OF AMERICA

O   0 9 8 7 6 5 4 3 2

PART I

Dislocation

CHAPTER ONE

Baltimore, September 1975

*E*lizabeth felt safer in the circle of light. She looked back down the alley to her car and it seemed very far away. When she had parked there and looked down this dark alley she had almost decided not to get out of the car. But the moment's foreboding had passed. She had convinced herself to be matter-of-fact, gathered up the heavy set of books and started down the alley, moving faster and faster until she reached the light over the door. From there she looked back. The alley was still reassuringly empty. It was a very narrow passage. Three men standing abreast would have filled it. For most of its length it was dark; only this back door of her office building was illuminated, and now Elizabeth was spotlighted as well as the door. She would have preferred the front entrance, but she only had a key to the back.

The night was quiet. It seemed to Elizabeth that in her youth downtown had been more festive and crowded, even at ten o'clock on a weeknight. She wasn't sure if the city had changed or if she had just gotten older and more timid.

She stood by the back door, under the light, going slowly through her key ring. She had never used this key before—she had never been to the office at night—so she couldn't remember what the key looked like, and could only find it by eliminating all the others. The old brick office building loomed ten stories above her head, obliviously, as if its back were turned to her. The bricks were old and worn, making the metal door look shiny by comparison.

There was a faint noise and the two heavy accounting ledgers Elizabeth carried slithered in her grasp. She almost lost one of them. The books were the reason she was here. She had worked for Empire Sales for only two weeks. It was a small company, not very well-run, but Elizabeth had been glad to be hired when she'd gone back into the job market at the age of forty-five. Her skills were rusty, but she was eager to make herself useful. Her boss, Roger Cook, always did the books himself. It was clear he hated that part of the job—he struggled and cursed over them—but apparently couldn't afford to hire a bookkeeper. Elizabeth had some bookkeeping experience herself, but her experience was two decades old. She wasn't confident enough to volunteer to take over the chore from Mr. Cook, but she wanted to be helpful and she wouldn't have minded getting a raise. This afternoon, when Mr. Cook had suddenly thrown down his pencil in disgust, Elizabeth had seen her chance. As soon as Mr. Cook left she had gathered up the account books and taken them home with her. Her idea had been to familiarize herself with his accounting system overnight and then, when she did volunteer to start keeping the books for him, astound her boss with how quickly she picked it up.

It had been an impulsive move and she had soon regretted it. Going over the books at home after dinner, she had quickly gotten lost in the figures. She couldn't follow a balance from one page to the next. Sums of money appeared from nowhere and then disappeared back into the same void. As soon as she thought she had found the main thread of the business's costs and profits it would disappear down an unseen rabbit hole. Finally, for reasons she couldn't articulate, the books had begun to make her uneasy. She didn't want them in her house any more. She didn't want Mr. Cook to get to the office before she did in the morning and find them missing. She had packed up the books again and returned to the office. By this time darkness had fallen and the neighborhood around the office building had emptied. Unconsciously Elizabeth had tried to muffle her footsteps and the jingle of her keys. It felt criminal to be here at night.

She finally found the right key, pushed the door open, and reached for the hall light switch, but stopped when she realized there was already light coming from the office down the hall. That was the Empire Sales offices, her offices, four small rooms off this little-traveled corridor.

Elizabeth caught the heavy street door before it slammed shut and eased it closed behind her. The books felt terribly heavy in her arms. She wished she'd never picked them up. She walked briskly down the hallway, in a hurry to drop the books off and get home again. This ground-floor wing felt divorced from the rest of the building. It was always colder and darker. At the end of this long corridor, where the hallway turned right and opened to the lobby and the front doors of the building, the air turned brighter and more comforting. Most of the offices in the other wing and on the upper floors were busier during the day with customers coming in and out, but Empire Sales did all its business through field representatives or by mail. They hadn't had a visitor in the two weeks Elizabeth had worked there.

As she came closer she wondered if the lights were always left on all night. But when she was halfway to the door she heard a voice, and stopped. Mr. Cook had returned. Elizabeth thought about turning and leaving again, but if he had already discovered the missing books it would be better to return them now than to let him think they were gone completely. When she stopped moving the books became an even heavier burden. She sighed. Mr. Cook might even call the police, and even when she explained he would probably still fire her. She was going to be furious with herself if this cost her her new job.

Elizabeth walked on more slowly, close to the right-hand wall. The corridor was narrowed by cardboard cartons stacked against the wall opposite her office door. It gave the hallway an unprofessional air, more like a warehouse than an office building. She edged past them to the door of the Empire Sales offices and peeked in. If Mr. Cook was in one of the other offices she might be able to slip the books back into place before he noticed her.

But it was the outer office that was occupied, and by more than her boss. The front office was the largest room, with more open space than the small inner offices. Its only furnishings were a secretary's desk and tall metal bookshelves against the wall opposite the door. The shelves were sparsely filled with bulky sample books and catalogues and two or three pieces of equipment that looked to Elizabeth like carburetors or other engine parts. She could smell their faint oiliness now.

Elizabeth stopped outside the door and looked in. She didn't want to interrupt Mr. Cook's business, whether it was personal or professional. But she was hopeful now that since someone else was in the office her boss hadn't had occasion to look for the accounting ledgers.

There were three men. During the day the room looked merely tacky, but tonight it looked harsh, like a cell. Mr. Cook was the only one sitting, in a hard-backed wooden chair. He looked as if he'd been drinking, and hadn't yet been home to change clothes after work. His tie was pulled askew, his white shirt crumpled, his hair falling into his face. But his eyes were alert. He kept them steadily on the second man, who paced in front of him. This second man was much more elegantly dressed, in a three-piece suit and tie, but that was not what made his appearance memorable. He was very big, tall and seventy pounds overweight, with heavy features and thick-fingered hands. One hand was very pale, the blood forced out of it by the force with which it was clenched into a fist.

Elizabeth didn't notice the third man at first. He wasn't rumpled at all. His three-piece suit fit him with no more wrinkles than appeared on his boyish face. His blonde hair was casually in place, dipping onto his forehead. Much the youngest of the three men, he leaned against the far wall, watching both the others. The other two men radiated tension, but this one was smiling slightly. Elizabeth was in his line of sight. She drew back until the slice of the room she could see contained only Mr. Cook and the big angry man.

Now the angry man stopped with his back to her. Maybe he assumed a more reasonable expression. At least his voice was calm. "You're not a good manager, Roger." It took Elizabeth a moment to realize he was talking to Mr. Cook. "I never should have thought you would be. I did think you could take orders. But you got in way over your head. I think it's time—"

"There's nothing wrong with the business," Mr. Cook said quickly. He sounded sullen. "We could make a profit. I just need—"

"It's not a business!" the big man shouted, whirling on him. "Are you out of your mind? What do I want with a profit? So the IRS can audit me? If you had the brains of a rat—"

"If you'd just listen—" Mr. Cook began.

Elizabeth heard the smack almost before she saw the big man's arm move, and when he stepped back there was blood on Mr. Cook's cheekbone. After this physical exertion the big man's shoulder's dropped a little. "I didn't come to have a discussion with you." His voice was softer now. "You're out, understand? I don't know if I need somebody dumber or smarter for this, but you're not it."

He turned and walked toward a briefcase sitting on one of the metal shelves opposite the doorway. Elizabeth drew back as he passed her position. She was gripping the ledgers tightly so that their covers wouldn't scratch against each other. When she looked back around the doorway she saw the big man again standing in front of Mr. Cook, extending some papers toward him. "Just sign this," he said. "You're selling the business to Danny." The big man nodded slightly toward the young man against the far wall, and the reason for the young man's slight smile now seemed apparent. "For the time being. We'll find someone with a little more—"

"You're nuts," Mr. Cook said. His voice had gone too shrill. "Why should I? I haven't screwed up anything. You don't have the right—"

The big man looked amazed at this show of defiance. But then his face swiftly reddened and the papers he'd been holding slipped from his huge hand.

"You bastard!" he yelled, lunging toward Mr. Cook. "You think I need you to sign? I'll just inherit it from you!"

Elizabeth saw him raise his fist high. Mr. Cook tried to dodge aside but the fist followed him and slammed into the side of his head with a thud that made Elizabeth take an involuntary step closer. Until that blow fell she had watched the argument from an emotional distance, wondering how its outcome would affect her. That slight worry fled when she saw Mr. Cook almost slide out of the chair and the big man grab him by the throat and hold him in place. He shook him until Mr. Cook's head flopped bonelessly.

The third man, the young one, came forward and looked on worriedly. Elizabeth didn't realize she'd made a noise until he looked at her. In stepping toward Mr. Cook she had exposed herself in the doorway. The young man put his hand on the angry man's arm and they both turned to look at her. She stood perfectly still, as if immobility would make her invisible.

The young blonde man smiled. "Come in," he said. "Don't worry, it's all right." He took a step toward her.

His step released Elizabeth. The ledgers slipped out of her hands and she ran. Not the way she'd come: the alley door had to be opened with a key from inside as well as out and there was no time to get her keys out. The other end of the corridor was shorter anyway. She bumped into a stack of cardboard cartons and one fell, almost tripping her as she scrambled toward the corner, desperate to get out of sight.

Even in such a seemingly dangerous situation, the first thing you worry about is your dignity. Maybe she hadn't really seen what she thought she had. Maybe she was making a fool of herself by running away, starting a series of jokes she'd never hear the end of. So it was a sort of relief when she heard the gunshot and saw the small hole open in the wall ahead of her. She could run in earnest then, nothing ladylike about it, scrambling, graceless, clawing handfuls of air out of her path. She could also scream, and hear the sound spiral through the empty building.

She turned the corner to the right before another shot was fired, and was running through the small lobby of the building. The front doors were to her right, the way she came in every morning, but they would be locked now. She didn't even veer toward them. To her left was the closed door of the elevator. As she ran past it she slapped her palm against the button, but the elevator was on a higher floor. She didn't slow down. Ahead of her was another corridor that entered the lobby perpendicularly to the one from which she'd just emerged. She had only been down that way once, when she'd come to apply for her job and didn't know which wing held the Empire Sales offices. She didn't know if there was another exit from the building this way. She just wanted to be out of sight before the man behind her came pounding into the lobby. The semi-darkness of the second corridor was welcome as she ran into it. She flung open the first door she came to, on the right-hand side of the hall, but her panicked body wouldn't stop there. She caromed across the hall to a second door, and through it.

Elizabeth almost screamed again when she saw that she was in an office. There was no other exit. She clamped her teeth together and remained quiet. There were heavy curtains on the far wall and silently she crossed to them. She could dive through the window even if it was locked. Elizabeth pulled one of the curtains aside and saw a blackboard, not a window. She turned and looked around the small dark room again, hunching down. The only way out was through the door. The door she'd left open. Elizabeth crumpled slowly to the floor, waiting for that doorway to be filled by the man with the gun.

The young man with the gun skidded to a stop in the lobby. He could no longer hear the woman's footsteps, so he knew she had run to earth somewhere. He glanced around the empty lobby. No place to hide there. He crossed it quickly and moved into the other hallway.

The first office door, on the right, was open slightly. He smiled a bit and kicked it violently open. He had seen too much television to allow someone to hide behind a door on him. The door hit the wall and bounced back toward him. He stopped it with his foot and stepped inside. He turned on the light. It was a small office. The only place to hide was behind the desk. He walked toward it slowly, still glancing around the rest of the room, then suddenly jumped behind the desk. He frowned at the emptiness.

There was a sudden noise in the building, the sound of the elevator arriving in the lobby. The man with the gun ran out of the office, leaving the light on, and took the four or five steps back to the lobby. The elevator doors gaped open, but no one was inside. He walked closer to make sure. The door closed in his face, but not before he'd made sure the elevator was empty. He frowned around the lobby and walked back into the hall-way, passing the lighted office he'd already searched. The next door, across the hall, was also open. He hit the lights and looked around. There was no one hiding behind the desk. This office was also empty. He took one more look around and stopped. He grinned again, aiming the grin at the toes of the shoes peeking out at the bottom of the heavy curtain behind the desk. He waited a moment, being careful, then shot two holes in the curtain, four feet above the shoes.

When Elizabeth heard the shots she slipped out of the first office across the hall, the lighted, already-searched office she'd slipped into when the man with gun had gone back to check the elevator. She ran noiselessly now in her stocking feet, into the lobby and toward the elevator doors. She ran inside the elevator cage, pushed the highest button, and ran out again, across the lobby and back into the first corridor.

The man with the gun had discovered that the shoes were empty. When he heard the elevator again he ran into the lobby and pressed the button, then stood watching the indicator, waiting to see which floor she got out on. There was no exit from the building on those higher floors. He had her now.

Elizabeth passed quickly along the corridor, glancing over her shoulder. She had heard the man run into the lobby and stop, so her plan had worked. Then she stepped into the light from the office doorway. When she turned, she saw Mr. Cook's body slumped on the floor, saw the big man looking disdainfully down at him, and she gasped. For a moment Elizabeth forgot the other man's presence, she was so startled by how obviously dead Mr. Cook was. But then the big man turned. He didn't make any other movement, and for a long moment their eyes held each other. Time stopped; they almost seemed to recognize each other. The frozen moment broke when he started toward her, barely raising his voice to call, "Danny! Danny, she's here."

Elizabeth ran down the corridor, fumbling her keys out of her purse again. She almost dropped them, but before they fell she juggled them aloft and found the right key at the same time. The lock on the back door eluded her as she tried to insert the key, and she realized her hand was shaking. She heard footsteps and looked back to see Danny appear at the far end of the corridor just as the big man stepped through the office doorway. He was in Danny's line of fire, which gave Elizabeth time to get her key in the lock and turn it. Danny was already pounding down the hallway, covering the distance twice as fast as she could run. Elizabeth fled out the door, leaving her keys dangling in the lock.

Danny was confident he could still catch her. As he came out the door he saw her at the end of the alley. He could run her down. Even if that was her car parked right there, she wouldn't have time to get in it and get away.

Elizabeth realized that. She didn't pause at the car. Besides, she no longer had her keys. The shortness of the downtown blocks saved her momentarily. She had less distance to cover to the next street intersection than Danny did coming down the long alley. By the time he emerged from it she had already turned the corner and was out of sight. Danny ran to the intersection and looked both ways. There was no sight of her. He didn't know which way to go until he saw her purse lying at his feet, the purse to which she'd clung through all the pursuit. He turned the corner by the purse and ran.

*E*lizabeth didn't hear running footsteps behind her any more, but she kept running even after she began to hope she was safe. She didn't have her house keys or car keys or enough money for a cab or even a phone call; she was alone downtown at night, without her shoes, but at least she was alive.

She had dropped her purse in panic because it was slowing her down. Then, in a burst of inspiration, she had run across the street and around the opposite corner. Elizabeth wanted to laugh aloud now at how well it had worked. She had never been pursued before, never known how elusive she could be, how quickly smart.

It was minutes before she realized she hadn't been smart. The killer wouldn't find her, but he would return to the office. He'd take the purse back to his boss, and they'd both be gone before she could bring police. Gone with her purse, her keys, her wallet.

Her name and address.

CHAPTER TWO

*E*lizabeth ran breathlessly through the night streets. She no longer looked back over her shoulder. She didn't hesitate at intersections, but flung herself out into the street. Scared to death that she wouldn't get to a phone in time, she was almost oblivious to potential dangers around her. She was thinking only of the real danger that had turned immediate again. The downtown streets seemed much brighter. Elizabeth ran past a group of black teenagers on a corner, but didn't notice that they turned to stare at her. At the mouth of an alley three startled faces looked up. One of the ragged men stood and started toward her. Elizabeth ran on. She was heading for a dimly-remembered police station that was blocks and blocks and blocks away. She kept her eye out for police cars too, but of course she saw none. The only cars that passed her looked shrouded and sinister.

At the next intersection she almost fell onto the hood of a car that skidded to a stop in front of her. Elizabeth didn't look through its windshield, just stood there breathing heavily, waiting for it to move on. But the car sat where it was. After a moment she ran around it. As she crossed the street she glanced up at the street sign. Only one of the names of the intersecting streets was familiar. She hesitated, turned, and kept running. Her feet hurt. Her throat was scarped raw by her ragged breath. But Elizabeth wasn't getting those messages. Her mind was too narrowly focused once she'd realized what might be about to happen.

Much later she ran up the steps of the police station, its lights already dismissing her memory of her run. Her unprotected heel came down on a sharp pebble but her ankle didn't turn. All her muscles were too tight for release. She slammed through the double doors. Without that noise her entrance would have gone unannounced. Her shoeless feet made only the slightest patter as she ran across the floor to the long counter. Behind it stood a white-haired cop whose bored expression didn't change, though he watched her closely. A black phone stood silently at his elbow. Elizabeth put her hands on the counter inches from it.

"I have to use that phone," she said.

The desk cop didn't even glance at it. He flipped the pencil in his fingers so that it pointed at the far wall. "Pay phone."

"I don't have any money." Elizabeth displayed her empty hands, keeping her voice calm. It would take even longer if she raved.

"This phone's for official business," the desk cop told her. He waited for her answer. She had piqued his interest, just a little.

"Someone's life is in danger," Elizabeth said tightly, but saw immediately that that didn't impress him. He heard people say that every day, ten times an hour. She started over: "I have a crime to report. A very serious crime, but I'm not going to do it until you let me make a call."

The desk cop inhaled, held it a moment, released it through his nose. "Calling your lawyer?"

She shook her head. "My husband. He's at home." Her voice rose slightly.

The cop considered that, and her, a moment longer. "What's the crime?" he finally asked. Her lips closed on each other. "You know it's a crime not to report a crime?" he said. She continued to stare at him. Her eyes were no longer just fierce; each held a cuticle of unshed tears. Finally she reached for the phone. The old cop put a hand on hers, stopping her. "Please!" she said, her voice no longer tightly controlled. The cop didn't release her hand. Finally he sighed, reached into his pocket, put a dime on the desk between them. He nodded toward the pay phone. She snatched up the coin and ran.

The phone rang three times. Elizabeth pictured it ringing in the room where his body lay unmoving on the floor. The image was only shoved a little way into the future when he answered.

"John. Thank God. Listen," she said.

"Where are you? I thought you'd be—"

"John!" Her voice, slightly higher, stopped him. "Listen. You've got to get out of there right now. Now, John. Mr. Cook has been murdered." She bit off the story. She was keeping him on the phone.

"At the office?" John said, his voice suddenly crisper. "Elizabeth, get away from there! You don't know, they might—"

"I'm at the police station. One downtown." She gave him the address. "I'm all right. But the men who killed him are on their way to our house. *Please*, John! Get out of there now." She turned and looked at the white-haired desk cop. He was leaning toward her curiously but couldn't hear what she was saying.

"Hurry." She hung up the phone so John couldn't say anything else. But she pictured him. John would look at the phone, glance around their living room, think about calling the police station to continue the conversation. The story about the killers coming to their house didn't make sense from what she'd told him; he'd puzzle over it. He'd stand there at the phone for a minute thinking. Finally he would start moving, but he'd stop at the couch to put his shoes on, glance at the television from there, finally start up the stairs to their bedroom, where he would collect his keys and his wallet and his loose change, then pat all his pockets to make sure he had everything. On the way out he would stop at the hall closet while he decided whether he should wear a jacket. At first he'd think no, he'd just keep the car windows rolled up if it was cool, but then he'd remember he was going to a police station, so he'd better look a little more respectable. He'd be thinking about Elizabeth, not himself, concerned for her but knowing she was already safe. Elizabeth knew all the things he'd do before he left the house, and a car might be pulling up in front during any of his little preparations. He probably didn't even have his shoes on yet, and he didn't know what was coming for him. She wanted to scream. She wished they had moved farther out into the suburbs as they'd talked about doing when their son was young, but they never had. Their house was only a fifteen-minute drive from her office building. It was convenient.

She walked slowly back to the desk, counting, imagining where John would be now, and where the other men would be.

"So what's the crime?" the desk cop said when she stood in

front of his counter again, looking down at the floor, forgetting where she was. "And don't tell me it's that somebody snatched your shoes."

"It was murder," Elizabeth said quietly. "I saw a man kill someone." She started shaking. When she said it it was as if they were in the room with her again, the big man staring at her with his cold eyes.

The desk cop was a little embarrassed about his joke. He covered that with details and paperwork. Elizabeth saw that her naming of the crime hadn't appalled him. He heard it every day. But it was her first murder.

He wanted her to go upstairs and talk to a homicide detective, but Elizabeth wouldn't leave the lobby. She kept watching the doors as she talked. Every time they opened her heart lifted and failed. The station stayed quieter than she would have thought. Like the downtown it served it was fairly quiet and uncrowded on a weeknight. The desk cop wrote as Elizabeth talked. After a minute he called someone on an intercom and a plainclothes detective came down to listen to her story. Elizabeth listened to her voice rising, and she couldn't stop it. She knew she had to keep the hysteria at bay, make herself sound rational. But the most she could do was to stop talking from time to time when her voice went too wildly out of control. She was deeply grateful to the desk cop when he dispatched a patrol car to her house, and another to her office building. She told the story in a shattered version, then waited out their questions. When John got there everything would be fine. They'd both be safe for that night at least. It would be up to her then to save their lives. She had to make everyone, including John, believe the danger they were in. She had to convince them or die.

John had still not appeared when the two patrolmen radioed in their report from the office building. Just as Elizabeth had feared, they found Mr. Cook's body but no one else. Her purse was beside the body, the wallet missing. The desk cop wouldn't tell her anything more. The patrolmen who had gone to her house called in to say there was no one there.

Elizabeth stood by the desk, not letting any nervous habits take over her body. She didn't bite her nails or toy with her hair. The cops thought she looked remarkably composed. But she seemed to be losing her hearing. They had to raise their voices and ask questions twice. She would start talking and then her answer would trail off when the door opened. Finally the detectives were looking in that direction too. Elizabeth stood with her fists clenched at her sides, staring at that door. When John walked through it everything would be all right. She was willing to stand there all night waiting for him.

CHAPTER THREE

*H*alf an hour passed, very slowly for Elizabeth. After the men had stopped asking her questions a new one came to her with a Styrofoam cup of coffee, a thoughtful but wasted gesture, because as soon as she took it from him she forgot she was holding it. The young man had palely sandy hair and a smear of freckles across his nose. You had to look at him twice to see he wasn't a kid, and Elizabeth didn't. He began to ask her quiet questions about the two killers. They needed descriptions or anything that would help identify them. Had she seen the men's car, its license plate? Did the men call each other by name? Danny was the only name she remembered, and that didn't seem to be much help. It was her description of the big man that interested the young detective. It wasn't a description that would have fit very many people.

"Was he going a little—?" the detective began, starting to raise his hands to his head. Then he stopped himself and asked instead, "What did his hair look like?" He had to stop himself from forcing the description on her. But when she answered, "Very black, balding back to about here," he looked satisfied. After two or three more questions he hurried away. Before he did he gently took the cup of coffee from her fingers and set it on the counter beside her.

That left two detectives standing with her at her vigil. "This man—" one of them was asking her a few minutes later. Elizabeth could *not* have given a description of any of the detectives who had questioned her. Her eyes remained fastened on the front doors of the station house. "—the big man, the one who did the actual killing—did he have any kind of accent?"

"I don't know," she said distractedly. His voice hadn't impressed itself on her memory, not the way his face had. "I didn't notice. If he did it wasn't a thick one."

"But if he did have one," the detective persisted, "what kind do you think it was? I mean, not necessarily a foreign accent, maybe it was American, like say a New York accent. Do you know what—"

"John!"

He had just walked in. He didn't see her until she called his name, and by that time Elizabeth was running toward him. His hands were in his pockets but when Elizabeth reached him and threw her arms around him he held her instinctively, the force of her emotion excluding everything else for a moment. "Thank God," she said into his neck.

He was afraid she was crying. "It's all right." He was reaching up to stroke her hair when he noticed the men in the suits standing across the room staring, which made him suddenly feel awkward. But Elizabeth's slight trembling was much more important than the strangers across the room. He held her protectively and stared back at the men defiantly, until they glanced at each other and turned slightly away.

"It's all right," John said to her again. Her brief explanation on the phone had made no sense to him. He wondered if she was at the police station as a witness or a suspect.

Elizabeth still clung to him. She was amazed by his solidness. In the last hour she had almost come to believe he existed only in her imagination. John was of average height but stocky. Anyone glancing at him would have guessed he did something physical for a living. He was in his late forties but his arms around her felt as strong as when they were first married. For a moment Elizabeth was reassured, until she realized how little strength would mean against guns, or against the mountainous man she had seen kill Mr. Cook with his hands. She remembered that it was she who had to protect John.

"I'm okay," she said. She released him from her hug but kept hold of his arm as they walked across the room toward the detectives, who were watching them again, noncommittally. They fell into step with Elizabeth, behind the counter and up a flight of stairs.

"We'd like you to look at some pictures," one of the detectives said.

The heavy book of photographs the detective brought to Elizabeth reminded her of the ledgers she'd been carrying earlier that evening. If she'd left the ledgers where they belonged she never would have gotten involved in this, but Elizabeth wasn't the kind of person who broods about turning points. She absorbedly turned the pages of the big book, giving each picture a careful scrutiny. She understood what finding the right picture would mean, but she didn't dwell on that either.

John sat nearby—there was nothing he could do to help. He had already brought her all the coffee she wanted. He glanced down at her feet. She had them curled around the rungs of the hard chair in which she sat, so he could see the soles of her stockings, which were absolutely black from the filthy floors of the station. That trivial detail of her shoelessness continued to bother him. He didn't like the way it made her look, like someone captured in a raid.

All Elizabeth's attention was on the photographs. At first John had looked at them with her, but within a couple of pages the faces had begun to look alike to him. Now he was looking around the squadroom instead. It was a large room but had a low ceiling that made it look condensed. The lighting was fluorescent tubes, a harsh light. In the corner one of the tubes flickered now and again. The floor was just concrete, bare and cold. Five or six wooden desks were scattered around the room in no particular pattern. Like the Empire Sales offices, the room looked like something else—a warehouse or machine shop—temporarily disguised as an office.

An older man—older than the young cops, at any rate—came into the squadroom. John hadn't seen him before. He was a tall man with his thick hair gone mostly grey on the sides, and the kind of weathered skin you can't get from a sunlamp. The man's eyes went straight to Elizabeth as soon as he came in. The other cops in the room didn't snap to attention, but they were aware of this man's arrival. They watched him for a signal but he didn't give any. After a quick study of Elizabeth he crossed the room and disappeared into an inner office with a pebbled glass door. One of the buttons on the phone by John's hand lit up.

John wondered what the man's arrival meant. The other cops had obviously been waiting for him. His quick passage through the room had set off a reaction in the detectives. They were gathered in a little cluster around two of the desks halfway across the room from Elizabeth and John. Before they had been lounging, chatting lazily, what would you expect of cops waiting for an identification in one more routine murder. Now they spoke in lower tones to each other and were more obviously staring at Elizabeth, almost urging her on with their eyes.

Elizabeth hadn't noticed. She continued to turn the pages of the book slowly, with careful attention. After a few minutes one of the detectives detached himself from the group. He seemed to have been elected their emissary to the civilians. It was the young cop with the sprinkling of freckles who had earlier asked Elizabeth the more precise questions about the killer's appearance. He strolled up behind her, nodded at John, and looked at the pictures over Elizabeth's shoulder. John didn't think she'd noticed him until she spoke without looking up.

"Maybe he's not in your pictures," she said. "Maybe he's not a criminal, just a business partner of Mr. Cook's. This could be the first crime he ever committed."

John saw the detective start to say something, check himself, and say instead, "Maybe so. But you said his associate had a gun. I wouldn't think most businessmen travel with armed bodyguards. At least I hope not."

Elizabeth nodded abstractedly, turning a page. John stood up behind his wife, put his hands on her shoulders, and rubbed them a little. His touch was familiar; she didn't look up.

John saw the detective glance down at the page of photographs. The killer *was* in that book somewhere: John was sure that's what the young cop had almost said. And this was not the first crime he'd ever committed.

The young cop glanced up again, looking almost guilty when he saw John had seen him looking at the mug shots. He smiled sheepishly. "My name's Dennison, by the way," he said. "If you need anything—"

"Going home would be nice," John said.

"Yes," Dennison said, but it was just general agreement, not a promise.

"How soon do you think we can? After she identifies someone will you go arrest him right away?"

"Yes," the young cop said again, but this time it wasn't an answer at all. "We'll certainly try. But I don't know if you'll want to be going home tonight."

John had been right that the cops were keeping some sort of professional secret from him and Elizabeth. She hadn't even identified anyone yet but the cops already seemed to know what was going on. John put his hands on his wife's shoulders again. From the time he had seen her in the lobby of the police station tonight it had seemed that the danger was already past. Clearly it wasn't. But they couldn't live in a police station until the murderer was found. John tightened his grip on Elizabeth's shoulders.

Elizabeth was paying no attention to his conversation with the young detective. She had been looking for a full minute at one photograph. Finally she tapped it with her fingernail. "That's him," she said calmly, and continued to stare at the photograph. It was a wide face with quietly murderous eyes, as if the man wanted to kill the photographer but disliked the effort involved. The expression was the same one he had turned on Elizabeth two hours earlier. "That's the man," she said again.

Detective Dennison glanced down at the picture. When he looked up at John again his expression was sympathetic. "Are you sure?" he asked Elizabeth.

"That's him," she said again.

The detective left them and walked quickly to the office with the frosted glass door. He went in without knocking.

John was looking down at the photograph as if surprised on the street by someone he had known a long time ago. He had never seen the face before. But his wife's identification had suddenly made a formless idea immediately real. Here was a man who actually lived. He had killed another man in this city, tonight, and then had discovered Elizabeth watching him. Everything John had seen, down to his wife's shoeless feet, fell together for him abruptly. He remembered the panic he had heard in her voice when she'd called him on the phone. This face flattened on the page was a menace to both of them. "That's him?" John asked, squeezing her shoulder again. She nodded.

The frosted glass door opened and the young detective emerged. "Would both of you come in here, please?" he asked. He walked back to them and offered Elizabeth his hand to rise from the chair.

"This is Captain Jerek's office," he said as he waved them through the frosted glass door. Elizabeth thought it odd that he put it that way, as if he were introducing them to the room rather than to a person. The detective didn't follow them into the office but pulled the door shut behind them.

The only other person inside the small office was the tall, greying man John had seen earlier. Unlike the squadroom, this office had a window. The man was standing at it, looking down toward the street. When he turned he hesitated almost imperceptibly, to flash one searching look at the Truetts. Then he was coming toward them around the desk, his hand out.

"Sit down," he said. "You must be tired." He motioned at the only two visitors' chairs in the room, facing the desk. They were slat-backed, hard-bottomed wooden chairs. Standing might have been more comfortable, but the Truetts sat, looking up at him.

"I'm Bill Jerek," he said, and he and John shook hands, firmly but quickly, no wrestling match.

John estimated that Jerek was a few years older than himself, just slightly past fifty. Where John's stockiness suggested a lifetime of physical labor, Jerek looked like he had once been an athlete and had never gone to seed. Maybe a tight end in college; he had the broad shoulders and large hands. John felt more reassured than he had in the squadroom full of young detectives.

Jerek sat on the front edge of his desk, then stood again. He kept straying back toward the window. John and Elizabeth were both staring at him. Elizabeth looked very composed, John noticed. Just sitting there expectantly, paying close attention like a good girl in school.

When Jerek began to explain things to them he had a tendency to rush. Then he would consciously slow himself down. It was as if he were taking John and Elizabeth somewhere and would keep running ahead, then come back to shepherd them along. When he moved it was in the same manner, with an initial quick movement and then a deliberate slowing down, as when he rose from the desk in a rush but then paced slowly toward the window. This didn't give John the impression of nervousness on the captain's part. No: it was eagerness. Jerek wanted to be off and running, but he was making sure to get all the preliminaries right.

"First of all," Captain Jerek said, "we have to be sure what we're talking about." He handed Elizabeth a small photograph. "You're positive this is the man you saw?"

Elizabeth gave the picture more than a perfunctory glance and handed it back to him. "No, I'm positive that's *not* the man," she said politely. John looked down at her, startled. Had she realized the danger she was in and decided on this way out? But Elizabeth continued, "That's not the picture I just identified, either. There's some resemblance, but that man—" she nodded at the photograph in Jerek's hand "—looks more like Curly on *The Three Stooges.*"

Jerek snorted a small laugh, looking down at the picture. "My brother-in-law," he finally said, and dropped the picture on the desk. "I'm sorry, stupid trick. But I do have to make sure." Again he seated himself on the edge of the desk, right in front of her, as he drew more pictures from his shirt pocket and handed them to Elizabeth. "Could you pick him out of this group, please?"

Jerek put his hands on his legs, leaning slightly forward. He was very still, but that suppressed eagerness was apparent.

Elizabeth spread the group of six pictures on her lap. "I just picked him out of a whole book of pictures," she said. "I don't see why—"

"But this is a similar physical group," Jerek said.

That was true, the six did bear a strong resemblance. John studied the pictures while Elizabeth did. Six broad, small-mouthed faces looked back at him. John thought he recognized the face Elizabeth had shown him in the other room, but she picked up a different photo and handed it to the captain. "This one," she said, and a moment later she handed over one of the other pictures as well, saying, "And this one too, I think."

Jerek only glanced at the two photos and then held them apparently forgotten in his hand as he stared at her, making no polite pretense otherwise, obviously deciding what he had to work with. Elizabeth stared back at him. She was forty-six; slim, with unconscious good posture that hadn't deserted her even tonight. Her back didn't touch the back of the chair. She sat there as if waiting for instructions. Jerek was impressed with her. He liked her, and because of that he felt sorry for her. Elizabeth saw both those emotions in his eyes, the liking and the fear, and she saw the emotions combine into longing—not for her, exactly, but she was involved in it.

John cleared his throat. Before that small sound died away Jerek was speaking. In the same instant he had moved again, back toward the window.

"The man you identified," he said, "is named Marco Galvan. Tonight is not the first time he's killed someone. Or robbed someone. Or extorted a business out from under a man.

But if he gets convicted of this murder it *will* be the first time he's been convicted of anything.'' He turned to face them, looking at John as well as Elizabeth. "You understand? His job is hurting people and he's very good at it because he enjoys it. He's better at it than we've been at making a case against him. He's a careful man—"

"He wasn't careful tonight," Elizabeth said.

"No. He gets carried away. He has a vicious temper and no conscience at all as far as I can tell. But so far it hasn't gotten him in trouble. That's the kind of man I'm trying to tell you he is: mean enough to kill someone on a whim, and smart enough to get away with it."

Jerek stopped talking. John found that he was holding Elizabeth's hand between their chairs. He couldn't remember having reached for it.

Jerek didn't seem to be waiting for a response—he had just gotten lost in his own thoughts. "If you're trying to ask if I'm willing to testify against him—" Elizabeth said rather loudly.

"Now think about this," John cautioned her, but he already knew she would do it, and that he couldn't talk her out of it.

"I know you will," Jerek said soothingly, already as sure of her as John was. "Besides, even saying you wouldn't testify wouldn't make you safe from him. It wouldn't make a bit of difference to him."

Jerek said "him" the way some religious groups won't give the devil a name. There was loathing in the pronoun.

"All right," Elizabeth said, mollified. "I said I will, there's no point in trying to scare me. If you're still worried that I won't be able to identify him, you could arrange a lineup. Isn't that what you usually do next?"

"That's what we usually do when we've arrested someone," Jerek said. "That's our problem. I sent a squad car to Galvan's house an hour ago, but no one's there."

"An hour ago?" John said. It hadn't been fifteen minutes since Elizabeth had picked out the photo of Marco Galvan.

"Young Dennison out there, who wants to be Sherlock Holmes when he grows up, thought from Mrs. Truett's description that it might be Galvan involved in this and he called me at home." Jerek paused, but went on with his thought. "It's pretty well known in this department that I have a strong continuing interest in Marco Galvan. Some people think he's my hobby."

"And he's already gone," John said, following the main thread of his own thoughts. "Does that mean he already—"

"I wouldn't call it conclusive," Jerek said. "But I have a strong feeling he won't be making any more public appearances. Not until he—until we find him."

But John and Elizabeth had heard him change thoughts in midstream. "And Elizabeth won't be safe until then," John said.

"She'll be as safe as I can make her." Jerek made one of those sudden moves and then was standing immobile beside the window—not silhouetted in it. He was staring out at the night not fearfully, John thought, but possessively. Jerek rested his hand, just the fingertips, on the glass of the window. There was some business out there he wanted to be about. It almost seemed that it didn't involved Elizabeth or John at all, that they were keeping him from it.

"How safe is that?" John asked bluntly.

Jerek looked at both of them. He hadn't planned to tell them, but now he thought maybe he should. It might do them good to be scared. John, he noticed, was starting to look defiant. But when he looked at Elizabeth he saw her staring back at him. She had moved her chair slightly so that the door of the office was no longer at her back. She had both it and the window in her peripheral vision. *She knows*, Jerek thought. She understands the danger perfectly. Her husband doesn't yet. He doesn't quite believe in it: he didn't see Galvan. John was still trying to fit life into a mold Elizabeth had seen shattered. They both had a right to know what they were up against.

"There's only been one other time I had a good case against Galvan," Jerek said. "I knew I finally had him. We had arrested one of his men on robbery and assault charges that would have been good for twenty years in prison at a minimum. He decided he'd rather make a deal. This guy had been an eyewitness to a lot of Galvan's business, including at least one murder. As a witness he wasn't what you'd call ideal, since he'd been in on it all himself, but he was a vivid talker. I think a jury would have believed him."

Jerek stopped. "But . . ." John prompted him.

"He didn't last three days," Jerek said.

Elizabeth spoke up for the first time in minutes. "He was murdered right here." When Jerek looked at her in surprise, she explained, "I remember reading it in the newspaper."

"Yeah," Jerek said. They could see it still pained him to admit it. "He was killed right in this building."

That put a stop to conversation for a minute as they all thought about how long Elizabeth had been inside the police station. Jerek's attention returned to the window. His fingers were on it again, pressing hard. Then his eyes shifted slightly and it was Elizabeth he saw reflected in the glass, as if she were hovering out there in the night, high in the air for everyone to see.

"So you have a new plan this time I hope," John finally said. "Someplace else to take her?"

"It could take a while, couldn't it?" Elizabeth said.

"It certainly could," Jerek said, but he was thinking that it would probably all be over, one way or the other, very soon.

"I was hoping we could get some things from home," Elizabeth said.

Jerek snorted. "You're not going near your house again, not until we find that—" He didn't finish.

"I know," Elizabeth said with a slight edge in her voice, and he realized he'd insulted her. "I hoped one of your men could pick up a few things—"

"He'd kill ten men before he realized you weren't with them," Jerek said bluntly. "He'll be too frantic tonight. No one's going to your house tonight. Unless—" He looked suddenly concerned. "There's just the two of you, isn't there? No children at home?"

"No children," Elizabeth said. Jerek hadn't noticed the slight pause before her answer. John felt her gripping his hand more tightly.

"Good," Jerek said. He came and stood in front of them, suddenly very tall. "Now our first problem is getting you out of here without being seen."

But the much bigger problem, Jerek was thinking, was that he still didn't know which member of his trusted circle had betrayed him the last time.

CHAPTER FOUR

Jerek kept his eyes almost constantly on the rearview mirror. There was one pair of headlights back there that had stayed steadily with him ever since he had turned onto the highway. It was too far back for him to identify the car.

There was movement from the back seat behind him. "Can we get up now?" John Truett's voice came muffled from under the blanket.

"Not yet," Jerek said.

The simplest plan had seemed the best, for him to take the Truetts himself, quickly, before Galvan could organize watchers at the station house. The trouble with the best plan, though, was that it left him isolated with his charges, beyond the range of help. If Galvan's spy had already been at the station, and had already alerted the gangster—

The headlights behind him turned off. Jerek put on speed. They could be following him in relays, one car keeping him in sight until another was in position. Jerek was outside the city now, the streetlights left far behind. He felt very alone in the night.

They were heading north, the direction Jerek had taken automatically. He had a hunting cabin in that direction, some twenty miles from Baltimore. The only times he ever left the city, that was where he went. He wouldn't go near the cabin tonight, but without thinking he had taken the route leading to it.

John's voice was irritable when it came again. "Can we at

least take this smelly blanket off our faces?" he asked, doing so without waiting for an answer.

"Don't sit up yet," Jerek warned him. There were few cars on the road and all he could see of the ones behind him were headlights. "They'll be looking for a car with three people in it."

John turned his head back and forth a few times, trying to get the kinks out of his neck. "Don't you think you're going a little overboard?"

"Yeah," Jerek said. "Last time I didn't do silly things like this."

That produced silence. Mrs. Truett, Jerek noticed, hadn't made any complaints about his foolish precautions. He didn't have to impress her with the seriousness of her situation. Her husband, though, might turn out to be a problem.

As he drove Bill Jerek kept ticking off the names and faces of the detectives who'd been at the station tonight. Two years ago there hadn't been one of them he didn't trust. Now they all seemed like strangers. All of them had had financial problems at one time or another—who hadn't?—which was just the kind of problem that might make them prey to a man like Marco Galvan. There'd been personal problems too, undoubtedly more than he had known about. Being a cop didn't immunize a man against acquiring a taste for something illegal. Quite the contrary. You rubbed up against opportunities every day. Galvan would be quick to take advantage of that too.

Less than an hour out of Baltimore Jerek turned off the main highway onto an older one that seemed deserted, and soon after that he stopped at an old motel with a permanent Vacancy sign. It seemed like a mistake to stop, but to drive on aimlessly would be a bad idea too. Memory lent an exaggerated weight to everything he did. The last time he hadn't seen the end coming at all. Now he saw it coming from every direction. He was confident, though, that he hadn't been followed out of town. Even if he had been it might be better to stop now rather than drive on blindly and let them pick the spot. Besides, he was tired. If he didn't get some rest he'd be more likely to do something stupid. There were undoubtedly people looking for him, but their efforts would probably be confined to the city tonight. Marco Galvan could raise a lot of manpower when he needed to but he wasn't the Mafia. He couldn't be everywhere.

Jerek had men combing the city tonight himself, but he didn't hope to find Galvan that quickly. Maybe Galvan had fled the city too, Jerek thought suddenly. Maybe he had run to ground in this very motel, peering nervously through the curtains right now and seeing Bill Jerek get out of the car and walk toward the office.

That's the way Jerek's mind was working tonight. In the motel office he rang a hand bell until the owner appeared from a room behind the desk, appearing irritated rather than happy for the business. Jerek paid cash in advance and signed a fake name to the register.

He hoped the sleepy owner was already back in bed when Jerek shepherded the Truetts into the room he'd rented. Elizabeth almost stepped out of the shoes he'd found for her in someone's locker at the station. As he took a last look at the motel parking lot and closed the door on it, Jerek had that same sinking feeling, that he'd forgotten something fatal.

*H*e spent the night in a chair. The Truetts lay on the room's only double bed, but Jerek didn't imagine they got much sleep either. He turned the chair so it faced the window. That put his back to the Truetts, but that was as much privacy as he could give them. Occasionally he heard them murmuring to each other, sounding almost like sleepy children. He was surprised when Elizabeth raised her voice to ask him about the last time, the other witness he'd had against Marco Galvan.

Jerek almost didn't answer, just let her think he'd fallen asleep in the chair, but then he heard himself talking about it. With his back to his listeners and the room dark and otherwise silent, it was like talking to himself.

"We already had him in custody when he decided to talk. I didn't think there'd be much problem. Only a few of us even knew about it at first. We didn't fall all over ourselves to make the deal, either. We had good charges against the guy—we weren't anxious to drop them just because he suddenly offered to give us Galvan. We weren't sure how much he knew anyway."

"What was the man's name?" Elizabeth asked quietly.

"Who?"

"The witness."

"Oh." Jerek had to think for just a second. He was getting very sleepy. "Kinsolving. His name was—Kinsolving." He couldn't remember the man's first name. He'd gone by some nickname.

"So we already had him at the station and that's where we

kept him. I wasn't going to put him up in a hotel. I still thought he might just be trying to set up an escape for himself. I kept him at the station instead of putting him in the general jail population, but I kept him in a cell. He said he had to have police protection and I told him he had it already." Jerek said that bitterly. The phrase "police protection" had become satirical for him.

"When we started working out the details of the deal and he started giving us a few teasers of information on Galvan more people got involved. D.A.'s, FBI, federal prosecutors. Some of the crimes were federal. People started getting excited. Kinsolving was like a celebrity, giving out interviews to every— And of course by then Galvan knew something was up." You had to admire his efficiency, Jerek thought. He got organized a lot faster than we did. And then did he use someone he already had in his pocket, or did he reel someone in specifically for that job?

"And in two days it was all over. Kinsolving was dead in his cell. Nobody heard a shot, nobody heard him scream. Just— Between one team of interrogators and the next somebody walked up and stood there at the bars and shot him in the heart. Kinsolving must've thought it was just another cop with more questions about Marco Galvan."

Jerek hadn't forgotten that day, of course. The whole circus collapsed in a matter of minutes. No more big case, no more federal prosecutions. And everyone looked at Jerek like it was his fault, because he'd been too stupid to do the only job he had, protect the witness. Marco Galvan had beaten him before Jerek even knew what the game was.

That had begun Jerek's obsession with Galvan. He'd known who Galvan was before that, the man had been a frequent suspect, and Jerek would have liked to catch him at something, but there were a lot of things like that he wanted, and Galvan wasn't near the top of the list. But after the Kinsolving fiasco it had turned personal. Not just because Galvan had managed with apparent ease to make Bill Jerek look like a fool, but because of the way he had done it. He had turned out one of Jerek's own men, one of his friends, made him into a traitor. And Jerek still didn't know who it was. Whoever it was had kept a low profile for the last two years, probably hadn't had any contact with Galvan at all. But the traitor was still within easy reach of Galvan, and Galvan would have more of a hold over him now than ever.

Jerek had stopped answering Elizabeth's question. Now he was just going over the story again in his own thoughts, which was easier. Jerek had been a cop so long he had in many ways lost the civilian touch. After a while you had more in common with the crooks than with ordinary people. You thought like a criminal, picked up their phrases. He would have had to translate for the Truetts' benefit. Like the phrase he'd used in his own mind to describe Galvan's forcing someone to betray Jerek: "turned out." It meant to make someone into a whore. Guys going off to prison were afraid that some pimp would come along in their absence and turn out their wives or girlfriends. It was a cruel life for the woman, of course, but occasionally the pimp did it only as a gesture of contempt for the imprisoned man. And Galvan had done it to one of Jerek's own, right in front of his eyes.

He leaned forward and looked outside. They were still in the same general part of the state as his cabin. Jerek had spent many nights outdoors around here, he knew what it was like this time of year. The air would be crisp and moving. It seemed to carry scents more clearly than during the heat of the day. The ocean was not many miles away to the east. It lent a tang to the breeze. You'd have a sense of it in constant motion there just over the horizon. Jerek had spent a week at his cabin last fall. Ostensibly he'd gone there to hunt, but after the first day he'd left his gun inside and just gone for long walks in the woods. It was more peace then he'd known in years, it let his mind stretch. But by the fourth day he'd been getting restless. He had wondered what it would be like to spend every day like that. He had enough years in for retirement and some days he had the inclination. But he knew he never would until he'd settled this business with Galvan. Cops who retire always leave cases dangling, but he wouldn't leave this one. Tonight's events had revived him. Anger made him young again.

He couldn't take the Truetts back into the city until he knew who Galvan's traitor was, and until Galvan was arrested. He couldn't turn them over to the federal witness relocation program or use any other usual channel. He had to cobble together his own makeshift protection network, and he had to do it tonight.

The room had fallen silent after he stopped talking. The Truetts were breathing easily, probably asleep. Jerek was sleepy too, very sleepy—he'd already been in bed tonight when he'd gotten the call hours earlier. It was stupid to spend this night sitting up in a chair, peering out between the blinds at nothing. He slumped down in his chair and rested his head against the back of it. He closed his eyes and let his thoughts roam over all the people he knew. There must be one somewhere he knew well enough to trust and yet who was far enough removed from Jerek's life that no one would ever think of the person when trying to figure out where Jerek had hidden his new witness. Jerek smiled briefly, remembering that his wife had come to see him for a minute that day at the station before the witness was found dead. For a few minutes after that he hadn't even trusted her. Thinking of other people he knew seemed repetitive. Nearly all his friends were in law enforcement, he realized. Not surprising, after his twenty-five years as a cop. But there must be someone . . .

Jerek came awake with a jerk, already standing at the window before he even realized he'd been asleep and that something had awakened him. Movement in the parking lot? No, there was nothing stirring out there. Maybe a car passing on the old highway. Jerek stood there thinking about the name he'd thought of. Maybe the answer had come to him in his sleep. He didn't trust dream solutions, but the longer he thought about it, not only did his answer make sense, but the alternatives seemed nil. He didn't have time to ponder it forever. The sky was already greying in the east. He needed to find a hiding place for the Truetts today and then get back into the city to direct the hunt for Galvan.

He slipped out the door into the motel courtyard. The air was clean and chilled. He was the only one who had breathed it this morning. Gravel crunched under his shoes as he crossed the parking lot to the pay phone on its stand on the far side of the lot. He could keep the room door in sight while he talked. He had deliberately brought a lot of change on this trip. He fed it into the phone, dialed eleven digits, and woke someone up.

When the motel door closed, Elizabeth's eyes popped open. Her heart raced when she saw that she and John were alone in the room. John was snoring, lying on his back in the strange room. The semi-darkness of very early morning made the few pieces of furniture look sinister. Elizabeth went to the window and saw Jerek across the parking lot, talking to someone on the telephone. And the thought occurred to her: why should we trust him? Just because the other policeman knew Captain Jerek was so interested in Marco Galvan that they called him as soon as the gangster's name came up? But isn't that just the kind of act someone secretly working for Galvan might put on?

She didn't gasp when arms encircled her. She had heard John's snoring stop and the bedsprings creak. He held her and she put her hands on his arms. They both stared out the window at the parking lot. It was that unfamiliar view that brought John fully awake. For a moment in the dark he had thought they were in their own bedroom. Now he didn't know where they were.

"I'm sorry," Elizabeth said.

"It's not your fault."

It was the first time they had been alone together since John had walked into the police station. It seemed they had been in headlong flight ever since. This was the first moment they'd had to reflect on how suddenly and completely they'd been uprooted. Elizabeth was thinking of their dark, empty house in Baltimore. Was someone creeping through it this minute, rifling through her letters and clothes or sitting patiently in the dark, waiting for her to return?

John was looking out the window at Jerek on the telephone. He turned Elizabeth so he could see her face. She didn't look afraid, just concerned for him. In the very dim light she looked twenty-five. "I love you," he said, and she smiled and came even closer to him. For a moment neither of them was troubled. They could have been at a nice hotel on a second honeymoon. But John caught another glimpse of Jerek, hanging up the phone. He spoke quickly.

"You know, he didn't do such a hot job with the last witness he had. Maybe—"

But Elizabeth had already resolved her earlier doubts. She was ahead of him. "Where else could we go?" she asked rhetorically, leaning back to look into his face. "We have to trust someone."

John, looking out the window, wasn't sure of that.

"*I*'m going to turn you over to someone else," Jerek said half an hour later when they were back in the car. "You'll be doing a little traveling. Maybe you'll feel safer once you're out of state."

"Where are you taking us?" John asked. "I mean, is it another agency, a person? I'd like to know just what—"

"Her name is Karen Boone," Jerek said. "She—"

"*Her* name?" John said, but Elizabeth didn't look displeased.

"She's a federal marshal in Ohio," Jerek continued. "I've known her practically all her life. Her daddy and I used to work together. She's never been a Baltimore city cop and she had absolutely nothing to do with the last witness we had. She's never heard of Marco Galvan, and you'll be safe with her until we can get him."

John's silence sounded unconvinced, but he raised no objections. Elizabeth asked a few questions about Karen. The highway slipped by. They were still going north, not west toward Ohio.

They crossed the state line and in Wilmington, Delaware, Jerek pulled to a stop in the train station. "We're taking the train to Ohio?" John asked.

"No," Jerek said. "And let's not do any talking for a while."

"*I* told Karen," Jerek explained to them in a low voice, once they were on the train, "that I want her to hide you someplace without telling anyone—anyone—what she's doing or that she's doing it for me. It won't be at her house or maybe even in her city. I left it up to her. I don't want to know. I'll be the only person in the world who knows she has you and she'll be the only person who knows exactly where you are. This way there'll be a buffer between us." Elizabeth wondered fleetingly how far Jerek thought Galvan might go in order to find her. But Jerek was hurrying on. "I won't contact her again until I have news. You'll be okay." And they should be, he thought; he saw nothing wrong with this plan, but that was what bothered him. No plan was perfect.

Their tickets were for New York City, but they left the train abruptly at the 30th Street Station in Philadelphia. Jerek had sat there as if just waiting for the train to start rolling again, but just before it did he hurried them out of their seats and out the door onto the platform. John and Elizabeth were taken by surprise, and that was the plan. Anyone else would have been too, Jerek hoped. He didn't see anyone follow them off the train, but of course some passengers had already gotten off. The three of them hustled down the platform and up the stairs to the waiting room, the men again pressing close to Elizabeth.

Out on the street the sun was momentarily blinding. September hadn't yet banished summer. Elizabeth felt the heat of the pavement through the soles of her borrowed shoes.

And when Jerek saw Karen waiting for them at the curb in front of the station, he realized he'd let himself forget how young she really was. *She's just a girl*, Elizabeth thought when she saw her. A nice-looking girl of maybe twenty-five, looking even younger without makeup. She turned toward them and Elizabeth realized how early she must have been awake this morning to meet them here. But her eyes brightened when she recognized Bill Jerek. She bounded out of the car energetically. She was wearing jeans and a loose jacket. A breeze was blowing her brown hair back from her face, making her look fresh and alert. Elizabeth noticed that when Jerek came up to her Karen stood very straight, almost at attention, looking up at him.

"Anyone follow you?" Jerek asked her without a greeting.

In spite of his manner Karen was smiling slightly. "Who would be following me?" she replied, and that was right, there was no reason for anyone to follow her here from Cleveland. No one could have known she was coming to meet Jerek and the Truetts.

But Jerek's eyes were sweeping the open area around them. He ushered John and Elizabeth into the car, saying, "I'll call you when I hear anything." He was in a great hurry. Elizabeth looked out the window to see Karen hesitating momentarily as if waiting for a farewell, but Jerek just said, "Go, go." Karen did, pulling away from the curb smoothly. Her eyes were on the rearview mirror. Elizabeth didn't think she was watching for pursuit, though. Looking back, she saw Jerek standing alone, staring after them.

Jerek put his hands in his pockets and tried to fade back into the crowd. He had hurried the three of them away from him as if he were the danger, as if he were glowing from radiation poisoning. Which was exactly how Jerek felt. He thought he stood out like a pillar of flame on the sidewalk in front of the train station. There were dozens of people in sight, all of them apparently watching him and the departing car. It wasn't going nearly fast enough to suit him. Already Jerek regretted letting them out of his sight, but that was the plan. Anyone who had managed to follow them onto the train almost certainly couldn't have had a car waiting in Philadelphia as Jerek had.

He watched the car turn a corner and vanish from sight. He hadn't seen anyone following it, but there was traffic going the same direction. That was Karen's worry now, though. He was out of it.

And again he had that feeling that he had forgotten something perfectly obvious.

CHAPTER FIVE

*A*nd then something terrible happened: nothing. Karen Boone and the Truetts reached Ohio without incident and the Truetts settled into hiding. Marco Galvan apparently did the same. As far as Bill Jerek could determine, Galvan had left the city as well. There was no trace of him anywhere. Jerek knew he was around, though, waiting for the information he needed. People asked Jerek about the Truetts, and he would say only that they were safe. Jerek continued to direct his own search. He felt handicapped. He couldn't disseminate plans generally among his men because that would send the plan directly to Galvan. He split his detectives up into two-man squads and had each report only to him. But he doubted the effectiveness of that isolation. Men who share a job will always discuss things with each other. So Jerek kept most of what he knew or suspected to himself. And when it began to seem clear that the usual police methods weren't going to turn up Galvan, Jerek set in motion certain plans of his own. One plan was for a turnabout: Jerek wanted to find or install a traitor of his own in Galvan's camp.

Through all this, Jerek scrupulously avoided any contact with Karen Boone. But he worried.

Karen worried too. She had been deliberately breezy with Jerek when she'd picked up the Truetts at the train station in Philadelphia, but his nervousness had communicated itself to her almost immediately. She had not stopped looking over her shoulder. It seemed completely unlikely that anyone could trace the Truetts to her, and yet—Time kept passing with no news from Bill Jerek and she wondered how long his makeshift arrangements would hold together. There was undoubtedly a relentless search going on for Elizabeth Truett.

Elizabeth knew that herself, of course. She and John spent all their time in the small, sparsely furnished house Karen had rented for them. There was nothing adventurous about what they did with their time. The longer that time grew, the more the odds seemed to favor Marco Galvan. The police should have turned him up in a matter of days if they were going to find him at all. The terribleness of the uneventful passing of time was that the police search would grow less intense with every day. Other crimes would call for their attention. Bill Jerek wouldn't be able to devote all his manpower to Marco Galvan for long. Galvan, on the other hand, would not be diverted until he had found Elizabeth. Time was not on her side.

Two weeks passed in that holding pattern, and then something did happen, all the way across the continent.

California

A few months earlier, this would hardly even have been a problem. Handling just this sort of thing had been their job then, they'd had the set-up and the personnel for it. Those teams had been disbanded and shipped out months ago, though, and the post returned to its normal routine. But then, no one else was equipped to deal with it now either, so the problem had been dumped into their laps, at least to begin with. Specifically, into the lap of Major Archer van Dyne. He couldn't trace the line of compromise and evasion that had brought it to him, but he did know that if he had been thinking more quickly, he would have shuffled it on to someone else, too.

Not that it was a terrible problem. It was simply unique. That meant there was no policy on it yet, so van Dyne would have to make decisions, chart an original course. It wasn't complex enough that he could expect a commendation out of it if he handled the thing brilliantly. No one would notice unless he screwed up.

Van Dyne left his office and started down the white corridor. He narrowed his eyes against the glare from the desperately shiny floor, which seemed to absorb heel marks and shine all the more brightly. If there was one person who did his job on this Army post, it was the janitor.

Every turn of the corridor took van Dyne deeper into the building. Bright fluorescent lights kept any latent claustrophobia at bay, but van Dyne still felt like a rat in a maze every time he came this way. He almost expected to find a huge block of cheese when he opened the door of the briefing room.

Instead he found nothing. The five chairs at the table in the center of the small room were empty. Van Dyne looked at the sign on the door whose knob he still held. He was in the right room. But maybe his—what, his patient? client? his responsibility, at any rate—hadn't found the room. Van Dyne looked around and then started back out, but he saw something through the crack between door and jamb that brought him back into the room.

"There you are," he said heartily, and closed the door.

His responsibility had pulled one of the chairs back into the corner behind the door. He still sat there, giving no response. He had found the juncture of two shadows, which crossed at the level of his head. With the contrasting brightness of the rest of the small room, his face was well masked.

"I didn't see you back there." Van Dyne still got nothing in reply. He took three steps to the table and set his folder on it. The man was still sitting in the shadow when he turned back. Van Dyne smiled at him in a way he hoped was reassuring and motioned for the man to join him at the table.

His face was still fairly well masked even when the man rose out of the shadow. Someone had dug up some fatigues for him that almost fit, but he hadn't shaved off the completely nonregulation beard that hid half his face like jungle brush. That he'd been able to hide from van Dyne for even a moment was quite a feat, because nothing could have looked more out of place in this antiseptic room. The man was not tall but very thin, his tendons prominently displayed when he moved. His skin was dark, but as if from stain rather than sun. He must have been thoroughly cleaned up and disinfected by now, but the man's skin gave the impression of being covered by layers of grime or camouflage that would never wash off. He came slowly toward the table and stopped well short of it.

"How are you doing?" van Dyne said, extending his hand across the long space between them. "Welcome home. I'm Archie van Dyne."

The shadow-scarred man looked the hand over before taking it loosely. His eyes had been hooded. He raised his head slightly and Archie saw his eyes were green, startlingly so.

When he looked at Archie for the first time his gaze held the major's. After a moment of silence he repeated the only piece of information he'd really given them in the day since he'd landed on the jet from Hawaii.

"My name is Bryan Truett."

CHAPTER SIX

*E*lizabeth and John Truett had often wondered exactly how their son had been lost. They thought they wanted to know, but if they could have seen it happen they would have wanted to forget it again immediately. The Army had pieced together an explanation months earlier but had spared the Truetts the details. The bearded man told Archie van Dyne a somewhat different story. His voice was unemotional, but once in a while when he paused Archie could see him remembering parts of the story he didn't tell.

*V*ietnam, 1973

He stared at the trail as he would at a coral snake he had to step over. He had learned to mistrust trails, and this one he hated personally. He looked for the spot that would kill him. Nothing was mined in Vietnam except the trails. The jungles were treacherous and the paddies loathsome, but the trails—the hard-packed, slightly reddish earth, the only places in the country where a man or a platoon could make good time—the trails were guaranteed to cut your legs off.

"I would have avoided the trail if I could have," the bearded man said to Archie. "I could have got to the village just as fast without it. But the trail was my assignment. We were all ringed around the village, and they expected when we converged that the trail would be the most popular way out. I didn't think there were any Vietcong in this village anyway, and I sure didn't think they'd be using any trail if they had to get out, but nobody asked my opinion."

"How many of you were there?" Archie asked.

"Three squads."

Three squads of strangers. Tripwire wasn't one of them. He'd come back to headquarters from far in-country because he had information about Vietnamese troop movements, and before he could leave again he'd been drafted to join this ridiculous mission. He didn't like it, he didn't like being part of a troop of American soldiers again, and he could tell he made the others nervous.

For months he had been what they called a Lurp, a long-range patroller working completely alone. He didn't have a regular reporting schedule, he usually worked without specific orders, and best of all he was on his own. The places he went, there was often not another American within fifty miles, and he'd come to like it that way. His job was basically spying, something a squad couldn't do. He couldn't count the number of times he would have been killed if he'd had even one other man with him. And now he was one soldier among three squads of soldiers ranged around the village. They thought they were sneaking up on it, and Tripwire imagined he could hear every one of them. The whole mission had an air of futility and doom over it.

"There was another guy with me, named Graham, and when I started—"

"Graham?" Archie said, making a note.

The bearded man said, "I'm sure that won't be in any record. Things were awfully confused about this time."

"Okay," Archie said agreeably.

"What are you doing?" Graham had whispered at him.

Tripwire didn't answer. He kept edging along the trail, staying at the right-hand edge so that a mine might blow off only his left leg. He looked closely at every spot before setting a foot on it, then stopped to peer farther along the trail. He wished there were children around. Children always seemed to know where the mines were, veering one step off a path without even slowing down when they ran. Sometimes, he was sure, it was the children who had planted the mines. But there were no children around today. The village gave off no sounds.

"Where are you going?" Graham whispered at him again. "We're supposed to stay here until the time comes."

He came clanking and jangling after Tripwire, making as much noise as Custer's whole Seventh Cavalry. Tripwire stopped him and they stood there together—two brown-haired, pale-eyed American boys looking terribly out of place. In the dry brown grass surrounding them their green and black camouflage suits were about as effective as "Shoot me" signs hanging from their necks. On top of that, Graham had encumbered himself with all the equipment he could carry, useless junk like canteens and a walkie-talkie. Tripwire stripped all of it off him except his rifle, left the junk lying on the trail and starting moving down it again.

"They'll steal it," Graham whined. He stood there indecisively until Tripwire was fifteen feet away from him, then he came running after him. Tripwire knew how Graham felt about him. Tripwire made no friends at headquarters—other Americans tended to avoid him as if he were something as alien and dangerous as the Vietcong themselves, but out here where it mattered Graham felt safer having him along.

Before Graham could ask another question Tripwire told him, "I'm going to check out this trail. I don't want to have to run down the whole damned length of the thing when the time comes." He couldn't study the trail while running. "And if you say another word or make another sound I'm going to cut your throat," Tripwire added. He could see Graham believed him.

*T*he next part of the story was one the bearded man didn't know. Archie knew it in rough outline, and told him in two or three sentences what they thought had happened. It was about what Tripwire had figured out later.

*E*lsewhere on the perimeter around the village the lieutenant in charge of the operation was on the radio. The radio operator stared frankly at the lieutenant's face. When he saw the lieutenant frown, the radio operator smiled. The lieutenant, who had been in combat only a week, was too gung-ho by far. His men already had a pool, broken up into hours, on how long he'd live. Their fear was that he'd take all of them with him when he went. The lieutenant wanted this mission, so when the radio operator saw him frown he hoped it meant the mission had been cancelled. Everyone else in the three squads would cheer that decision. One mission scratched meant one less chance to get killed.

The lieutenant was still frowning when he signed off. "Call the men back."

"Yes sir!" The radio operator stood up to shout to the next man along the circle. The lieutenant grabbed his arm.

"Not that way. Quietly. Go tell him."

"But sir, if the mission's been cancelled—"

"There's no need to let Charlie know that. You go tell that man and send him around the circle. You circle the other way. Quietly."

"We could use a flare, sire."

"No. Tell them we're ordered to fall back. Meet here. Quickly. We're needed somewhere else. The day isn't over yet."

"Yes sir." The radio operator set off at a trot, putting on his helmet and then holding it in place as he ran. He gave the word to the first man he encountered, then started back the way he'd come, running, grinning, letting his equipment rattle. The radio operator didn't worry about mines or snipers, not when a mission had just been cancelled. That made him invulnerable for at least twenty minutes.

Graham and the other one, the Lurp, were not where they should have been. The radio operator frowned, advanced a little way along the path they had been assigned to cover, didn't see anything, and stopped. He had almost completed a half-circle of the village now. Any minute he would meet the first soldier he'd told, who had circled the village in the opposite direction. The absence of the two men slowed the radio operator down, and he didn't like it. When he stopped running he lost some of his invulnerability. He took three more steps along the path and stared ahead to where it disappeared in shade. No one would have been crazy enough to pass into that shade before he had to. The radio operator felt a coolness on the back of his neck, as if a cold stare were lodged there. He turned slowly, saw no one, and was not reassured. The first soldier must have beaten him to this spot, he decided. He and those two were already on their way back to the lieutenant, leaving the radio operator alone here, as far removed from his fellows as he could be. He turned back the way he'd come, trying to look clumsy, inoffensive, not worth killing. He was in the open, in sunshine. It didn't warm him. In this country, shadow was warm, shadow that kept out cold, invisible stares. The radio operator began running again, once in a while throwing a little zigzag into his stride, dodging a bullet before he heard it, knowing you never do hear it coming.

"*T*hey were pulled out in such a hurry maybe the lieutenant in charge forgot about you, since you weren't one of his regulars," Archie said. "He got killed later that day, so we don't know. They were sent about twenty miles south as reinforcements in a firefight no one had been expecting. It turned into a bloodbath. Not everyone was accounted for. There wasn't even a record you were part of that mission. Frankly—" He trailed off.

"I was," Tripwire said. "I was still back at that damned quiet village, hiding in the bushes, waiting for everybody else."

*T*ripwire was in a hedgerow, looking into the deserted village common area. He felt safe. He had already traversed the whole length of the trail, he was out of sight in the hedgerow, and there were still five minutes before he had to step out into that village. Graham, beside him, did not look as happy. His head kept swiveling.

The five minutes passed quickly. Tripwire was listening for noise. Not from the village. He expected silence there. Vietnamese seemed to move in a slightly different dimension, any sounds they made were unhearable by American ears. Tripwire was listening for the sounds of the other soldiers in his squad moving into position. He heard nothing. He was surprised by how quiet they all were. Tripwire had been silent himself, and he had managed to make Graham shut up. But now he was suspicious of the silence. He didn't think the rest of the men were capable of it.

He looked at his watch. It was time to move into the village. He looked out of the hedge. Nothing. No soldiers appeared. From where he squatted, Tripwire should have been able to see someone enter the village. No one did.

He and Graham looked at each other. Graham's eyes were the most visible objects for miles around. He looked over his shoulder, then back at Tripwire. They both turned to study the village. Still no one appeared, Vietnamese or American. Tripwire's skin was tingling. Had they all been killed on their way in? Were he and Graham the only ones left alive?

No. He was a strong believer in Vietnamese stealth, but

thirty men couldn't die so silently. He would have heard
something. They must all be here, still waiting, still—

He suddenly realized what must be wrong. He hadn't seen
anyone step out of hiding. But no one had seen him, either. No
soldier would come out until he saw another American, so no
one would ever come out. Tripwire grinned humorlessly. All of
them sitting in their own sweat, waiting for everyone else. That
fearless lieutenant was probably shivering in the bushes, frozen
with indecision. Someone else had to take charge.

Graham saw the Lurp grin and it scared him, but not as
much as Tripwire's standing up and stepping out of concealment. Graham tried to grab his leg, missed, and almost fell
on his face. Tripwire stepped out confidently, rifle leveled,
trying to look both fierce and matter-of-fact. Graham was
certain he'd lost his mind. Tripwire took a step or two into the
village, waiting for the others to join him. They would all be
smiling slyly, acknowledging their embarrassment that they'd
been afraid to step out.

No one joined him. The hot sun found no white American
teeth gleaming in the square. Tripwire remained all alone.

It was time to fade away. This mission had been jinxed from
the beginning. He'd tried to do his part but the others had
botched it up somehow. They could do it without him now. The
hostility of the silent village pressed in on him. It made the
bush seem friendly.

He turned back toward it and saw Graham staring at him
with a stare that was too fixed. When Tripwire moved toward
him Graham's eyes didn't move correspondingly. Then the rifle
fell out of Graham's hands and clattered to the ground.

Tripwire looked up and saw a brown face just above
Graham's very white one. Even as Tripwire swiveled his rifle
around to bring it to bear he saw another face in the bushes and
another. Here were the silent Vietnamese he'd been expecting.

He fired off one shot just to make them duck out of the way,
then plunged back into the bushes ten feet away from them,
throwing himself on luck to pick the right spot.

But there was no luck today. He shouted as he entered the
bushes, and the shout was cut short by the machete blade
striking his temple. Tripwire's voice stopped then, but he didn't
fall unconscious. He was falling backward, but the ground
wouldn't come up quickly enough. The pain of the blade
slicing into his skull was awful. It wouldn't end. Tripwire
closed his eyes, but unconsciousness wouldn't come. He felt

the blade going deeper, and the pain growing worse. He couldn't stand it. Why wouldn't his brain let him escape into senselessness? There wasn't even any blood yet, time was passing so slowly. The blade continued to cut more deeply. The force of the rage behind the blow must have been enormous. Tripwire feared that rage as much as the pain. He wanted to die, now, to pass into a state where vengeance could not be taken on him. The pain continued interminably. Tripwire wanted to scream again, hoping only that the effort would erase his last bit of strength. But he was no longer in touch with his vocal cords. He was trapped in this tiny box of pain, a brain that refused to let go of its awareness. This last moment of life was so terrible; why did his body insist on clinging to it?

The machete blade was retreating now, causing a new sort of pain. Tripwire's fall was finally pulling the blade free. He calmly longed for death, but it wasn't quite ready for him yet. He felt the ever so slight pain of his body hitting the ground, a totally unnecessary indignity. He was ready to die long before then.

CHAPTER SEVEN

Karen

*K*aren tried to remember the way ordinary people behave. She sat at her desk on a weekday morning looking, she hoped, perfectly normal, but routine had fallen away from her so completely she could hardly fake it any more. Her assignment from Bill Jerek took precedence over her regular job, but no one else could know that. At first she had planned to take a leave of absence, but had immediately realized that would be a mistake. Her life had to appear unchanged.

Karen had deliberately acted light-hearted when she'd seen Jerek, suppressing her nervousness in order to reassure Jerek that he had chosen wisely when he'd called on her for help. But even in the brief moment she'd been with him his worry had infected her. She knew how much making this case meant to him, and she knew she was now the only link to Elizabeth Truett.

She and the Truetts had had a few hundred miles in which to get to know each other on the drive from Philadelphia. Elizabeth had talked freely. She had even mentioned their only son Bryan, missing and presumed dead in Vietnam. Karen had seen from John's startled expression in the rearview mirror that it wasn't a subject Elizabeth ordinarily broached to strangers. It was as if, Karen thought later, Elizabeth were trying to leave an oral record of her whole life during that long drive. By the time they reached Ohio Karen felt close to her. That was something she hadn't counted on: a personal relationship with her charges. It made her own responsibility seem that much heavier.

It was ironic that Karen had to strain now to recreate the routine of her job. Usually the dullness of that routine was the major complaint she had about her work.

Karen Boone was twenty-six. It sometimes seemed to her that the most significant fact of her life was that she was a cop's daughter. That was how she knew Bill Jerek: he and her father had been partners in their early days on the Baltimore force. Karen's father had moved to Cleveland because it was her mother's home town and because he'd been offered a better-paying job there as an insurance investigator. After a year of that he'd realized the money wasn't as important to him as being a cop was, and he'd joined the Cleveland Police Department. Karen had spent many summer days at the station house, and the stories she heard when they had company at home were police stories. She'd grown up with the unspoken idea that that's what adulthood was. When she'd graduated from college with no particular ambition, she had discovered— not much to her surprise—that contacts were as important as education, and her father knew every law enforcement officer in the city. It seemed her only decision had been what type of law enforcement to choose.

Not that she'd been railroaded into it. She liked her work. There were days of boring paperwork, but there were also days when even a routine chore like serving a subpoena turned into a task that required planning and imagination. She even liked the challenge of being one of the few women federal marshals; it made her feel like part of an elite group. It's just that she hadn't intended to make a career of it. It had just been something to do until she decided what to do. When she'd started she thought that after a year or two she'd go to law school, but her job now required her to spend a good deal of time in courtrooms, and as a consequence she had no great respect for lawyers. It wasn't worth the sacrifice of four or five years of night law school just to become one of them.

Karen's job became more important to her after the great romance of her life blew up. She had started dating Jeff in college and they had fallen together so comfortably that they had become a couple almost without any will of their own. After college when dating was no longer enough they had drifted toward marriage—drifted so far in fact that they actually set the date. But as it approached Karen realized she

didn't want to spend her life with him. She was just settling
into a comfortable niche. But what a terrible thing to do to
herself, to both of them: starting out life with love already
ground away to nothing and only familiarity holding them
together.

She began picking on him about faults she hadn't noticed in
years but that suddenly began to irritate her enormously.
Finally one of the fights she started took, and the breakup
lasted. A year later Jeff married someone else. Karen's reaction
was surprise that what she'd thought she wanted had actually
happened, and of course there was some jealousy. But a few
months after his marriage Jeff had called her from a bar to tell
her he'd made a terrible mistake. But Karen hadn't, and she
didn't make one that night either. It gave her a sad sense of
triumph to know he still wanted her.

She had thrown herself into her work. She was good at it and
it was generally satisfying, but far in the back of her mind was
a hope that if she did her job better than anyone else some day
she would be recruited to an even more elite force. Now in a
way that had happened, with this assignment from Bill Jerek.
Though there was nothing official about it, no vast secret
organization behind the mission, that only made it all the more
important to Karen that she make no mistakes. She was very
flattered that Jerek had thought of her. He must have chosen
her not only because of what her father had told him, but
because he had seen it firsthand, she thought.

When Karen had gone to the F.B.I. Academy in Virginia to
take her marshal's training, she had been surprised to find Jerek
an instructor there. She had idolized him when he and her
father were partners in Baltimore, but she had been only a girl
then. The fact that he was a guest instructor at the academy,
though, meant others thought highly of him as well. He
remembered Karen and at first he'd treated her half like a kid,
taking it a little easier on her than on others in the class. She'd
tried to impress him and maybe she had. Her last night there
they went out for a few drinks together. They talked about her
father, their respective jobs, and it was mercifully *not* like old
times. But it wasn't an initiation ritual, either. It was as if
sometime toward the end of the course he had accepted her as
an adult, and a colleague. She was proud of herself. She began
to look at him differently too, not as her Uncle Bill. She was
glad to see that she hadn't been wrong to be impressed with
him when she was a girl. When he walked her back to her dorm

room he had put a hand on the small of her back going up the hill. It was a light tough but she could feel the strength of his hand. Her skin grew slightly damp under her clothes, under his touch. Feeling at last his equal as an adult had paradoxically made her feel awkward and teenagerish again. It was a good thing they didn't linger long at her doorway. She was starting to lean imperceptibly toward him but, "Take care of yourself," was all he said, and touched her shoulder and went off down the hall. Karen had gone to bed and lain awake for a long time thinking how much a little space of time could change things.

But she had forgotten that night until Jerek called her in the very early hours of morning. Hearing his voice and gazing sleepily at the clock she had been reminded of Jeff calling her from the bar. Jerek's voice was crisp, though, not drunken, and he had only wanted her help. Speeding through the night toward their meeting in Philadelphia she had thought how much more welcome Bill Jerek's middle-of-the-night call had been than Jeff's two years earlier.

She could do this job better now if Jerek hadn't made her so aware of its importance. She had been startled by his furtiveness—fearless Bill Jerek, looking over his shoulder and staring suspiciously at a passing bag lady. After that she'd driven back to Cleveland with her eyes so constantly in the rearview mirror that she'd almost run into the back of a truck. She was sure she and the Truetts hadn't been followed after they'd left Jerek; Marco Galvan had never even heard of Karen Boone. But there was always the chance someone would get the information out of Jerek. The more time that passed the farther afield the killers would search Jerek's old contacts. Karen had no control over that and no way of knowing. She hadn't spoken to Jerek again since their meeting at the train station. He'd said he wouldn't risk contacting her unless he had something very important to report. Karen had found a newsstand on her way to the office that carried the Baltimore *Sun* and she'd started buying it every day, being careful to let no one see her reading it. But by the time she'd gotten involved in the case the story had already moved off the front page, and it soon fell out of the paper altogether when there was no progress in the hunt for Marco Galvan.

Karen glanced at the office clock high on the white wall behind her desk; eleven thirty in the morning. She took a quick look around the large office. No one was paying her any undue attention. The other marshals were starting to think about lunch. They looked up, stretched, strolled to other desks. Suddenly Karen didn't want to share anyone's company over a sandwich. She had a more important errand and this would be a good time to slip away. Before anyone could ask her plans for lunch she was out the door. At the end of the short corridor she looked back. No one had followed her.

*I*n fifteen minutes she was on the highway. It had been a week now, and this was the first time she'd gone to see Elizabeth and John. Her original plan had been to install them out of town a comfortable distance away and then not go near them. She'd rented a house for them but did not provide a car. She cautioned them to go out as little as possible. Elizabeth's face had appeared in a wire service photo that might have cropped up in other papers besides the *Sun* on a slow news day. There was no telling who might see them. Karen had provisioned the house thoroughly enough to last out the seige, she thought, but she hadn't planned on it lasting this long. She'd had no idea Marco Galvan could disappear so thoroughly. Today John had called her at the office, pretending to be an informer who wouldn't tell anyone else his name, as Karen had instructed. She got calls like that once in a while; no one would inquire too closely. After he got her on the phone John told her starvation was going to force them out of hiding. He was joking, but not by much. Karen had promised to bring groceries. Better for her to go to them, she thought, than for Elizabeth and John to become known in the small town outside Cleveland.

She had soon left Cleveland behind as well as the main highway, and was on a narrow two-lane blacktop. Another advantage to having the Truetts hidden out of town was this road itself. It was narrow and little used, so she should have no trouble spotting someone following her. The road curved often enough that if a following car stayed far enough behind it wouldn't see her. But then she wouldn't see it, either, so Karen had devised a system to prevent any surprises.

There was no one behind her when she turned off onto a small dirt road, little more than a pair of ruts. She travelled about half a mile down it and turned her car around in the yard of an abandoned farmhouse. Then she waited. She rolled down her window and listened. She was far enough from the blacktop road that she wouldn't be able to hear a car passing, but she could hear if one was coming down the dirt road.

After five minutes of silence Karen started her car again and went tearing back up the dirt road, her wheels throwing up a tall curtain of dust. She encountered no other car there or when she was back on the two-lane blacktop. Anyone following her would have driven past and lost her by then. The extra precaution didn't embarrass her. She was not going to be the one to make a mistake.

In half an hour she was on her way to the Truetts' rented house with bags of groceries on the back seat. Daytime traffic was light in the small town of Chagrin Falls, but Karen stayed careful. Once she completely circled a block, and again she half-circled one and headed back in the opposite direction. There was no other car in sight when she finally turned onto the Truetts' street, a residential block indistinguishable from the blocks and blocks around it. She pulled into the driveway and got out of the car carrying one of the bags of food. Her other hand was in her purse, which held both the keys to the house and her revolver.

She hesitated on the porch for a just a moment before knocking, and when there was no immediate response she reached for her keys. Jerek had emphasized to her the relentlessness of the man who wanted Elizabeth dead, and exaggeration was not one of Jerek's failings. In spite of her care Karen couldn't help thinking Galvan could have found a way around her. She was afraid of what she might find when she opened the Truetts' door.

CHAPTER EIGHT

Tripwire

"*T*hat's where we lost track of you. In the records, I mean."

The bearded man looked coldly back at Archie, as if everything he had been through were Archie's fault. Because of course it wasn't only in their records that the Army had lost this man.

His eyes were not the quick, darting ones Archie would have expected in someone who had come out of the jungle alone. They seemed almost lazy instead. When he and Archie had walked into the room the bearded man's eyes had made one slow sweep of the whole room, then came to rest on Archie and stayed there, as if he had isolated Archie as the only potential danger to him.

"A lot of men were killed that day," Archie went on. "And we never were sure if you had even been there. No one who lived could confirm it. And since you didn't even belong to that outfit—"

"No. I should have been far away from that botch."

"But at least you're alive," Archie said. "After all."

The bearded man didn't answer. Major van Dyne subsided and looked into the coffee he was stirring. There was one stubborn speck that wouldn't dissolve. Non-dairy creamer. Found on a shelf in this deserted rec room, it was probably months old. Probably had developed some sort of non-dairy, dehydrated, low-fat disease by now. A mutant strain that would kill Archie van Dyne in about two more sips. If it did, the man sitting across from him would watch without emotion while Archie choked to death, then probably finish his own black coffee before stepping over the body to leave the room.

This Bryan Truett had Archie thoroughly cowed. Archie didn't know how to approach the returnee. Whatever kind of horrifying ordeal Truett had survived had caused him to forget all the social conventions still hanging on back home in the good old U.S. Like answering Archie's friendly little implied question about being alive. Even if Truett was going to tell him to go fuck himself, he didn't want to talk about it, he should have done it right away, not subject Archie to half a minute of that hard stare first, as if Archie had been trying to stroke his thigh.

"By the time I came to I had a festering scalp wound and a high fever. Damned near no clothes, and I didn't know where I was."

Archie looked up in surprise. Truett was answering him after all. Just like him to make Archie feel like a fool for having asked the question, and then answer it anyway, minutes too late. There was that hesitation in everything he did. Hold out your hand to him and he'd stare at it, then glance at your face to see what you meant by it. Perhaps something would finally remind him that this was the custom in his native land, and he'd take the hand and shake it perfunctorily. He didn't have a soldier's grip. He seemed to want to get his hand clear again as soon as possible.

"The ones who had captured me kept me with them. We headed back north to their base camp. I stayed there for months." He stopped abruptly.

"Must have been inconvenient for them to hang on to you," Archie said curiously. "It's a wonder they didn't just kill you on the spot."

The bearded man gave him that glare again. "Are you asking if I talked?" he said. "Spilled my guts? Sold out my country to save my own miserable life?"

"I didn't mean—" Archie tried to say.

"Damn right I talked. I talked like a speed freak. I was hoarse for a month. I told them everything I knew and more. Trouble was, I didn't know much. I'd been detached for so long, working so far north—. I knew more about their army's movements than I did about my own."

"Anyone would have talked," Archie said quietly. What others higher up the chain of command might think of this confession was another matter, but Archie didn't feel inclined to condemn.

Truett ignored him. "We were already back at their camp by the time they realized I wouldn't be any more use to them. And then they kept me anyway. I'd become a sort of—" He didn't finish that thought. "They kept me so long they got careless, and one day I escaped. But by that time there was no place to escape to. I headed south, expecting any day to run into American soldiers, but there weren't any by then. I was the only one."

Archie pictured that. He must have stood out like a helium balloon. That he had escaped the country was miraculous. "How did you get to Malaysia?" Archie asked cautiously.

"In Saigon I found a boatload of South Vietnamese who were getting out. I went with them and that's where we drifted, Malaysia. We were stopped by gunboats outside the harbor. They had too many refugees already. That night I swam ashore and found the U.S. Embassy." That had been the first place he'd used the litany that had taken him this far: "My name is Bryan Truett. U.S. Army serial number 449-88 . . ."

"And from there it was just a few hops to us. But Saigon—it must have been a madhouse. How'd you talk 'em into letting you on that boat? You have any money?" Truett laughed harshly. "Then, without a bribe, I don't see—"

"They had some idea that having an American with them might do them some good when they got wherever they were going."

"Oh. What happened to them?"

"I don't know."

Again Archie realized how essentially alone Truett had been for so long. No one had survived the adventure with him. Archie was backtracking through the story. Other officials had debriefed Truett thoroughly, he was sure, but it was all new to Archie. "What about Graham, the kid who was with you?"

That hesitation again. But this pause wasn't as cold as the previous ones. The bearded man's eyes shifted away from Archie. "He died on the trail, just a day or two after we were captured."

"He was wounded that badly? Or did they—?"

"Sometimes people's imaginations kill them. You know? Graham was scared to death of reaching a prison camp."

There was no contempt in his voice, only understanding. Archie let a little silence pass for Graham.

"His body was never recovered either."

"They made me bury him. We made a little party out of it."
A deathday party. "They said to me, 'Now he's a good
American.' You understand? They got that phrase from us."

"Yes," Archie said. "I'd better remember to notify his
folks. They'll want to know for certain what happened to
him."

"I don't think they'd want to know much of it."

Archie stopped trying to hold back the silence. It jostled in
and crowded the empty room while the two men sat with the
thick white mugs cupped in their hands. Archie noticed that
Truett had hardly tasted his. "How's that coffee?" he said.
"Bet you wished for some a few times when you were out in
that jungle." Archie winced at how insensitive that sounded.

The man across from him took a sip, as if he hadn't thought
about the quality of the coffee until asked. "Coffee isn't one of
the things I missed," he said.

He surprised Archie by smiling. Damn, the guy might be
human after all. The smile was even a good one. Good old
American teeth that had endured months in the jungle without
toothpaste or floss and come through shining, protected by
years of fluoridation. Archie smiled back at him.

"Let's go for a walk."

Archie led them out into the sunlight. As they went out the
door he said, "Oh, Truett, wait a minute, we have—" and the
man kept right on walking. More hesitantly, Archie said,
"Bryan?" and the man took another two or three steps before
turning. That was the moment when he looked most out of
touch, Archie thought, as if he hadn't understood what Archie
was saying.

Truett shook his head. "Not used to being called by my
name," he said. "You know it's been—been a hell of a long
time."

They started walking again. "You have a nickname over
there?" Archie asked. "Before you were captured?"

"Yeah." The man produced that familiar hesitation, as if he
were afraid the information might be used against him. "Some
of 'em called me Tripwire."

"Tripwire," Archie said. "Why was that?"

"For one thing, I had this obsession about getting out with
my legs still attached. I went around—you know what a
tripwire is?"

Archie nodded. "I've seen them. A thin wire stretched

across a trail or some place, close to the ground, attached to a mine so that when you broke it—''

"Just lying there waiting for some big American boot to come along,'' Tripwire said. "They'd say sometimes you could feel it snap just before the mine comes bouncing up to about waist level and the next thing you know—. I hated the things. I went around with my eyes on the ground all the time. And that's how you get a name. Sometimes they name you after what you love and sometimes they name you after what you hate.''

They fell silent as they walked. The sunshine was strong, and Archie looked at his charge to see if he showed any reaction to it. Maybe the sun had become a personal enemy to him, so that even this milder version would remind him of jungle heat. But the young man was walking easily, without sign of discomfort. Those slow green eyes were half-lidded. In fact from the way he walked, with his head slightly bowed, it looked as though it was actually his ears that were absorbing all the information available. The distant grunting of trucks, the chatter in the buildings around them and in the phone lines overhead. The silent tread of Cong feet, always close at hand.

Archie had never been to Vietnam. He would have been a colonel by now if he had. But by the time he'd come out of basic training and Officers' Candidate School the war had already been winding down and Archie had had a family. It was possible to avoid the war, but his feeling toward it kept alternating. Some weeks he was on the verge of requesting transfer, hungry for the chance to move up in rank on the strength of combat experience, to go to war and return with that distant glare and listening posture of the men who had lived on one of the hundreds of front lines. Other times he was glad to go home to his family every night. He didn't really want to leave them and risk coming back in a box, shocking his children with the fact of his mortality.

He had developed strong feelings toward the men who had gone to the fighting. He resented those who, less able than he, had been promoted over his head after spending a year in Saigon bars. Archie always walked away from their laughing war stories that featured only whores and black marketeers. But for the grunts, the foot soldiers who had actually fought the war—grimy, misled, often dead before they knew it in a country there'd been no need for them ever to hear of—for those men Archie had a respect that always threatened to tip into awe. He couldn't meet one without thinking that this was the very man who had taken his own place on the line. If Archie had had the nerve to go do his duty himself, this man could have been spared.

There was more to it than that. The war always changed a man. That one year of living with death every day became a black hole in the man's lifetime, its gravity warping every preceding and subsequent year toward that Vietnam tour of duty. Nothing could happen thereafter that he couldn't relate back to "When I was in 'Nam . . ." and demonstrate how that experience had changed his attitudes. Archie had the demeaning feeling that he himself would have gone through the whole war untouched, coming back as the same man. Because he had never gone to Vietnam that is in effect what he had done: come through the war unchanged.

He always found himself looking for a sign of the change when he met a combat veteran. He had been watching Truett since yesterday. He didn't disappoint Archie. Cold, quiet, he somehow made the face that should have still been boyish look sinister. Truett was only, what, twenty-one? His face was in fact almost unlined, but the beard and the eyes shrugged off the whole question of age.

Archie cleared his throat. "You know, shave that beard and you'd look pretty official again." His listener stared at him again. "I mean, they'll probably want you to shave it, for new pictures."

"Now who would want my picture?"

"Oh, you know the Army," Archie said lightly. "Everything verified, in triplicate. Pictures with all the forms. Before and after . . ."

The man raised a hand to touch his beard. He smoothed it down, perhaps unaware that it sprang up again as soon as his hand passed.

"I've gotten so used to it," he said. He tried his smile again, and Archie quickly returned it. "I'm not sure I've still got a face under here."

"Well—" Archie wasn't going to order him to shave. He'd be a civilian again in a matter of days, anyway.

They walked on, past the post library. A private passing them with books under his arm edged Archie and his charge closer together on the sidewalk. The private stared curiously at Truett, who didn't appear to notice him.

There seemed to be a good deal, in fact, that escaped Truett's attention. In Archie's experience, most of the returning POWs had been intensely interested in all sorts of things. Television, movies, varieties of food. Tall white women striding around town. Archie remembered one man who had been fascinated by sidewalks; he had forgotten them in his three years as a prisoner. Archie had been answering barrages of questions when taking other former POWs on this same walk. Their eyes were eager to take in birds and buildings and passing cars. Truett showed no such interest. He had yet to ask Archie a question about anything he might have missed. Truett had developed the attitude of a guerrilla fighter. Anything that didn't relate to his immediate survival was trivial. Only danger would bring him to alertness. The rest of the time he was sleepwalking. That was Archie's theory.

"We're going back to the administration building, by the way. A little paperwork . . ."

"When am I getting out?"

Archie hesitated. Nobody had told him anything about Truett's release date. "Pretty soon. You know the Army. Things always—"

"And when am I going to see my parents?"

Longer hesitation. "Should be any time now."

The bearded man stopped walking. "Taking a hell of a long time already, isn't it? I've been here for two days, and you knew I was coming for days before that. I expected you'd have them here waiting for me. But we haven't even talked on the phone yet."

"Yeah. Well, to tell you the truth, Bryan, we're having a little problem. People are working on it right now—"

"What problem? I gave you their address. 1605 Montclair Avenue, Baltimore—"

"Right, right, we've got all that. We're trying to contact them there, but nobody's been home."

Truett was looking at him coldly. He had this trick, Archie had found, of remaining silent when an obvious question should have been asked, but staring as if he had already asked it, and was waiting impatiently for an answer.

"Maybe they're on vacation," Archie said lamely.

"They don't go on vacations."

Truett's face had hardened into the old expression. Archie didn't think he'd see him smile again.

"They're just not there right now, Bryan. You know, they

didn't know you were coming, there was no reason for them to wait. They don't even know you're alive.''

"And you're saying you can't find them to tell them? The Army, the government? Have you checked with the police in Baltimore?''

"It didn't seem called for," Archie said. "We figured they were just out of town for a few days—''

Truett was shaking his head angrily. "No. They don't do things like that. You check with the police, you find out what's happened to them.''

"We will," Archie said soothingly, trying to start them walking again. "In the meantime—''

Truett stayed rooted to the spot. "And what about my back pay? Why's that taking so long?''

"The paperwork I told you about," Archie said. "And the sooner we get to it—''

Tripwire looked at him as if he'd made an obscene suggestion. "You just get me to my parents," he said flatly. "You find out where they are and you take me to them. That's not too much to ask, is it?''

Without waiting for an answer he turned and strode rapidly away. "Tr—" Archie began, and stopped. "Tripwire," he'd been about to call. The name fit when the man was angry. "Truett," Archie called after him, but he didn't stop walking, and Archie let him go. After all he'd been through, Archie didn't have the heart to harass him over a few forms to fill out.

CHAPTER NINE

*B*ill Jerek sat in his office with the door closed. A few weeks ago that would have been unusual. His door had been always open, his office just a part of the larger squadroom outside. Now the closed door was standard. He no longer felt like one of the detectives, and he knew he made them uneasy. It hadn't taken them long to understand that they were being deliberately excluded from the secret of the whereabouts of the witness against Marco Galvan, and they knew what that exclusion meant. Jerek's suspicion had communicated itself to all of them—there had been a lot of searching looks in the first few days of the investigation. But the men didn't really believe it. Most of them had worked together for years. Thinking that one of them was a traitor and a spy required too great a restructuring of their assumptions. So they fell back into familiar patterns. You go to lunch with your partner like always, talk about the Orioles and Earl Weaver, and for half an hour at a time you'd forget that your partner might be the one you were all wondering about. After a while, when the suspicion had failed to take root in their minds, it faded away altogether. It was much easier to believe Marco Galvan had learned about the first witness some other way, through someone else.

Only Captain Jerek held on to his suspicion. The men began to resent him. They had dismissed their mistrust, why hadn't he? Men in the squadroom would look up from a joke or from typing a report and find Jerek staring at them from his office.

The laughter died, the talk faded away to mutters. The men would glare angrily at everything except their captain. When the detectives met for a drink after work it wasn't Marco Galvan they talked about, it was Bill Jerek.

So Jerek's door came closed. He knew the effect he was having on his men. He didn't want to make it any worse than it was. But the fact remained—though only he seemed to still grasp it—that one witness was already dead, killed in this building, and not by an outsider. There'd been no outsiders. The killer hadn't necessarily been one of the detectives, Jerek knew. The station had been full of any number of beat cops, federal agents, assistant d.a.'s. But now that the situation was ripe for Galvan to strike again it was Jerek's own detectives that he could least afford to trust, precisely because they were closest to him. Here in the day-to-day madness of the investigation was where he was most likely to let slip a clue to the Truetts' location, so it was here among his own men that he had to be most guarded. That was another reason for the closed office door, for Jerek's own peace of mind. While he was watching the men, someone was very likely watching him.

It had been two weeks since he had delivered the Truetts to Karen Boone. Jerek was tired. The constant weighing of the factors and the possibilities had finally left him a little numb, aggravated by the fact that he couldn't share this burden with anyone. He felt as if he were playing a gigantic chess game, with himself as one of the pieces. Because, while Jerek was the only one still obsessed with Galvan's capture, Galvan knew Jerek was the only link to the witness who could put him in prison. One way or the other, Jerek was going to be the catalyst that produced the ending to the match.

Now he had something new to consider. He thought it might be best just to ignore this new element, but he didn't think he could. He sat there with the clipping on the desk in front of him and didn't see how it could do him anything but harm.

The pebbled-glass of his office door distorted everything outside. The men in the squadroom were reduced to shadows that passed across the light, receded or expanded to huge proportions when a man came to knock on the door. When a man came that close his features would almost be visible through the glass, but enlarged and disfigured by the pebbling, so it looked as if a huge misshapen monster stood at his door. That happened now. He had been vaguely aware of raised voices and movement in the squadroom, and then a man came briskly through Jerek's door without knocking. Jerek's first impulse was to put a book over the clipping on his desk, but there was no point in trying to hide it. It had, after all, come from this morning's newspaper. It wouldn't be much of a secret to those who understood it. Jerek just sat where he was and said, "Hi, Fred. Feel free to barge in any time."

Fred Tyler was an FBI agent who had grown up in Baltimore, gone away for a while to the academy and assignments in other cities, then in a miracle of bureaucratic acumen been reassigned to his own home town, where he'd remained for four or five years now. He and Jerek were pretty good friends in a nonpersonal, business way. They had managed for the most part to overcome the natural antagonism between federal and local police.

"Came to offer you some help again," Fred said pointedly. He was shorter and a little heavier than Jerek, always casual, usually in a good mood. He perched on the corner of Jerek's desk now and unabashedly looked over some of the papers there. His eye didn't linger on the newspaper clipping.

"Professional help, or personal?" Jerek asked. He was leaning back in his chair, as relaxed as he ever got these days.

"Well, I don't want to put a damper on your day," Tyler said. "But your very few friends are saying that what would profit you most right now is psychiatric help. I stood up for you, though. Said you don't need a shrink, all you need is a nice vacation at some quiet place in the country, where friendly people take care of all your needs during the day and strap you into bed at night. I have some brochures . . ."

Jerek didn't laugh, but his mood lightened. No one had joked with him in two weeks.

"Seriously," the FBI agent said, "don't you think it's time the Bureau stepped into this? Galvan's obviously long gone, out of the state, maybe out of the country."

Jerek shook his head. "He hasn't left town."

"Oh really? You can smell him, I suppose?"

"I know him," Jerek said, standing up, walking around the desk. "He's too damn arrogant to let something like this drive him out of town. He'll stay here and try to handle it. Besides, he thinks this is his city. He thinks he owns the place."

"And it's really yours, isn't it?" Fred Tyler said lightly. Jerek didn't reply and Fred didn't follow up on it. Instead he said, "You know, the federal prosecutors are interested in Galvan too. They're looking into all kinds of possibilities.

Income tax evasion for one, if he was taking money out of that business where he killed the guy. Besides, they think he might be connected to even better organized criminals, if you know what I mean. They might be interested in striking a deal with him."

"No deals," Jerek said flatly. "Not on the murder charge."

Fred didn't argue. All he said was, "Well, luckily, you don't make *all* the decisions," and added quickly, "but that's not what I came to talk about."

"What did you?"

"That," Fred said, stabbing his finger down toward the newspaper clipping while still looking straight at Jerek, across the room. "Interesting little story, isn't it? So small and inconspicuous, too." He picked up the short clipping. "Just a little wire service story. You'd think the local paper would be interested, wouldn't you? Baltimore boy thought dead turns up alive halfway around the world? And so soon after his mother witnesses a murder?"

"I don't think they made the connection," Jerek said.

"And maybe you still have a few friends who are willing not to make a big deal out of it right now in return for a better story when it becomes available. But I don't care about the newspapers. I want to know what you plan to do about this kid."

"Nothing, if I can help it. If he's who he says he is he'll be better off out of the way 'til this is over. If he's not—" Jerek fell silent for a minute, staring out the window. Coming out of his thoughts he said, "Either way Galvan would like nothing better than to have me take this kid to see his 'parents,' so that's exactly what I'm not going to do."

"Even if he is their son?"

Jerek shrugged.

"You're getting awfully cold in your old age," Fred said lightly. "Look, if he is Galvan's it should be easy enough to check out. Where could he have come from? Probably some out-of-work actor from right there in California. His story would—"

Jerek was shaking his head. "He *was* in Malaysia. That's as far back as anyone can verify his story, and from there forward it checks out. No one's going into Vietnam to try tracing him back to some prison camp."

"You have been looking into it," Fred said with faint approval. He looked again at the clipping in his hand. "Not even a fuzzy wire service photo to go with the story? Malaysia?" He fell silent. Jerek looked at his office door. A shadow had passed over the pebbled glass but there was nothing there now. "That's a long reach for Galvan, isn't it?" Fred said, regaining Jerek's attention.

"I don't know," he said slowly. "No one even knows where Galvan is from originally. Maybe California, who knows? We do know he deals drugs, among other things. Southeast Asia was a big heroin connection during the war. If Galvan had a network there it could be operating . . ." Jerek trailed off and glanced at Fred but Fred was listening seriously. So Jerek went on. "There's a whole community of Vietnam vets over there who never came home. In Bangkok, Singapore. Malaysia. You could find someone to fit any description you wanted. And for the right money . . ."

Jerek shrugged, started to say something else, but the FBI agent interrupted him. "Think of those men over there," he said thoughtfully. "Who wanted to stay near that hell rather than come home? Must have had something terrible waiting back here. Or just couldn't stand to let go of the excitement—"

"Whatever." Jerek's voice had grown crisp. "I'm not taking a chance of letting one of them get near my witness. He's on the other side of the country, let him stay there."

"But it'll be easy enough to find out," Fred Tyler said again. He was growing animated. "The kid has fingerprints, doesn't he? And I assume the Army has—" He glanced at the newspaper clipping. "—Bryan Truett's prints on file."

"I'm arranging for that."

"I'll take care of it for you," Fred said, moving toward the door. He seemed again as cheerful as when he'd walked in.

"I can do it."

"Don't take on the world, Bill. This happens to be just the kind of thing the Bureau is well set up to handle. I wouldn't be surprised if we have an office or two even in California. Probably got a bunch of hippies running 'em, but they can probably take a fingerprint. I'll get you a few sets, and some good photos."

"All right," Jerek said. It was true he couldn't handle everything himself, and he was determined that this new element would sidetrack him as little as possible from his main job.

Fred was rereading the newspaper story before laying it back on Jerek's desk. "Be a hell of a story if it's true, wouldn't it?" he said almost to himself.

"Could be a hell of a story either way," Jerek said. "But I don't want to be in it."

"Suit yourself," Fred said. "You always do." At the door he turned back. "I'll have the pictures and prints for you in a day or two. In the meantime, if you decide you're not the Lone Ranger after all and you want some help finding Galvan—"

"I'll keep you in mind," Jerek said. Fred shrugged and smiled and went out, and the pebbled-glass door closed behind him.

PART II

Homecoming

CHAPTER TEN

Tripwire

*A*nother day gone and he was no closer. He'd been a fool to expect any help from the Army. When had it ever come through for him?

And today something had changed. It was already early afternoon and Tripwire hadn't had a visit yet from van Dyne. For two days the man had been his constant companion, and today he had backed off completely. Tripwire sat up suddenly on his bunk. Sunlight streamed unobstructed through the small window. He advanced on it slowly, as if he heard voices outside, but the view from the window was empty.

*A*rchie glanced up from the report he was writing, searching for a word, and drew in his breath sharply. "Truett," he said heartily, but didn't seem to have anything to add. "Didn't hear you come in," Archie finally continued. "Sit down, sit down. Good to see you."

Tripwire closed the office door without a sound and without taking his eyes off the major. Archie glanced at the closed door. It occurred to him that one of the clerks outside should have buzzed him on the intercom to announce Truett's arrival. Archie resisted an urge to pick up his phone and listen for a dial tone, to see if he was still connected to the outside world.

"Glad to see you," he said again. "What can I do for you today?"

Truett didn't respond. They looked at each other in silence. Archie found himself thinking of the man's nickname: "Tripwire." Archie knew a little bit about how people got tagged with names in the Army, and he thought there was more to this one than the story Truett had told him about being afraid of mines. Confined with him now in the office Archie thought it might refer as well to the way he made people feel—afraid to take a step. Cross him and he'd blow up in your face. It wasn't the kind of name a man's friends gave him. It was a name men would say behind him as he passed by.

"Sorry I haven't been around to see you yet today," Archie said. He smiled. "Frankly I thought you'd appreciate the rest. I know I've been running you ragged with all these questions and tests and reports. But you know how—"

"My parents," Tripwire said abruptly. Archie just looked at him politely, still smiling, but as if he didn't understand. "Yes?" he finally said.

"Have you found them?"

Archie hesitated before admitting, "No. I'm sorry, we haven't. But of course we haven't given up. In fact, we've enlisted more help. They're coming to talk to you tomorrow, as a matter of fact."

"To me? Why? I've been out of touch for a while, you remember."

"Just starting at the source, I suppose. Background material, you know." Archie was looking down at the paper clip in his hands that he had been twisting back and forth ever since Tripwire had walked in. Archie was a lousy liar. They both knew it.

"Look," Tripwire said. "Someone knows where they are. Right? Someone official. They didn't just run off on their own. And you know who knows." He didn't make that a question. "So someone can take me to them. Everything else can wait."

"I'm sorry," Archie said. He wasn't lying about that, but if he'd kept talking he would have had to lie again, so he didn't. The silence grew until it made Archie curious and he looked at the other man's face again. He almost flinched from what he saw there. The ex-P.O.W. seemed to be staring stonily at him with the coldest look Archie had ever seen, as if wondering if killing Archie would solve his problems. But as the stare continued Archie saw that the bearded man wasn't looking at him, he was looking *through* him—through the wall behind him as well, and across a great distance, calculating.

"But look," Archie said hastily, standing up, interrupting the stare and the calculations. "I do need your help with something else, if you don't mind." He crossed to a filing cabinet and after a short search drew out a thick, battered file. He set it on the desk in front of Tripwire and opened it. On top of the stack of pages was a photograph of a very young soldier with an uncertain grin. "Know him?" Archie asked.

Tripwire glanced at the picture. "No."

"He's still missing over there," Archie said. He was no longer lying and his voice resumed its normal, slightly eager tone. "MIA. He disappeared from the same general area you did. Here's some information on him." He lifted the picture and underneath were a few typed pages. Archie riffled all the pages in the file. "They're all missing. Everyone here. We hoped you might have some more information about some of them. You were over there for a long time, and more recently than anyone else we have. We thought—"

"We didn't hold reunions, you know," Tripwire said in a harsh but quiet voice. "Walk into a bar and say, 'Hey, anybody from the old 22nd Airborne here?' After I escaped I tried to avoid other prison camps if at all possible."

"I know. Still—" Archie said without apology. "We ask all the ex-P.O.W's to look through this. You might have come across one of them, you never—"

"All right." Tripwire slipped the file under his arm. He hadn't tabled the real issue, though. "And I'll talk to whoever you want me to talk to tomorrow. Once. After that somebody better tell me something. I'll wait one more day."

And Archie believed him. Tripwire was a better liar than Archie was.

*T*ripwire made his way back across the post, walking slowly, apparently not paying much attention to his surroundings. He already knew all the roads and fences and guardposts. That wasn't a problem. A Stateside, peacetime Army post wasn't designed for keeping anyone in. The only problem was letting no one know when you left.

They had assigned him to a very small barracks that stood alone between a parade ground and a street. The barracks seemed to be a hastily-converted office, three small rooms containing a bunk, a desk, two chairs and a television. Tripwire didn't share it with anyone. That was either a thoughtful gesture, someone realizing he wouldn't be used to constant company, or a way of quarantining him until they could isolate the diseases, mental and physical, he might be carrying. In any case, he'd been glad of the solitude, and had retreated to the rooms whenever he could. He didn't like the way the little building stood all alone, though. It made him feel like a target.

He spent most of the rest of the afternoon going through the file Archie had given him. The histories had a dismal sameness to them. Lost when patrol was ambushed. Lost on his second day in-country. Lost the week before he was going home. Lost while out looking for a missing buddy. Lost, lost, lost. The faces, too, were all superficially similar. All very young, American, trying to look tough or sporting nervous grins. Tripwire could read the degrees of fear and hostility under the expressions. And they'd all been right to be scared and angry, hadn't they? None of them had come home.

Only he had. He lay on his bunk and felt dusk gathering outside. He was perfectly relaxed, muscles smooth and easy. He might have lain there forever. Lately he had been winding down like a mechanical toy. Things had gotten too easy for a while. He couldn't adjust to that. Life had been for too long a constant struggle to hold onto life. Idleness and ease were too much like death, or imprisonment.

Now he had been given a challenge. He was glad for the sudden obstacles, glad that it wasn't going to be easy after all. He had something new to press himself against.

The shade of the window was drawn, but he knew when dusk had come. He rose from the bunk and went into the other room. The photographs lay scattered on the desk, but he didn't look at them again. They made him feel like the only survivor from a lost company. He didn't expect any trouble, but just to be sure he glanced out a side window before going to the door.

There was a soldier leaning idly against the nearest building, fifty yards away. No apparent reason for him to be there. The soldier just stood there smoking a cigarette, facing Tripwire's building. He carried a rifle.

Tripwire drew back from the window and returned to the room with the bunk. Its window was on the opposite side of his small building. He looked out and saw another soldier. This one, also armed, was even more obviously on guard, because there was nothing near him, no reason for him to be there. He stood on the edge of the parade ground, at ease but facing Tripwire's building.

Tripwire went to the front and back doors of his building and saw no more guards, but the two who were there were placed far enough away that they had between them a view of the whole building. They could see him leave from any of its four sides. Their strategic placement removed his last doubt that they might be there for another reason.

Archie had believed him when he said he wouldn't do anything for another day, but Archie was no longer in charge.

Night falling wouldn't help. There was nothing but flat ground around the building, not even a bush for cover. There were buildings a hundred yards in front of his building and more a hundred yards behind it, but he didn't have a chance of reaching them unobserved. He thought about climbing out a window and walking straight up to one guard, keeping the building at his back so the other guard couldn't see them. The guard he approached would probably be unwary enough to let Tripwire get too close; after all, it wasn't an enemy soldier they thought they were guarding. But Tripwire had no way of knowing that the guards wouldn't be changed every hour. Even if he took out one of them and got away, an alarm would be raised very soon. The point was to leave without their knowing he'd left.

Of the two waiting guards, one was getting bored and the other one nervous. The bored one looked at his watch and saw that it was almost seven. He wasn't going to be relieved for another four hours. He lit another cigarette and sat down against the wall of the warehouse he'd been leaning on.

The nervous guard on the other side of the house grew more alert as darkness fell. The shadows seemed to change the contour of the ground, to provide cover where none had been an hour ago. He stared at the house intently. But a few minutes later he saw a bird fly down into the deepest shadow, land, and peck at something on the ground. Even in that shadow, the soldier could see the bird clearly. He relaxed.

Both guards sprang to attention when the front door of the house opened and the man they were guarding came jauntily down the front steps. The smoker threw away his cigarette and scrambled to his feet. The birdwatcher stiffened. The man they were guarding didn't glance at either of them. He walked straight up the sidewalk away from his front door, looking down at the ground and patting his pockets as if to be sure he hadn't forgotten anything. He looked like a man leaving for the office in the morning.

The two soldiers kept their distance but followed. When they got clear of the small house they could see each other, a hundred yards apart, with the guarded man in the middle. The guards looked at each other and the smoker shrugged. Their orders were not to confine him to quarters, just to keep track of him, unobtrusively if possible. It was hard to be unobtrusive walking along on his flanks carrying their rifles, but the man didn't seem to notice.

The guards drew in closer as the man approached the nearest buildings in his path. They were two long administrative buildings, side by side with a covered breezeway running lengthwise between them. This time of day the buildings were closed and dark. They weren't his destination, obviously, he was just cutting through to head toward the center of the post. The movie theater, the library, and the PX were all in that direction.

The nervous guard grew a little more nervous when Tripwire glanced in his direction. The guard understood his orders to be that the prisoner shouldn't realize he was a prisoner. The guard didn't know if that was from a sense of diplomacy or for another reason. He did, however, know a little of the history of the man he was guarding. Maybe he'd be dangerous if he knew he was being watched. The guard tried to look nonchalant. He put his head down and hurried along as if on business of his own.

Tripwire disappeared into the covered breezeway.

The two guards, who were much closer now, looked at each other and shrugged again. If even one of them followed him into the small breezeway it would be obvious they were following him. The breezeway would also be a good spot for the guarded man to prepare an ambush if he already knew he was being followed. They didn't think he knew, he had looked too casual, but still—

The nervous guard motioned with both hands and then quickly walked around to the backside of the administration building on the right. The other guard did the same on the left. They walked along at a brisk pace. Even if the guarded man ran through the breezeway, they'd reach the other end soon enough to see where he went.

The nervous guard reached the far end of the building. The guard who'd been smoking was already there, looking at him. There was no one else. They stood there for a minute, looking at the mouth of the breezeway, but no one emerged.

Finally they cast subterfuge to the winds and ran together. They met near the mouth of the breezeway. It was dark inside there, they couldn't see to the other end.

"You think he knew?" the smoker asked.

"We better go call somebody," the nervous guard said.

"Wait a minute, wait a minute, we ain't lost him yet. How far could he have gone?"

The nervous guard just peered into the breezeway.

"Look, he's gotta either come out this end or he doubled back and come out the other end again," the smoker reasoned. "He couldn'ta gone into the buildings, they're locked."

They stood there for another few seconds, feeling time hurrying by. The smoker said, "All right, here. I'll go back around on the outside. You wait a minute and then come through the whatayacallit, the tunnel there."

"The breezeway. But what if he sees me? What if he's still in there?"

"Then he sees ya. At least we'll find him again. Nobody said we haveta be secret about it. Okay? Okay?"

"Okay," the nervous guard said after a pause, and the smoker took off at a run, back around the building he'd just come around.

The nervous guard stood there for a full minute and more, staring into the darkness of the breezeway. He wished the other guard hadn't called it a tunnel. The nervous guard was a little claustrophobic, especially at night. He unslung his rifle from his shoulder and held it. If he looked foolish, okay, he'd look foolish. But he was going to shoot anything that came at him in that dark tunnel. Slowly, he walked down the slight incline and into the mouth of the breezeway.

The guard who smoked ran hard around the administration building, hard enough that he gave himself a mild coughing fit and had to stop. He wasn't worried about getting hurt, he was worried about looking like a jerk. Guard duty was about the most simple-minded duty a man could draw, so what did that make you if you botched it? He was trying to think of how he could put the failure off onto the other clown.

Then he came around the end of the building and his coughing turned into laughing.

There, walking back up the steps into his own little house, a hundred yards away, was the man he was guarding. The smoker stopped running and just stood there. The guarded man was patting one of his pockets again, irritably, as he opened the front door and went back into his house. A light came on inside. The guard lit another cigarette.

Almost five minutes passed before he was joined by the nervous one. "What took ya so damned long?"

"Just being careful," the nervous guard said, trying to keep his voice level. Finding nothing inside the breezeway had been almost worse than finding something, making him advance more and more slowly, adrenaline hitting his heart like a punch in the chest. "Did you find him?"

"Yeah," the smoker laughed. "He went back inside." He indicated the small house with the light burning inside. "Musta forgot something. Look, when he comes back out—"

"When he comes back out *you* follow him through the breezeway and *I*'ll go around."

"Whatever you say," the smoker said, looking at him peculiarly. But they stood there for another five minutes and nothing happened. "I don't think he'd coming back out," the smoker said. "You think he's coming back?"

For answer, the other guard just walked away, back toward his original post.

"Musta just wanted a stroll," the smoker said, walking back to his own spot by the warehouse. When he got there he could no longer see the other guard, but between them they could see all the angles from which a man might leave the small house. They fell back into the dull routine of guard duty.

By that time, of course, Tripwire was long gone. After doubling back to his front door he had stood there until the guard could see him, then he'd gone into the house, patting his pockets and shaking his head like a man who's forgotten something. He had turned on the desk lamp and then gone straight out the back door of the building. With the building between him and his guards it had been easy to get clear. By the time the guards took up their all-seeing posts again the house they guarded was empty.

The point was to get away without their knowing you were gone. He didn't think anyone would check on him tonight. The guards would stay there all night or be replaced and tell their replacements everything was fine. He hoped he'd given himself a ten- or twelve-hour head start.

He ran easily across the Army post, avoiding the main-traveled ways. The sun had been down for half an hour. Shadows had recaptured ground they'd lost during the day. He slipped through them.

The post remained quiet. No alarm sounded, no extra lights

sprang up. Tripwire moved south with no regard for the layout of the post. He wasn't following the roads or making for a specific spot on the perimeter. He wanted to avoid the official exits, but that was easy. There was a great deal more fence than there were guardposts.

When he reached the fence he didn't even slow down. The fence was only a few strands of wire, and the interval between the lights was slightly too large: the circles of light didn't intersect. There was no one in sight. Tripwire ran toward the fence, unaware that his lips were stretched into a smile. He hit the ground, rolled under the wire, let the roll bring him to his feet, and was moving again as if his run hadn't been interrupted.

He crossed a street, the asphalt jarring. Soon he was loping through a residential section, weaponless, empty hands swinging out. The night was cool, lying on him like a friend's good wishes. Dogs confined to back yards smelled him, but he was gone before they knew what they were barking at. He ran easily, the smile on his face again. Behind it he was thinking, the planning as effortless as his run.

They would be looking for Bryan Truett, but how hard would they look? He was a hero of sorts and, as Major van Dyne had said, almost a civilian anyway. His hitch had been up long ago. They might not even consider this a desertion. He suspected that van Dyne would be glad to be rid of him, but from what the major had said this afternoon, there was someone else who had taken an interest in him.

The name Bryan Truett had brought him this far. It would be a hindrance now. The running man didn't think of himself that way. He thought of himself by the name he'd been given in Vietnam. Tripwire. The trigger of a hidden mine. That name had meaning.

Night silence, unwitting canine patrols. Something alien to this neighborhood crossing the quiet front yards. Shadows all around him, shadows he thought of as his friends.

CHAPTER ELEVEN

Jerek

*F*rom the moment he returned to his daily routine after slipping the Truetts out of town, Jerek was followed everywhere he went. That was a matter of course; Jerek accepted it. Galvan had no way of knowing that Elizabeth was gone from the city. It could have been that Jerek wanted to keep her close at hand, maybe even consult with her from time to time. Not likely, of course: Jerek wasn't going to lead Galvan to Elizabeth and Galvan knew that, but there were some options you just had to keep covered. One of the givens in this game was that Jerek was the only one constantly visible. Galvan and Elizabeth had both vanished from sight, but Jerek had to be out there every day. Consequently he had a constant shadow. It was just one of the rules.

But Jerek didn't have to follow the rules. One day not yet a week into the hunt he found himself staring into his rearview mirror at a brown Buick three cars behind him. He recognized the driver, a man named Bigelow who worked for Galvan. Bigelow wasn't being subtle about what he was doing, either. When Jerek pulled into the left turn lane Bigelow followed, even though it meant there were no longer cars between them. He probably knew Jerek could see him in the mirror, but he just sat there behind the wheel looking bored.

Jerek went slowly down the next block. He had nowhere to go. He wasn't following up any leads to Galvan's whereabouts because there were no leads. After turning the next corner Jerek picked up a little speed. His tires squealed on the hot pavement. The Buick fell back but kept plodding after him. It was offensive: Jerek had no idea where to begin looking for Galvan, but Galvan was keeping contant tabs on him.

Jerek continued to speed up. There were cars again between him and the Buick. Jerek suddenly swung into the mouth of a narrow alley and hurtled down it. Back on the next street he slowed as if confident that he'd lost his pursuit. But as he turned into another alley he caught a glimpse of the Buick two blocks behind him, keeping up, just as Jerek wanted.

Bigelow turned into the next alley and saw Jerek's unmarked car parked and empty. He drifted past it, looking at the buildings on both sides. The building behind which Jerek was parked was a restaurant. He could smell the kitchen even with his windows rolled up. But on the opposite side of the alley was the back door to a suite of empty offices. Bigelow knew the neighborhood. He knew the For Rent sign on the front door of the office was faded and peeling.

He parked his own car and ran back. The back door into the office building hadn't quite caught when it closed. Bigelow eased it open. He didn't take his gun out of his belt, yet. He had just been told to follow Jerek. No one thought he'd get a chance to do the main job itself. But if the opportunity came his way . . .

He stepped into a sort of storeroom and closed the door behind himself, leaving him blind in the dimness. There was a light on somewhere deeper into the offices. Bigelow walked quietly toward it.

When he stepped through the door into a hallway Jerek stuck the barrel of a pistol into his ear.

Bigelow jumped a foot, then grimaced when he saw it was the cop. Jerek gestured and Bigelow handed over his gun. Jerek patted him down and found the knife, too. Bigelow shrugged.

"So I'm a dope, okay, so you caught me following you. So what? What're you arresting me for, breakin' and enterin'? The door was open."

"Who said it's an arrest?" Jerek said, and hit him in the side of the head with the gun.

Bigelow went down on the dirty floor. He looked up at Jerek with honest surprise, but didn't bother to say anything. Obviously Jerek wasn't trying to make a legal arrest. That meant there were no restraints.

"That office down there," Jerek said, gesturing with the

gun, but when Bigelow tried to rise Jerek kicked his feet out
from under him. Bigelow started crawling toward the office
doorway, trying to crawl fast enough to get away from Jerek
and back on his feet, but Jerek stayed right with him, kicking
him the length of the hallway. Bigelow fell into the empty
office. "What's the matter with you?" he shouted, his voice
rising and cracking at the end of the question.

Jerek didn't answer directly. "How long you think it'll be
before they find you here?" he said instead. "Real estate agent
doesn't even bother to show this place any more. Could be
months. Know what a body looks like then? I found one once
in an empty tenement. It starts to swell up with gas when it
rots. And if there's no wound for the gas to escape from your
body'll just keep bloating until it finally explodes your guts all
over the room. The smell alone'd make you puke.

"The point is, nobody's going to connect me with the mess
that'll be left of you when you finally turn up. Especially since
I'll be conducting the investigation."

"You're terrifying me," Bigelow said sarcastically, but
when Jerek stepped toward him he slithered back against the
wall. "What's the matter with you?" he repeated. "You got
nothin' against me. I just work for him."

"Brilliant," Jerek said. "And he's the one I want."

Bigelow's eyes opened wide. Jerek had surprised him again.
"You don't think I know where he is? Christ, don't you think
he'd plan for something like this? He wouldn't take a chance
on me givin' him away."

Jerek didn't answer. He reached down, hauled Bigelow
halfway to his feet, and kneed him. As Bigelow was falling
down again Jerek clipped him on the ear with the gun. Bigelow
fell onto his face. When Jerek kicked him in the ribs he rolled
over and stared up at him. Bigelow was groaning, one arm
protecting his ribs and the other cupped over his bleeding ear.
Jerek planted a foot in his stomach and just stood there,
looking down.

"You know I don't know." Bigelow was trying to shout but
with the little breath he had left it came out a moan. "What're
you gonna do, kill me for the fun of it?"

He looked up at Jerek's face and thought that he'd hit on the
reason. Jerek knew; he was just going to take out his frustration
on Galvan's only henchman within reach.

Bigelow started crying.

And Jerek knew he was telling the truth. Bigelow was a big,

hard guy, used to having people glance his way and edge away from him. He probably hadn't cried since he was four. It wouldn't even occur to him to fake that. He lay on the floor blubbering, eyes and nose running, belly shaking.

As Bigelow had said, Galvan would know something like this might happen, and he had protected himself against it. "Well, hell," Jerek said, and walked out. The sound of crying didn't cease all the way down the hall.

*T*hat didn't end the surveillance, of course. Some days Jerek was almost glad to see it. As a week passed with him no closer to finding Galvan, Jerek sometimes began to wonder if he was the only one still playing the game, if something had developed behind his back that had already put an end to Galvan's hunt or soon would. So for that reason Jerek found being followed a comfort. It meant Galvan was doing no better than he was.

But today Jerek had something to do and couldn't afford company. When he left the station he drove a couple of aimless blocks until he could spot who was following him today. It was easy. It was the brown Buick with Bigelow driving again, making no pretense of doing anything except sticking with Jerek. In fact he was edging closer to him through the traffic.

Jerek turned, and turned again. When he'd speed up so would the Buick. No subterfuge was going to work today. Jerek glanced in his mirror and saw Bigelow hunched over the wheel, glaring at him.

Jerek found a block that was lined with cars and a few pedestrians. He wanted witnesses. Jerek parked at a fire hydrant, the only empty space on the block; the Buick had to double-park behind him. Jerek got out and walked back toward it, keeping his hands in plain sight. Bigelow opened his own door and stepped into the street. His eyes were full of hate. The bruise on his cheekbone had turned yellow, Jerek noticed. He kept walking toward the car. Bigelow reached inside his jacket.

Jerek hadn't counted on how much Bigelow hated him. He was oblivious to the passersby. A man sweeping a storefront sidewalk fifteen feet from Bigelow looked up, saw the big man's intention in an instant, and hurried inside his store. Suddenly all the other pedestrians seemed to have vanished as well.

Jerek stopped. "Easy," he said, putting his palms out. Bigelow sneered. His hand was emerging from beneath his jacket.

The police car Jerek had called on the radio came to a stop behind Bigelow's car and gave one short wail of its siren. Bigelow froze, his hand still out of sight inside his jacket. He looked back over his shoulder at the police car, from which two young uniformed officers were emerging. Their revolvers were still holstered. Bigelow turned his glare on Jerek again. Jerek saw him weighing the time he had.

"Not again," Bigelow said in a low, fierce voice as Jerek reached him.

"No," Jerek said. There was sight movement under Bigelow's jacket. When Jerek took his arm and gently pulled his hand out into the open it was empty. To the uniformed officers Jerek said, "This car is double-parked illegally and this gentleman, I believe, is carrying a gun. I'd be surprised if he has a permit."

One of the officers took Bigelow's arm and began frisking him. Bigelow never even glanced at him. He was still watching Jerek. Jerek reached inside the Buick, took the keys, and tossed them to the second patrolman. "Impound it," he said.

Bigelow looked almost comforted. This was all standard procedure this time. He knew where he stood. He'd be back on the street by afternoon. As Jerek turned away Bigelow said, "I wouldn't want to be you." He didn't sound angry any more. He sounded almost cheerful, in fact.

"Be gentle with him," Jerek said to the patrol officers. "He's very sensitive."

He drove away alone. By the time he got near his destination he'd put Bigelow out of his mind. He circled a couple of blocks to make sure no back-up had followed him, and parked three blocks from where he was going. He still had that feeling in the back of his neck that someone was watching him, but he'd had that feeling every minute now for two weeks, even alone in his own bed at night. He felt confident he was unwatched for the moment.

The building he entered was a two-story roominghouse so dilapidated it seemed ready to fall down of its own volition before a wrecking crew got to it. A block down the street three rowhouses that had been in equally bad shape a year ago now sported bay windows and new paint; a Volvo was parked in the street in front of them. In this neighborhood, they looked like a threat.

Jerek went up the creaking stairs and into a room on the second floor without knocking. Inside, the only furnishings were a narrow bed and a desk. The man at the desk looked up, startled, and swept something into a desk drawer and closed it. "What do you think you're doing?" he said then, but his outrage was manufactured. Jerek ignored it. He walked to the one window in the room and looked out at the three refurbished rowhouses.

"They're going to urban renew this place right out from under you, Paul," he said.

The man at the desk was probably not yet thirty and looked forty-five. He was wearing only boxer shorts and an undershirt. His cheeks were heavily stubbled and though it was the middle of the afternoon he looked as if he hadn't been awake long. Jerek's appearance had made him very alert, though. Jerek saw him eyeing the open door.

"Close it," Jerek said.

The man walked slowly across the room, hesitated at the door, and closed it.

"I want to make a deal with you," Jerek said.

Paul laughed. It was a short bark of genuine surprise, not amusement. His eyes still looked scared.

"What I want—" Jerek continued mildly.

"Everybody *knows* what you want," Paul interrupted, then corrected himself: "*Who* you want."

"Good. That'll save us a lot of boring explanation." Jerek had stepped away from the window, toward the center of the room. The other man still stood by the door.

"What makes you think I could help?" he asked nervously.

"Let's skip over that, too," Jerek said briskly. "Just because he's hiding doesn't mean he can afford to let business slide for this long. You've done business with him before, you can let it be known you want to do it again. He'll see you."

"All right," Paul conceded. "But why are you wasting your time? You know I won't do it."

"You don't know what—" Jerek began.

"What could you possibly promise me?" Paul said. His confidence grew as he talked; he convinced himself. He stepped away from the door. "Or were you just planning to threaten me into it? Because let's not be silly. Whatever you'd do to me would be a picnic compared to what we both know he'd do to me. You must be desperate, man."

"You'll do it," Jerek said, his voice rising. His careless facade fell away instantly. He seemed to grow taller with rage. Paul stiffened. For a moment he thought he might have been wrong about the contrast between what Galvan would do to him and what this cop would do. "You'll do it," Jerek went on, "because I'm sick of this! He turned out one of my own men for that last job. Now, *I'm* going to have a spy working for me."

His fist was clenched and he was walking very slowly toward the other man. Paul had backed up against the wall again.

"But not me," he said, as firmly as he could. Scared as he was, he meant it. He'd have to be crazy to try that with Galvan.

"You're declining the assignment?" Jerek said quietly. He had regained his control, which made Paul no less nervous. He nodded.

"All right," Jerek said. "Then get your pants on. You're under arrest."

The younger man looked as if he hadn't heard right, or thought Jerek was making another joke. "You got no reason to arrest me."

"I know. I'll realize that after we get to the station. After I make sure a few key people know I arrested you. Then after you and I sit in my office a little while I'll let you go again. And the same people will know that."

Paul knew what he was saying immediately. "Nobody'll fall for that," he said. "They'll know you're just trying to set me up, make it *look* like I made a deal with you."

Jerek came toward him again. "Yeah, you're right. They probably won't fall for it. But let's try it anyway." He reached for the smaller man's arm.

"Wait a minute, wait a minute," Paul said. His mind was racing. *Jerek could make the trick work, he thought, at least well enough to get me killed.* Because Galvan was not only a cautious man, he was—excitable. It meant nothing to him to have somebody killed. He'd do it if he had the slightest suspicion a man planned to betray him.

But maybe Paul could just stay away from Galvan. Let Jerek try his scheme of making Paul look like a cop spy. If Paul went nowhere near Galvan after that, he couldn't get in trouble.

The trouble was, he probably couldn't stay far enough from Galvan to be safe. Jerek was right, business had to go on. And doing Paul's kind of business in Baltimore these days meant doing business with Marco Galvan. Any of Paul's other contacts would also be contacts to Galvan. It would still look like Paul was trying to get to Galvan.

Paul glanced up at Jerek, who was a good six inches taller and at least that much broader than the younger man. Jerek probably didn't know what he'd done to the city in the last two weeks, Paul thought. Or maybe he did. When a man like Marco Galvan wanted something as badly as he wanted this witness, it gave everybody a bad case of nerves. And with Jerek wanting Galvan just as badly, the whole city was a silent battleground. A man could get killed.

Paul hated it, he *hated* the idea. Not just making a deal with a cop, that was bad enough, but what he hated more was being drawn into the war. He wanted only to sit it out until this one was over. But he could see from Jerek's face that that was no longer possible. And if a man was going to be in a war he'd be a lot better off having one of the generals on his side rather than having both of them out to get him.

"I hope to God nobody saw you come in here," he said.

Jerek smiled. "I think you're making a good career move, Paul. I'll remember this for a long time."

"Yeah," Paul said unhappily. "Let's hope *I* do."

"You could call me at home when you know something," Jerek said, businesslike again. "That'll be safe. Or if I don't hear from you in a few days I'll just drop in again here."

"For God's sake be careful if you do."

"Why thank you, Paul. You be careful too."

Paul gave a melancholy laugh.

After Jerek left Paul stood staring at the door, hoping it would never open again. The best thing he could think of to hope for was that somehow this would all be resolved before he had to do anything. That was the only way he could see to survive this war.

CHAPTER TWELVE

Tripwire

As guards, the soldiers he'd escaped from had been amateurs. The next ones turned out to be semi-pro.

The Army post lay side by side with a small city. He didn't even know its name, but it was big enough to have an airport, if he could find it. He couldn't just take a cab. Not only did he not want to leave anyone behind who knew where he'd gone, but he had no money at all. That lack was like a physical handicap. It would slow him down badly, just when he most needed speed.

On the fringe of the more populous streets he came across a gas station closed for the night. Under its canopy darkness had settled heavily enough to make the oil slick look like a deep black pool. Tripwire tried the door and found it locked. But the door was mostly glass. Through it he could see a rack of maps. One of them should tell him the way to the airport. He laid a palm on the glass and found it thicker than he had expected. He also noticed the wide grey wire of a burglar alarm running through it. He stood there for a moment weighing the risk, and glaring headlights swept across him.

His instinct was to run but he stood stock still. Turning to look into the headlights would both blind him and give the driver a good look at his face, so he stood with his back turned until the headlights passed over him. When he turned to look it wasn't a police car, just a man turning the corner. He did think the driver glanced at him curiously.

That put an end to that plan. He walked away, forcing

himself to move slowly. The area was too crowded; the next car that passed might be a police car. There was almost certainly one close enough to respond quickly to a burglar alarm.

He got through the sleeping residential streets and found a livelier downtown area. He wasn't sure how much good that would do him either, without money, and his instinct was to shy away from the lights. But darkness had taken him as far as it could for the moment. He forced himself out into the glare of a streetlight and shuffled across the street, head down and hands in his pockets.

Tripwire was still dressed in his fatigues. As he crossed another street he saw in the next block a small clump of soldiers. One of them waved and called to him but he walked on. He didn't want to get caught in conversation, but he was glad to see he didn't look out of place in this Army town. That emboldened him to slip into the next bar he saw, after looking in to make sure there were no other soldiers inside. He didn't want to be befriended. There looked to be slim chance of that in this place. There were only five or six customers inside, all men, each one sitting alone, head lowered over a beer with an occasional shot glass beside it. The ones who glanced up at Tripwire, including the bartender, looked sullen. They all seemed to be gathered here waiting for bad news. Tripwire added a slight sideways lurch to his shuffle and slurred his words a little when he leaned on the bar and motioned the bartender to him.

"How does a guy get to the airport in this town?" he asked.

"He calls a cab," the bartender said. A wit. One guy at the bar grunted, the dim equivalent of a laugh. The bartender seemed to appreciate the response.

Tripwire shook his head. "I got a car. All I need's directions."

The bartender couldn't think of a funny answer to that so he just leaned on his own side of the bar and looked hard at Tripwire. The bartender was a beefy middle-aged man with a big, spongy-looking nose and hair that was receding faster than it was greying. Tripwire hoped he didn't look that distinctive himself. The bartender probably saw a lot of soldiers every day and if Tripwire was lucky they all looked alike to him.

"What would a soldier be wanting with the airport?" the bartender finally asked. "Won't the Army take you where you want to go?"

"Got to pick up my mom. She's flying in to meet me."

The bartender considered that. Without answering he took the pencil from behind his ear and began drawing on a napkin. When he had a rough map drawn he explained it. The bartender still sounded sullen—Tripwire wondered briefly if he was giving him completely false directions. He hardly cared any more, he was just very itchy to get outside. Everyone in the place had by now turned to look at him.

The bartender reluctantly parted with the napkin and Tripwire put it in his pocket with thanks. Before he could leave the bartender said, "Don't you want a drink before you go?"

Tripwire tried to look as if the idea appealed to him before he looked at the clock above the bar and said, "I'm already late. I'll stop in on the way back. Mom'll like this place."

The bartender looked neither appeased nor surprised. The other customers kept their fixed stares on Tripwire until he was out the door again. He walked briskly away. No one followed, as he'd half-expected someone might.

Ten minutes later someone *was* following him.

He had reached the outer fringe of downtown, an area more of warehouses than of stores or bars. The streets were not only deserted, the streetlights were farther apart. Tripwire was a little lost, but he felt back in his own element. He breathed more easily.

When he stopped at a corner and looked both ways down the cross street his peripheral vision caught a flash of movement a block behind him. When he turned to look directly there was nothing there. He waited, but when nothing came into sight after a minute he walked on. At the next corner he looked back again and wasn't surprised to see no one. The block held doorways and the mouth of an alley, any number of good hiding places. But he could feel his follower now. Halfway along the next block he glanced back over his shoulder and saw him, just before the guy ducked into a dark doorway. That quick glimpse was enough to identify him. A skinny kid surely not out of his teens, wearing dark pants, black T-shirt, and a bandanna around his forehead. And one hand had been behind his back as if holding something. A mugger.

A godsend.

Tripwire put the slightly drunken roll back into his gait as he walked on. His steps remained silent, but he wasn't even aware of that; it was second nature. So was the strategy. He walked faster to draw his pursuer out of hiding. He passed a long stretch of blank wall with no openings in it, and when the footsteps behind him told him the would-be mugger had reached that stretch of wall Tripwire turned and got a better look at him. The kid had nowhere to hide and just stood there foolishly, stopped in his tracks. He definitely had a weapon in his hand, probably a knife, possibly a heavy piece of pipe. Tripwire pretended not to see him and made a show of retying his boot while the kid finally ducked behind a mailbox.

At the next intersection, though, there was a streetlight, and after Tripwire crossed through it the kid did too, deliberately letting himself be seen, even whistling in a great show of fake casualness. Tripwire wondered what the point of that was. Possibly to scare him. Obligingly, Tripwire put on a small display of panic, like blood in the water, to draw him in.

But it didn't.

The kid maintained his distance. When Tripwire speeded up so did the kid. When Tripwire tired of the game and slowed down, pretending to stumble, the kid hung back, making no move to close in. He stayed almost a full block behind.

When Tripwire had first realized he was being followed his body had responded joyfully. It knew what to do. Tripwire had felt cramped and inhibited for a week. His run-and-hide instincts kept his nerves constantly at war while he sat in a chair or lay on a bed or walked across a compound in broad daylight. But here in the dark with a shadowy pursuer behind him he had felt at ease again.

Now, though, he was getting irritated. The mugger wasn't behaving as he should have. Tripwire had done everything but lie down on the sidewalk, but the kid wouldn't close in. It was as if the kid had been assigned to keep track of him and no more. Tripwire wondered if it was possible this kid was a back-up to the guards he'd eluded.

Just before he stepped into the trap, he realized the mistake he'd made.

It was the setting that threw him off. If he'd found himself being followed down a jungle trail, with a ravine or an especially thick stand of trees ahead, he would have recognized the makings of an ambush at once. But he didn't associate those tactics with city streets and empty looming warehouses. He might have been better off if he'd closed his eyes and imagined himself back in Vietnam.

He finally realized what was happening when he saw the street was coming to a dead end. There was a building on his right which ended at a narrow alley twenty yards ahead. On the far side of the alley the street came to a fence and stopped. Across the street another building ran all the way up to that fence, so there was no way out except he way he had come or into that dark alley. The spot was ideal and the kid behind him had herded him right into it.

Tripwire heard the footsteps behind him finally pick up their pace, but they were still some seconds behind him. His most obvious move would be to turn and meet his attacker, but that would leave his back to whatever lurked in that alley. Better, he decided immediately, to plunge ahead unexpectedly, leaving the known danger at his back to be dealt with later.

The alley mouth was still twenty yards ahead of him. Tripwire deliberately made his steps heavy and slow. He even bumped against a trash can, sending it rattling into the street. At the corner ahead of him a bare sliver of face appeared, then hastily drew back. As soon as the mugger's hidden ally had judged Tripwire's pace, Tripwire changed it. He ran, silently. Behind him, the first mugger started running too.

Tripwire came around the corner low and hard. The hidden man wasn't where he had expected, he had drawn back farther into the alley, so even though Tripwire's sudden appearance was a surprise, the guy had time to react. For a frozen moment they were staring at each other as they closed in. But the mugger's hand holding the knife was already drawn back and before Tripwire could reach him it had started forward.

But he was starting from a dead stop and Tripwire had come around the corner at a run. It was no contest. The mugger's arm appeared to be moving in slow motion by comparison as Tripwire lowered his head and butted him in the stomach. Tripwire slammed him back against the brick wall and breath gushed out of the mugger's body. His knife-holding hand dropped to his side. Tripwire grabbed that wrist and forced the hand behind the guy's back. But at that moment the guy's other hand came up and clamped on Tripwire's throat.

They stood locked like that. Tripwire heard a voice shout, "Randy!" Pounding feet sounded close at hand. He'd be around the corner in another few seconds. The guy Tripwire was holding smiled at him thinly.

But Tripwire's hand was still moving behind his back. The mugger hadn't dropped his knife, but Tripwire had control of the guy's wrist. He turned it, and the handle end of the knife touched the wall, so that the knife was standing out from the wall at a ninety degree angle. The mugger lost his smile as he felt the point of the knife touch his back.

Tripwire pushed.

The original mugger came pounding toward the corner where the drunken soldier had disappeared and Randy had been waiting. That was the plan and it should be all over by now, but the drunken soldier hadn't looked so drunk there just before he went around the corner, and Randy wasn't answering his friend's shouts. The first mugger's throat tightened, but it wasn't from fear, it was from eagerness. He wanted to be in on the kill. His knife was out and steady in his hand as he ran. Breathlessly, he came around the corner.

And stopped dead. "Randy?" he said.

In the dimness he saw Randy standing there, staring at him. His knife was hanging at his side, and it was wet. "Randy?" the first mugger said again, starting toward him.

Tripwire, standing behind Randy and holding him up with one hand gripping the fabric of Randy's shirt, gave a push and Randy toppled forward into his friend. When Randy fell out of the way, the first mugger could see that it wasn't Randy's hand holding the bloody knife, it was Tripwire's.

Tripwire pushed forward, but as a shield Randy wasn't ideal. He was heavy and his feet dragged. And his friend was cat quick. Startled as he was, he saw at once what had happened and stepped aside. Tripwire was in danger of falling over Randy's feet and going down. He let go and the mugger crashed to the ground. Randy groaned and his limbs moved slightly, but his standing friend didn't even glance at him. He and Tripwire stood there three feet apart, both holding knives.

But Tripwire was no knife fighter. That was for city boys, and it seemed like a long time since he'd been a city boy. The city boy facing him, for example, looked confident. He held the knife easily in his hand, like an extension of his flesh. So Tripwire threw his own knife away.

He made a placating gesture with his free hand, stepped back half a step, and threw his knife straight up into the air. He put both hands up, palms outward, surrendering.

The kid didn't believe it for a second, of course, but he couldn't help himself, he was worried about where that knife was coming down. He looked up.

Tripwire was on him at once. He didn't leap at the kid—you lose speed if you leave your feet, and you have no leverage when you reach your destination. He just ran, so he had momentum by the time he reached the mugger and the kid had none. By the time he got his eyes down Tripwire was already driving him backward. Tripwire's hand was clamped around the wrist of the hand holding the knife, but the kid was good, he started twisting even while he was being pushed back, and he might have been able to wiggle free, but before he could they had reached the corner of the building and Tripwire slammed his arm against that brick-hard edge.

The kid screamed and fell on his back on the pavement. When his first wave of pain passed he looked up to see Tripwire kneeling, his knee barely pressing down on his chest. For the first time in his life the kid wished there were cops around. The soldier picked up the knife and brought it toward the kid's throat, muttering what sounded like a valedictory wish:

"I hope you had a good night."

The kid misunderstood that until the soldier started patting at his clothes, then he said helpfully, "Here, here." He made the mistake of moving his bad arm and the pain shot through him again, but through clenched teeth he said, "The shirt pocket."

Tripwire found the roll of bills there. It was obvious from the size of it these kids *had* been having a good night until the last few minutes. It must have been payday at the post, and Tripwire was not their first planned victim. The money in the roll of bills could take someone a good way across the country.

And the mugger certainly wasn't going to report the robbery. He lay there on the pavement looking very young suddenly, a schoolboy, the few hairs of his wispy moustache made oily by the sweat on his lip. It was a warm night but the kid was shivering. His arm no longer hurt him. He looked up at the soldier, who was staring at the roll of bills as if it were his own recovered money. In his other hand he still held the knife. His attention returned to the kid under him and he looked momentarily undecided.

"We wouldna hurt ya," the kid said unconvincingly. His remark left the soldier unmoved. His eyes looked opaque, nothing behind them. The kid turned his head away from that expression and closed his eyes.

The rage the fight had induced in Tripwire was fading. But his heart was still pounding. He suddenly drew back his arm and hurled the knife as hard as he could in a high arc, so far away he couldn't hear a sound when it landed. By that time he was running again, around the corner and through the dark streets.

An hour later he boarded a plane. He took the first one leaving rather than wait for one going in the direction of Baltimore. That wouldn't fool anyone for long. They knew where he had to go. He wondered who would be waiting.

CHAPTER THIRTEEN

John

*J*erek would feel a lot better after he had a spy of his own in Galvan's camp. As it was he had no idea what Galvan was up to or how much he had learned. There was still that nagging feeling that he'd made a mistake at the very beginning, that somehow Galvan had already bypassed him and was closing in on his victim. Every day Jerek resisted the temptation to call Karen Boone and make sure she and Elizabeth and John Truett were safe.

*S*ilence had recaptured their lives. During her visit Karen had literally brought a breath of fresh air into the house. It had been the only time since their arrival that the door of the house had opened. Karen had sat there unknowingly holding them enthralled with the most mundane trivia. Her remarks had conjured up streets, buildings, *grocery stores*, for God's sake! They sensed that Karen was a little bored with her life. But John could teach her something about boredom. Hadn't she seen how he and Elizabeth had hung on her conversation like clotheslined sheets longing for a breeze? Now, in the three days since her visit John had been living on the glory of his twenty-foot trip to her car to carry in a bag of groceries. Karen had been in the kitchen with Elizabeth. He knew she wouldn't want him going outside, so he felt like a kid sneaking out. But it had been wonderful to feel something underfoot besides carpet or linoleum. He had been able to look all the way to the corner, where a car had been passing. A new model Buick John had seen only in TV commercials. Just the air itself had been revitalizing, air that had never been breathed and re-breathed behind a prison of walls. It had held more smells than he could assimilate in his brief moment of freedom. Fresh cut grass. The barest taste of wood smoke. Even the hint of dog shit had been appealing. Well worth the reproachful look from Karen when he'd gone back in with the groceries.

Elizabeth passed through the room and into the kitchen. John sat up and opened his mouth. But he had nothing to say. That was one of the properties of prolonged silence, he had discovered. At its beginning it could be shattered by anything, a glass scraping or a TV show. The clearing of a throat would do it. But as the silence lengthened its importance grew, until it could only be broken by something of equal importance. Let the silence go on long enough and no statement seemed consequential enough to throw up against the quiet. For a moment he imagined that he couldn't speak now if he wanted, that any sound would be absorbed by the sandbagged walls of silence that had grown up in the house.

When they first came to this house there were moments when it seemed like a second honeymoon, in spite of the danger. No; because of it—the danger and the isolation had made them even closer. They saw no one else, they didn't set foot outside, there was no reason to get out of bed in the morning. That first week they made love more often than they had in years, more than since they were first married. It almost seemed as if they were newlyweds again, just starting out in a barely furnished house that wasn't theirs yet because they hadn't filled it with memories.

John had felt fired with purpose when they'd first come here. It had seemed likely the murderers were close on their trail. He had felt like a guardian rather than one of the protected—the last line of defense between Elizabeth and the killer she had seen. But as the days slipped away so did his sense of danger. His days were too quiet. John hadn't seen the murder, or Galvan in the flesh; hadn't run terrified through the streets. It was all second hand for him. By now the threat was less immediately real to him than his restlessness.

He drifted into the kitchen. Elizabeth was still there. He touched her arm in passing and she smiled. Elizabeth sensed his restlessness, and he knew she took it as an indictment of her. She had put them in this spot. He had tried to tell her differently, but she still felt guilty. He couldn't help that.

He opened the carton of milk and sniffed at it. There was no way to adequately provision a house for a full week. Things went bad. He was used to stopping on the way home from work for a quart of milk or a loaf of bread. John was already away from the refrigerator, groping in his pocket for car keys and wondering where the nearest convenience store was, when he remembered he had no car and he couldn't go out. Old habits constantly reasserted themselves that way: he couldn't keep constantly in mind his new restrictions.

But as he walked back to the bedroom he thought, why not? A short walk to the store wouldn't expose him to anything more threatening than bad drivers. If the killers knew they were in this town they would have already found them by now; they would have followed Karen to the house three days ago. No one knew them here, almost a thousand miles from home.

In the back of his mind he knew he was only rationalizing his way to doing what he wanted, and accepted it as such. Already a tiny resentment was growing because he knew Elizabeth wouldn't accept it.

His wallet lay on the dresser in the bedroom. He pocketed it along with some change he hadn't had the chance to spend in two weeks, and, as an afterthought, the keys to this house, which he'd never had in his pocket before. He slipped on thin-soled mocassins that were really meant as house slippers but that would do for a short trip to the store. He realized as he left the bedroom that he was already trying to walk without making a sound, like an Indian scout, and he grinned at himself, feeling foolish but determined.

Now for the hard part. In the living room he said, "Elizabeth?"

She came out drying her hands on a dish towel. He saw her look momentarily uneasy at finding him there jingling the keys in his pocket, but she didn't say anything. Her hands didn't stop moving under the dish towel. "Yes?"

"I'm going out and find a store," he said quickly, but he didn't try to slip slyly away as soon as he'd said it. He stood there waiting for the inevitable confrontation.

Elizabeth just looked at him. "It'll be okay," he said. "I'll just be gone a few minutes."

"I hope so."

"Look," he began, and realized that was too loud. "They're not out there. We're too far away. If he's got people in every town in America then we might as well give up, we're dead already."

She didn't respond, and John regretted his choice of words. "I'm going nuts in here. I've just got to get out for a little while. Ten minutes."

"I know you are," she said. John started to speak but she continued. "But that's not enough reason to take unnecessary chances. We don't know anything about him except that he's a powerful man and he's desperate to find—us. I'm sorry—"

There was a short silence. John wanted to say that it wasn't an unnecessary chance, or that he was desperate too. It would be silly to make such a comparison, he knew. He wanted to say that if they stayed huddled here forever inside this tiny house then their lives—the lives they knew—were already lost. What he said instead was, "I'm not doing this just to provoke you, you know."

"I know." Elizabeth lowered her eyes. They both looked at her hands, still covered by the dish towel. Like the preliminary to a magician's trick; in a moment a pigeon would burst from the concealment.

"Look at us," John said with a short, artificial laugh. "Can you even imagine this argument? About a walk to the Seven-Eleven?"

That drew only a wan smile from her. Still without looking up at him she said, "I wish—" but the futility of wishing fell on her before she could complete the thought. She turned back toward the kitchen. "All right," she said faintly.

John stepped toward her, his throat already warm with his raised voice. He didn't want just a concession, he wanted an acknowledgment that he was right. He wanted to argue and win.

Elizabeth had already passed through the doorway out of sight. He stopped, the words unspoken. His shoulders drooped to their natural level. The argument would be futile. The way to win it was to do what he proposed—go out and come back safely.

It wasn't fair to be mad at Elizabeth. He turned and walked to the front door. It was no more her fault than his.

As he went out the door he said, "I love you," but it

sounded melodramatic, too significant. He hoped she hadn't heard it.

At the sound of the door opening Elizabeth ran out of the kitchen and through the living room, but she got to the front door just in time to see it close and hear the locks turn again. She stopped dead. She wouldn't follow him.

She wandered into the back of the house, to the bathroom. She stood in front of the mirror over the sink, but it wasn't herself she looked at. She couldn't expect John to feel as she did, when she was even beginning to forget herself. It was so hard to hold on to the terror of that one night. It had really lasted only a few minutes, and like a bad dream it was slipping away from her. For the same reason a dream fades: there was nothing to link it to the rest of her life. The whole thing—the killing, the chase, the murderer's scowl—was so alien that it detached itself from her memory and floated away into fantasy.

But Elizabeth knew it had been real. She knew she was still in danger. Like an athlete exercising every day to stay in shape, she made herself remember.

What she was looking at on the mirror was a small photograph taped to the upper left corner. It was a slightly blurred photocopy of a police file photo, but still sharp enough for her to make out the image. The face was that of Marco Galvan. He hadn't been holding his head up when the picture was snapped, so the double chin showed under the broad, flat face. The lines of his face fell naturally into a sneer. Nothing animated the features. It was Elizabeth's imagination that made the eyes leak hate. She knew that face so well by now that she could project it in front of her at any time of the day, place it on John's head or Karen's. Galvan had become almost a member of the family, but only as a photograph. Elizabeth remembered him as one remembers a grandmother who died during one's childhood: the photograph overlaid the actual memory. She wondered if she would recognize the real man if she saw him now. John almost certainly would not. He probably never glanced anymore at the picture taped to the mirror.

John stiffened as soon as he closed the door behind him. He immediately turned his back on the outdoor scene while he twisted the locks closed. He was trying to look immensely casual, and of course failing. Everyone in the houses across the street must have spotted him by now. *Hey! Come look!*

Somebody's coming out of that house over there, the one where they never come outside. See him? Quick, go call Fred and Ethel next door, tell them to look too!

Stop that. Nobody was watching, no one gave a damn if he came or went. They probably weren't even home over there. They had better things to do than watch for him all day long. Even if they had at first, they would have gotten bored with it by now. No one would have waited around at the window this long for him to appear. John turned, pocketed the keys, and gave one searching glance to the houses he could see. There were no faces in the windows. Their curtains didn't move. He started down the driveway to the sidewalk. His hands were in his pockets and his shoulders slumped as if they'd like to crawl in after the hands.

But that was stupid. He *would* draw attention if he made himself look like the most suspicious character in town. John deliberately straightened his shoulders and paused on the sidewalk to look up and down the street. No one in sight. Unbunching his shoulders allowed the sunlight to sink into his skin. He breathed deeply, testing for all the smells he'd gotten bare tastes of three days ago. They were all there and more, too many to classify. He smiled, smiled at himself for smiling, and started walking.

He could feel the warmth of the sidewalk through the thin soles of his moccasins. If he stood in one spot too long the feeling would become uncomfortable, but while he kept moving it was pleasant. The sidewalk was old and full of cracks. Occasionally there was a slab that had been convulsed out of place and now stood at a slant, like a ship about to rear up and slide beneath the green waves.

John continued to see no one. He was not to the end of the block before his uneasiness returned. He couldn't keep Elizabeth's fears, and his own, at bay. he pictured her at home waiting at the window for him. Abruptly the walk lost its pleasure and became a test. How long did he have to stay out to prove to both of them that it was safe? How soon could he go back home and lock himself in? If he got killed in this senseless display of bravado he'd feel terribly guilty. If they got him they would also get the house keys in his pocket. And Elizabeth might be standing at the window in plain view because of him.

He walked faster. The sinister houses watched him. Every window was a good spot for a sniper with a high-powered rifle. Every window he passed safely brought him into range of a

new one. There was no way to tell which posed the real danger.
Maybe all of them. Why were they toying with him?

All right. Stop. He stood at the corner and looked both ways
for a long time, using the interval to calm himself. He took his
hands out of his pockets and swung his arms as he crossed to
the next block. He didn't smile at himself again, but he did
slow down and become a stroller rather than a fugitive. He
glanced at the windows he was passing. Most had blinds down
or shades closed. Some had potted plants inside on the sills.
Those windows didn't hide any assassins.

On the other hand, they didn't offer any refuge, either. Why
was everyone hiding inside, leaving him alone on the street?
He couldn't rush up to any of those closed, locked doors and be
taken in. He would still be beating on the door when the bullets
cut him down. The street was empty of people. When the black
limousine came gliding down it John would be the only human
in sight, an obvious target.

All right, now that wasn't Elizabeth's fault, he was doing
that to himself. All those damned TV shows he watched all day
for the last two weeks. Reruns of *The Untouchables* and
Gunsmoke. In a minute he'd see Jack Palance step out of a two-
car garage, spread his fingers as he pulled the black glove tight
on his hand, and tell John to go for his gun. Be sensible. No
one was going to gun him down on this quiet street. (Yeah, a
little *too* quiet.) (Cut that out.)

Still, it summer, and the middle of the afternoon. Why
weren't there children out playing?

He had walked three blocks now. When he managed to
dampen his imagination he realized the character of the area. It
was an older neighborhood. All the trees were grown tall, good
for climbing. But the children who might have climbed them
had grown tall themselves, and left home for neighborhoods of
their own. Back yards would be empty now, bearing the
imprint of dismantled swing sets given to the Salvation Army.
The only children he'd seen on this street from his window
were high school age. Of the children left in this neighborhood, the youngest would be teenagers.

The simple mystery solved, John's walk turned pleasant
again. The tall old trees provided frequent respites from the
sun, the sun a warm renewal when he came out of the shade.
He saw through an undraped window a woman vacuuming,
then an old man outside watering his lawn. The old man
returned John's wave. John took two steps on the wet grass, a

relief to his feet, just as it had been in childhood when he'd gone everywhere barefoot.

The houses were mostly old wooden frame houses, not elaborate by their own standards but looking quaintly stylized by comparison with stark modern structures. John didn't have modern tastes. The houses gave him a comfortable feeling. Most were kept up nicely, but here and there was one that had given out, particularly susceptible to the wasting disease that afflicted the whole neighborhood. Weeds grew in the yard. Cardboard patched broken windows. Not all of these houses were vacant.

John turned right at the next corner, and two blocks brought him to a broader, busier street. Here were the children he had missed. They were in cars, driving up and down the boulevard, calling to each other at the stop lights, pulling off into the parking lots. Children drove everywhere they went these days.

Consequently, their feet wouldn't be as hot and sore as John's were. It had been a stupid gesture to go out wearing the moccasins. He turned right again and walked beside the busier street. There was no sidewalk; he stepped carefully along the gravelled shoulder. City planners didn't expect pedestrians here. He had to watch his feet carefully to avoid shards of broken glass. Sharp pebbles bruised him through the thin leather of the shoes.

When he came to the next cross street he looked up and waited for the light. Across this street was a small but crowded shopping center with a grocery, record store, small bar, dime store. In the center, next to the bar, was a hardware store. As John watched, a young man came out carrying a small stack of two-by-fours. He managed to open the door of his car and get the wood inside, but the boards were too long, he had to leave the other ends sticking out the window. The young man tapped them tentatively, as if commanding a newly-trained dog to stay.

On a normal outing John would have at least stepped into the hardware store, assessed its order and its smells, but today he looked at it as if it were a trap deliberately set for him, and gave it a wide berth. He glanced back over his shoulder as he ducked into the grocery store.

It wasn't the pleasure he had anticipated. Everyone seemed to look at him either suspiciously or as if his name were on the tips of their tongues. Carts came at him suddenly around corners. He got the quart of milk and didn't even take the time to look around for a good dessert. The checkout clerk's automatic pleasantries made him duck his head and mumble.

John was hurrying as he crossed the street toward home. He paid close attention to his feet on the roadside. It wouldn't do to cut his foot so that blood would be the first thing Elizabeth saw when he got back. At the next block he turned down a quieter street. Something was trying to catch his attention, but he didn't notice it until he made that turn. A car engine was turning over slowly behind him.

He had been hearing the sounds of cars all along the boulevard, but those had been racing, rising to a roar just before they rushed past him, then fading into the overall buzz. This new sound remained constant, a few feet back of his left elbow. A car was following him.

John didn't let his imagination panic him again. He was probably wrong. If not, there was another explanation. Maybe it was a police car, with a cop so familiar with the neighborhood John stood out in it. He glanced back casually as if he were about to cross the street. Then he turned back and kept walking, forcing himself to keep the same pace and watch for broken glass. It was no police car following him, it was an old blue Mustang, with those impenetrably tinted black windows and windshield. John had always hated that stuff, had refused to carry it in his own hardware store even though people occasionally asked for it. It made cars look sinister, darkly intentioned, not like instruments of human transportation.

The car didn't pass him. it stayed hovering back there. He could hear its engine thrumming. John was worried, but he didn't feel doomed. He was out in the open, surrounded by people, not yet back in the unpopulated streets of his own neighborhood. He looked around at all the passing traffic, trying to find allies.

The trouble was that he had turned back toward home, and there were no allies. Even among all these people there was no other pedestrian, and all the cars drove by unconcernedly. Drivers don't notice walkers, unless the walkers get in the way of their cars. Sometimes not even then.

John forced himself not to look back, then looked back anyway, forgetting his determination not to do so. The Mustang was still there. Yes, its headlights looked like eyes, its grill like a sinister smile, its black windshield like a mask behind which a madman sat and ruled the world. All that idiot stuff, made real here on the midafternoon street. John saw no good reason now why he shouldn't panic. No one was noticing him anyway. Maybe panic would draw the attention he needed.

He almost laughed, thinking of the Mustang. It wasn't what he had pictured. He had been thinking the killers would come in a long black limo, or maybe the late model Buick he had seen the other day. By why not a five-year-old Mustang? Who said gangsters had to follow television's rules?

His feet hurt like hell. He would have stopped to rub them by now if he weren't being pursued. Maybe he should stop and see if the car would glide past. But no, that was probably what they wanted, one good shot at a still target. John wasn't used to making plans that affected his survival. Even now he couldn't concentrate on the problem. His mind veered off into self-recrimination. Elizabeth had been right. Even if this hadn't happened, had this walk been so damned wonderful that he should have risked both their lives for it? The one thing he could do now was try to make sure the killers wouldn't find her through his idiocy. He took out his house keys and, screening the action with his body, flipped them into a bush as he passed. At least they wouldn't find them on his body, use them against his wife.

It was time to run. There was no point in continuing to play their waiting game. He didn't want to lead them any closer to the house. John was walking beside a vacant lot. As he veered off into it he heard the car's engine being gunned. He looked over his shoulder. The passenger's window was open and something was emerging. John ran. He looked back once more and saw an arm out the window and something coming toward him. He dived to the ground and the object shattered beside him. There was a sudden reek.

Of beer. The hurled object had turned into broken brown glass on the ground beside him, and some of the beer left in the bottle had splashed onto his shirt. The car was roaring away now, trailing teenage laughter. John lay panting on the ground, as shattered as the beer bottle. His feet were killing him.

CHAPTER FOURTEEN

Tripwire

*T*ripwire was on an airplane for the first time since returning to America, and he didn't like it. He hung above the country like a slow-moving target, and all his twitches and fears couldn't force the plane to go any faster or into any evasive maneuvers. It was against all his instincts to be inside a big, visible vessel with its destination known to anyone who cared to look at a flight schedule.

Nor did he like being trapped in a confined area with his fellow passengers. It was three o'clock in the morning; most of the lights were off. Rare puddles of light spotlighted the reading heads of strangers who couldn't sleep on planes either. Tripwire had his own light turned off, but these shadows were not his friends. They were disconnected from the ones he knew on the ground: the sanctuary they offered was patently false.

The carefully controlled air inside the plane felt to him too close. He had broken into a light sweat. When he did close his eyes the passenger compartment seemed to grow even smaller. He pictured the other passengers turning to look at him and slowly rising from their seats to creep closer. He could hear their soft tread.

His eyes snapped open. A stewardess was just passing him in the aisle, glancing from side to side. Her hands were empty. No one had made any requests of her on her late-night round. Tripwire watched her progress. She slipped behind a curtain and did not reappear.

After a moment he followed her, through the parted curtains

to the front of the plane. His eyes roamed over the features of the plane: the overhead compartments, the emergency exits, the small closet opposite the door through which the passengers had boarded. In front of that closet the stewardess sat talking quietly to another stewardess. Before they saw him Tripwire withdrew. He still wore his Army fatigues and his beard, and knew he made a too-memorable figure.

He retraced his steps slowly down the aisle, past his own vacant seat toward the back of the plane. The seats of the late night flight weren't half filled. Some passengers had a row of three seats to themselves. Tripwire studied each face he passed. The passengers didn't look as affluent as those on a daytime flight would: kids in jeans, a couple of family groups, an occasional man in a suit. Nearly all of them were sleeping, or pretending to sleep.

A woman's eyes flickered open and held his. She gasped; she had no way of knowing how long he'd been standing there. Tripwire hurried on, not looking back.

No one looked any more or less suspicious than anyone else, to a man who had seen old women handle automatic weapons and three-year-old children wired with explosives. Tripwire took a seat near the back of the plane and watched the aisle mistrustfully.

When the plane began to descend, the change in pressure started waking people up, and the stewardess's too-cheerful voice completed the job. "The captain has informed us that we are on our final approach to Houston Intercontinental Airport. We will be stopping in Houston for approximately fifteen minutes. Those of you going on with us to Atlanta, please remain in your seats. For those who will be disembarking here, welcome to Houston."

When the wheels touched the runway few of the passengers followed the stewardess's instruction to remain seated. Tripwire, who had returned to his original seat shortly before her annoucement, clogged the aisle with the rest of the passengers. He wanted to be in the midst of the crowd when they disembarked.

In the terminal was a man in a blue suit doing a favor for a friend. The man was in his thirties, of average height but with broad shoulders, his stomach growing a little too heavy. He spent a good deal of time in the airport, especially late at night, looking for nervous people traveling alone, carrying hand luggage and flying in from Miami or Los Angeles. Tonight he was also keeping an eye out for a young soldier with a beard who might be on a flight from California.

The man in the blue suit had a partner who had picked a bad time to go for coffee, because the plane landed as soon as he left.

Tripwire strode through the swaying umbilicus tube into the terminal. "These things give me the creeps," the man next to him said. "Like being in the belly of a big metal worm."

Tripwire agreed and said so. He walked closer to the man and asked about his destination, so when the two of them emerged into the terminal it looked as if they were traveling together. A small disguise but sometimes effective. A man looking for someone traveling alone will surprisingly often let his eyes glide right over small groups.

The man in the blue suit made that mistake initially. He was leaning against a column scanning the small crowd emerging from the California plane, looking for a young soldier traveling alone. The passengers were spreading out as they came toward him. They blocked his view of the later-emerging passengers. He kept twisting his head.

Tripwire spotted him immediately. The man's eyes were alert but his face expressionless. There was no anticipation of seeing someone he knew. Tripwire now felt trapped in the crowd he had planned to use for cover. He kept his head turned toward his fellow passenger but his neck was tense, waiting for the gaze of the man in the blue suit to settle on him.

A moment later it did. The man stood up straighter but didn't take a step yet. He didn't want to alarm the soldier.

As soon as Tripwire knew he'd been seen he raised his right hand and gave a big wave, breaking into a grin and a trot. He was looking far across the terminal. The man in the blue suit turned and looked as well. There were a couple of small family groups there, coming toward the passengers, smiling and waving. The watching man was momentarily flustered. He was used to intercepting people who were alone and nervous. He didn't want to break up a family reunion.

When he looked back, the soldier was gone.

The instant the man had looked away across the terminal Tripwire had turned and gone back the way he'd come, fast but not fast enough to draw attention. He had maybe two seconds until the man turned to look for him again. But Tripwire knew the way a watcher's eyes work. The man had seen Tripwire starting to run, so when he looked back for him his mind made an automatic adjustment and he looked where the run would have taken the soldier in that short time. By changing his course and speed, Tripwire had vanished.

But the trick was good for only seconds, not long enough to get him to an exit from the terminal. Tripwire ducked into a men's room, the only refuge in sight. Inside it was bright and open, the lights reflecting off the white tile, offering him no protection.

The man in the blue suit came away from the pillar, eyes tracking over the whole terminal. The passengers had thinned out enough that he could be sure his quarry was no longer among them. He said something under his breath and started for the exit from the terminal. But he stopped. He had enough confidence in himself to be sure the soldier hadn't gotten that far. Besides, his partner was out there, should be on his way back by now, and he too knew they were watching for a bearded soldier.

He started across the terminal, and didn't see the men's room door open a crack. Tripwire stood behind that door. He had turned off the light. When the man stepped into that darkness Tripwire would have the advantage.

But the man in the blue suit had another destination. He knew the California flight was a through flight to Atlanta. He reasonably assumed the soldier had reboarded to resume his journey. He disappeared into the tunnel.

Tripwire came out of the men's room, ran softly across the terminal, and through the door into the main corridors of the airport. When he reached that safety he slowed down. The corridor was long, white, and futuristic, dazzling after the darkness in the men's room. Tripwire looked back over his shoulder and so didn't notice the tall man emerging from a snack bar carrying two Styrofoam cups of coffee and looking at Tripwire curiously.

But even though he felt safe for the moment Tripwire ran through his usual tricks out of habit: stepping up his pace and then abruptly slowing down, ducking into doorways and looking back the way he'd come, turning randomly. The corridors behind him remained nearly empty. He went around one corner, loudly stepped faster, then turned about completely and went quietly back around the corner.

He bumped into the tall man, no longer carrying two cups of coffee.

They both stepped back, startled. The fingers of the tall

man's right hand disappeared inside the jacket of his grey suit, then stopped as the man caught the reflex. He smiled. He had a craggy, trustworthy face that fell naturally into a gracious expression as he said, "Excuse me. Shouldn't be in such a hurry, I guess." But Tripwire knew what the man had instinctively reached for inside the jacket. He'd felt it when they'd run into each other: the gun at his belt.

"Sure," Tripwire mumbled, and edged past the man. The tall man went on around the corner. When they were out of sight of each other, Tripwire ran. At the sound, the tall man reappeared, the startled look back on his face. He ran too, down the diminishing corridor after Tripwire. In his hand he carried not the gun but a walkie-talkie. He talked as he ran.

The corridor's lights seemed to have intensified. Tripwire turned the first corner he reached, but he was still pinpointed under the bright lights, against the whiteness of the walls and floor. He ran past water fountains and restrooms, snack bars and television monitors listing arrivals and departures. None of it concerned him. He wasn't, of course, getting back on the plane.

But his pursuer didn't know that, Tripwire suddenly realized. He began making his way through the white maze back to the plane. Behind him the tall man came on, slowed by caution every time Tripwire turned a corner, but keeping him in sight on the straightaways.

Tripwire's time sense was skewed; it seemed he'd been dodging through the airport for half an hour. But he knew it hadn't been that long, and hoped his flight hadn't left yet. He nearly tripped over a mop left leaning against a wall, kicked it to spill its bucket of soapy water across the corridor, and ran on. After he turned the corner he heard a smack and a curse.

His own terminal was in sight ahead of him. The debarking passengers were long gone, the ones boarding here for the flight to Atlanta already in their seats. There was no sign of the man in the blue suit. He had apparently been drawn away by his partner's call on the walkie-talkie. Tripwire ran to the tube that still tethered the plane to the terminal. At its entrance he stopped and looked behind him. A moment later the tall man came into sight. Tripwire let himself be seen, then ducked into the entryway.

He skidded along the boarding tube to the door of the plane. A stewardess frowned at him, her stern look out of keeping with her perky cap and the short skirt outfit that showed off her long, thin legs. "You shouldn't have left your seat, sir. We're about to leave." Her frown deepened when Tripwire ducked around her toward the pilot's cabin. He stepped around the small closet into the flight attendants' cubicle he had discovered earlier, darting a warning glance at the stewardess as he disappeared from sight.

"Sir, you can't—" she began officiously. Tripwire's face reappeared around the corner, his finger to his lips. She could barely see him, and someone entering the plane could not.

The stewardess shrugged and stepped to the door, ready to disengage the aircraft from its moorings. As she reached for the handle the tall man came aboard, panting.

The stewardess frowned at him too. "You almost missed it," she said sternly. "Let me have your boarding pass."

He ignored her, staring down the aisle. No one was standing. The tall man had his hand inside his jacket but didn't pull out his gun, not wanting to alarm the passengers. He moved cautiously down the passenger aisle, still breathing deeply, eyes darting from face to face. He straightened the shoulders of his suit.

Behind him, the stewardess was reaching for the door handle again. Tripwire, his finger at his lips, came out of hiding and stepped through the doorway just before she closed it. He was off the plane, and he motioned for her to close the door. The stewardess stood with her hands on her hips. Tripwire gave up on her and ran like a thief.

"Sir!" she shouted after him. "Sir, we're not going to hold the plane!"

The next moment she caromed off the closet wall and fell in a heap, her perky cap falling over her eyes, as the tall man slammed past her and out the door. The aisle filled with heads looking with interest at the fallen stewardess. No one offered to help her up.

Out in the airport corridors, the chase continued. The people Tripwire passed looked up curiously, but no one interfered. If they had, they would have done so on behalf of the man in the suit. Tripwire was the one who looked like a criminal, in his beard and dirty fatigues.

A man being pursued has a problem: he wants darkness, but he doesn't want to be caught alone in the dark with his pursuer. Tripwire avoided doors and stuck to the sparsely-trafficked halls. He stayed pinned under the lights, never getting out of sight of the tall man for more than a few moments. And the tall man was on the walkie-talkie again. Tripwire kept twisting around corners, trying to stay ahead of the directions his pursuer was giving, but he knew he couldn't keep that up for long.

He didn't. He turned and at the end of the next short corridor, waiting for him, was the man in the blue suit who had been waiting for the airplane originally. He was standing easily, rested, not displaying a gun, but his hand was inside his jacket.

Tripwire heard the tall man's panting breath behind him as the man came around the corner, saw his partner, and slowed to a walk. Tripwire slowed down too. To his left was a wall of windows with a view of runways. On his right was a blank wall leading all the way to the man in the blue suit. They had picked their spot well. Tripwire looked behind him and saw the tall man approaching. The man in the blue suit held his ground, letting them both approach him. Tripwire looked at him, shrugged, and raised his hands slightly.

The man in the blue suit stood at the head of a flight of stairs going down. The stairwell stretched ahead of him, toward Tripwire, but the man in the blue suit was protecting the top of the stairs. A white stucco wall, waist-high, surrounded the stairwell. As Tripwire came closer the man walked along that wall toward him, but he was careful not to come all the way to the end, where Tripwire might have a chance to push him over the wall down the stairwell. He smiled as if he realized that was what Tripwire had had in mind.

Tripwire shrugged again, picked up his steps a little, and raised his hands higher. The man in the blue suit took his hand out of his jacket and reached toward Tripwire. They were both beside the waist-high stucco wall. Just when the man in blue was at his most confident, when he almost had hold of Tripwire's arm, Tripwire lowered the other hand to the top of the wall and vaulted over it, plummeting down the stairwell.

He was lucky not to break a leg. The stairs were concrete with metal edges for traction. Tripwire landed on one stair, slid down two more, turned before he completely had his balance, and leaped down the rest of the stairs.

He had a good head start on both his pursuers. Startled, they first stood staring down the stairwell, then ran back to the head of the stairs and down.

Tripwire found himself running through a dark, short

corridor. He burst out of it into the bagagge claim area. Three conveyor belts snaked around the floor and back out through a doghouse-sized opening covered by plastic strips. Only one of the conveyor belts was moving, carrying a small, grim assortment of bags that looked as if they'd never be claimed. Two security guards looked up from their stations and started slowly toward Tripwire. Security guards don't like running men. They were between him and the outside doors. Behind him, he could hear the first two pursuers almost upon him. Tripwire darted aside, toward the suitcases moving on the conveyor belt. Without slowing down he dived onto the belt. Each plastic strip covering the opening was the width of a razor strap. In his panic they seemed to cut his face like knives as he went through. Behind him, there were cries of "Hey!" and "Stop!" from the security guards.

That chorus was taken up on the other side of the conveyor belt opening by baggage handlers unloading a cart. But they didn't pursue when Tripwire scrambled up and away. Someone did. Behind him he heard suitcases being knocked aside, and renewed cursing. He looked back and saw the man in the blue suit rising from the conveyor belt, and his partner just coming through the opening behind him. Tripwire ran. He turned a corner of the building and was safe again for an instant. He was outside. To his right were the runways. Airplanes, gigantic now that he was outside them, stood patiently under the care of their handlers or lumbered toward the runways with a slowness so terrible it denied they would ever be airborne again. Tripwire turned the other way.

He came around the end of the terminal building to see hope and danger. The hope was the parking lot: more cars than rush hour in a small city, enough for him to lose himself in. He thought if he got that far he could dive headlong into all those cars as into a cooling sea, never to be seen again. The bad part was what loomed between him and the parking lot: fifty yards of open ground, and a wooden fence.

He reached the fence just as his pursuers came around the corner of the building. They had their guns out now, pointing up into the air, but there were no people around. The man in blue lowered his pistol, sighting.

The fence was low enough to vault and Tripwire did so. He seemed to hang in the air forever, like a small plane himself, a perfect target. He tried to pull himself down. As he went over the fence, a small spike on the top scraped the inside of his wrist. The sudden pain burned his nerves, the physical equivalent of the sound of fingernails on a chalkboard. Blood is so close to the surface in the wrist: it flowed. Tripwire stumbled and fell.

The fall was good for him. It made him stop and think, for the few seconds he had to think. The wooden fence hid him momentarily from the view of the men chasing him, but when Tripwire pressed his face to a crack between two boards he could see them. The younger man, the one in the blue suit, seemed more eager and less tired than his partner. He had outdistanced the tall man, and as Tripwire watched he put on a burst of speed and widened the gap. He still had his gun in his right hand. He put out his left to jump the fence.

Keeping low, Tripwire shadowed him, pressed against the fence. When the man in blue came over the fence Tripwire was directly under him. There wasn't even an exchange of blows. Tripwire just cut his legs out from under him and the man landed on his head. His pistol went flying, skittered across the sidewalk, and Tripwire's groping fingers were too late to keep it from falling down a sewer opening. He looked back and saw the tall man's head. Tripwire would have liked to follow the gun down the drainage shaft, but the opening was too small. Luckily for him, the tall man was slower to come over the fence. Tripwire managed to reach the parking lot, ran a short way up a row of cars, leaped between two of them, and without hesitation hit the ground, rolling.

The tall man in the suit *did* hesitate to fling himself down on the oily pavement. A moment after Tripwire disappeared his pursuer had reached the spot. Cursing again under his breath, he knelt awkwardly and peered under the car next to him, his head going low, preceded by the pistol.

"Come out from there," he said bitterly, sounding like a parent.

But Tripwire wasn't under that car. He was under the one next to it, staring at the broad expanse of cloth stretched across his pursuer's rump. Carefully slithering out, Tripwire planted his foot in that easy target and pushed, hard. The tall man's forehead rammed the side of the car. He lost his precarious balance and his gun and fell, again face first, full-length on the pavement.

Tripwire grabbed the gun and stood over him, but the man didn't move. Tripwire knelt beside him. The tall man's breath was coming in long, slow pulses, those of a man who would not soon awaken.

As he knelt there, Tripwire had an idea. He hated the idea, because it meant going back inside the airport rather than running away. While he tried to talk himself out of it he went through the fallen man's pockets and found his wallet. An ID card identified him as an officer of the Drug Enforcement Agency. That made no sense to Tripwire, but at least the man was official. That clinched Tripwire's idea. Reluctantly, he rolled the man under the car, out of sight, and returned to the first agent.

No one in the pre-dawn darkness had discovered him yet. Tripwire found him also unconscious. He too carried an ID card in his wallet. Tripwire looked at the man's face for a long moment. He was young, only a few years older than Tripwire. He had blonde hair and almost nonexistent eyebrows. He looked very clean-cut. Tripwire, with his beard and scowl, looked older. Sighing, he picked up the agent and went looking for a place to hide him.

*H*e got lucky. There was no plane leaving for Baltimore in the next few minutes, but there was one leaving for Washington. Baltimore and Washington are less than an hour's drive apart. The plane wasn't boarding passengers yet, but Tripwire managed to slip down the tunnel and find a stewardess. Before she could shoo him off the plane he had shown her the younger DEA agent's ID card and ushered her into her small alcove behind the cabin.

"There are going to be two men coming aboard this flight," he explained in a low voice. "They may or may or not be sitting together. They've checked their bags through to Washington. We've let them think we don't know what's in them."

"What is it?" the stewardess whispered. She was bending low because Tripwire was keeping his face down and turned away from her. "Heroin?"

"It doesn't matter. What's important is that there's a slight— very slight—risk that they already know we're on to them. They may try to take over the plane once it's en route and divert it to another destination. It wouldn't be the first time."

The stewardess's eyes widened. "Why don't you arrest them now?"

He gave her one sharp glance and she felt reproached.

"Because we want their contact in D.C. Don't worry. That's why I'm going to be aboard, just in case they try anything—which we're pretty sure they won't." He nodded at the ID. "You keep that, if you will. I'd just as soon not have it on me."

The stewardess was staring at the ID photo and at what she could see of Tripwire's face. "This isn't a very good picture of you," she said slowly.

He looked at her. She blushed, afraid she'd said something stupid again. Tripwire tapped the card. "It's possible they know that face," he said significantly.

Her eyes widened again. "Ahh—you're in disguise. It's a very good one."

"Thank you." He kept his face averted. "Unfortunately, they may have spotted me like this, too. That's why I wanted to warn you ahead of time. I'm going to go away now, and when I board the plane with the rest of the passengers I'll look completely different. If you *do* spot me, for God's sake whatever you do don't let on. Understand?"

He looked sharply at her and she nodded. Her eyes were bright. This was going to be the most exciting flight of her career.

"And hide that!" he said, pointing at the ID card. She hastily put it out of sight.

"Thanks for your help," he said in a kinder tone of voice, and as he slipped out the door she whispered, "Good luck."

When the passengers boarded a few minutes later she was true to her word and didn't give any signs, but she stared hard at the few young men on the flight. Two or three of them were flattered.

Long before the plane reached Washington it received a message from Houston that a Drug Enforcement agent named James McCollum had been knocked unconscious and had his ID card stolen. The fugitive who had stolen the ID had been headed for the Baltimore–Washington, D.C. area. It took two messages—one from Houston, one from an FBI agent in Baltimore—to convince the stewardess that the man she'd talked to was an imposter. She admitted he was aboard. An FBI agent and three Baltimore cops met the flight in Washington.

*F*or a brief time, after the law enforcement team had delayed and thoroughly outraged all the passengers on the Houston-to-

Washington flight, Tripwire enjoyed a reputation as a master of disguise. They had thought the chase was over once they realized Tripwire was masquerading as a DEA agent, not deducing until too late that there had been another layer to the deception. By that time they had made the mistake of relaxing their surveillance at the other entrances to Baltimore. Tripwire came in without trouble on the train from Philadelphia, having taken a slightly later flight than the one that was intercepted in Washington. It was morning in Baltimore and he walked out into its streets unhounded. He was skeptical. He had no faith that he had thrown off his pursuit for long.

He was right about that. He wasn't being followed. But he had already been anticipated.

CHAPTER FIFTEEN

Galvan and Danny

*D*anny watched Marco Galvan sip tea. In Galvan's hand the delicate cup looked like something from a little girl's doll set. Galvan handled it with the daintiness it deserved and the occasion called for. The old lady sitting on the sofa opposite him looked pleased. She had gotten herself all done up for the occasion, in a long-sleeved, dark green dress that looked hot as hell; it was probably the best dress she owned. Her thin hair was arranged in tight little purpled waves all over her head. She was still wearing house slippers, as if she'd forgotten to get fully dressed. Her feet were swollen, she had explained to Danny—the slippers were all she could wear. He had assured her Mr. Galvan wouldn't be offended.

Danny stood well behind her, near the front door, as the old lady and Galvan had their tea. It was the most grandmotherly room Danny had ever been in. The brocaded chair in which Galvan sat had doilies on its back and arms. It was a massive chair, bigger than Galvan even, but everything else in the room looked spindly. The little coffee table was so covered with bric-a-brac, mostly little glass animals, there was hardly room on it even for their tiny cups. Prominently displayed on the mantelpiece was a hand-lettered Mother's Day card one of her sons had sent her from prison. Near it, hanging at what would be eye level for the old lady, was a calendar with a picture on it of a very white cross and Jesus with a shining face.

"I'm so glad I could finally do something to return a favor," the old lady said.

"It's terrible to impose on one's friends," Galvan said.

The old lady knew who Galvan was. There was no chance of her giving him away. The old lady hated cops. Cops had killed her husband and imprisoned her sons. She loved Marco Galvan, on the other hand. Galvan paid her rent every month, an agreement he had made with one of the sons in return for silence, but the old lady thought it was an act of simple kindness. It was an Old World sort of arrangement Galvan enjoyed making, the kind of thing Danny would never have done. He would have just had the son killed before he could talk.

Danny looked out the crack between the curtain and the window. The man on the opposite corner wasn't looking at Danny, he was looking down the street. He was the only one Danny could see, but as long as the man was standing there it was safe.

Danny had mixed feelings about being in Baltimore. It was dangerous, of course, and stupid. He had told Galvan there was no reason for Galvan himself to come into the city. He could have stayed in the relative safety of thé house on the Eastern Shore, at the end of its private road and guarded by their most trustworthy men—made more trustworthy because they were all also guarding each other, and because none of them was allowed to leave the estate or use the phone. Danny didn't even like that arrangement. He kept telling Galvan to go to Florida, go to Puerto Rico, leave Danny in charge until this was all over. But Galvan not only wouldn't go, he insisted on making occasional gestures like this trip into town, just to show everybody that he was still the boss and wasn't afraid of anything. Maybe Galvan realized that if he ever put Danny in charge and went away he could never come back again.

That was the pleasant side of Danny's mixed feelings. While they were in the city something might happen. Cops could be on their way right now. Danny, always light on his feet, was confident of his ability to get away. Giant Galvan, though, looked more like he was wearing this room rather than sitting in it. Galvan wouldn't be able to move two feet in this tiny, cluttered rowhouse before the cops would be all over him. Danny could escape and Galvan couldn't: both thoughts made Danny smile.

Galvan wore a pleasant expression, but his eyes were hard when he glanced over the old lady's head at Danny and jerked his eyes sideways, toward the stairs. Danny came forward and touched the old lady's arm.

"If you wouldn't mind leaving us alone now, ma'am," he said politely. She gave him a regretful smile, whether it was because she had to leave or because she wasn't forty years younger he couldn't tell. Old ladies always smiled at tall, blonde Danny with his boyish face.

Galvan stood when she did. Her hand looked as small as the tea cup, and he held it just as lightly. "Thank you again, Mr. Galvan."

"Not at all. Thank you for your hospitality. I'm sorry to put you out."

She murmured that it was no trouble and turned away. Danny helped her as far as the stairs, next to the fireplace, where she released his arm and smiled at him again. He thought she was going to touch his face, but she didn't. She went up the stairs slowly, one at a time, stopping to rest on every third or fourth stair. When she had climbed high enough that her head was out of sight she must had thought she'd turned invisible, because she stopped for a longer rest.

Galvan stayed on his feet. He paced through the most open area of the room, moving more easily through the glass-filled room than Danny would have imagined. After a minute of silence passed Danny jerked his head up toward the retreating old lady and said, "They say she was a real Bonnie Parker back in the thirties. Shot a deputy sheriff to death, they say. But her boyfriend got blamed for it and they fried him."

Only the old lady's slippered feet were still in sight. They hesitated as if she might come back down and correct or confirm this story, but then she shuffled on upstairs.

"When will you contact our man?" Galvan said, ignoring Danny's historical foray.

"Three-thirty. Fishermen's Market."

"Does he know anything new?"

"I'll find out then."

Galvan kept staring at him as if that answer were incomplete, until Danny added, "He couldn't know anything great or he would have wanted to meet right away."

"Jerek hasn't told him anything?"

"Jerek doesn't tell anybody anything," Danny said. "And our guy can't ask questions without making him suspicious—which he is anyway, of everybody. But our guy's checking out something. If Jerek did what he thinks he did, there may be a way to find out."

"How soon?"

"No way to tell. Few days, maybe. Maybe never."

He said that last just to goad Galvan, and it worked. Galvan made a noise in his throat and turned away. His right hand was clenched hard behind his back, Danny noticed. He stood stock still for a moment as if he might bring the fist down on that spindly coffee table and smash its herd of glass figurines into splinters. But then Galvan walked on, out of the room back toward the kitchen.

Danny stayed where he was, listening. He could hear the old lady shuffling upstairs, Galvan turning on the water in the kitchen, kids playing on the stoops outside. Danny felt perfectly poised for whatever was coming. He was still in good shape, still fast and light; it had been only a few years ago that Danny had looked like an Olympic athlete. He'd had that very trim, almost undernourished musculature, not the gross weight of a professional. His skin had looked golden, as if TV cameras were trained on him all the time. He had boxed in the Golden Gloves and he had been good, but there were enough hard-edged black guys in the tournaments, even more desperate to get out than Danny, that he hadn't had a chance of going very far. The only other sport he was good at was swimming, and there was no money in that. School was something he had already left far behind. Danny was only eighteen when he realized that he would never be a world-class anything. The knowledge had left him in an almost constant rage, ready to kill someone. That's when Marco Galvan had appeared, like the devil after his soul, and given Danny the chance to do just that. "I plucked you out of the gutter," Galvan said to Danny once years later, but that wasn't exactly true. Galvan had just made him more polished at what Danny would have turned to on his own anyway.

Danny had risen quickly to become second in command. Everybody knew he was the golden boy, the heir apparent, but Galvan was not old and was not ready to relinquish any control. Danny didn't have the knack of accumulating secret allies. He thought he could seize control if Galvan were out of the way somehow, but in the meantime he didn't trust anyone enough even to approach them with the idea of overthrowing Galvan. Besides, he didn't want a power struggle. Danny wanted Galvan's power but he wanted it intact. If it turned into war that power would be fragmented. Others would seize some of it, carve out their own niches. Danny wanted it all. He wanted Galvan simply to disappear, leaving Danny in his place.

So Danny had waited, biding his time, until this business had come along. He was sure now that this was his opportunity, but he hadn't figured out yet how to grasp it. One problem was that his interest coincided with Galvan's at least to the extent that they both wanted this witness, this Elizabeth Truett, dead. She had seen them both. Danny was pretty sure she hadn't identified him because Danny didn't have a record, his picture wouldn't have been in the police books. But if she ever saw him again she'd know him, and that was bad enough. And Galvan would find a way to bring Danny down with him if he knew he'd been betrayed. So Danny's interest in the hunt was as great as Galvan's, but he had other angles to consider as well. He hadn't seen his chance yet, but it kept him thinking all the time.

"Danny." He knew Galvan hadn't raised his voice, but the word came flat and true from the kitchen. He walked back there.

"Yes sir."

Galvan was looking out the window in the back door. Three wooden steps led down to a tiny back yard surrounded by a five-foot-tall board fence. Beyond it was an alley, beyond that more fenced yards. The alley could already have been full of cops. Danny wouldn't go that way. He'd go over the fence into one of the neighboring yards, gun drawn, and over several more side fences before he'd venture toward the alley or back toward the street. Galvan would be left behind, bellowing like a bull in a chute. He might be able to knock down one of the fences, but he sure as hell couldn't go over it.

Galvan turned and looked at him. He didn't say a word for a long minute, just stared at Danny as if he knew exactly what the younger man was thinking. That trick didn't work with Danny, though, because Galvan had given him the same look plenty of times when Danny wasn't thinking anything at all.

"Nervous?" Danny said with a thin edge of malice, but it only had the effect of making Galvan look smug again. He smiled.

"I have too many ways to win," the big man said.

Danny just nodded. He wouldn't ask a question or let Galvan see him scowl. He turned on his heel and walked out, but as he walked back across the living room he *was* frowning. He hated it when he didn't know everything that was going on. He wouldn't put it past Galvan to try to set *him* up, have the cops tipped off that Danny was the killer. But the cops would never go for that, would never accept Danny with his clean record in place of notorious Marco Galvan. Still, Galvan was up to something, which maybe meant Danny should speed up his own plans.

He looked out at the sliver of street he could see from the front window without moving the curtain. The street corner was empty.

Danny moved his head trying to see more of the street, and just as he was starting to panic there was a knock at the front door, almost touching his shoulder. He jumped back. His gun was in his hand as if it had grown there, he didn't even remember reaching for it.

But then the knock came again and he recognized it as the signal. Danny grimaced. Stupid business—secret knocks, recognition codes—but at the moment it was reassuring. He kept his gun out and opened the door a crack. Their man from across the street was in front. He just nodded at Danny and stepped aside, returning to his post. His departure revealed the other man on the front stoop, a short, thin man looking very dapper in his white summer suit. Danny motioned him in and hardly had to open the door wider to accommodate him. The man sidled inside and stopped. Danny frisked him perfunctorily and put his own gun away.

"Sorry about all this dumb stuff," Danny said, "but the boss, he's a little jumpy, you know."

"Who wouldn't be?" Paul said.

Danny stood looking at him, smiling. "You're looking pretty spiffy, Seligson."

Indeed, Paul Seligson looked much better than he had when Bill Jerek had walked into his room three days earlier, but he felt much worse. He nodded his thanks for the compliment to his white suit. "I shouldn't even be wearing it, you know," he said. "Labor Day was two weeks ago."

"Yeah," Danny said, wondering what the hell that meant. "Come on back," he added.

In the kitchen Galvan rose to greet him and extended his hand. The kitchen had about as much clear space as an elevator—if they had all tried to cram in they would have looked like a dozen midget clowns in one of those tiny circus cars—so Danny hung back in the doorway.

"I'm glad to see you, Paul," Galvan said. "It's nice to know all my friends haven't forsaken me in my vicissitudes."

"Well, this too shall pass," Paul said. "In the meantime, life goes on, right?"

"Yes," Galvan said. "I think we'll be able to help each other." He sat at the table again and motioned Paul to the other chair.

"I hope so," Paul said. He glanced over his shoulder at Danny in the doorway behind him. For a goon, Paul thought, he almost looks like he's thinking.

CHAPTER SIXTEEN

Jerek

"*M*y report, Captain." Dennison stood stiffly in front of Jerek's desk. He bent at the waist to lay the pages on the desk and, very faintly, clicked his heels.

"Yuk, yuk," Jerek said. Dennison didn't smile. Maybe he'd laugh when he got back out into the squad room with the others. He turned smartly on his heel and walked out.

Jerek glanced at the report. It might as well have had NOTHING printed on it in big red letters. According to the report Dennison and his partner had interrogated a pimp, staked out a house, put out feelers to all their contacts. Maybe they had; maybe they had just sat in a bar all day concocting the report: "Yeah, that's good, put that in." Jerek had done the same thing himself when a superior had made unreasonable demands. No one believed in this case any more except him.

And one other, he reminded himself. Among those detectives out there who had stopped talking to him except with sarcasm there might very well be one who knew exactly what Jerek wanted to know. Jerek was more interested in that knowledge than in bringing Galvan to "justice" for the murder. That was the only piece of information he wanted from Paul Seligson. That would cancel out Galvan's advantage.

Later that afternoon he was about to go out when Fred Tyler, the FBI agent, cornered him in his office. It was a momentary pleasure for Jerek to have somebody come through his office door without the stony expression that had become standard.

Fred was in his usual good mood, though he didn't have good news.

"We lost young Truett."

Jerek looked at him as if he were deliberately being stupid. Fred ignored that and explained what had happened in Houston. "Two DEA agents had him, then all of a sudden they didn't."

"DEA?" Jerek said.

"Doing a favor for the local FBI agent. Those drug enforcement people spend all their time in airports anyway, and besides no one really expected to see him. We can't have somebody in every airport in the country."

Jerek didn't answer. Fred was sitting on the edge of his desk again, glancing at all the papers while he talked.

"Very neatly done, actually. The way he threw all the dogs off his trail. He must've been a very nervous boy in the air when he took another plane, if that's what he did, but it worked." Fred paused and looked at Jerek, who was leaning back in his chair with a hand covering his mouth. "I'm not getting much response to my little narrative here."

Jerek said, "What do you want me to say?"

"I want to know what you're going to do about him. He must be on his way here."

"I told you before: Nothing. Can you prove who he is? Any description?"

"The description's more useless than the lousy pictures. The stewardess thought he was a master spy. And he took off before we could get prints in California."

"So," Jerek said, shrugging. "If he's their son he can wait. If he's some little scheme of Galvan's I'm not going anywhere near him. Either way he's not my prime concern."

They stared at each other. "What if it was your son?" Fred Tyler finally said. "And you thought he was dead but he wasn't?"

"Then what I didn't know wouldn't hurt me."

Fred pursed his lips and looked at Jerek as if trying to tell if he was serious or just striking a pose. Finally he pulled a piece of notepaper out of his shirt pocket and dropped it on the desk. "Just do me one favor. Call the Army and tell them why we're not rushing to arrange a happy reunion on network TV."

Jerek didn't reach for the paper. "Haven't you already told them?"

"It's not my story to give," Fred said, standing up. "But

they're calling me every day. I don't see why I should take the heat for you any more."

"All right, I'll call," Jerek said.

"Now. You won't do it if I'm not standing over you. I'll dial it for you."

He did, coming around the desk and dialing the number without unfolding the paper. He looked at Jerek as if that should impress him with how often he'd seen the phone number on messages. Jerek didn't react. When Fred pushed the phone at him Jerek hesitated, then took it.

"Hello? Yes. I need to talk to a, just a minute, please." He unfolded the message. "A Major van Dyne, please. All right, I will." To Fred Tyler he said, "This is the one you've been talking to?"

"One among many," Fred said.

"Hello. Major van Dyne? This is Captain Bill Jerek—I'm with the Baltimore Police Department. I'm calling about someone you had there name of Bryan Truett."

That apparently set the man on the other end of the line talking. Fred watched Jerek fall silent for a minute, nodding. "Well, I'm sorry about that, sir," Jerek finally said. "We weren't deliberately being uncooperative about this."

Fred Tyler snorted.

"We've got a unique sort of situation here," Jerek continued, and explained briefly and in no detail.

Three thousand miles away, Archie's face as he listened: expressions following hard upon one another as he tried to absorb this new information while maintaining his conviction that people are as basically nice and uncomplicated as he had always thought them. "I can't believe it wasn't him," he said more than once.

Jerek didn't have an opinion one way or the other, but he felt argumentative with Fred Tyler staring at him derisively. "Why else would he have run?" he said to the man in California.

"I just figured he got impatient with us," Archie drawled. "We sure weren't telling him much. But that wasn't really our fault now, was it?"

Jerek didn't respond to the rebuke. "I don't suppose you got his fingerprints," he asked.

"Didn't occur to me." Archie leaned back in his chair, wishing the boy had waited a couple of days, wishing he could talk to him now that he knew something about his parents. "We had no reason to doubt he was who he said he was."

"Wouldn't it have been standard to do that?" Jerek asked, wondering how far Galvan's reach was.

"I don't think we *have* a standard procedure for someone who's escaped alone out of that hell and finally clawed his way back home. Whatever it is, it wouldn't be to treat him like a criminal. Bad enough we don't have a parade and a brass band to welcome him home. At least we don't have to act like we doubt everything he says." Archie was growing animated. "And I'll tell you one thing. Whoever the boy was we had here, he had definitely served time in Vietnam. And as a P.O.W., too."

"How do you know?" Jerek asked, hoping for some inside information that would clear this up.

"I know," Archie said. "We had a lot of them through here."

Jerek didn't question the major's expert opinion. When he hung up a minute later he sat silently, thinking about the soldier. It took him a moment to remember the FBI agent in the room with him. When he did he spread his hands and said, "Satisfied?"

"Never," Fred said. "What else are you going to do about him?"

"I don't see that I have to do anything. He's gone, isn't he?"

"But you know where he's coming. Whoever he is. We can find him. We've still got the Truett's house wired, if he goes there."

"Fine," Jerek said. "Then you handle it. You wanted to help, didn't you?"

"And what're you going to be spending your valuable time on?"

"Little project of my own," Jerek said.

*I*f he'd been a rural cop he might have seen vultures circling. In the city it was junkies.

Jerek had finally gotten rid of Fred Tyler and had left the office himself, through the silent squad room. One pair of eyes followed him more closely than the rest but Jerek didn't notice because he kept his head down.

It was another day when he didn't want to be followed. He went down to the underground parking garage, came out going fast in an unmarked car and drove around aimlessly for a while. Once in a while he passed a patrol car. He instinctively trusted the uniformed cops, just because they weren't highly placed enough to have been worth Galvan's trouble to recruit them. But he still didn't want anyone near him today.

There didn't seem to be. Galvan's men had for the most part given up their fruitless surveillance of him. That could be bad news, meaning they had other leads, or it could mean just that they had realized he would never lead them anywhere. He finally drove, slowly, through an old residential neighborhood near downtown, so decayed it looked bombed out. There were big taped Xs on most of the windows, but people still lived here, people who were glad when the Condemned signs went up because that meant they didn't have to pay rent any more. Others had moved into the neighborhood only after the Xs had appeared, furtive men who looked condemned themselves. They had more pressing concerns than where they might sleep tonight. Home was a mattress on the floor. Jerek drove past two or three men glimpsed in alleys, sitting against a wall or slumped over, sleeping during the day when it was warm. They were dispossessed even by the standards of this neighborhood. Even the slums have slums.

Jerek drove through that neighborhood because it was like a radioactive zone. There was almost no traffic, so he could get a good look at any cars behind him. None followed him. Satisfied, he turned toward his destination.

Again he parked blocks from Paul Seligson's apartment and walked. A patrol car passed him and he stared straight ahead. The cops' eyes passed over him and went on glancing at the storefronts and down the alleys. Jerek hurried.

He didn't notice the junkies at first when he got to Paul's block. But when he crossed the street their movement as they pulled back out of sight caught his eye. He walked to where he could get another look at them and they were still there, muttering and looking up at the building. It was a very small crowd, three men, but for junkies, who didn't have much of a social life, it was like an opening night on Broadway. Jerek cursed under his breath and went in the door of Paul Seligson's building.

What could draw a crowd of junkies was the smell of easy money. A drunk or heart attack victim passing out on the street. A burning apartment just after the family fled and just before firemen arrived. A dead man with pockets to be gone through.

They would also come, like ants to a picnic, it they sensed a major drug deal, and Jerek hoped that was the case here. But when he got to the top of the stairs he saw Paul's door was ajar,

and a moment later it was flung wide open and the bravest
junkie came stumbling out. Even in warm September he was
wearing all the clothes he owned, including a long red stocking
cap that hung halfway down his back. The junkie didn't even
see Jerek. He was hunched over almost double, making
retching noises. He fell, caught himself, and staggered on,
almost bumping Jerek in his haste to get away. Jerek caught
one glimpse of the junkie's horrified expression and then the
man was hurling himself down the stairs, still gagging.

It might have been fear that produced that reaction. There
might be someone inside the apartment with a gun who had just
let the junkie escape with his life. Jerek didn't think so, but he
went in slowly with his own gun drawn. As soon as he saw the
vivid object in the middle of the room, though, he forgot his
caution.

Paul was hanging from a pipe on the ceiling. Not by his
neck; the rope went under his armpits. He was displayed there,
like a scarecrow. He was dead, and he was the worst thing
Jerek had ever seen. There was blood on the floor under him so
he had probably died there, but Jerek guessed most of the work
had been done elsewhere, some place where there were no
neighbors to be bothered by noises and a man could work in
private for a long time.

Paul had been a small man to begin with, but he was much
smaller now. He was missing some fingers, and both eyes—
Jerek stopped cataloguing the damage as his own stomach
heaved and he turned away. He closed his eyes tightly and ran
to the window across the room. He pulled it open and took a
deep breath. The fetid outside air tasted fresh by comparison.
Throwing up would be a rookie's stunt. He managed to avoid
it, but not by much. Jerek had seen quite a few corpses in his
time, but never one that shrieked pain the way this one did. He
stood at the window and from the corner of his eye looked at
the body hanging there like an accusation.

That's not what it was, though. It was a warning. Jerek
looked out the window and saw the junkie in the long red cap
reach his companions across the street. He said a sentence or
two and pointed up to where Jerek stood. The other junkies
turned frightened faces toward the building and then looked
away quickly as if avoiding a curse that had fallen on someone
else. They all turned and ran faster than they had in years.
Jerek should try to question them about what they'd seen, but
he knew he'd never catch them. What they had seen would be

all over the city by nightfall. Jerek could keep it out of the newspapers, but that's not where the people at whom this was aimed got their news. Every petty crook in town would hear what happened to somebody who tried to screw Marco Galvan. Jerek would never be able to recruit another potential spy. Galvan was laughing at him again.

He wondered what Paul had done to give himself away. Maybe nothing, maybe Galvan had just suspected anyone who tried to deal with him during this time and that suspicion had been enough for him to act on. Whatever it had been, it hadn't been Paul's fault. He'd had no training for the job and he certainly hadn't volunteered for it.

He deliberately cut off that line of thought. What he'd done had been necessary. He turned back into the room. He didn't look at the corpse directly again, but the smell couldn't be escaped. The body moved slightly. Jerek thought about cutting it down, but the medical examiner would probably want to see it in position. Not that they'd learn anything. As Jerek stood there with his thoughts moving very sluggishly he heard a floorboard creak in the hall outside.

Jerek automatically stepped back, out of the line of sight from the door of the room in case it opened suddenly. His hand crept to his belt where he had replaced his gun.

Jerek suddenly realized an assumption he'd been operating under without ever thinking about it. He knew Galvan would do anything he had to do to find Elizabeth Truett and kill her, but Jerek had assumed that he himself was safe.

What had given him that idea?

CHAPTER SEVENTEEN

Jerek

*H*e stood frozen, not knowing what to do. It was hard to think in the shadow of that hanging corpse. He tried to block it out of his mind but that was impossible. The face seemed to wear a ghastly, inviting smile, as if Bill would soon be joining it.

That thought spurred him into motion. There was no phone in the room and his car was parked blocks away. He had worked hard to be sure no one knew where he was. He had cleverly arranged his own murder.

He wouldn't go meekly. His gun was in his hand as he looked out the open window to the empty street. He backed away. Outside the other window, he remembered from his first visit to this apartment, was a clanky old fire escape, but he didn't like the idea of being pinned there against the side of the building for the time it took him to reach the street. There could be a man with a rifle in the building across the street. Or a man could be standing in the recessed doorway of this building, from which he could keep both the fire escape and the inside stairs covered. It would be much better for Jerek if he could lure the man inside.

A board creaked again. There was definitely someone in the hall. Someone moving toward the room, from the sound of it. Jerek stepped toward the sound. His hand clenched around the grip of the gun was tingling as if it had been asleep.

The door to this room was also recessed. Coming in, one passed through a very short hallway, maybe five feet long, before emerging into the room itself. Anyone coming in would be effectively trapped, but Jerek would also have to expose himself in order to get a good shot. He decided to avoid that.

Just inside the room, to the right of the short hall from the door, was a closet. On its door was a full length mirror. Paul Seligson, a dapper man, must have stood in front of it often, putting the last perfect touches to his appearance. Now his reflection was hanging in the mirror with his shoes three feet off the ground. Jerek caught another glimpse of him as he opened the closet door, moving the mirror. The door had a tendency to fall shut, but when it was open wide enough it would stay open. Jerek swung it open all the way, so the mirrored closet door blocked off the short hallway, facing the front door of the apartment. A man coming into the room would see his own reflection. Jerek moved the door back to a different angle, then stepped across the hall opening and pressed himself against the wall. In the mirror he could see the front door of the room. He looked into the mirror, then stepped back to change its angle slightly. He returned to his concealed position and checked the line of sight again.

Danny watched all this with amusement.

Jerek got the angle just right, so that he could stay out of the line of fire from the door but still see in the mirror anyone who came through the front door. Of course, that also meant that the man coming through the door would be able to see Jerek in the mirror, but he still wouldn't have a direct shot at Jerek. Jerek thought the man's first sight of the mirror would be disorienting enough to give Jerek time to reach around the corner and fire, exposing only his hand to a return shot. It would be almost like one of those trick shots sharpshooters in the wild West shows used to do, aiming in a mirror and firing backwards, but Jerek would only be five feet from his target and he didn't think he'd miss.

But he didn't want to stand there all day getting nervous. Now for the lure. A moment later the man in the hallway heard: "Hello. This is Jerek. I'm at 329 Annapolis and I've got a stiff. Get a medical examiner and send some detectives right away. I need three men and I need them here ten minutes ago. Right. I'll be here."

Jerek "hung up" just by dropping his hand back to his side. He felt like a fool talking into his clenched fist, but he figured the killer hadn't been in this room long enough to be sure there wasn't a phone, or he might believe Jerek had a radio.

Thinking reinforcements were on the way should force the man's hand.

But Danny wasn't in the hall. He was on the fire escape, watching Jerek through the window. Danny found this even funnier, to see Jerek talking into his hand like a kid playing soldier. Danny wished he could have shot him at that moment, so Jerek would die knowing someone had seen him making a fool of himself.

But the window worried Danny. He was afraid it would deflect the bullet if he fired through the glass. Then his second and third shots would be through the falling shards of glass, blocking his vision and possibly the bullets. If he first smashed the window with his gun and then fired, the sound would give Jerek an extra moment's warning, and Danny would still have the problem of falling glass. Jerek was standing there with his gun already in his hand, so Danny didn't have much extra time to give away. Only the element of surprise was working for him.

But the window wasn't locked. Danny knew that because he had come out the window to begin with. Jerek had surprised him, arriving almost contemporaneously with the murder—though by the time Danny actually killed Seligson the little man was so far gone, after the night he'd already spent with Danny, that he didn't even feel the last pain. Danny had been warned by the sound of the junkie creeping down the hallway. That had made him go to the window, and from there he'd seen Jerek coming along the sidewalk. Danny knew the police captain, though Jerek didn't know Danny. Danny had waited until he came inside the building, then Danny went out the window just as the junkie came in the door of the room. Danny had softly lowered the window and gone up to the roof. He had planned to escape from there to an adjoining roof, but once he had paused he had realized the chance he was passing up.

Galvan didn't want Jerek dead. He wanted him frustrated and humiliated, but not harmed in any way. Galvan wanted Jerek's hunt to die from lack of event. Through his pipeline Galvan knew that Jerek's superiors didn't believe whole-heartedly in the case against Galvan; they knew Jerek's personal grudge against him. Galvan wanted nothing to happen until those superiors were convinced Jerek was hunting the wrong man. Then they might bring Elizabeth Truett back out of hiding. That was Galvan's hope, anyway, in the event he couldn't find Elizabeth first. But the hope depended on nothing happening to make Jerek's bosses think Jerek was right about Galvan. Jerek's getting killed would make his suspicions look dead accurate.

But what Galvan wanted was not always the same as what Danny wanted. He didn't want the heat on Galvan to simmer down. He wanted it turned up even hotter, in fact, so Galvan would be forced to flee or better yet get arrested or killed. Either would leave Danny in charge. And what would be more likely to intensify the hunt for Galvan than the murder of a police captain? Everyone would be sure it was Galvan's work. It might even make the captain's fellow cops mad enough that they wouldn't settle for an arrest and trial. They would want Galvan dead.

The idea pleased Danny. It had brought him back down from the roof after Jerek had looked out the window, and Danny had been watching him ever since. He waited to see if Jerek might do or say anything useful. His presence here already corroborated Danny's hunch—it had been no more than that—that Paul Seligson had been trying to set Galvan up. That would have been all right with Danny, except that Seligson knew Danny too. Besides, Galvan had also been suspicious of Seligson—he had ordered the interrogation, and the interrogation had produced a confession. Of course. The little man had been easy. He'd been ready to babble as soon as Danny touched him. He just hadn't known anything. It had taken a long while to convince Danny of that.

Now Danny crouched outside the window and waited for a good clear shot at Bill Jerek. He decided it would be best to raise the window. He remembered that it had opened and closed quietly—Paul Seligson must have regularly used the fire escape as a back door himself when he had unwanted visitors. The window was still open a crack at the bottom. Danny would only have to raise it another few inches.

All Jerek's attention was focused in the opposite direction. Nothing seemed to be happening in the hall. Danny carefully pressed his fingers against a crossbar of the window and waited. When Jerek stuck his head around the corner to look curiously at the door of the room, and took a step toward it, Danny pushed upward. Whatever slight sound the window made as it rose didn't carry to Jerek's distracted ears.

Danny had raised the window six inches for good measure. He retrieved his gun and crouched at the window, making sure the barrel was at the opening. He didn't have the best shot

because he couldn't hold his arm straight—he had to shoot
more or less from the hip, looking through the window but
firing through the opening. By the time he got settled Jerek was
moving, and he waited for him to stand still.

Jerek was moving because the mirrored closet door was
moving. Danny's opening the window had created a cross-
ventilation that was making the door swing slowly closed. For
a few moments Jerek, who expected someone to come through
the door of the room any second, moved back to keep that door
in sight in the mirror. He had his back to the window and was
backing toward Danny. Danny almost didn't want to take the
shot. It was too easy. Jerek finally stopped when the closet door
swung further closed, picking up speed. When Jerek stood still
Danny had the perfect shot. He crouched even lower to put his
eyes behind his gun.

Paul Seligson saved Jerek's life.

The closet door was moving faster now. The floor in the
room was uneven, making the door fall shut. Jerek stepped
across to catch it, momentarily exposing himself to sight from
the door of the room if a man came through it. Jerek
concentrated all his attention on that front door, gripping his
gun. He made it across the opening safely and just as he
reached for the closet door his own reflection flashed through
the mirror and behind him that of the man with the gun outside
the window.

Jerek spun aside. Danny cursed at having waited too long,
but he still had Jerek in his sights. He swung his gun hand in a
short arc, keeping it trained on Jerek, and fired.

But by that time the hanging body was between the living
men. Danny's bullet hit the corpse in the leg. The impact made
the body twist on its rope and turn to face Danny. Danny cursed
again and kept firing.

Jerek returned fire, shattering the window inches from
Danny's face. Then he ran the short distance into the bathroom
next to the closet.

Danny pushed the broken window up and was stepping into
the room when Jerek's hand with the gun came around the edge
of the bathroom door and fired. It was a blind shot, hardly even
close, but it stopped Danny. He fired savagely back, three shots
into the bathroom door, and the hand withdrew, but Danny had
lost his favored position. To rush Jerek now he'd have to
expose himself to that fire. It wasn't worth it. The gunfire
might already be drawing other cops. Danny fired again to

keep Jerek in the bathroom, then backed out the window and ran down the fire escape. He didn't even look back over his shoulder, trusting his speed to get him safely out of sight. He was right. He reached the bottom of the steps and when he looked back up there was still no face peering down at him.

That made Danny decide to take one more chance. He was just around the corner now from the front door of the building. Jerek might be coming down the inside stairs in a hurry. If Danny could find a hiding place he would get another shot. He slipped inside the front door into the gloom within. It took a moment for his eyes to adjust.

And in that moment a gun barrel pressed against the side of his head just above his ear. A voice said, "Hold it."

Danny froze, except to raise his hands slightly. His gun was still in his right hand. "Okay, okay," he said hastily. He could see the man from the corner of his eye. A young man in a suit. He should have expected Jerek to have a back-up.

"Damn it," Danny said. Caught. His first arrest. Even if he got out of this, he'd have a record from now on. It made him feel stupid. His shoulders slumped.

The other man relaxed slightly when Danny put his hands up. He reached for the gun. Danny struck.

That's what had made Danny good as a boxer—quick hands and no hesitation. He had learned how fast a hand can move before the opponent can react. Even a hand encumbered with a gun. The man in the suit fired but Danny's head was no longer in the line of fire by then. In the next moment Danny's gun smashed into the guy's face and he went down in a heap.

Danny exhaled a long breath, straightening the shoulders of his jacket. He could hear Jerek moving upstairs. Danny didn't have time to wait for him now. There had been too many shots fired, there would be cops on the way. And the shot this guy had just fired would warn Jerek that someone was down here at the bottom of the stairs. He'd be cautious. Too bad. It had been a good idea, killing Jerek to stir up the hunt for Galvan, but it had been just a fleeting thought for Danny. He let it go.

He had already started out the door of the building when he glanced back down at the young cop, who was stirring slightly on the floor, moaning, and Danny realized it was still a good idea. As quickly as the thought crossed his mind Danny aimed and fired into the guy's chest. And again to be sure. He was dead before Danny ran out the door. One dead cop should be as good as another to heat up the search for Galvan, Danny thought. As he ran it occurred to him that he might have made a mistake, but he didn't spend much worry on it.

Jerek found the body at the foot of the stairs. He almost stumbled over it. At first he thought it was the guy who'd been shooting at him, and that mystified him. The light was bad in that cramped place. Bill pushed open the street door and a slice of light fell across the young cop's face.

"Dennison," Jerek said, still mystified.

He couldn't imagine how the detective had gotten here. His first thought was that Dennison must have been the spy in the department—he must have been following Jerek to see what he could learn. But that couldn't be right. Galvan's man wouldn't have killed Galvan's spy.

When the squad car arrived one of the patrolmen explained. "He had us watching you. A bunch of patrol cars, enough so's you wouldn't notice just one following you." Jerek remembered the patrol car that had passed him as he'd walked toward this building. They had alerted Dennison, who'd followed him into the building, first upstairs to the hall, then back down to his meeting with Jerek's assailant.

"Why?"

The uniformed patrolman who was explaining looked a little too old to still be driving a beat. There were lines stretching from the corners of his eyes into his hairline. He stood at an angle, looking searchingly at the building across the street rather than at Jerek or at Dennison's body.

"He thought Galvan might try something. Said if he told you you'd just laugh him off. But he thought, maybe he could spot someone following you and he could follow *them* back to Galvan. Or maybe—"

Or maybe just be there to protect me, Jerek thought. A few people had appeared on the sidewalk and the uniforms walked away to exercise some barely necessary crowd control. They seemed glad to withdraw from Jerek, leaving him with the body.

Jerek had known Dennison for eight years, ever since he'd joined the force. He was thirty-two years old. He had a wife and two young daughters. Jerek had seen their pictures on Dennison's desk every day for years. Now Jerek would have to be the one to call the wife or go see her. She would probably blame him, and she might be right. He knelt and pulled

Dennison's coat up over his face, then stayed there with his hand on the body, his throat getting constricted.

He knew just what would happen now. There would be an outpouring of concern for the widow and children and a fund would be raised that might be adequate to pay their rent for two months. People would promise to keep tabs on them for Dennison's sake, but no one would. When she came to the station to pick up his things other cops would look at her and feel guilty themselves, because she reminded them of the responsibilities they were forsaking whenever they risked their own lives. She'd pack up the pictures of herself and her daughters and after she went out the door they'd never see her again. If she was lucky she'd marry someone else, who wasn't a cop.

The other predictable reaction would be the rage. Jerek felt it in himself now. He wanted to smash his fist into the wall. No, he wanted to smash it into Galvan. "Damn you," he said to the body, and to himself, and most of all to Marco Galvan.

He was deadly calm again by the time the medical examiner arrived.

CHAPTER EIGHTEEN

John, Elizabeth, Karen

*J*ohn still woke at the same time every day. His eyes would open automatically and the first thing he'd see was the clock reading 6:25. For a fuzzy moment he'd be back in his real life, but before he moved to throw back the covers he'd remember where he was. Sometimes then he'd manage to roll over and go back to sleep, but usually after a few wakeful minutes he'd get up, even after one of those nights when sleep had eluded him until far after midnight. Those nights were coming more frequently, partly because of the inactivity of his days. But he'd rise at that early hour and go through his usual ritual—shower, shave, make coffee—but that was where his day ended now. By 7:30, the time he used to leave for work every day, he had nothing more to do.

His restlessness was real. He had gone out for another walk after the beer-throwing incident, to reassure himself that that had been a fluke, and sure enough nothing unusual had happened. The fantasies were fading but there were still moments when he literally twitched from the desire either to fight or run. Adrenaline coursed through his system to no purpose, leaving him shaky and mad. There was no one to fight and they couldn't run any farther than they already had.

The days passed slowly but they accumulated. It had been two and a half weeks. John suspected that if Marco Galvan hadn't been captured yet it would be a long time before he was. The hunt for him would have been most intense at its beginning. The more time that passed, the more cases would pile up, the more police attention would be diverted to other matters. Meanwhile, Galvan was probably living pretty much as he always had, while John and Elizabeth's lives were completely gone.

Elizabeth seemed less maddened by the situation than he did. Though hers was the life at stake, she somehow managed not to dwell on it. She didn't pace the house the way John did. She could sit and read the newspapers and magazines Karen had brought. John couldn't relax. They didn't grow into the house because there were no homey touches they could add to it. It remained foreign, kept reminding them they were out of place.

Sometimes a day would pass with John and Elizabeth hardly speaking to each other. They had nothing to say. There was no news from day to day except what came on the television, and that seemed insignificant.

One day in the middle of that third week, though, it was Elizabeth who was unaccountably distracted. John walked into the kitchen at mid-morning, already thinking about lunch, to find her puttering around with nothing, straightening the few dishes in the cabinet. She knocked over a cup when he said her name.

"Oh," she said. "You startled me," But she didn't appear startled. Her movements were slow and deliberate as she laid a hand over the clattering cup, stilling it. She was staring at the door of the cabinet, where the thin lines of the wood grain diverged and joined again.

"What's the matter?" John said. It sounded like a stupid question. They were fifteen hundred miles from home in a strange town, their lives shattered and a murderer frantically trying to find them, and he had to ask, Is something troubling you? But he could see something was, something other than the obvious.

"Nothing," Elizabeth said, a lie. He kept staring at her until she turned and faced him. She crossed her arms and tried to look composed. "Don't you know what today is?" she asked.

John didn't. He didn't even know what day of the week it was. He glanced around the kitchen, but there was nothing in the whole house to tell him. The newspapers they had were a week old. His watch had stopped days ago and he hadn't bothered to rewind it.

"It's September 20th," Elizabeth prompted.

It was Bryan's birthday. When he'd been a baby Elizabeth

had made parties for just the three of them, or three of them and a set of grandparents. When Bryan was older she would have some of his little friends to the house, in the afternoon before John got home from work, and he'd come home to find remains of cake and ice cream and wrapping paper, and Bryan often as not half-sick from the food and the excitement. Even after he was a teenager and would rather be with his friends Elizabeth had always made him a cake with candles on it. They had twenty years of snapshots of him blowing out the candles. She had even sent one cake to Vietnam before he'd been lost.

As all that passed through John's mind he saw that Elizabeth had already been brooding about it all morning. Her hands were clenched tight. That's why she'd been in the kitchen opening cabinets and rattling dishes. There was no cake to make, nothing to do but feel helpless.

John looked out the window. Sunlight made the back yard look especially empty. There was nothing to be seen out there but his thoughts. Elizabeth knew what they were. Just as she blamed herself for their current danger, Bryan was John's fault. It was John who had driven him out of the house and into the Army—had killed him. Not deliberately, but inexorably just the same. It had caused a rupture between John and Elizabeth, and Bryan's death made it a wound that would never quite heal. Elizabeth had never blamed him in so many words, but he knew. If nothing else, she sensed the guilt he felt.

She was looking at him now so intently she was almost glaring. Sometimes it was best not to touch her. Sometimes when she was angry or sad it would pass if she was left to her own devices, but if John tried to comfort her, her emotions would soar and she would break down even harder. But today John needed the contact and he thought she did too. He went and held her. Her body remained stiff for a long moment and then she put her head on his shoulder and her arms around him and he knew she was crying. He held her without saying anything. He wanted to protect her from this too, but he was equally helpless to do so.

He was gripped again by the unfairness of it. They were ordinary people, their lives already stained once by tragedy when their only child was lost. Now they were lost themselves, driven out of their home and their home town. Elizabeth had never done anything wrong in her life, and now a man who did nothing but wrong wanted to kill her. John wanted to kill somebody himself. He held his wife as tightly as he could, as if he could keep everything, even her emotions, at bay.

When Elizabeth drew back and looked at him her eyes were wet but she managed a wan smile, as if to say the worst had passed, or would soon. She looked like she was going to apologize. Before she did he said, "Let's go for a walk."

She shook her head automatically. "Please," John said. "It'll do you good, I promise."

She shook her head again, but she was thinking, Why not? What more was there to lose? Her caution seemed silly.

She left his arms and walked slowly to the dining room window. Sunshine didn't penetrate the shade around the house, but Elizabeth could see the street dancing in it. Even from there the sunshine made her squint a bit. A child, pre-school age, walked slowly in front of the house, making a game of walking. He followed the course of something in the air Elizabeth couldn't see, then found his eyes resting on her house. Elizabeth waved to him. He didn't see her or didn't want to respond, but he kept looking toward her window. Elizabeth flinched as the boy suddenly turned and ran back across the street, not looking anywhere except straight ahead. When he gained the safety of the opposite side he turned to face her. After a moment's serious watchfulness he returned her wave once, formally, then turned and ran out of her field of vision.

John's two ventures outside the house had frightened her. When she was alone she felt watched. But by whom? Probably by everyone who wasn't there: John, Karen, Bryan. All the ghosts watching to see what she did with herself when alone. Marco Galvan was well down on the list of watchers. He was hardly more real to her now than he was to John. But she still felt a sort of generalized threat when she was alone, as in the days when she had first started sending Bryan to school. The fear was not for herself, but that she couldn't be there to protect the ones she loved. She had never accepted Bryan's death, but she knew she couldn't help him. She felt the same way about John when he went out alone.

She turned back into the house's sparsely-furnished interior. It was terribly dark. The sunlight had given her blind spots, and so managed to dazzle her again after she turned away from it.

"John?" she said. He had disappeared behind the flaring lights.

"Here," he said. He was standing at the front door, holding a hand out to her. She joined him. When he opened the door she flinched back, but nothing rushed in at her. They went outside and locked the door behind them. He put his arm around her and they walked along the sidewalk. After half a block they were walking more briskly and John was talking about where they might go. The day turned overcast and warm, but it was the most beautiful day Elizabeth had seen in two and a half weeks. She smiled.

Behind them, inside the house, the sudden whistling of the tea kettle testified to the spontaneity of her decision to go out. In the bathroom Marco Galvan's photo glared at nothing. When the tea kettle's whistling died down the house remained silent.

*D*anny swore he hadn't been the one who killed the cop, but Galvan was still furious. As Danny had expected, the killing had intensified the flagging search for Galvan. The FBI joined in. Men scoured more than Baltimore now; they were covering the whole state, and beyond. They had probably gotten close to Galvan's Eastern Shore hideway a time or two, but Galvan still had the advantage of knowing most of their movements. Still, it made Danny nervous to be near him, and Galvan kept him close all the time now. That was only one of the good reasons Danny didn't simply make an anonymous call to the police telling them where Galvan was hidden. The best reason was still that witness. She had seen Danny with Galvan at the scene of the murder. When Galvan finally got caught Danny wanted to be completely clear of him, he wanted no witnesses connecting him. So not until she was found and taken care of would Danny's interests and Marco Galvan's completely diverge. And Galvan had a much better chance of finding her than Danny did on his own.

"We may be very close to finding her," Galvan said to him the day after the shooting in Paul Seligson's building.

" 'May be'? How?"

"Remember what I told you about knowing everything," Galvan said. "When the time comes. Assuming we aren't both arrested first. Thanks to that stupid cop-killing—"

"I swear," Danny said earnestly. "I dumped Seligson's body and got away clean. There musta been somebody else hanging around, hoping to rob the apartment or somethin'. Some junkie with a gun. When the cop showed up—"

"All right," Galvan said shortly. "I'm not questioning you."

They were walking in the woods that surrounded Galvan's house. In places the woods were so thick that sunlight never reached the ground. Fallen leaves formed a thick, mushy carpet, sometimes covering roots or holes. Danny stepped carefully, not wanting to get gunk on his city shoes. Galvan was gotten up like a country squire in a tweed suit and lace-up boots, and he carried a walking stick. He seemed at ease. Danny's hand would flash toward his gun every time he heard scurrying under the leaves.

Once in a while they'd come across an armed man. So far they had all been very watchful. Danny had the feeling if they found one nodding off Galvan would kill him and leave his body as an example to the others.

"What makes you think you're closer to finding her than you ever were?" Danny asked. From Galvan's dark tone the first time Danny had asked how, anyone else might have thought it was dangerous to ask again. But Danny knew Galvan had no one else to talk to, and he liked confiding in Danny, showing off how smart he was. "Jerek's obviously not letting anything slip. It's been two and a half weeks."

"Exactly," Galvan said. As Danny expected, Galvan smiled slightly. "He could not have expected me to elude him this long, so he wouldn't have known the woman would have to stay hidden this long. We are counting on Captain Jerek to make a very simple mistake soon. He may have already made it. When he does, we will be this close to finding her." He held his thumb and index finger barely apart.

"How close is this?" Danny asked, mimicking the gesture.

"Any day," Galvan said. "Maybe by tonight."

Galvan smiled at Danny's look of surprise. "*Then* I'll tell you just what you need to know," he said smugly.

They went back into the house. Later that night, Galvan got a phone call and sent Danny into the city.

And Karen, the eye of this storm, didn't know anything. No one kept her informed. Bill Jerek hadn't contacted her once. She hadn't expected him to do so, but she hadn't expected it to last this long, either. Two weeks and four days since she had picked up the Truetts at the Philadelphia train station. She had thought there would be a frantic, massive search that would produce Marco Galvan in a day or two, after which she could

bring her charges safely home. She hadn't counted on this
being a long-term assignment. She knew nothing about the
progress of the search except what she could infer from the
Baltimore papers, which was very little. The story of one of
Jerek's detectives being killed was on the front page. Reading
it made her go cold. She assumed the killing was related to the
hunt for Marco Galvan and Galvan's hunt for Elizabeth Truett.
It was still a killing matter.

Karen wanted to go see John and Elizabeth, to check on their
safety and to reassure them. (That would have to be with lies,
because the little news she had all sounded bad.) On the other
hand she wanted to stay away. Because she did know this
much: Marco Galvan wasn't going to find Elizabeth Truett.
There was no longer a direct connection between anyone in
Baltimore and Elizabeth. When Galvan discovered what Jerek
had done it wouldn't be Elizabeth Truett he found, it would be
Karen Boone. For that reason Karen stayed away from the
Truetts and Jerek made no contact with her. That left Karen
alone in the middle, not knowing if anyone was coming for her
yet. Jerek would surely warn her if he knew Galvan had found
out, but what if Jerek had let something slip without realizing
it?

She sat at her desk in the office shuffling papers, not making
a very good pretense of reading. She looked up at the clock
high on the wall and then kept staring in that direction without
seeing anything as her mind went into other fantasies. Suppose
Jerek were killed or badly injured. That would leave Karen the
only person who even knew Elizabeth Truett was alive. Should
she call the Baltimore district attorney's office to tell them their
witness was safe? If she did that they'd want more information,
and Karen couldn't afford to trust anyone. But if she didn't tell
them, might they drop the case against Galvan for lack of
evidence? That would leave Elizabeth in official limbo.

But of course nothing had happened to Bill Jerek. As far as
Karen knew. She wondered how soon she'd learn about it if
something did happen. What if Galvan got tired of waiting and
just kidnapped Jerek and tortured the information out of him?
There was no question he could do it. Jerek was as tough as
anyone Karen knew, but anyone could be made to talk.
Probably the only reason Galvan hadn't done it already was
that it would be obvious he was behind it and he didn't want to
be caught at any more capital crimes while trying to cover up
this one. Not while there was a chance of discovering the

information less violently. But he might do it if he got desperate, and two weeks and four days could produce a lot of desperation in a man of Galvan's temperament. If he did, he could snatch Jerek at night, have the information from him before morning, and easily keep the news of Jerek's disapperance out of the newspapers for one day, long enough for any number of Galvan's men to fly to Cleveland and find Karen. She pictured Jerek's mutilated body in a shallow grave in the basement of a condemned building, and menacing strangers coming up the stairs of her building.

She stood suddenly and walked out of the office. Her heels clattered in the hall. She was moving faster with every step, as if she could outrun the horrible fantasy. The walk was good for her. By the time she got outside she had slowed down. It was a bright, clear day. The sun had lost little of its summer power. Karen realized she was prey to this paranoia partly because of her physical inactivity. She was mired in place, nothing she could do to help herself or the Truetts. That was her job, to stand still and wait.

She walked past the row of white government cars lined up in the first row of the parking lot and thought about taking one of them home instead of her own, but there was no point to that. As long as she went home she could always be found, and she had to be at home so Jerek could reach her if he had to.

She drove slowly in the direction of home. No one seemed to follow. When she finally pulled into her driveway she picked up the control of her automatic garage door opener, but then paused. The car still running, she sat and thought.

There was another reason she hadn't been back to see the Truetts. She'd seen the story in the *Sun* about the soldier who'd appeared on the west coast, claiming to be Bryan Truett. She had expected to hear from Jerek then, but it had been almost a week now with no call and no more newspaper stories about the young soldier. It must have been a trick and Jerek hadn't fallen for it. Or maybe it had been their son, quickly taken into separate protective custody, kept from his parents. Karen felt an obligation to tell the Truetts if their son really was alive. But suppose she did tell them and they wanted to do something crazy, like rush home to meet him? And if it was a trick then *she* would be the one who had fallen for it, betraying Jerek's careful plans. She needed more facts.

She glanced at her watch. It was late afternoon in Baltimore. Jerek would be at his office. She didn't like what she was thinking about doing, but she liked even less the idea of another restless night in ignorance. Slowly she put the car in gear and backed out of the driveway without ever having opened the garage door.

*T*raffic had thinned out by the time she reached a mall halfway across town from her house. Dusk was beginning. The sun didn't seem to be fading away, instead it looked as if the color of its light was changing from yellow to gold. Karen circled the parking lot, undecided if it would be better to park in the middle of the cars or away from them all. This wasn't her kind of work.

She found a phone at the edge of the parking lot, near where the cars were parked for the Sears auto shop. Fifty yards away the bay doors were open and men in coveralls still working, but not in any haste. A few of them had time to stop and stare at her as she got out of her car.

She put a ton of coins in the pay phone, producing loud clinkings in the receiver. The phone was one of those new ones completely exposed to the elements except for a short shelf of roof and two narrow wings of clear glass. She wondered what had ever happened to phone booths. She stood there on the asphalt feeling very exposed, so much so she almost decided not to call. But she did, turning into the phone and hunching her shoulders. She forced herself to look more natural, but she stared all around her as the phone started ringing on the other end. She almost hung up when someone answered.

"Captain Jerek, please."

She waited for what seemed a long time, long enough for someone to have started tracing the call. Finally a gruff voice said, "Jerek."

She couldn't recognize his voice from that one short word. "This is Sears catalog service," she said, looking at the Sears sign while she said it. "Is this the William Jerek who ordered the bedspread from us, sale price $49.95?" The particular words didn't mean anything, and she felt like a fool saying them. The pause from the other end of the line was long enough that she thought she had the wrong person.

But when his voice came again it was recognizable, and recognizably angry. "Yes it is. Is anything wrong with the merchandise?"

"I'm afraid we don't have that item in stock right now," Karen said, improvising. They hadn't worked out an elaborate code in advance, just something for her to say at the beginning if she absolutely had to call. "Would you like us to back order it for you, or would you like to make a replacement order?"

"I don't know anything about all this," Jerek growled. "It must have been my wife. Call my home instead."

"Yes sir, I'll do that." Karen hung up the phone hastily and was glad to walk away from it. Even if someone in Jerek's office had traced the call to Cleveland, they'd have no reason to pick her out of the whole city. Her previous connection to Jerek was very thin.

It was a close enough connection to make her nervous, though, as she drove home. Dusk came over the horizon and covered the city. Streetlights blinked on. Karen lived halfway down a long residential block with the closest light far away at the corner. It was one of those neighborhoods that had sprung up to house veterans returning from Germany and the Pacific, and now it was in a state of flux, some of the houses remodeled extensively and some sagging slightly under their weight of years. Karen's was one of the latter, well-tended but never remodeled. It looked very dark when she pulled into the driveway, the only lights her headlights. She should have left a porch light on. She pressed the button on her garage door opener and there was a long hesitation, as always, before the door went clanking up. Her father had installed the door opener when she'd moved into a house of her own, and he insisted that she keep the garage cleaned out enough that she could park in it and not have to walk from the driveway to her front door. He had been a cop for a long time, long enough to picture his daughter as the victim of any number of horrible crimes. Karen had thought his precaution silly, but she was glad for it now. She drove into the cluttered garage, where there was barely enough clear space for the car to fit, and didn't open her door or turn off the headlights until the garage door had closed behind her. When she got out it was into darkness. She stumbled over a box getting to the inside door.

That let her into the kitchen, where she turned on the light and immediately felt spotlighted. She had broad kitchen windows and a small backyard with an alley behind it. She walked quickly out of the kitchen and checked the front door to be sure it was locked as she had left it this morning. The house felt sinister to her. Darkness seemed to slink reluctantly out of each room as she turned on the lights. She hadn't even made it back to her bedroom yet when the phone rang.

That would be Jerek. His saying to call him at home had actually meant that he would call *her* at home, as soon as he got to a phone he knew he was safe, that much they *had* worked out ahead of time. His response told her where to go to receive the call. That was the extent of the code they had worked out that first night Jerek had called her from the motel, long ago. Eighteen days ago.

"Hello, Karen Boone," she said, and the silence on the line made her think she shouldn't have said her name. Then Jerek's voice came through reassuringly, if angrily:

"What the hell do you want?"

"Uh—" Now that she had him on the phone, nothing she wanted to know seemed important enough to have taken this risk. Then she got a little mad herself. "I'd just like to know what the hell is going on. When I took this job I didn't know it was going to be a lifetime assignment. If this is going to take a lot longer I need to make some—"

"Excuse the shit out of me," Jerek growled. "I didn't mean to inconvenience you. I guess I'll have to start making more of an effort."

"Hey I'm a volunteer, remember? Don't bark at me."

There was a pause. "Sorry," Jerek finally said. With the anger gone from his voice he sounded tired. "All I can tell you is we're still looking. I don't even know how close we're getting."

"Any developments?"

"Yeah. One of my men got killed two days ago. So did a guy I was hoping to use to find Galvan."

It was Karen's turn to say she was sorry. After a moment of silence she said, "What I really wanted to know about was this soldier who's supposed to be back from Vietnam. Is he really Bryan Truett? I have to tell them something."

"Everyone keeps asking me that," Jerek said tiredly. "The answer is I don't have the slightest idea. He ran off from the Army post and the FBI lost him crossing the country. He's probably here by now. The next sound you hear'll probably be him sneaking up from behind and strangling me. But who he is I don't know. If he gets close enough I'll find out. Either way, there's not a chance in hell I'll bring him to your people until this is all over."

"Maybe if you find him I could tell them and they could come up with some test questions to give him to see if . . ."

She trailed off, feeling silly again. "Of course, I guess you could just fingerprint him."

"That had occurred to me."

She said hurriedly, "Look, just let me know if you hear anything more about him. I want to be able to tell Elizabeth and John something. Who knows, maybe he can find them." Find me, she meant. "Maybe they accidentally left some clue that only he would recognize. Sounds crazy, but the whole thing's—"

"I'll let you know," Jerek said.

"All right." Karen was winding down. "And listen, be careful, okay? Think of the fix I'd be in if you got killed."

He chuckled. It sounded hollow, coming from so far away. "It's sweet of you to care."

They talked for another minute. Just as he was about to hang up she said, "Bill—I mean it, take care of yourself." She didn't make a joke out of it this time.

When she put the phone down she realized it was the first time she'd ever called him by his first name. It hadn't been calculated. She wondered if he'd noticed. She was glad she had made him laugh. It was probably the first time in three weeks. She wished there was somebody around to cheer her up. She thought about the Truetts. She hadn't learned anything, but there was still the urge to tell them something. Distracted again, she started unbuttoning her blouse and walked down the dark hall to her bedroom.

CHAPTER NINETEEN

Tripwire

*T*he house no longer looked like part of the neighborhood. It looked like an implant, erected on this quiet residential block for some sinister purpose and imperfectly disguised. Looking at it gave Tripwire that old jungle feeling of staring into impenetrable shade and wondering what was within. The house looked not so much watched as watchful. There was nothing but dimness inside the front windows. He crossed the front yard feeling conspicuous and turned left to walk back beside the fence. The house was on a corner lot so there was no other house on this side, only a street. At the end of the house's back yard fence he came to the alley. There was a detached carport and storage room one entered from that alley. He could see from here that the carport was empty and the storage room padlocked. He crossed the side street and walked in a wide circle back the way he had come, until he was standing across the street looking at the front of the house again.

Some attempts had been made to pretend people still lived in the house, but they were unsuccessful. The front yard had been mowed, for example, but not edged. The sidewalk leading to the front door had grown thin from encroaching grass. The porch light was burning, though one could hardly see it in the daylight. At night it would probably look even more artificial, with the house dark and silent behind the one light. There was nothing obviously wrong with the house, but it gave the impression that several major things could go wrong at once: the rain gutters come loose, the windows crack, the roof collapse. Slam a door and everything would come tumbling down. Only the front of the house was visible. The rest was surrounded by a redwood fence that started near the front of the sides of the house, so the house looked like a dowager showing only her face to the world, a high collar covering everything below her chin.

Tripwire was sure the impression the house tried to give of harboring secrets was a false one. A bus pulled to a halt, cutting off his view of the house, and opened its doors. He climbed aboard, dropped coins in the box until the driver looked satisfied, and found an empty seat. He was looking the other way as the bus left the house behind.

The bus lumbered to the end of the block, turned, and was soon out of the residential neighborhood. Scenery flowed over Tripwire's eyes in the same way it threw fleeting reflections across the windows of the bus. Nothing tugged his eyes from the path of their gaze. A vision running on the inner surface of his eyes turned the outer surface opaque. Baltimore didn't register on him.

Rowhouses became interspersed with coffee shops and doctors' offices, then gave way completely to stores and office buildings. The bus passed the railroad station, the first thing to take Tripwire's attention. His gaze fell abruptly from the street level to the tracks forty feet below, with an impact almost as shocking as if he had made the fall himself. He stood slowly, like a man expecting pain, lurched into the aisle, and scrambled out at the bus's next stop.

He was almost downtown, he had come too far. He turned around and started back north. Tripwire didn't mind walking. His strides grew surer and he began to notice his surroundings. He crossed the street, went three blocks up a side street, and turned north again.

*D*rugstore with peeling sales signs on its windows. Third-rate department store: mannequins with twisted limbs. Liquor store, its metal gates folded back. Closed hardware store.

Tripwire stood looking in the window. He saw no explanatory notice, just "Closed," on a weekday morning. He tried the door, but the sign was telling the truth. The size of the locks was appropriate to a hardware store. There was one dim light from the back of the store, inside the storeroom, whose door was ajar. The open door gave the impression someone would emerge from the storeroom any moment, but no one had appeared in the fifteen minutes he had stood there, even when he knocked on the glass.

There was still a display in the window, power saws and burglar alarms, but there was an undisturbed layer of dust over everything. The display cases still stood inside, full of merchandise, but there was no look of expected customers. It was a ghost store.

Tripwire turned his back to the glass and looked around. A few people walked the sidewalks, fewer still stopped to look in windows. Some black kids bunched on the corner across the street reminded him for a moment of Vietnam. Wearing torn T-shirts and Taiwan-made tennis shoes, and backed by the cheap merchandise in the novelty store window behind them, they could have been in Saigon. Tripwire had a sudden inclination to get away. This neighborhood, though, was the only other place he had to go in Baltimore. He turned and walked quickly, but only as far as the liquor store.

It seemed as dim there as the hardware store, but this place was open for business. Tripwire dawdled in front of the wine while two old men bought pint bottles and shuffled out. When he stepped to the counter Tripwire saw that the clerk was younger than he was. He looked like he belonged in high school. The kid drummed his fingers on the counter in a complicated rhythm, his head cocked as if listening to make sure the other members of the band were keeping up. It took Tripwire a moment to realize that the kid's "Help you?" was directed at him.

"Uh, let me have a pack of cigarettes."

"What kind?"

That took up another minute. Cigarette brands seemed to have proliferated faster than bad neighborhoods. Tripwire didn't care what he bought, but the kid demanded precision.

When he got the pack and his change Tripwire didn't move away. He stood at the counter unwrapping the pack and removing one. The kid looked at him, flipped a book of matches onto the countertop, and resumed his drumming.

"You know the man next door?"

"What?"

Tripwire pointed.

"Oh." The kid shook his head, starting his lank blonde hair swinging in a counterpoint to his drumming. "Naw, there isn't anybody there."

"Did you know the man who used to be there?"

Another head shake, reinforced by a frown. "Naw, man, there's never been anybody there. That place's been empty forever."

"Oh." Tripwire still stood there. He was glaring a threat, but the kid had never once looked him in the eye. "How long have you worked here?" Tripwire finally asked.

"'Bout a week."

He walked out and passed the hardware store again. Still no one had come out of the storeroom door. On the other side of the store was a lunch counter. Tripwire went in and sat on a stool near the door. The place was all white, or had once been. Now the floor was darkened by the marks of many heels. The stains had gotten a running start and begun climbing the walls, a few marks reaching shoulder height. Only the ceiling and the countertop retained their original unsullied whiteness.

And the man who came toward Tripwire with two menus. White hair, white cap, T-shirt, apron, pale skin of arms and face. Not a mark on him, except the marks of age. "Breakfast or lunch?"

"Excuse me?"

"Breakfast or lunch?" The man presented each menu in turn.

"Oh. Um, just let me have a hamburger. Coffee."

"Lunch," the man said definitively. He looked over his shoulder at the clock perched high on the wall, shrugged, and moved to the grill. Tripwire found an unlit cigarette in his hand and put it in an ashtray.

"Coffee," the counterman said a moment later as he set the cup in front of Tripwire.

"Hamburger," a few minutes after that. "Will there be anything else?"

"No, not any—"

"Check," he said, laying it down and starting to move away.

"Wait a minute." The counterman turned back with an expression of unsurprised weariness. "There is something else," Tripwire said.

The man picked up the check and stood waiting.

"No, nothing else to eat. I just want to ask you something."

The old man put the check down again. "I'm a busy man. You want directions, ask a cop."

Tripwire looked around. There was only one other customer in the place, drinking coffee at the other end of the counter.

"You get any busier, you're going to be out of business like the hardware store next door."

The old man stopped, his back to Tripwire. When he came back he did not look particularly angry. He leaned on his side of the counter and looked steadily at the young man. "I'm a talkative old man," he said. "Get me started, I'll talk your ear off. I try to control myself, so I don't scare the customers off, but you I don't mind scaring. You got me started, it's on your own head.

"You happen to have come in at an in-between time, that's how come we're not busy in here, just a couple of bums who apparently don't have jobs and so can come in here when it's not breakfast time or lunch time either one."

Tripwire took a bite of his hamburger and sipped the last of his coffee. The old man kept talking while he fetched the coffee pot.

"As for the hardware store next door, I might go out of business some day, God forbid, but not like that. That was a very funny set of circumstances. Who are you, by the way?" The question was abrupt.

"Bryan Truett. It was my father's store."

The man looked at him sharply. "I know John. You used to work there yourself, didn't you? Summers when you were a kid?"

"Years ago. A few times."

The old man nodded but continued to study him. Tripwire stared back and the old man dropped his eyes a bit. He reached out and moved a hand under Tripwire's chin as if swatting a fly. "Beards. It looks crummy, take my word for it, I don't care if the girls do like it. What have you got to hide?"

"Not a th—"

"Now that you're here, maybe you can tell me what happened to your father? One day he's here, doing business as good as you can expect, the next I never see him again. He doesn't come around complaining about the location, wringing his hands, 'What am I going to do?' He's just gone. Very funny business."

"I'm looking for him myself."

"You don't even know where they are?"

"I was gone—"

"Yeah, kids, running around, don't even call your parents often enough to find out if they're dead or alive."

"I was in Vietnam."

"You really?" He fingered the sleeve of Tripwire's fatigue jacket. "I thought you were just being stylish. Well, I'll tell you, young Truett, you don't need to be talking to me, you need to be talking to maybe the police, maybe the C.I. of A." He paused and looked significantly at Tripwire, who said nothing.

"That doesn't bring a question from you? So, I'll tell you anyway. One day about three days after he's not open any more I decide it's time to find out what's the deal. So I owe your father a little money, nothing much, I bought some hinges and I didn't have the change in my pocket. So on this day I take the money from the cash register, tell my idiot who comes in part time not to steal me blind while I'm gone, and I go next door. The door says closed but it's not locked, so I go in, making noise, I don't want to be shot for a robber, calling, 'John, John, I got your money.' I figure this will bring him on the run.

"But what it brings out is this big man wearing a suit, but the suit should have 'cop' written all over it, as much as this man's going to fool anyone into thinking he's a civilian. And he's glaring at me, waving his arm like he can push me out the door from all the way across the store, and saying big, 'Out, out, we're closed.'

"'*We're* closed,' I say, 'That's funny coming from you, since you're not the owner of this store and he happens to be the one I'm looking for.' Well, that shuts him up for a minute but then he says, 'He's gone, Mr. Truett isn't here, he's on vacation.' 'Very interesting,' I say. 'Maybe you can tell me where, so I can write and ask him what he found out about this neighborhood to make him vacation so suddenly, maybe I'll want to take a trip myself.'

"So then this big cop dummy starts giving a song and dance to kill vaudeville all over again, says he don't know where John went, nobody knows, I should forget it. He won't even take the money I owe, tells me to mail it in to the store. *Mail* it to next door, when I'm standing right there already. So I put my money in my pocket, I come back to my own business, and I mind it from then until now."

"How long ago was this?"

"Three weeks? Maybe two. You got any more questions, keep 'em to yourself, because if I didn't already answer them I don't know the answer."

They looked at each other for a long moment, the silence feeling like an alien atmosphere. Before they started choking in it Tripwire said, "Well, thanks. I guess I'll have to look somewhere else."

"Try the cops, they'll know."

"Yeah. Thanks." Tripwire stood and put a hand in his pocket.

"It just so happens," said the man behind the counter, "that the price of your sumptuous meal comes to the same amount I owe your father. So when you find him you should pay him for the hamburger."

"Thanks again."

"No thanks involved, just business."

The old man's tone was brisk, as if had chores to get to, but when Tripwire went out the door the man stood still, watching him move off down the sidewalk. "That Vietnam, that was a bad business," he said quietly. He raised his voice as he moved down the counter toward his lone remaining customer. "It almost makes me glad my own rotten son was a draft dodger, the little worm." He shook his head and looked back over his shoulder.

*H*e had taken care to come up on the house from the back, to wait for the neighborhood dogs to stop barking, and to be sure no one saw him when he slipped over the fence into the back yard. So he jerked visibly when he was peering through the window of the house and a voice directly behind him said, "Hello."

It was one of those hellos with too much emphasis, that meant something more than a greeting. In this case it was inquiring who he was and what he was doing. Tripwire mastered his surprise and turned slowly, ready to lunge in any direction, and was surprised again to find no one else in the yard. The woman who had spoken was on the other side of the fence, peering over. She looked like a puppet in the process of being assembled. Only her head and her arms from the elbows to the fingers showed above the fence. Her chin was nestled in a notch of the fence top and she looked very comfortable there. Her blonde hair was cut short, with two points sliding down her temples. Tripwire took in what information was available: wedding ring on the appropriate finger, tanned face and forearms; the eyes beginning, with only a few twigs now, to build a nest of wrinkles for themselves. The woman was probably edging into her forties, as calmly but cautiously as she was looking over the fence.

"Hello," he said, taking a step toward her. She didn't react, so he took another.

"Thinking about buying it?" she asked. One of her detached hands moved to rub her eye. "I don't really know if it's for sale or not, actually. You can see there's still some furniture inside. The people that lived there took off so fast—. Of course you probably know, you must have talked to a realtor."

She looked at him steadily. Her eyes were more suspicious than her voice. He took her for the kind of bored housewife who spends time staring between her blinds or through the chinks in her neighbor's fence. She was staring at him with an absolute confidence in being where she belonged, and as if he, on the other hand, needed to explain himself.

"I don't want to buy it. It's already mine." He took another step toward her, coming out of the shade of the house. He was within ten feet of her, but she only looked curious. She shaded her eyes with her hand, studying him.

"My name's Bryan Truett. It's my parents' house."

Her eyes widened under her shading hand. She strained forward slightly to get a better look at him. He moved closer.

"I just moved in a few months ago," she said, "I never—. But I've seen pictures of you. But I thought—Do you have a brother?" He shook his head. "But I thought someone told me you were—"

"Dead?" he said gently. He took another step toward her. She put her arms down from the fence and stepped back.

"Well, lost," she said. "In Vietnam? Was that just one of those crazy things that get started?"

"No, that was true. But I got out finally."

"That's wonderful," she said, but it was obvious she didn't swallow the news in one great gulp of belief. She became suddenly aware of how close he was. Even in the sunlight his eyes were shadowed. She thought he was staring straight at her, but then she saw his eyes flash with movement. She resisted an urge to look back over her shoulder. Her back door was unlocked, she was sure.

"But your mother's not here. It was so sudden, like—. I didn't talk to her before she left, but it was in the paper that she'd seen that murder. Have you talked to them yet?"

"No, not yet. There hasn't been anyone around the house here since they've been gone?"

She might have been insulted by the fact he assumed she would know anything that had gone on at her neighbors' house, but she wasn't thinking about that. He had moved up next to the fence now and she had taken another step back from it. The fence was five feet tall, the boards pointed on the top, but she felt as if they were standing there with nothing between them. She didn't look directly into his face any more.

"Oh, you know, there was some activity the first week or so, men coming and going, but I haven't paid much attention since then." Some of those men had looked hard and grim, but they hadn't worried her the way she was worried now. She felt herself shrinking, trying to grow small and insignificant. She hadn't felt this way since she was a child.

He asked no more questions. She could feel him just staring. From the corner of her eye she saw him put his hands on top of the fence.

"Well, welcome home," she said hurriedly. "I'm sorry there's—Is that my phone?"

She turned jerkily and walked briskly toward the house. In two steps she was running. She saw the back door ahead of her and wished it opened inward so she could just fall through it and slam it shut behind her instead of having to stop and pull it open, because when she did stop she could feel him close behind her. She could almost see his hand reaching past her and holding the door shut. She pulled it too hard, hitting her shin, and stumbled through, pulling it closed and scrabbling at the lock. When it locked her panic abated. She was embarrassed as she stooped ruefully to rub her shin. She wondered if he was staring after her flabbergasted, but when she looked through the window in the back door she saw no sign of him. He was no longer leaning over the fence. She stopped dead still, listening. Quietly, not even breathing, she backed away from the door. She knew the front door was locked but she ran softly through the house to check it anyway. She heard a sound outside but couldn't tell if it came from next door or her own yard.

She hadn't bothered to call the police when she'd seen those other men snooping around the Truetts' house after the murder. She has assumed they *were* police, for one thing. But this one was no policeman. She tried to pin down exactly what about him had frightened her. Even if she believed his story, it gave him a ghostly quality. If she had known him before it probably would have been worse. And if he *wasn't* the son . . . In any event the police would want to know, she thought. She wanted to call them. She picked up the phone, peering out the blinds of her front window.

"Hello, operator?"

She drew back from the window. He had suddenly appeared, walking between her house and the one next door. He paused in the front yard for a long moment, looking at the Truetts' house.

"Get me the police, please. Yes, it is."

He began walking away. Not toward her house. He didn't even look in her direction. He walked unhurriedly, hands in his back pockets. From this distance he looked boyish, his head down and his feet scuffling through the leaves at the curb. She began to feel silly.

When the police dispatcher came on the line she hung up and went to make herself a drink instead.

CHAPTER TWENTY

Bryan

John and Elizabeth were returning from another walk, carrying grocery bags, laughing together, when they saw the car parked in their driveway. John panicked worse than Elizabeth did, because he felt not only frightened but guilty. He was supposed to be the protector; he had screwed up. He dropped his bag of groceries and took Elizabeth's arm, starting to turn, wondering where they should go. But there was no time. Someone had been watching through the dining room window, and before he could take a step the front door opened.

Karen stepped out onto the front porch.

John felt relieved, then foolish, then guilty again. Karen had warned them not to go out. But we have to eat don't we, he thought. He stooped to pick up his spilled groceries while Elizabeth walked on toward the house, calling a greeting. Karen didn't respond, but she didn't look angry, exactly. She had a look like a mother sometimes gives a child: you've hurt me with your thoughtlessness.

John and Elizabeth's leaving the house was not what weighed on Karen's mind, though. She was thinking about what she had come to tell them. Their absence had reinforced her idea that she should. Maybe her news would make them more cautious.

"Well come in, come in," John said heartily as he walked past her. "Don't stand out here on the porch all day. This time we've got food to offer you."

"I hope you were careful," was all Karen said, and

Elizabeth immediately responded, "Oh, we were, we were."
"We disguised our voices at the checkout stand," John added,
and he and Elizabeth laughed.

Their high spirits made Karen happy one moment and
uneasy the next. They were adapting to captivity; she didn't
know if that was good or bad news.

They offered her coffee and cake and the three of them
settled in the living room, John and Elizabeth acting for the
first time like hosts instead of like prisoners getting a visit from
outside. Karen almost decided just to make pleasant conversation for an hour and go away. But it was their secret more than
hers. She had decided she had no right to keep it from them.
She wasn't their parent. Besides, she thought there was danger
in ignorance. Karen would have felt more reassured herself if
she had more information. At least she thought so.

It was John Karen watched later as she worked her way into
the story she had to tell them. Elizabeth's reactions were
perfectly conventional, and plainly written on her face. It was
almost painful for Karen to watch the succeeding emotions
announce themselves there. John's face was both more puzzl-
ing and easier to study.

"I haven't been able to think of a graceful way to start telling
you this," Karen began, wishing Elizabeth wouldn't look at
her as if she thought this the beginning of a funny story. "A
few days ago, almost a week, someone showed up on the west
coast claiming to be your son. He said he had been a prisoner
of the Vietcong for some time, ever since his supposed death.
They held him after the end of the war, until he escaped and
made his way to our embassy in Malaysia."

She kept talking because she wanted to get the whole story
out before Elizabeth's face found an expression. She was
staring at Karen, her features drawn inward, but she had the
look of a woman about to burst into a smile, or tears, and
Karen wanted to finish the explanation to give Elizabeth the
chance to choose the right response.

"Now, we know that at least the last part is true. He did turn
up at the embassy, saying he was Bryan Truett, and he was
transported to an Army base in California. We didn't tell you
about him because we hadn't verified his identity yet. We still
haven't. And I'm not supposed to be telling you about him, but
I thought it's time you knew."

"Bryan," Elizabeth said. It wasn't a question. John sat
perfectly still.

"The trouble is he's dropped out of sight now. And we're still not sure . . ."

Karen talked on, watching John for the most part now. Elizabeth followed her narrative intently, leaning forward, urging the story on through every twist toward some kind of conclusion. Her expression was hesitantly hopeful and very watchful.

John, on the other hand, hardly seemed to be paying attention. It looked as if the first mention of his son's name had dropped a spell over him, setting him at a remove from the world. His eyes stared placidly and his head was cocked slightly as if he listened for something other than the sound of Karen's voice. Karen watched him closely without gaining any idea what he was thinking. His face reminded her of an ant colony: cold plate glass with dozens of movements just under the surface.

"But the point I want to emphasize is, we don't know who he is. There's no official position. Chances are it's not Bryan. And if it's not—"

"Then it's a trick to find me," Elizabeth said.

"Yes." Karen wished the coldness out of her own voice, but it wouldn't leave. She wanted to offer sympathy, but she could only go on mechanically, like a news ticker. "That's the main reason I decided to tell you. If he somehow finds out where you are, gets around Captain Jerek and me and manages to contact you, I don't want you to be so startled and happy you just blindly assume it's your son. Probably it's not. You have to be more careful than ever." Careful even of your emotions, Karen thought. And from the looks of them the Truetts were being emotionally careful. They'd made no outbursts. She saw them look at each other, start to speak, and then say nothing, glancing at her. She understood that her visit was over.

"Maybe I shouldn't have said anything," Karen said when she rose. "I thought you'd rather know than not." But now, looking at them, she was afraid she'd been wrong about that. She had yet to see an unguarded reaction to her news.

Elizabeth finally bestirred herself to look at Karen. "Thank you," she said. "We're glad you told us. I hope it doesn't get you into any trouble." Karen detected no life in her formal tones.

Elizabeth walked her to the door. "Please let us know everything you hear."

"I will. Of course. Well—Goodbye." Karen raised her

voice enough for it to carry into the living room, where John still sat, but there was no response. Karen hadn't expected to leave so soon. The women looked at each other apologetically.

Elizabeth closed the door behind Karen and came back into the living room. John hadn't moved. He sat hunched slightly forward, elbows on his knees, his hands clenched in each other's fingers. Elizabeth stood looking at him. He was aware of her presence, but didn't look at her even when she spoke.

"John?"

"I don't know." His hands gripped each other more tightly.

*I*f time were not so maddeningly constant, there are many moments in which we would choose to linger. But time trivializes every instant of our lives by giving them all equal duration. Decisions which should be pondered are never made at all. We are hurried along, embarked on a course before we know a course must be chosen.

John and Elizabeth sat in mutually exclusive remembrances, with a sense of time rushing past them in all directions. They thought they had to reach a decision, but for the moment they couldn't even clarify the question. There seemed to be no time. Time hurried on, as fast as it had through the brief years of their son's life.

Bryan seemed to have used up, in his short childhood, his whole life's allotment of happiness, and love. He had been a very cheerful boy, causing them no trouble ever. An only child, he had seemed for that reason to fit more easily into his parents' lives. There was no need for them to slip Bryan into a separate, children's compartment of their concern. The three of them simply comprised a family, without divisions. Bryan went everywhere with them, trailing his mother through all his early years when she had no other job than raising him; waiting in the front yard for his father to come home. Sometimes he spent whole days at the hardware store, aping John or inventing games of his own when the slow atmosphere of the store grew too static for him. After he started school the store became a regular stopping place for him. He and John often came home together, Bryan explaining to his father the fine points of spelling or long division. John knew more of the principal exports of Brazil than any other father he knew.

Bryan didn't need to look beyond his own house for love. His closeness to his parents drained off his need for friendship. He had plenty of acquaintances, enough to fill a birthday party, but friends came and went in rapid succession, leaving no impression on the triumvirate of Bryan and his parents.

So it had been hard for them to see when he was no longer happy. The very ease of their relations to each other had caused them to drift apart, assuming each other's happiness. But Bryan was no longer an easy boy by his last high school years. His mother had gone back to work, and he spent more time alone in the house. He often imagined himself an orphan as he waited for his parents to come home. Bryan was not naturally solitary. He didn't know how to spend the time alone, but he had never learned how to keep friends. He didn't like school. He didn't want school to end.

Choosing a life for himself had been a distant threat for the last few years. Now it began to look as if it would really happen, and Bryan was secretly terrified.

There began to be arguments. John and Elizabeth sometimes felt that the fights with their son were forced on them, and they were right. Bryan projected the arguments directly from his own mind, assigning his parents one side and taking the other for himself. There was no agreeing with him, because he could argue either side of the proposition. After a while John and Elizabeth grew interested in the arguments for the sake of what they were trying to find out. Then the arguments became real, and began to center around one topic: what was Bryan going to do with his future?

Elizabeth was less emphatic than John, but Bryan could see that she sided with his father, and he felt betrayed. First she had left him alone for a career she didn't really need, then she had gone over to his father's side in the fighting. He lost heart for the arguments, no longer responding to his parents' questions. He seemed completely indifferent, unwilling to face the fact that the steady flow of days must bring changes.

His parents saw only the indifference, not the hidden fact that the question of his future troubled Bryan as well. They badgered him about it, and he grew more defensive. He was a surly ghost in their lives, usually in the house but seldom in their sight, and seemingly with no purpose except to haunt them. He absorbed all their bewilderment, anger, and all their love without visible effect. Bryan had gotten the idea that he was being goaded out of their lives and into one of his own, one he wasn't ready to choose. Time. . . .

Bryan said he wanted to go to college. Elizabeth was pleased. She would have been more pleased if he'd seemed to have some idea of what he wanted to do in college. The fear that he was just trying to prolong his school days was a small one in the back of her mind. She was willing to let him do so, if it came to that. She was sure that Bryan would pull himself out of his tailspin, given time. College would probably do it. He would find interests there. Maybe friends.

John had much more mixed feelings. At first he wouldn't discuss any of it with Bryan. "Whatever you want," he said, trying to sound genial and failing. When he and Elizabeth were alone, though, John would say the word, "College." Conclusively, flatly, with all the weight of his dying respect for education. He had spent years of his life regretting his own lack of college. Now what he saw as the antics of the latest crop of students convinced him that it had become institutionalized time-wasting for the congenitally immature. His history of thought on the subject gave strong but mixed feelings, the contempt of a hard-working peasant for a drunken lord. He could drop the entire weight of his feelings on the one word: "College."

There was more to it. Bryan worked summers in the hardware store, up through his last summer after high school graduation. John had expected him to come into the business, an idea so basic to him that he had never voiced it. Seeing his son making a sale at the counter gave him a prideful feeling of continuity. He saw no reason that Bryan shouldn't continue there. It wasn't as if he had other ambitions of his own.

But Bryan didn't like the hardware store. He said nothing, and worked there without complaint, but he had no intention of continuing in the store. That would have been too much like settling down to his parents' lives forever, never making a decision of his own. Through the years of questions and quarrels the one thing that had hardened in him was the resolve to find the life of his own he was being compelled into. He hadn't found his direction yet, but he had found the determination.

When the question finally came up, casually, John's and Bryan's tacit expectations met head-on. Their disagreement was all the more vehement for the fact that they had never before realized that they disagreed. John took Bryan's attitude for a slur on his own occupation. Bryan thought his father was trying to smother him. They quarreled.

They argued incessantly, turning the house into a battleground when they were together. Even when one of them was absent the other would carry on the fight, through Elizabeth.

"What does he want from me?" Bryan asked her again and again, as if she had a reasonable explanation to give if he would only keep at her long enough. "What does he want me to do?"

"He just wants you to be happy," she would murmur.

"Come on," Bryan said, turning away angrily. He was always saying that to her: Come on; tell me the truth; be serious. As if she were keeping anything from him.

Bryan paced around the living room; always in a rush, even when he didn't leave the room. He pushed back the long hair that was another point of contention with his father. His hair had darkened with age, but the summer sun had lightened it considerably. He became a boy again in the summer.

"What does he want?" he said again. "I thought he'd want me to go to college. He never seemed to dislike the idea before. People are supposed to be proud when people want to go to college."

Elizabeth heard John's voice saying the word: "College." "He is proud," she said. "He wants whatever you want. He's just not sure that you really want it."

"I want it. Why else would I do it? It's hard work, you know. A lot harder than hanging around in the crummy store."

"I know," she said. "I know." Always conciliatory. There would have been no time for Elizabeth to get angry herself, even if she'd been inclined. The other two pre-empted all the angry time in the house.

"What's he said to you?" John would ask her, sounding like his son.

"Nothing."

"You must talk some time, when I'm not here. He must tell you something about his plans."

"Nothing he hasn't told you." They were in bed, keeping their voices low. The sound of the television came faintly from the living room. Elizabeth put her hand on John's neck and held it. He didn't seem to notice; it didn't change his tone of voice. "Don't worry about him so much," she added, massaging the taut muscles.

"How can I help it? He's so—listless. Isn't there anything he wants to do?"

"Just don't—Don't rush him into anything."

John was silent for a moment, and when he spoke his voice

had changed, grown momentarily hopeful. "Maybe he is planning something. Maybe he does have something—he just doesn't want to tell us about it yet."

"Maybe." She was willing to believe it, especially if it would leave both Bryan and John happier.

"Maybe," John echoed her, the brief hope no longer present in his voice.

Bryan went to college. He lived at home for one semester and part of the next while going to a local school. Elizabeth saw John doing his best to be fair, to give the enterprise a chance. When he came home and found his son watching television he would greet him pleasantly and settle in a nearby chair with nothing else occupying his attention, waiting for Bryan to tell him something. Sometimes John would sit like that for half an hour before picking up the newspaper. Bryan never volunteered anything. One would have thought he had spent the whole day in front of the television. Elizabeth would catch John's look and shrug in return.

John began to ask questions, kindly at first, doing his best to show Bryan his genuine interest. How was school? What was he taking? Did he like it? What were his professors like?

Bryan continued indifferent. "All right." That was his most common reply. Everything was all right. He hadn't chosen a major and didn't seem close to choosing one. None of his classes excited him. John's questions grew sharper. Soon they were arguing again. John thought that he had given the experiment time enough and it had failed. Half a year, Bryan would reply. Only half a year and his father was ready to give up on him.

They bellowed at each other. Elizabeth couldn't see sometimes what kept them from coming to blows. Perhaps it was her own intervention. Each of them was again coming to her with his arguments when the other wasn't there to contradict. She agreed with them both while trying to make them more reasonable toward each other. She felt, justifiably, caught in the middle of their fights; everyone's secret counselor, no one's ally. Sometimes, rarely, she wanted to scream at them both, but she never had the opportunity. She had to remain the voice of reason in the household.

Bryan began to declare to her that he couldn't live with John any more. The words didn't carry much conviction at first, though they were loud enough. Elizabeth brushed them away, while secretly believing it. Neither she nor John had been living at home at Bryan's age.

The arguments grew in intensity. The last, worst of all, was over Bryan's registration for the second semester. His course load was a mishmash leading to no degree or showing any concentrated interest. He might have chosen the classes deliberately to goad his father. They stormed at each other for a week, until Bryan went suddenly silent. For three more days he spent very little time in the house, most of that in his room. On the fourth day Elizabeth came in from working late to see him sitting in the living room wearing his coat, suitcase at his feet. John was in the chair near him. She saw Bryan's profile and the back of John's head. They weren't saying a word.

"I've been waiting for you," Bryan said quickly, standing. He carried the suitcase near her. "I got an apartment near school. It'll be easier." He stood in front of her holding the suitcase, anxious to be off but apparently looking for some sort of ceremony.

"An apartment," she said. "How will—"

"He's got a job, too," came from John in a neutral tone. He didn't turn his head. Bryan looked at her and shrugged, half-smiling. The silence gathered a little more weight until John said, "Ask him where he got a job."

She looked at Bryan. His half-smile became half-grimace. "In a paint store," he said. Elizabeth felt inclined to laugh, but didn't.

"In a paint store," John repeated loudly, finally turning around. "Ask him where he learned anything he knows about paint."

Bryan hefted the suitcase higher and got a better grip on it. "I've got to go. I'll see you, Mom." He brushed her cheek with his mouth and let the forward motion carry him past her.

"Come back," she said. "Sometime. When you want a good meal."

"I will," he said without turning, and went out. They heard his car start.

She heard from him once in a while, usually on the phone. His life on his own didn't last long. She asked him, gently, about school and his job, and got the old answers. All right. Yes, no, all right. She sensed that he missed his father's resistance. Without it neither the job nor college held much interest for him. He found it hard to support himself and keep up with his course work. Before the semester was over he had dropped out.

He was drafted then. There were no more college deferments, but his dropping out seemed to be the sign the Army had been waiting for. Bryan was nearly twenty. It was 1972, the war was winding down, not as many young men were being drafted. Bryan probably could have avoided it if he had tried, but he sounded almost happy when he told his mother the news. It was the most excitement she had heard in his voice in a long time. John allowed, when she told him, that the Army might do him some good.

Bryan came to the house one last time, in a strange spirit of hidden bluster, as if he were already a warrior. They all managed to get along without arguments. At the end of the day Bryan hugged his mother, shook hands stiffly with his father, and was gone. That was the last time they had seen him. Almost two years ago.

It was strange to think of Bryan alive in the world again. For John it was a harder adjustment than for Elizabeth, because Elizabeth had never quite given up believing her son was alive. But John had buried him. John had loved his son, loved him living and dead, but more than that, he had invested in Bryan. Lifelong hopes had died with his son. Life had shifted into a lower gear after Bryan's death, everything stripped of one aspect of significance. It was painful for John to think of him again.

And he could hardly bear to sit in the same room with Elizabeth knowing *she* was thinking about Bryan. John was afraid. The worst time of their lives had been after Bryan joined the Army. In the year before that Elizabeth had seemed eminently reasonable, always moderating between them. But after Bryan left she had turned slightly cool, as if she'd really been on his side all along. No, that wasn't fair; it was as if she *had* been neutral, until John had gone too far and driven their son away from them completely. John tried once or twice to explain that he'd never intended it to go that far, but she wasn't receptive. Her coolness just had to pass, and it did—until Bryan joined the Army.

John was alone when he found the telegram saying Bryan was lost. It was lying opened on the dining room table and Elizabeth was gone. She stayed gone for a whole day; John never knew where. He was torn in suffering between the loss of his son and the apparent loss of his wife. When she returned it was clear that the decision to stay with him had not been an easy one. She never said a word of blame: *You killed him. If it wasn't for you he'd still be here.* But John felt it.

They didn't comfort each other through that time. They bore their grief separately. Only after it receded were they able to come together again. They didn't reconcile exactly; they just lived past it. That rift hadn't closed. It was still there, deep and threatening, and now, it seemed to John, they were being pushed toward it again.

"What are we going to do?" Elizabeth finally said aloud.

"What she told us, I guess. Wait and see." But what John was thinking was that this was his second and final chance. It hardly mattered whether this soldier was really Bryan. John couldn't fail his son again, no matter what.

CHAPTER TWENTY-ONE

Tripwire

*T*ripwire sat on the patio of the Truett house in Baltimore. There had been no surprises this time. After his encounter with the next door neighbor that afternoon he'd walked conspicuously between their houses and then stood in the front yard for a long minute, making sure she saw him leave. But he hadn't left the neighborhood. By the time he returned there was a car in the driveway next door. He hoped she wouldn't be peering out her windows with her husband home now.

This time Tripwire came over the fence more carefully, on the side away from hers. No one saw him. He drew a lawn chair back into the dimmest corner of the patio, next to the house, and sat waiting. He sat while the sun went slowly down, dragging color out of the world with it. He sat while the stars struggled into focus and a cool wind came up. He heard the sound of another car pulling into the driveway across the street. A front door opened and closed. Life went on normally around him.

He was waiting for the neighborhood to settle down. Let people sink into their houses and easy chairs and turn on the television, cover any unusual noises. He would have preferred to break into the house during the day, when the area would be more sparsely populated and he'd have had light to work with. That had been his plan when he'd been interrupted by the neighbor. So now he waited.

He didn't acknowledge that he was putting off going into the house because he didn't expect to find anything helpful there, and because once he had exhausted this possibility he would have run completely out of ideas.

Finally he stirred. He stood at the glass patio doors looking in, his nose almost pressed to the glass. The doors were uncurtained. There was furniture inside, looming in the darkness like obstacles on a course.

Sliding doors were easy. It didn't take a burglar to break in. On the patio he found a metal rod, the broken leg of a wrought iron chair, and he used it as a lever to pop the lock. He looked at his reflection in the glass as he worked, and when the door slid open it was as if he disappeared.

He stepped into a paneled den with bulky leather furniture. A heavy, old-fashioned television sat on the floor, filling one corner. There was no mantlepiece full of pictures, no desk to be rifled. Tripwire stood letting his eyes adjust to the deeper blackness, saw another doorway across the room and started toward it.

He hadn't quite reached it when there was a click and the room filled with light.

He froze for an instant, then leaped through the doorway ahead of him, which could have been a mistake but luckily no one waited there. He paused. He would not make any more foolish mistakes. He couldn't believe someone had waited in the den so silently that he had walked right past him before the man had turned on a light. The house could be full of waiting men. Or maybe there was only one, who had come in through the patio doors behind him. So he stopped, his body still trying to hurry even though he was standing still, and peered back around the doorway into the den.

It was empty.

A lamp had been turned on next to the recliner that faced the television. The light revealed the TV section from the newspaper resting on the arm of the chair. The chair was empty, but he could see the depressions in the cushions where someone had sat for many hours. It looked like an invisible man sitting there staring at him.

Tripwire looked back at the patio doors. He had closed them behind him and they were still closed. The light had turned them black; he couldn't see into the back yard any more. But the room was reflected now, so Tripwire could see both sides of the sofa and the two chairs. There was no one crouching anywhere in the room.

Some kind of remote control, someone playing games with

him? Tripwire walked cautiously back into the room. That was dangerous, with the possibility of someone right outside those patio doors, but it would also be dangerous to go deeper into the house without finding out what he was leaving behind.

No one rushed in as he reached the lamp and checked it for, perhaps, long wires leading elsewhere. What he found, near where it was plugged into the wall, was a small plastic box with a dial. A timer. Obviously, it was set to turn on the lamp just after sundown and that was also the time Tripwire had waited for to break in.

With the light on the room seemed inhabited. It looked like someone had just gone to the kitchen or bathroom during a commercial. Tripwire would have liked to turn it off, but someone might notice that. He left the room. The rest of the house downstairs consisted of a small formal living room, dining room, and a kitchen. On the living room wall was a family portrait, John, Elizabeth, and Bryan dressed up and smiling stiffly. On an end table was a grouping of more natural pictures: Elizabeth at a picnic table setting out paper plates, smiling to herself. John sawing a board while twelve-year-old Bryan held one end, trying to steady it. Bryan holding a football, arm cocked, just turning toward the camera as the picture was snapped. Bryan in a cap and gown, looking cross-eyed at the tassel. His face changed slightly from photo to photo, even the ones from about the same age. Tripwire's eyes returned to the family portrait in which everyone was smiling but looked strained, caught out of their natural habitat and spotlighted together. Like the living room he stood in they looked too formal to be comfortable. It was obvious that the life of the house was in the den but the family was trapped here, the ghosts who haunted this house. Tripwire's hand rested momentarily on the sofa but then drew back as if the stiff brocade had bitten him. He backed slowly out of the room. When he reached the doorway he ducked his head and hurried away from the staring family pictures.

Lights had come on upstairs too. It was almost worse ascending into that light than it had been having it come on in the room behind his back. He almost called out as he went up the stairs, but didn't. There was that sense again of palpable presences, that he was invading people's ongoing lives. But there was dust on the banister and a slightly musty smell to the air. The house smelled the way it would when the family came home from a summer vacation. Disused but not abandoned.

He stood in the doorway of the master bedroom. What he noticed about the room was its haphazardness. It was neat but hadn't been cleaned for inspection. There we e dress slacks laid out on a valet with shoes underneath. The closet door was open and there was a gap between two dresses as if Elizabeth had gone through her clothes looking for something to wear. There was no keychain or wallet on the dresser, but there was a jewelry box. The toothbrush rack in the bathroom was filled. A shower cap hung on a hook just inside the shower stall. No one had done any packing.

That made him realize the futility of his search. The Truetts probably hadn't even come back here after they knew they were leaving. They couldn't have left a message or clue if they'd wanted.

He glanced into Bryan's room—Bryan who certainly couldn't have left any clues. The dust was more noticeable in here, but there were still posters on the wall and the twin bed made up neatly, as if Bryan were expected home. But there was no one to meet him. Tripwire had a momentary urge to lie on that bed and sink down into unconsciousness until someone came home to find him. Anyone.

He went downstairs and had that same feeling in the den. The furniture looked comfortable from years of use. It would be so easy to turn on the television, lie on the sofa, and sink into a semblance of normality until someone came to get him. He turned off the lamp and the room looked less inviting, hostile even. Tripwire walked stiffly to the patio door and out, closing the door behind him.

He only got as far as the patio before he sank down into the same wrought iron chair at the far edge. There was no place for him to go from here. He knew his immobility made him vulnerable, but he welcomed the danger as something to live for. The darkness seemed a familiar ally close at hand.

The mindset of the long-time prisoner was clamping down on his thoughts. He couldn't move. Morning would find him sitting here, frozen to the spot by a purposelessness as effective as arctic cold. If he had been thinking he would have recognized that feeling. It was the same inertia that had settled over him during his second week as a prisoner of war. A feeling like coming home. He had finally achieved what he had been seeking ever since coming to Vietnam. What had appealed to him most about being a Lurp was that he *was* alone and far from other American soldiers. Because it seemed to him that all Americans in Vietnam were marked for death. They advertised for death. They were so out of place in the jungles they glowed. When he got away from them he felt safer—quieter, harder to find, and responsible only for his own mistakes. Sometimes when he had been out on his own long enough he could even pretend he no longer was an American. He could almost become a native. It was that subconscious desire that had made him so docile after his capture. He had stopped trying to escape. He longed to be one of his captors, brown and silent and emotionless.

The Cong had soon lost interest in him. He was so harmless they took no notice of him, sometimes forgetting to feed him for days at a time. His attempts to gain their attention were pitiful. He was like a dog the children of the family have outgrown. If someone kicked at him he took it as a sign of affection.

Until one day they left him almost alone in their compound. The war was over, though he didn't know it. The lone Vietnamese ostensibly guarding him was in fact ignoring him. Tripwire had had the freedom of the compound for months. The guard sat at a table almost dozing, his back to the American. There was a knife stuck in his belt in the back. Tripwire had stared at the knife for a long time, trying to remember. He had begun to think of his captors as a higher, bloodless order of beings. Only weaklings like Tripwire could bleed. Finally he walked slowly up to the table, silent as a ghost himself, took the knife from the belt and curiusly, experimentally, drew it across the guard's throat. When the Vietnamese bled Tripwire was filled with contempt, and then with rage. He stabbed the guard in the heart. It was as if at the sight of the blood Tripwire was reoccupied by his spirit, absent so long. But in all those docile months that preceded his escape he hadn't been faking. They would have known.

What he had lost now was the sense of mission he had found that day. Finding the Truetts had been his mission, and he had failed.

Sitting on the patio, he lit a cigarette and saw its glow reflected in the patio doors. Funny cigarettes: long and brown, almost cigars, but much too thin, and they seemed to burn forever. He had found himself bemused by the variety of cigarette brands American held now. He probably just hadn't noticed before; he hadn't started smoking until Vietnam.

The patio had been left completely furnished. The area was

very cluttered, as he could dimly see in the darkness. There were three other black wrought iron chairs, mates to the one in which he sat. At his elbow was a base for what should have been a glass-topped table, but the glass was missing. What accounted for most of the clutter were the plant accessories. Pots of various sizes were everywhere, some sitting on the concrete, some with stands of their own, some hanging. A few still held plants, some dead and burned now to dry twine. Most were empty. One hanging stand, empty of its pot, hung directly behind his head. That was probably what kept him from drifting off. He could feel it moving, almost bumping the back of his head. Its threat sent a steady message along his nerves.

There were also empty glass jars lying around. They had been used for a few beginning plants, seedlings. Dirt still clung to the insides of most of them. A few were full.

He watched his glowing cigarette tip. That was all he could see reflected in the glass doors; he was invisible behind it, the perfect magician's assistant. He saw the tip begin to fade, then suddenly go nova as he dragged on the cigarette.

Darkness had clamped down on the whole neighborhood. It was so quiet Tripwire heard the slight buzz all the way across the yard. He turned his head quickly and saw nothing. But the sound had brought his senses to such alertness that he flinched as from a sharp pain when he heard the buzz again and this time saw the tiny light accompanying it.

A firefly. Tripwire relaxed back into his chair. His senses remained enough on edge that he could almost follow the insect through the darkness, and he saw the tiny natural light when it came on again, closer to the patio. He could hear the crackle that accompanied the light. An almost-unheard buzz and an instant's flash: the thunder and lighting of a dust-mote world. Tripwire continued to watch as he smoked.

At first he could trace the insect's trail only by connecting the lighted points. But then he began to see the spot of deeper darkness even when it was not lit, as the firefly circled closer to the patio. It suddenly turned on its light close to his head. Tripwire saw two points of light reflected in the glass doors.

He laughed softly. In the dark the insect's flare and the glow of his cigarette were indistinguishable. The firefly must have thought he had found another of his kind, this one with an intriguing aroma. Tripwire inhaled, making the cigarette flame more brightly, and was gratified to see the firefly respond, only a few feet away. He began to wave the cigarette in tight circles and arc-filled patterns, drawing the firefly in. Tripwire chuckled again, wondering if he was performing an erotic firefly dance.

*F*red Tyler, FBI agent, pulled into the alley and cut his engine. Fred the fed. It was too good to resist; even others in the Bureau called him Fred the fed. His brother Benjamin had been the first. Benjie was dead now, victim of a hit-and-run driver, but the tag he had hung on Fred remained clamped to him as if it had been sewn into his underwear. It was such a habit that Fred even used it himself sometimes, especially when he was on ridiculous duty, as now. He thought, Fred the fed coasts quietly into the alley, eagerly anticipating the capture of a mysterious fugitive.

The alley was paved and the car was dark and quiet. Fred brought it to a stop behind the house and sat there for a moment letting his eyes adjust to the darkness. He had only himself to blame for being here. Fred was always near the phone when the alarm went off at the Truett house. And going over there wasn't a job anyone fought him for. Most likely what had happened was that a door jamb had warped slightly, moving just far enough from the door to set off the sensitive alarm. Or perhaps a cat or a squirrel had crossed the roof too heavily. This was the third time already the alarm had gone off and the first two times had been just because the system was too sensitive.

This time, though, Fred had reason to be wary, because it was very likely the soldier was in Baltimore by now and no one had spotted him yet. They still didn't know whether he was the son he claimed to be, but Fred wanted him. Son or not, he might well have come to the Truetts' house. The silent alarm wouldn't have scared him off. He could still be there.

Fred had waited long enough. He picked up his revolver from the seat beside him and eased out of the car. He was beginning to get heavy but he sill carried it well. The extra flesh hadn't made him clumsy. Looking down, he remembered he was wearing a white shirt, and grimaced. J. Edgar Hoover had insisted his agents dress like gentlemen, and the tradition lingered. White shirts might be good for impressing witnesses Fred questioned, but they were lousy for nightwork. He pulled his jacket closed and buttoned it, then moved up beside the garage to the back gate. He stood there listening for a moment and heard a faint sound he couldn't identify. It wasn't nearby. He opened the gate and slipped through.

There were lights on upstairs in the house. They illuminated the back yard enough for Fred to see it was empty. He hurried toward the corner of the house, around which were the patio and back doors. He glanced at the ground to be sure it was clear of obstacles, kept the gun out away from his body, and watched the house as he moved quickly toward it. The slight light from the house was hurting his night vision, but he could see well enough. Fred reached the corner of the house, an experienced man moving quietly.

He looked around the corner and instantly pulled his head back, then stood silently as he examined the mental snapshot he had just taken. The patio doors had been closed and the patio full of dark shapes. It was even darker there, under the roof. There could have been several burglars huddled on the concrete. But Fred knew the shapes had been flower pots and chairs. There had been nothing to break the darkness—

Except the pinprick glow of a cigarette.

Yes. Fred saw it clearly in his memory. One of the dark shapes had been background for a tiny flare, and Fred could smell the cigarette from here. He was preparing himself before he had even reached the conclusion that someone was on the patio. He had taken two more long, quiet breaths. He exhaled now, gripped his pistol tightly, and stepped around the corner.

Apparently he went unnoticed. If the man on the patio could see no more clearly than Fred himself, then Fred had the advantage. The glow of the cigarette gave away the other man's position perfectly. His head must be directly behind it, the body in the chair . . . Fred got two steps closer and leveled his pistol. He could almost reach out and touch the light.

"Don't move," he said. "I have a gun."

What Fred had covered was the firefly. Tripwire had captured it in one of the glass jars and left it on the plant stand that had hung just behind his head. Now he was ten feet away, to Fred's left, crouched at the edge of the patio. The flower pot he hurled struck Fred's gun hand and shattered. Fred shouted and dropped the gun. The second pot, which Tripwire threw with his left hand, wasn't as successfully aimed. It glanced off Fred's knee. Before it hit, Tripwire was covering the distance that separated him from the intruder. Fred was just realizing where his opponent was really coming from, and reached for him. Tripwire stopped short and kicked Fred forcefully behind the knee. As the agent began to fall backward Tripwire aimed a blow, his fists locked together as if he were holding a baseball bat, at the back of the flailing man's neck.

He missed a little, getting more of the shoulder than the neck. Fred bent forward at the waist as he was falling backward. In fact the blow almost restored his balance. He was going backward on his heels, not quite going down, straining to remain upright.

Both men were still working in the dark. Tripwire saw that his opponent wasn't going down for good, and rushed toward him. Fred, grabbing for anything within reach to stop his fall, found one of the wrought iron chairs in his grasp. He gripped it for balance and pulled it in front of him, directly in Tripwire's path.

Tripwire hit the front edge of the chair with his left shin. The pain was sharp as a cut, but he still managed to get his right foot high enough to climb onto the obstacle, then use it as a springboard to launch himself at the taller, heavier man in front of him. Fred reached for him, Tripwire got one hand within reach of Fred's throat, and they went down together.

Tripwire landed full on his opponent as they hit the concrete patio. But Fred had managed to get his fist into Tripwire's stomach, and the impact drove it deeper. They were both stunned for a moment. Tripwire rolled off his attacker, desperately trying to draw a breath. He had that sick, dry feeling deep in his throat, as though his lungs had quit for good. He crawled away, still gasping.

Fred remembered that his gun lay somewhere on the patio. He pulled himself up to a sitting position and peered into the darkness, looking for movement. He saw Tripwire directly ahead of him, still on his knees ten feet away. He had obviously remembered the gun too. As Fred scrambled up into a crouch he heard the man he had never seen clearly say, "Ah."

No time. Still crouched, Fred took two running steps and dived toward his man.

That's what Tripwire had been waiting for. He turned and pulled the chair beside him into position. Fred had launched himself by that time. He had no chance to see the trap or avoid it. His forehead smashed into the metal chair. He didn't move at all after he hit the concrete. Tripwire grunted softly and went back to his search for the gun.

*T*here were no degress to Fred's return to consciousness. Even before his eyes opened he was fighting again. He reached out, straining—But when he did open his eyes he saw he was alone on the patio. He groaned and tenderly touched the lump on his forehead. It was sticky. Fred looked around confusedly. He didn't see his gun. He hoped like hell the soldier hadn't taken it. Always embarrassing to lose your gun.

The patio doors opened and Fred looked up. Danny stepped down out of the house. He had Fred's gun in his hand.

"Yeah, he's gone," Danny said. He was smiling. "This just isn't your night," he said to Fred.

CHAPTER TWENTY-TWO

Night

*B*ill Jerek had gotten in the habit of having no habits. He no longer let it become a matter of routine for anyone to follow him. He kept odd hours, left the house at different times, returned home by no usual schedule or route. Some nights he didn't go home from the police station at all. Anyone can be killed if someone wants it badly enough and is patient, but Jerek wasn't going to make it easy for them to keep track of him.

There were faint sounds out in the squadroom as men closed desk drawers and started for home. The noises diminished. Jerek stood at his office window looking beyond the roofs of the nearby buildings. It was that time of day when the sun is already below the horizon and the dusk balanced so delicately that it can turn to darkness in an instant. As Jerek watched, that instant came and passed. His view darkened. The streetlights didn't snap on; they hadn't yet been retimed for the shorter days of fall. For a few minutes the city would be as dark as it ever got. The buildings were only vague hulks now. Memory and imagination filled in the details.

The way to own a city is to know it better than anyone else. Jerek had been born in Baltimore and had never left. He felt proprietary about it, not like a mayor or an industrial baron, but like a janitor or a night watchman, someone who knew the city in unguarded moments, without a facade. Not that Baltimore ever put on much of a facade. Jerek knew it as a muscular, working-class town. All the glamor was in Washington, a city where everyone came from somewhere else.

What had drawn him to being a cop was that sense of knowing the city. Not the power or authority. He hadn't liked wearing a uniform, it made him feel conspicuous and clumsy. And he had no ambition to be chief of police. That was a political job. All he wanted was that sense of ownership that came from being part of the life of the city on every level.

He developed a personal grudge against Marco Galvan because Galvan was an outsider who thought *he* owned the town. His manipulations subtly changed the character of the whole city. Jerek could feel his city being turned out the way one of his men had been, into something with a tacky glamor, into the kind of city that didn't work so hard for a living and wasn't content with a couple of beers after work. What was most galling was that it was being done by Galvan, who didn't even know the city he was trying to reshape in his own image. He had no stake here, no claim—he could as easily have been doing the same thing in Miami or Denver. It sometimes seemed that the worst crime Galvan had committed was being from out of town.

Jerek turned away from the window and began gathering up reports to take home with him. It had been a busy couple of days. As Danny had hoped, the murder of Detective Dennison had set off an explosion in the police station. Dennison's heavily attended funeral had been like a very subdued pep rally directed against Galvan. There was grief, there was sadness for the widow and children, but there was also a strong undercurrent of rage. Dennison had been popular. There was at least enough evidence to convince his colleagues that his killing had been cold-blooded. Jerek had heard the long space between the shots; it hadn't been a shootout; and the medical examiner reported that Dennison might have been unconscious when he was killed. There was also a component of personal fear in the police response. What had happened to Dennison could have happened to any of them, and still could as long as his murderer was loose.

In the days following the funeral the city swarmed with cops. There weren't more of them than before, but they all worked longer hours. Double shifts were unremarkable. The search covered the city and expanded. Hundreds of people were questioned. More than a few civil rights were violated. All to no avail. All the cops had to go on was Marco Galvan, and they still couldn't find him. Not only couldn't they turn him up, they couldn't find anyone who knew where he was. And some of the evidence they uncovered was bad for their own case against Galvan. He had an alibi for the original murder, the one Elizabeth Truett had witnessed. A restaurant owner and a dozen waiters and patrons said Galvan had been eating at the restaurant across town at the time of that killing. Jerek didn't believe them for a second, but objectively they blew a big hole in his case. None of the witnesses had a police record, and he could only find previous connections to Galvan for three or four of them.

The attempt to reconstruct the last days of Paul Seligson turned up an old lady whose rowhouse had been used for a meeting between Seligson and Galvan. At first the old lady had gone into a gun moll act from the thirties, saying nobody could make her squeal. The detectives questioning her found it hard to continue when her responses drew them into the act and they started sounding like an old gangster movie even to themselves. They remained amused even when they looked up her record and found she came by the pose honestly. No one had to use a rubber hose on her, though. They just mentioned her son in prison, and that he didn't have much hope for parole when his mother was such a bad citizen. She talked after that, but she wasn't much help. She didn't know anything about Galvan.

Her one piece of new information was that Galvan had been accompanied by a young blonde man. Elizabeth Truett had observed the same thing the night of the original killing, but she hadn't been able to pick the young man out of the file photos and neither could the old lady. Her description was no use either. She'd been too vain to wear her glasses while Galvan was in her home. The sketch the artist drew from her description could have fit any young blonde man in the city.

It was enough, though, to give Jerek the idea he'd seen him too, at the scene of Dennison's murder. That was the link to Galvan. But Jerek's view of Dennison's killer had been too fleeting. He didn't know if he'd recognize him if he saw him again. It just added one more blank piece, gave his men a few more unanswered questions to ask when they interviewed useless witnesses.

The crime rate in the city dropped. Several career criminals left town, and others stayed home at night. It wasn't safe out there. The cops were everywhere and they didn't ignore other crimes during the hunt, because there was no telling what petty

thief or burglar might have a connection to Galvan. And God
help anyone who got arrested if the cops thought there was the
slimmest chance he knew something about Dennison's killer.
The poor bastard's bail bondsman wouldn't hear from him for
days.

Jerek knew all this activity could backfire on him. Galvan's
alibi was bad news, and so was the fact that even with all these
hours of police overtime piling up they hadn't found any new
evidence against Galvan for either of the murders. Jerek had
already gotten some strong hints from higher up that they
should question Elizabeth Truett more extensively. They
wanted her brought back to town. And they didn't like Jerek's
being the only one who knew how to find her. If the search
didn't uncover something new soon, the hints would turn to
orders.

Jerek walked out of his office with a file folder under his arm
and was struck by the emptiness of the squad room, as if all his
men had left hours before. All the detectives from his shift
were gone and only a couple of men from the next shift had
trickled in. They muttered greetings but didn't look at him.
Jerek's men had either hurried home or already ducked into the
nearest bar. No one stuck around to invite him along.
Dennison's death and the determination to find his killer hadn't
drawn Jerek and his detectives together again. They still
resented his suspicion. And in a way, he knew, they blamed
him for Dennison's death. It was Jerek's pet project that had
gotten Dennison killed.

He turned out the light in his office, leaving it dark, and
walked down the hall under the harsh white lights. No one was
around. He could have been a visitor from out of town. When a
desk sergeant barely glanced at him and said, " 'Night,
Captain,'' Jerek acknowledged it gratefully. He took the stairs
down to the underground garage. The air was cooler there, and
it was quiet. It was that time between shifts when most of the
cars have been checked in but not yet checked back out. Most
of the engines were still generating heat—he felt it on his face
as he passed them—but his own wasn't. It was his personal car,
not a city one; it had been sitting here all day. He touched the
cool metal of the hood as he passed.

As he opened the door he heard footsteps from somewhere
else in the garage. He waited to see if anyone was coming after
him, but no one appeared. The sound faded. Jerek slid behind
the wheel, having to push papers aside as he did so. The front

seat was a mess. When he settled in he saw that a slip of
notepaper had slipped down behind the seat and he rescued it.
It was a note from Marge, a week old. He sat there for a
moment reading it, a reminder to pick up something on the way
home. He smiled sadly. No need for it now, Marge was gone.

When he looked up he noticed the silence again. Still no one
around. Jerek's eyes swept slowly across the ranks of parked
cars. Suddenly he turned and looked behind his seat into the
back of the car. No one there either. He smiled at himself, glad
no one was there to see him so jumpy, and finally started the car
and drove off.

He arrived home to a quiet house. Maybe it was being alone
that made him think later in the night about Paul Seligson
again, and his lonely little apartment. "Why don't you just kill
me yourself?" Paul had said when Jerek had forced the
assignment on him, and it would have been easier for Paul if he
had. The war was open now, with dead scattered in the field.
Maybe it was Jerek himself who had unwillingly escalated the
violence with the beating he'd given Bigelow. But that had just
been humiliation. Galvan dealt in something more.

Look what he'd done to Paul, whom he probably only
suspected of trying to betray him. What then would he do to
Elizabeth Truett if he could? This might turn out to be a golden
opportunity for Galvan, in fact. He could send a terrifying
warning to anyone who might *ever* consider testifying against
him. Jerek remembered Elizabeth in his office, the calm way
she had said of course she would testify. She was not just the
pawn Jerek and Galvan had both made of her. If Galvan got her
it would be exactly as if the bastard dragged her out of her own
home and murdered her in the street. If Jerek let it happen his
city would become exactly that kind of place, a town where that could
happen to an innocent.

He still had a powerful urge to retaliate. Galvan's men must
have understood that. They no longer followed him openly.
Jerek didn't know what he would do if he caught one of them
alone again.

After Dennison's murder he was afraid to go home. Not for
himself, for his wife. Every time he opened his front door he
remembered opening the front door of Paul Seligson's apartment. When Marge rose from her chair to put her arms around
him it was like an embrace from a ghost. He already pictured
her dead. Finally he had asked her to go stay with her sister for
a week or two. She could be traced easily if anyone wanted her

badly enough, but he didn't think Galvan would. She was safer than at home.

That was only one his worries. They made for a lot of sleepless nights, and Jerek had one tonight. All the lights were off in the house. He sat smoking and staring out his back door into the yard. The night was quiet. He was reminded of the night he had spent with the Truetts in the motel, staring out the window just like this.

And abruptly it came to him. What had almost come to him when he'd gotten off a different exit of the expressway on his way home tonight, avoiding his usual one. What had been nagging at him ever since that first night. He finally realized the mistake he'd made that night.

It was a mistake that couldn't be corrected now. If he was lucky he'd find Galvan in time and nothing would come of the mistake he'd made.

But he didn't feel lucky.

*F*red Tyler's forehead throbbed in alternating bands of pain and numbness, like the concentric circles of a target. He groaned again and rose to his hands and knees, but the effort made him dizzy and he stopped there, staring down at the concrete patio rather than up at Danny.

"I was hoping you'd at least hold him up long enough for me to get here," Danny said, still with that undertone of enjoyment in his voice. "I wanted to talk to him."

As a matter of fact, Danny was at least as curious about the soldier's identity as Jerek was. If he really was the son he would be easy enough to deal with. If not then he was some ploy of Galvan's, and that raised troubling questions. Why hadn't Galvan told Danny about him? Was Galvan perhaps planning to replace him with the soldier? But Danny had a great capacity for dismissing troubling thoughts while he was enjoying himself. He held Fred's gun easily and stepped away from the patio doors, toward the man on the ground.

Fred was checking his pockets. He thought his wallet was missing but then he put his hand down on it in the dark. He checked to see that his FBI identification was still there and returned it to his pocket. He managed to get to his feet but stood there hunched over, hands on his knees. As Danny came forward the pistol poked into Fred's line of vision.

"Give me that," Fred said harshly, straightening up.

Danny smiled again. "Why? It doesn't seem to do you much good."

Fred glared at Danny, hating him. Danny could see that clearly. He kept smiling. Fred stepped forward and put out his hand. Danny looked at it like a joke he was supposed to get and didn't.

"Don't be cute," Fred said, and took the gun. He put his safety on and stowed it in the holster at the back of his belt.

"Wasn't much use to you with him, was it?" Danny said again.

It was his familiarity Fred hated. Fred hadn't counted on opening himself up to this kind of talk from a petty, stupid thug like Danny. Other than that, Fred knew what he himself was and could live with it. He didn't have an image to live up to. Since his younger brother's death Fred was nobody's hero.

It was Benjie's death two years ago that had started it. Benjie dead literally in the gutter, victim of a bad driver. Somewhere there was a car with a battered grill, maybe a broken headlight, but they had never found it. That was hard enough to bear, and so was his mother's grief. But what had really driven Fred crazy over the unfairness of it was that his mother who had worked like a dog all her life didn't have enough money saved to pay for a funeral. Neither did Fred. Nor did he have extra money to help support her the way Benjie had done.

When the money came Fred knew who it was from but he took it anyway. He told himself he'd just never do anything in return for it, so there wouldn't be a problem. And Marco Galvan had left him strictly alone for a long time. When he finally did come looking for Fred it was to offer him more money than he'd ever expected to see in one lump sum, enough money to keep his mother comfortable for the rest of her life. In exchange for what? Killing another criminal. Hardly anything wrong with that. Galvan had made it sound like a straight business proposition. No one said if you don't your bosses might learn where you got the money to pay for your brother's funeral. But they had both known what they were talking about. Fred had thought he could live with it. He had stood at the cell door staring in at the witness, who had grinned back at him lazily, a man who had made his deal and could afford to look knowing. It had been gratifying to see his face fall and his eyes turn pleading when Fred had pulled out his gun, and then there hadn't been time to think because Fred had to shoot him before the man cried out. The gun had a silencer but Fred could hear, almost feel, the bullets hitting the witness's chest. He had stood there transfixed as the man flopped to the floor. He had almost stood there too long, staring, until he made himself drop the gun and hurry unseen to a different part of the station house, so that a few minutes later he was just one of the dozens of cops asking what had happened.

And sure enough he had been able to live with it. He almost never thought about it afterwards. It was easier without Benjie's hero worship to live up to. And again Galvan had left Fred alone for a long time, until this extremity. And now it wasn't another criminal Fred was supposed to help find and point out to Galvan's killer, it was an innocent woman. But the other difference was that there'd been no offer of money this time. The blackmail was explicit.

And the worst part, for Fred, wasn't thinking about the woman. It was that this punk could stand here in front of him and smile and make snide remarks like Fred was just one of the gang.

"You seen Jerek lately?" Danny asked conversationally. Fred could see his face in the light now spilling from inside the house. "Looking over his shoulder a little more than he used to? Not getting enough sleep because he's wondering if somebody's right outside his window? But I guess he doesn't confide things like that to you any more, does he?"

Fred didn't respond, but his expression was pleasure enough for Danny. "You said on the phone you might have something else for the boss," he went on. He almost said "our boss," but that would have been pushing it. Fred knew what he meant, anyway.

"I said I might have soon," Fred said. "If Jerek did what I think he did that first night when he took them out of town." Fred didn't identify "them" as Elizabeth and John Truett. He didn't want to give them names.

"What do you think he did?" Danny asked.

Fred almost didn't answer, but he wanted the information to get back to Galvan, that Fred the fed was on the job, doing what he'd been paid to do. He knew Danny was as close to Galvan as he'd get while all this was going on. Galvan wouldn't come out of hiding to talk to Fred.

"Everybody knows Jerek left town that night," Fred said tonelessly. "But nobody knows which way he went. But I know him. Bill Jerek works all the time, and he's lived his whole life in Baltimore. The only times he ever leaves town are to go hunting at a little cabin he's got up north. He wasn't stupid enough to go to the cabin that night, I've already checked on that, but what I'm counting on is that that's the direction he went, just out of habit. And he must've stopped somewhere, I know he didn't just keep driving all night."

"So what?"

It was Fred's turn to smile, just barely, just enough to tell Danny what a moron he was. "So I've been checking motels in that direction, seeing if he checked into any of them that night. And if he made any phone calls."

Danny mulled that over. You can almost see the rusty gears turning, Fred thought. Finally Danny said, "Sounds okay. Why's it taking so long?"

Fred looked at him. "You know how many motels there are in the world? And I sure as hell can't assign anyone else to help look. I'm just assuming it's narrowed down to this one highway, or it would be flat impossible."

Danny was nodding. "That's it? That's what you want me to tell Mr. Galvan?" Maybe a slight emphasis on the "Mister," mockingly.

Fred kept his voice flat. "No, that's not all. I've got one piece of advice you can give him. Tell him it might be best for him just to keep lying low and give up trying to find her. Maybe it's better if nothing happens to her."

"How's that?"

"Because Jerek's having problems from higher up. He's using up a lot of manpower and getting nothing for it. The only new evidence he's got is bad for his case. They're not going to let it drag on much longer. Some people in the department think Galvan was never involved in the first place, that Jerek's just working on a private grudge of his own. The longer nothing happens here and nothing happens to her, the more convinced they're going to be. If Galvan can wait, they might drop the case, or they might bring the witness right back here."

"I don't know," Danny said. "Mr. Galvan's not a very patient man, you know. And I don't think he'd put much faith in cops' good sense."

"Suit yourself," Fred said, some of the anger edging into his voice. "I don't give a shit."

"Just keep doing your job," Danny said jovially. Fred glared at him again.

They started walking out of the cover of the patio roof. "By the way," Danny said. "What'd he look like? The soldier boy?"

"Looked like a blur to me," Fred said, touching his forehead.

"You think he's really the son?"

Fred chuckled, making Danny wonder if he was in on the plan, which was just what Fred wanted him to wonder. It helped restore his feeling of superiority as he walked back to his car and drove away.

After Danny left as well, and the sound of his motor was fading in the distance, a shadow on the roof emerged from the other shadows there. The patio roof of the Truetts' house was a rather flimsy affair that had been added years after the house was built. At its edge it went under the original roof of the house, creating a narrow hiding space. Because the patio roof didn't quite reach the outside wall of the house, the spot was a natural listening post as well. Tripwire came out of that narrow manmade tunnel and dropped to the grass of the back yard. He couldn't have followed either Danny or Fred if he'd wanted, he didn't have a car. But his thoughts had already turned in another direction. Behind him the Truett home looked like just another sleeping house in the sleeping neighborhood, with the family comfortable and secure inside.

CHAPTER TWENTY-THREE

Jerek at home

*T*he next day Bill Jerek came home early (for him), about six o'clock. He'd been thinking about his wife, stuck at her sister's house and worrying about him. He thought he might go home and call her. He was wasting his time at the station anyway. Nothing seemed about to break in the Galvan investigation. Jerek was just sitting at his desk thinking, and not doing that very well. He seemed to be getting more annoying phone calls than usual. Finally he had decided to call it a day.

It took him half an hour or so to drive home. He lived in a house built in the late forties that had undergone several permutations in size in the almost twenty-five years he'd lived there. When he and Marge moved into it with two toddlers in '52 it seemed plenty big enough, after the apartment and the tiny rented house where they'd started their marriage. But the two toddlers had turned into three children and the house shrunk. The three bedrooms and living/dining room couldn't contain them all. That's when they had turned the garage into a den. At least that's what Jerek had thought it would be, but it had instead become what Marge called the family room. The kids took it over. Their schoolbooks were always lying on the pool table, and the TV or stereo or—usually—both were too loud for Jerek. But that left the living room to him so it was okay. Now with the kids gone the house had expanded again, all on its own. Jerek and Marge hardly ever went into the family room. The extra two bedrooms had been imperfectly altered. The middle one was supposedly a sewing room but it still had a bed in it and Marge's sewing machine remained covered for months at a time. The room had an abandoned air. The back bedroom was in theory Jerek's study—it had a desk in it—but Marge used it as much as he did.

Jerek came in the front door, glanced into the living room to see that he was, in fact, alone, and went into the master bedroom at the front of the house. He put his holstered pistol high on the second shelf of the closet, a habit left over from having kids in the house, pulled his shirttail out, and walked back to the living room, yawning and scratching in the really satisfying way you can only do at home alone.

And found a bearded kid in Army fatigues standing in the middle of his living room.

For just a moment Jerek thought one of his sons had come home. That's what the kid looked like, standing there almost at ease, as if he had once belonged here but no longer quite did. Then that image fell away and Jerek put the face together with the grainy photograph he'd seen of the young man who claimed to be Bryan Truett. Jerek stopped dead.

"I'm Bryan Truett," the kid said.

Maybe so, Jerek thought. Or maybe Galvan's getting desperate. "That so?" Jerek said. "Well, my name's Jerek." And took another step toward the kid. Jerek thought of his own gun on the top shelf of the closet. If he went for it now the kid would have plenty of time to get away. Where had he been hiding anyway? Jerek's eyes stayed steady on the kid, but in his mind he was counting the exits from the room. Back away, or close on him?

"I'm glad you turned up," Jerek said, moving still closer. Behind the kid the curtains covering the patio doors were open and it was still broad daylight outside. The kid was outlined in the sunlight pouring into the room so Jerek didn't have a very good look at him. He moved to the side and the kid turned too. Jerek got a better look at his face. He didn't look like such a kid there. His eyes had that tired but watchful look combat soldiers get. He looked authentic. Whether he looked like Bryan Truett Jerek couldn't say.

"You certainly took the hard way getting here," he said.

"Seems to me you were the one making it hard on me. You and the rest of the government."

"All you had to do was to wait at the Army post—"

"For how long?" Tripwire said. "Without knowing anything about what was going on?"

Except for turning to keep facing Jerek, Tripwire hadn't moved. He stood in the middle of the living room, feet slightly spread, his thumbs hooked in his belt. Jerek had circled more but come no closer. He wasn't sure of his next move. He was within grabbing distance but Jerek didn't think that would be a good idea. Jerek was a few years past his prime and the kid was either a soldier who'd just made it out of Vietnam alive or a professional killer. Without a gun Jerek wasn't sure he could hold him.

Tripwire stared at him as if he knew just what Jerek was thinking. But that was impossible, Jerek's thoughts were going in too many directions. "Where is she?" the kid asked, his eyes hard, as if he had dropped any pretense.

Jerek spun out an evasive answer. He had forced himself to dismiss the idea that this was Elizabeth Truett's son. He didn't want to believe it; Bryan Truett was no use to him. But if he was Galvan's man he might still be in touch with his boss, in case he learned anything useful. He had to know where Galvan was.

Jerek thought again of what Galvan might have to gain by killing Jerek. The investigation would be thrown into chaos for a while because Jerek was its coordinator, the only one who knew all the leads. It would sever the department's only link to Elizabeth Truett. They might be reduced to issuing some general plea for her to come home. As everyone scrambled to find her it would be Galvan's spy who fell into the information first. Jerek pictured the events that would follow his death in a detached way, like a non-participant—or like Marco Galvan. In these last desperate days Jerek had forgotten that Galvan might be desperate himself.

"I could help protect them," the soldier was saying.

Jerek was moving back now. The kid's eyes flickered down to Jerek's feet and then beyond him toward the hall doorway. But he still didn't move. He looked poised standing there in the middle of the carpet with the patio doors close behind him. If Jerek broke and ran for the closet now he could probably beat the kid to the gun but he couldn't get to the gun in time to stop the kid if he chose instead to go out the door. Jerek was torn between his desires for escape and capture.

The kid's eyes lighted on his face and Jerek thought the kid saw his dilemma.

"But their security isn't what it could be, is it?" the soldier said. "Seems like someone's been talking too much."

Jerek's eyes narrowed. The kid smiled at him ever so faintly.

"Maybe you could tell me who it is," Jerek said, testing.

The soldier stepped toward him. He looked as if he might be considering it. Jerek stepped back. His leg bumped an end table.

The kid was still coming toward him. "Maybe an exchange?" he said. "The loudmouth's name for her location? I can give it to you."

Jerek put his hand to his mouth and looked down as if he were considering the offer. What he was in fact considering was the heavy glass ash tray on the end table next to him.

"I'm her *son*," the soldier said with sudden intensity.

Jerek nodded. He looked directly into the kid's eyes. The kid stared back. His hands were out away from his sides, open.

"All right," Jerek said suddenly. "The spy's the one I want. If you can really give him to me . . . Elizabeth Truett's not in Baltimore anymore," Jerek said. "I'll write it out for you." He bent, his back to the soldier, and opened a drawer of the end table. There were pens in the front of the drawer and paper farther back. As he fumbled through the drawer Jerek's other hand fell on the heavy ash tray. His fingers curled under the sharp edge.

He never got it off the table. Suddenly hands gripped his ankles and then his feet were no longer under him. He flailed forward, knocking over the lamp, losing his grip on the ash tray. His face hit the table top.

He felt the kid lean over him and say something sharply into his ear. Jerek almost made it up off his knees, but by then the soldier had a powerful grip on his neck and the back of his head, and slammed his forehead down on the table top again.

Jerrek fell sideways to the floor. The detachment with which he considered his own death consumed him like darkness. Vaguely he could hear noises but didn't even try to interpret them. He faded.

He came to abruptly, already moving. He rolled to his hands and knees and was lunging through the hall doorway before he had even fully risen. No one blocked his way. For a moment he allowed himself to think he'd be okay. He fell through his bedroom doorway and didn't even look around the room before he was at the closet, fingers scrambling along the shelf for his gun. Then he had it in his hand and the grip was reassuring.

The silence was not. He couldn't hear a thing, as if he'd gone deaf. He shot a glance the length of the hall to his study. It was dark down there, but none of the shadows moved. He returned instead to the living room. The light was better in there, the sunlight of late afternoon fell evenly across the whole room. "Damn," Jerek said aloud.

The room was empty. At the back of the room the sliding door stood open, the flimsy curtains billowing out into the back yard as if the speed of the soldier's passing had pulled them out of the room.

Jerek walked cautiously across the room. His hearing was returning but he heard only the faint, normal sounds of the neighborhood. He looked out the patio door, darting his head out and back in again until he was sure no one was standing there just outside. He stood in the open door. There was no hiding place close to him. He lowered the gun to his side. The back yard was fenced all around, the kid could have gone over it in any of three directions. Jerek heard a dog barking somewhere in the next block. The kid could have been that far by now. Jerek had been out for only a couple of minutes at most, but that was plenty of time for an escape.

He pulled the curtains back inside and closed and locked the patio door. His heart slowed a bit, and when his blood stopped racing he realized how groggy he still was. He stood still for a moment trying to reconstruct the last few minutes.

And abruptly he remembered what the soldier had said to him as Jerek had slumped on the verge of unconsciousness. His attacker had raised his voice as if to make it follow Jerek down into the darkness. What he had said was, "I already know where she is."

Adrenaline rushed through Jerek again, but coldly this time. His skin tingled the way it had just before he'd stepped into Paul Seligson's apartment for the last time. He ran out of the room and down the hallway to his study. Even that short run left him panting. Not true, the soldier couldn't know.

But he could, Jerek knew. It was possible someone could have figured it out by now. He remembered again the mistake he had made that very first night. But he didn't berate himself again. He was thinking instead of Karen Boone. She had to be warned. Even if it was a lie, she had to know.

On Jerek's desk beside the phone was an old-fashioned directory of his personal phone numbers, one of those flat metal boxes with a pointer that slid along the edge indicating the letters of the alphabet. Jerek slid the pointer to *B* and pressed the button so that the top of the box flipped up on its hinge, revealing a page of *B* names. Karen's name was at the bottom of the page. Before all this he'd only had her home phone number. Now her office number was scrawled under it in recent pencil.

He picked up the receiver on his old black desk phone and dialed the first digit. He was reaching for the second number, the first number of Karen's area code, when he suddenly jerked his finger back as if he'd been about to stick it in a snake's mouth. He slammed the receiver down and glared at it.

Maybe this had been the reason for the kid's parting words. To panic him into calling Karen too hastily, from a phone that could no longer be trusted. No telling where Galvan had contacts. Certainly the phone company didn't have such tight security Galvan couldn't have bribed someone.

Karen still had to be warned. Jerek pulled a message pad close, started to write on it, then instead tore off the top sheet and put it flat on the desk when he wrote, so as not to leave an impression on the sheets underneath. He had seen detective movies too.

He wrote both numbers and stuck the paper in his pocket, then closed the metal phone directory. He walked hastily out of the room. Now was when they were all most vulnerable. He had her phone number in his pocket. But Jerek was getting mad again. He almost hoped someone was waiting outside to try to jump him. His grip was tight around the gun in his pocket. God help any of Galvan's men who fell into his hands now— especially the soldier, who might know Galvan's hiding place.

The sound of his steps grew fainter and the front door slammed. Jerek's car started up and rolled down the driveway. Only after those sounds faded too did Tripwire emerge from the closet in the study. As he stepped out of the closet he felt that tiny chill he always felt the first moment when he emerged from hiding. That was his best thing, hiding. For the last year it had been his life. Maybe if he ever found the ideal hiding place he'd never come out again. The closet had certainly not been ideal, but he'd counted on Jerek in his dazed condition accepting the evidence of the open patio door.

At the desk he pressed the button on the phone directory and the top flipped open to reveal the *B*s. Tripwire had been in the house for some time before Jerek got home. He'd found the flat metal box beside the phone and had realized the name he wanted was probably inside. It was only a matter of making Jerek show it to him.

He had seen Jerek write down two numbers. Only three of the names in the Bs had two numbers listed, and only one of those looked as if the second number had been recently added, in pencil instead of the original pen. That was the only one of the three names with an out-of-town address, too. *Karen Boone*, it said, *Fed. Marshal's Ofc*, and under that: *Cleveland*.

He stared at the name for a long minute before writing it down along with the phone numbers. Her home number might be unlisted.

He closed the directory and stood at the desk a moment longer. The house was still, but it was in the middle of a neighborhood full of sounds. Children, dogs, cars passing. It was still light outside. He could imagine suppers cooking, older children setting tables, fathers settling into easy chairs with newspapers. He felt very alien standing there in his fatigues inside someone else's house.

The front door was locked with a deadbolt and if he went out the patio door he couldn't lock it behind him. If he went out either of those ways Jerek would know when he returned that Tripwire had left the house after he did, rather than before as he had led him to believe. So he went out the same window he'd come in this afternoon. When Jerek found it unlocked he'd think only that Tripwire had gotten *in* that way. Tripwire walked a block to his rented car and drove away slowly, well under the speed limit. He was watching the dying light in the sky, looking west toward Cleveland, making plans.

He would wait until he got to Ohio to buy a gun.

PART III

Reunion

CHAPTER TWENTY-FOUR

Karen

*T*he phone kept ringing. The sound turned shrill in Jerek's ear. He had been hearing it all night. Karen didn't answer. She had already left her office when he'd tried there, and apparently she never got home.

He kept driving to different pay phones and trying her number again, for hours. He circled the city. Night fell but warmth lingered. Wind came through his car in a hot rush. He would drive like hell from phone to phone, always in a hurry until he got to the next one and again heard Karen's phone ringing without interruption. His empty stomach growled but he didn't stop for food. Between calls he would think about his options. His concentration seemed to diminish them.

By eleven o'clock he was no longer driving aimlessly; he was headed for the airport. He took the soldier's claim more seriously in light of Karen's continued absence from home. There had been time by now for the soldier to fly to Cleveland and find her. Plenty of time. Jerek saw no choice but to follow. It was too late to warn Karen, but maybe he could find some clue to the Truetts' whereabouts. He hoped not. If there were a clue to be found, then the soldier already had it.

It was almost midnight when he tried her number one last time from a phone outside the airport. To his surprise, there was an answer. The voice was muffled and unintelligible.

"Karen?"

"Yes?" The voice came clearer.

"Are you all right?" Hearing her voice made the urge to run

to her grow suddeny stronger rather than diminish. "Is someone there?"

"Bill?" she said groggily. It was sleep that made her voice muffled. She had come home half an hour earlier and gone straight to bed. She hadn't been sleeping well lately, but tonight the drinks she'd had with dinner had dropped her deep into slumber the minute she'd hit the pillow. She looked at her glowing alarm clock and for a long moment the numbers meant nothing to her.

"You're all right," Jerek said, more certainly.

"I'm fine," she said. She realized suddenly that this was the first time he'd called her after entrusting the Truetts to her care. She sat up and threw the covers back. Her sleepiness lifted.

"Where the hell have you been?"

"I had dinner with someone from the office," Karen said, apologetically before she realized she had nothing to apologize for. "We talked for a while. Is that all right?"

"I had a visitor," Jerek said. In a rush, shearing off most of the details, he told her about the soldier. Still waking up, Karen pictured Jerek with the murky vividness of a dream. She could imagine him very clearly, standing at a phone, shoulders hunched, speaking low; but she couldn't picture his surroundings at all. He stood in a heavy fog in her mind.

His voice slowed as he talked. By the end of his narrative he sounded more normal. Obviously his mind was still racing, though. The concern for her she'd heard in his voice at the beginning of the call had almost gone now. It was only belatedly that she realized that's what his anger had been: worry for her.

"I didn't believe him when he told me he already knew and I don't believe him now."

"Why?" Karen asked, sitting in the darkness of her small house and feeling it grow smaller around her. She was listening for sounds beyond the phone.

"If he'd been telling the truth you'd be dead by now," Jerek said slowly, as if he was just realizing it himself. "He wouldn't have given me time to call and warn you. I'm sure he was just bluffing. He didn't hear it from me, and who else—" Jerek didn't finish the sentence, and instead followed it by the word he kept using: "But there's no sense taking chances. If you go near the Truetts, for God's sake be careful."

"Why would he have been bluffing?" Karen asked. Her voice had lowered almost to a whisper.

"So I would make a mistake. And it almost worked, too. Look, Karen, I was just about to get on a plane to Cleveland. And I'm sure I would've been damned easy to follow."

A long pause followed, so long that both of then said, almost simultaneously, "Hello?"

"Yeah, I was thinking," Karen went on hastily. "Just in case—You want me to tell you where they are?" She held her breath through the short pause that followed.

"No," Jerek said, and that was the most reassuring thing she could have heard from him. He wouldn't take a chance with his witness. So he must believe that Karen would be okay. "There's no reason to change our plans now. Maybe that's what they want. They obviously know how to find me."

Karen pictured Jerek again, still in heavy fog, surrounded. "All right," she finally said. "Listen, why don't you go stay at the station house tonight? Just so I'll be sure where to find you."

"I think I might."

Either of them could have dropped a tender caution into the pause that followed but neither did. The pause had to serve.

"Well, good night," Jerek said, which brought a short laugh from Karen. She spent the rest of the good night sitting up in bed with her pistol in her hand. The one time she dozed off she woke with a start, feeling a warm hand on her face. It was the sun, glimmering through the curtain.

*K*aren looked over her shoulder.

Nothing but wall.

She jerked her eyes forward again. A co-worker was watching her with his face perfectly blank except for a slight pursing of his lips. Karen grimaced and shook her head for his benefit as she looked down at her desk. She picked up the phone, dialed two digits, and dropped the receiver in place again. She picked up the pencil she had been toying with and slammed it down on the desk, snapping it. "Damn!" she said, as if it had been an accident.

Her co-worker's stare was not the one that worried her, but she walked out of the office to escape it. Her heels made a tattoo on the polished floor.

She worked not in the big federal building downtown but in a three-story satellite building near a mall. It housed the overflow from several other departments as well—highway patrol, probation officers. It was usually busy with all kinds of people coming and going, but Karen knew that after five o'clock the building got much smaller and darker. She didn't intend to be here by then, but she didn't look foward to being at home, either, which had turned into a very small, dark place indeed since Jerek had called the night before.

She walked to the end of the corridor and stood at the bank of windows from which she could see the parking lot. The roof of her white Mustang twinkled in the sun. It was almost swallowed up among all the other cars in the lot. No one stood near it. No one was watching it from anywhere, that she could see.

She hurried downstairs and down the rows of parked cars. When she reached her own she stooped to look under it and under the cars near it. When she stood again a man in a suit was staring at her. Karen recognized him as a probation officer. The car door he was closing was emblazoned with the insignia of the department. "Afraid there for a minute that it was flat," Karen said brightly, and drove away while he watched. As far as she could tell he was the only one watching, but the traffic was too heavy to be sure. She went to the mall and an early lunch. No one spoke to her.

All day long she'd remembered Jerek's words: "If you contact the Truetts, for God's sake be careful." So she hadn't contacted them at all yet. She felt she had to warn them, but the act of warning might be what doomed them. So she had done nothing but jitter. Jerek had very effectively communicated his worry to her. But, she thought now, the night had passed, and half the day today, with nothing happening. Everything was normal. The soldier had had plenty of time to get to Cleveland and her. It was beginning to look as if Jerek were right; it had been a bluff.

After lunch Karen was back brooding at her desk, making time pass slowly. Still, it did pass: something should happen. A mischievous spirit was at work on Karen, drawing all her nerve endings out with tweezers, until they extruded all over her body. She felt every current in the air. Shadows shifted behind her, where there was no window. She looked over her shoulder. Nothing.

She went to the bathroom.

The tension was different now, because they knew someone was out there. The knowledge was oddly reassuring. At least it eliminated paranoia as a possibility. *Some*one had visited Jerek in his living room.

Every half hour or so she reached for her phone to call the Truetts. They were the ones who needed warning. If the soldier somehow managed to get around Karen (or through her) Elizabeth and John would be next, and have no idea that Jerek thought he was an imposter. If the soldier somehow learned their phone number without their location he could call them, pretending to be Bryan, and they would probably happily tell him where they were. They would even rush to meet him. She needed to tell them something that would hold them in place.

But there was no phone she trusted. Oddly, it would be better to go see them in person. At least you had a good chance of seeing anyone following you. There was no way to spot a trace on a phone line.

She left the office abruptly in mid-afternoon and drove. She didn't head straight for the Truetts—first she drove almost aimlessly around the city. But that was no good, there was too much traffic. There seemed to be a hundred cars following her.

Finally she grew bold enough, or worried enough, to head out of town. When she turned toward the Truetts' small town the highway narrowed and traffic fell off, but there was still some. It was late September, but many people hadn't let go of summer yet. There were still tourists on the roads. The heat lingered too. Karen's blouse was sticking to her back. She rolled down her window and hot air jostled into the car. The wind pushed her hair forward. One strand kept creeping into her right eye.

She paid so much attention to her rearview mirror she barely saw the road ahead. The highway began to twist, cutting her off from the cars ahead of and behind her. Anyone following would have to move in close now. One or two cars did, but they had family groups in them. Karen let them pass.

She seemed to be alone on the road when she turned sharply into the rutted dirt tracks where she always turned off and waited. She raced up the bad road and was out of sight by the time the next car came along.

It was a rented car and Tripwire was driving it. He saw the dust hanging in the air above the little dirt road turnoff. It might have gone unnoticed by anyone else, but he was trained to notice trails. Fear had taught him to watch for them. He speeded up, driving past the dirt track, going down the highway faster and faster. He overtook a blue station wagon he'd seen pass Karen's car, but he didn't catch her. So he turned back toward the dirt track. He parked out of sight of it and walked into the trees that bordered the rutted path.

At the end of the track Karen sat in her car in the yard of the abandoned farmhouse. She waited longer than usual. No car had followed her in. The point of this turn-off was only to let any car following her go past and get lost. It didn't require a very long wait to be sure of that, but today Karen sat in her car at the end of the track for a long time, waiting. She left her window open and listened. The sound of cars passing on the main road was an insect-like buzz from here. None of the cars turned toward her hiding place.

Karen had realized that if there were killers coming for the Truetts they might not be content just to follow Karen to them. More likely they would come directly to her for the information. This would be a good spot for that. Then as nothing happened she let herself grow momentarily more confident, but she still sat clutching the gun in her lap. The breeze grew cooler as the sun declined behind the trees.

Tripwire stood in the woods watching. He saw the very unused look of the farmhouse and two small outbuildings. He would reconnoiter here, but he sensed that this wasn't where the Truetts were hiding. He watched Karen, waiting for her to lead him.

After almost half an hour Karen started her car and crept back along the dirt track to the highway. No car was in sight when she emerged. She sat there, knowing she had to move quickly, but still undecided. She was fairly sure now that she hadn't been followed. If she had been, she had lost them. But still she sat there. She had a very uneasy feeling. She knew the feeling would get worse the closer she got to Elizabeth and John's hiding place. Probably this was nothing more than the uneasiness Bill Jerek had passed on to her like a communicable disease. But it felt wrong, when there was even a chance she was being followed, to go straight to the Truetts.

A car passed, startling her. Kids looked out the back window, waving. Hastily she pulled out, not wanting anyone else to see her there. She didn't have time to think about which way to turn, it was only instinct. Instinct headed her back into Cleveland.

All the way home she kept an eye on the rearview mirror. She never saw anyone, but her nerves kept tingling.

*F*red Tyler walked into the office of a motel north of Baltimore. He looked a little stiff. It wasn't his feet that were sore, it was his butt, because he'd been driving so much lately. And the fight on the Truetts' patio hadn't helped.

This motel looked as run-down as the highway outside. It was the old highway, the county didn't spend much on its upkeep any more. Fred had found it almost by accident. He thought he'd already checked every motel on the interstate between Baltimore and New York. Those motels were relatively new, glassy affairs without personality. After a few days of walking into them Fred had begun to feel he'd passed over a border into a different country—the nation of Holiday Inn, with its own flag and citizens and a consulate on every stretch of road. This older, slightly seedy place was a relief.

The man who came out of the office in response to the bell on the desk was tall, slightly stooped; old before his time, like no one bothered to maintain him any more either. He didn't give Fred a professionally cheery smile and bright greeting, and Fred appreciated that.

Fred showed him his FBI identification first. He let the man study it, because it was perfectly legit. He always let people take their time soaking in the ID, gave them a few moments to worry what they'd done wrong that had brought the FBI down on them. Everybody had some guilt, usually over income tax. Fred's way gave the questionee a great feeling of relief when Fred began asking about someone else, so they were always eager to help.

Fred put the photograph of Bill Jerek on the desk next to his ID. In the picture Jerek wore a white shirt and tie but no jacket. He was stiff because if was an official picture. After a day or two of showing it Fred had noticed that Jerek had begun to look more like a crook than a cop.

"I seen him," the motel manager said.

Fred was startled. He no longer had much faith in this enterprise, he'd just been going through the motions. He looked at the manager to see if he was joking, but the guy looked serious. "When?"

"Two, three weeks ago?" The manager looked at him as if Fred would give him the right answer. "We don't get that much traffic through here any more, you know, they stand out. Especially that one. Checked in in the middle of the night, woke me up, then hustled another man and woman into his room. He didn't think I was watching, but I was. I wondered what was going on with them three. Not surprised the cops're after him."

Fred tapped the photograph so the man looked at it again, matter-of-factly, like it was someone he knew. Fred said, "Could you check your records and tell me if he made any phone calls?"

"I can tell you he didn't," the man said cheerfully. "Not from one of our rooms. No phones."

"Oh." Fred's face fell. He had finally succeeded, and all he had learned was where Jerek spent the night with the Truetts that first night. All this time for nothing. But at the same time he was glad.

"Only phone for the guests is that pay phone outside," the manager said, pointing at a side window. He and Fred both looked at the phone standing on its pole outside. "Ah ha," Fred said. His response was so mixed it was no response at all. He just thanked the manager for his trouble and went outside to write down the number of the pay phone. He tried not to think. He had been successful at that for the last three weeks. When he'd come up with this plan it had been abstract, the way to find a random, unidentified person. Implementing it, he'd been able to fall into the routine of investigation. Ask questions, get no answers, check off one possibility, move on. Seeing Danny at the Truetts' house had brought him up short, reminded him of who he was working for. He would have liked to smash Danny in his stupid smiling face. Now this brought him up short again. He would have bet a month's salary Jerek had used this phone to arrange the hiding place for his witnesses. The information was almost in Fred's hands. He wondered if he'd really hand it over to Galvan. It would be just like handing over two lives. He knew he would. He felt himself growing abstract again, just a good investigator doing his job.

He wrote down the number and went off to find the local phone company.

CHAPTER TWENTY-FIVE

The Next Day: Jerek and Galvan

"*I*'ve got something for you, Bill."

Jerek didn't recognize the voice at first. The words and the tone made it sound like one of his junkie informants: nervous but trying to sound straight. There was some kind of noise in the background.

"What have you got?" he said.

"I've got Galvan, maybe."

Jerek paused. That sentence didn't sink in, but the voice did. "Fred?"

"That's right. Could you speak up a little, Bill?"

"Where the hell are you calling from?" There was a surge of noise on the line, clattering and a voice shouting but then it cut off abruptly as if someone had quieted them or closed a door.

"Pay phone in a restaurant," Fred Tyler said. "I don't have your dedication, I still take time out to eat."

Fred sounded like he was joking, but grew impatient during the pause that followed. "So are you still interested or have you gotten involved in something else?"

"I'm interested," Jerek said. "You going to bring Galvan in yourself, or do I have to go somewhere to get him?"

"I'm not joking, Bill. I think I've found out who your spy is."

Jerek stiffened. He looked out the open door of his office to where three or four men lingered in the squadroom, none of them looking at him.

"If we play it right we can get him to lead us to Galvan," Fred went on. "I think they're meeting today."

"Not on the phone," Jerek said. He was listening hard to all the background noises, both over the phone and his own building.

"No. You can meet me." Fred told him where and they hung up.

Jerek walked out through his men, nodding, saying a word to a couple of them. He was surprised they didn't look at him strangely, because that was how he looked at them. He had almost forgotten his suspicions since Dennison's death, because he couldn't bring himself to believe that anyone who had worked with Dennison could have arranged that. Now his suspicions came back in full force, backed with the hatred Marco Galvan himself inspired in him. He had to keep a tight rein on himself to get out of the room without glaring at them all.

He didn't tell anyone where he was going.

Fred Tyler hung up the phone in the manager's office of the restaurant in Little Italy. The restaurant was at an intersection where Italian restaurants stood on all four corners. Fred had walked into the wrong one first when he'd come to this meeting. It was afternoon, the kitchen was still noisy. Someone had closed the office door during his call. Fred looked up and said harshly, "Well?"

"That was fine," Marco Galvan said. "Thank you very much."

After Fred had delivered the name and address he'd learned, Galvan had asked for one more small "favor." Fred was in no position to refuse. He never would be. He had made the call. Now he just wanted to be far away. Galvan's politeness grated on him as much as Danny's insolence, but at least Danny wasn't here today. No one was saying where Danny was. Having made the call to Jerek, Fred had a good idea.

*I*t was a bad place for a meeting for a man whose lunch had been a dry tuna fish sandwich at his desk. The sandwich had tasted more like the plastic it came wrapped in than like any identifiable food, but Jerek had just wanted it to soak up the gallon of coffee in his stomach. Now his stomach was rumbling like he hadn't been fed in days.

The Fisherman's Market was a huge high-ceilinged warehouse of a building, crowded with stalls and visitors like a convention center. It was a convention of food. You could make a dozen meals by taking as many steps into the building. The name had become something of a misnomer, because while seafood still abounded the building also offered every kind of food Jerek had ever imagined. Some of it was raw—great whole fish, some of them longer and thicker than his leg, perpetually staring, still surprised by their capture—but most of it made it to be eaten on the spot: Vietnamese egg rolls and rice, Greek gyros, boiled shrimp, shishkabob, deli sandwiches, foot-long hot dogs with sauerkraut, fresh hot potato chips, fried fish and chips, Maryland beaten biscuits, crab cakes, steamed crabs, tamales, tacos. The smells clashed and combined. It was a riot, a continuing festival of eating.

Fred wasn't there yet. Jerek was a little early. He had half a dozen oysters standing at one of the tall tables in front of the oyster bar. You could watch the sweaty man in the T-shirt and apron prying open a shell and a second later feel the shell's inhabitant sliding down your throat. His nostrils stung with the gritty tang of the rock salt. He moved on deeper into the building. Fred hadn't said exactly where to meet. You could get lost quickly. The food stalls were packed closely together, leaving only narrow aisles on the concrete floor that was spread with sawdust in some places. Jerek walked slowly, his head raised to see above the crowds, but there was no place from which he could see very far. The stands were too tall and too loaded.

Marco Galvan was a phantom in Jerek's mind, flitting insubstantially behind other thoughts. Fred's phone call had raised no expectations in Jerek. He'd had too many leads go nowhere. Galvan was no longer even real to him. He was only an idea of evil, like the devil. Jerek was more interested in Fred's claim that he had discovered the traitor. Jerek's first thought—that it must mean it was an FBI agent—had faded. Fred could have come by information on anyone. No telling how many phones the FBI had taps on in this city alone. Supposedly the Bureau had cut way back on its domestic surveillance after Watergate, but anyone who believed that would believe Richard Nixon was going to be punished for his crimes. Besides, cops were always fair game, cops should expect to be bugged and followed. Assuming the traitor was a cop.

It was early evening now, but it was summer and so still light. But the crowds were thinning out a little in the Market.

Jerek looked at his watch. Fred was almost half an hour late. He hoped nothing had happened to him. Fred had sounded very nervous on the phone. Maybe he was standing somewhere now watching to make sure Jerek hadn't been followed to their rendezvous. Jerek looked around more intently and walked faster.

Past one of the booths, through a slit between rows of fresh fruits, Jerek saw a very big man in a dark suit. Jerek looked at him sharply, but he didn't see more than a slice of the man's shoulder and back before he passed out of sight. Jerek started in that direction and stopped. It wasn't Galvan; Jerek just had Galvan on the brain. If every big man startled him now, he was in the wrong place. He could turn his head and without trying spot three other men who fit Marco Galvan's physical description. If somebody wanted to hold a spontaneous convention of big fat men, the Fisherman's Market would be the place to start.

Jerek craned his head, looking for anyone else he might recognize, or almost recognize, like a blonde young man. Jerek suddenly thought that the Market would be a good place for a professionally done killing. The crowds, the narrow aisles. A handgun with a silencer. The victim goes down choking and before anyone realizes it's not a heart attack or a bad oyster the killer is miles out the door.

It was too late. Fred wasn't coming. Jerek wondered flickeringly, like heat lightning in the brain, if he'd been set up.

He touched his gun, on his hip under his jacket. A killer would be wearing a jacket too, that would be the way to spot him in this summer crowd of tourists in shorts and T-shirts. Jerek was too hot in his own jacket. He would have liked to take it off.

As he thought that he saw a thin man in a lightweight summer suit coming toward him in the aisle. The man's eyes were lifeless. Until he got close and saw Jerek looking at him. Then he smiled, nodded, and walked past. The aisle was narrow, they both had to turn sideways. As Jerek watched the man in the summer suit pass on out of sight he saw again, three stalls away, the tall heavy man in the dark suit. This time Jerek got a glimpse of the forehead where black hair was slicked back, receding from the forehead, to leave an arrowhead of skin at the temple. Jowls of pale flesh that would have darkened readily if the man ever got any sun. A nose much too narrow for that heavy face. Small, almost prissy mouth.

Galvan. Jerek was sure of it.

Come to spectate as his enemy was murdered? Jerek whirled away from the vision of the fat man to make sure no one was behind him. When he turned back Galvan was gone.

Jerek could almost believe he was going crazy. He was no authority on what Galvan looked like. He had only seen him once in person, someone else had pointed out Galvan having lunch in the window of a restaurant across the street from where Jerek was standing at the time. Jerek had seen dozens of photographs lately, but pictures were never quite true to life. Mostly Galvan's image existed in his own imagination.

Why would Galvan come here? He wouldn't risk it, even to see Jerek killed. Jerek kept walking toward the spot where he'd last seen the big man. He had his hand inside his jacket and he kept turning his head. He remembered to look up, into the dark upper recesses of the building. He couldn't see if there were catwalks up there.

In the week since Dennison's murder Jerek had sensed no threat to his own safety. It was as if only that one day had been open season on police and the menace had taken Dennison instead and passed on. Dennison had been sacrificed for him. Jerek couldn't escape that feeling. Maybe it was his sense of guilt, not just his feeling of safety, that had made Jerek less cautious in the week since. Today, for example. The Market was only a few blocks from the police station; Jerek had walked it. And he hadn't told anyone where he was going, but that was because of Fred Tyler's message. There was no one Jerek trusted enough to say, I'm going to find out who the traitor is. Cover me.

Maybe under those conditions Marco Galvan would feel safe in being here, especially if he had his own pet cop with him.

Jerek kept twisting through the narrow aisles. At that he was as likely to pass Galvan as to catch him. He needed a place to stand and survey the crowd. Inside a booth selling candied apples, popcorn, and cotton candy, he saw a fat woman in a pink dress sitting on a high stool looking exhausted. Jerek looked for a way in and found a little gate in the stand's wall. When he unlatched it and stepped inside the woman said "Hey!" and stood up, which was convenient. He stepped up onto the stool she had vacated. She said "Hey" again, but more curiously. The stool wobbled under him and she steadied it. "Thanks," he said distractedly.

From that height he could see across the heads of the crowd.

He also made himself a better target. But if someone wanted to shoot him unobtrusively, now wouldn't be the time to do it, while Jerek was already drawing attention. He risked it for a few seconds.

Thirty yards away, in the heart of the crowd, he saw a fat man. In his dark suit he still stood out in the crowd of touristy pastels. And now he was one of the few people not turning to look at Jerek.

Jerek vaulted directly from the stool over the railing of the stand to the concrete floor. The impact jarred his knees. He ran as best he could through the crowds. Some of them turned and yelled after him. One man wanted to fight, until Jerek let his jacket slip back to display the gun on his hip. He hadn't taken it out yet because he didn't want to panic everyone, but his hand stayed near it.

He wondered where Fred Tyler was. It didn't matter now. Jerek needed backup, other cops. This was downtown, there were probably some close at hand, maybe passing in the street outside. There were no phones, of course, in the food stands. There must be phones somewhere in the building, but he had no idea where. If he went looking for one he'd lose Galvan.

He reached the spot where he'd seen the fat man. Jerek leaned over the wall of the nearest food stand, grabbed the arm of the little proprietor, and said, "Big fat man in a black suit. Where'd he go?"

The little man gibbered back at him in Vietnamese.

Jerek let him go and turned. The few people near him shrank back from his expression. He felt Galvan slipping away just as he was in his hands.

He ran, caught a glimpse of him buying a sausage on a stick, and grabbed his arm at the same moment he realized this was the wrong fat man. Jerek let him go and ran on.

He stopped in a narrow aisle momentarily empty of people. The stand on one side of him was already closed for the day. A sudden premonition made Jerek spin around. A young man in a dark blue windbreaker was coming toward him, his hand going inside the jacket.

Jerek went for his own gun and got it out first. When he pointed it the young man made a small frightened sound and dropped the wallet he'd been reaching for. Jerek stepped close to him, pulled the windbreaker open, saw no gun. He pushed past the young man and kept running.

He reached one wall of the building. A maintenance man in

coveralls was pushing a ladder on wheels. Jerek stopped him, showed his badge, and scrambled up the ladder. It was a very tall metal one, two ladders leaning together to form a tall, narrow triangle. The rungs shook under his feet. Eight feet in the air, feeling like a target, Jerek stopped and scanned the crowd. A few people were staring back at him. He didn't see anyone raise a gun.

He saw Galvan in the thick of the crowd near him, turning away. "You! Stop!" Jerek shouted. Everyone stopped except Galvan, who turned casually away.

Jerek started down the ladder. It teetered. He jumped clear of it and the maintenance man fought to hold it upright. Jerek was running again. His heart hammered with the mixture of exhilaration and fear. If he could just reach Galvan before Galvan's men reached him. Jerek was sure now it was a trap, but at that moment he was willing to die if he could just get to Galvan first. They'd both die then.

The tourists parted for him. The crowd had diminished somewhat—it was closing time at the Market. The food smells were no longer so appealing. They had a deadened quality. Half the stands were closed already.

Ahead of him, turning a corner, Jerek saw Galvan. Jerek shouted something again, something inarticulate, almost animal. The man didn't turn to look at him. He quickened his step.

The worst moment was when Jerek almost had him. The two fears crescendoed as he reached for the man's arm, the fear of losing him and the fear of dying. He would grab the man and turn him and see a stranger's face again. Or Galvan had a man standing close by who would put a bullet through Jerek's eye as soon as he touched Galvan.

Jerek grabbed the man's huge arm and spun him around. At the same time Jerek circled, trying to use the man as a shield in every direction. For a moment it looked like they were dancing.

The fat man turned all the way around and they were face to face. "Yes?" the man said, as insouciantly as a British butler in the movies.

It was Galvan. They stared at each other for a long moment. It was a moment Jerek had hungered for for so long that he knew something was going to go wrong.

"You're under arrest," he said.

Galvan looked at him, unperturbed. "For what?" he said.

Jerek was surprised, up close, at the size of the man. He was taller than Jerek and Jerek's big hand barely half-circled the upper arm he was gripping. Galvan could rip free of that grasp with a shrug. Jerek had his gun out but it seemed small and inadequate. Fastidiously dressed as he was, there was still something distasteful about Galvan up close. He gave off a faintly sour odor, and a thin line of sweat, mixed with his hair oil, ran in a brownish trickle down one temple. Jerek didn't like touching him, but he overcame the feeling and began patting him down. Galvan could have concealed any number of weapons in his tent-sized suit. Not that he'd need them. In spite of the tingling in the back of his neck, Jerek had to concentrate all his attention on Galvan.

It seemed best to keep moving. Jerek couldn't even feel Galvan's resistance when he began hauling him through the aisles toward the exit. A security guard came running up. Jerek kept his gun out, not trusting the man's uniform. "Police officer," he said shortly, and showed his badge. The guard skidded to a stop.

"Call for a car, will you?" Jerek said, and the man went running off. Jerek followed him slowly, holding his gun out to the side. Galvan made no move for it.

"What made you come here?" Jerek asked. He didn't expect answers. "Who were you meeting?"

"I was just having a snack and seeing some friends," Galvan said. "Ask around, I often come here."

"Not lately." Jerek glanced back over his shoulder at the darkening food stands. There were little flickers of movement everywhere.

"No, not lately," Galvan agreed. "I've been out of town for the last couple of weeks, on business."

Jerek didn't bother to answer. He walked very close to Galvan, hoping to discourage shooting. Galvan went on talking.

"I got back into town this morning and I've been perfectly visible since. I'll give you my itinerary and you can check. I've seen dozens of people today."

"Sure," Jerek said, still turning his head. He was hardly paying attention to what Galvan said.

But a few paces later the information struck him. What Galvan said made it all fit. Why *had* Galvan been strolling casually through the crowds of the Fisherman's Market? Why had he been captured so easily? Why was no one shooting at Jerek right this minute?

Jerek stopped dead and turned to look at Galvan for the first time. Galvan looked back at him blandly, but behind that expression was another, self-satisfied smirk. Galvan let Jerek see it for just an instant. He couldn't resist letting the cop know he was beaten.

Jerek dragged Galvan with him. The fat man was a heavy weight, like a chain around Jerek's neck.

The security guard was waiting at the wide front doors of the building. A patrol car had appeared promptly in answer to his call. The security guard waved at it like a doorman. Jerek pulled open the back door of the car as a very young uniformed patrolman stepped out of the passenger side. His face was vaguely familiar.

"Captain Jerek," Jerek said, showing his ID. The patrolman nodded nervously. "This," Jerek went on, pushing Galvan forward a step, "is Marco Galvan. You know who he is?" The patrolman nodded again. "Good. Take him and book him. I'll be there in a minute. Got it? If he's not in a cell when I get there—"

Jerek shoved Galvan toward the car. He seemed almost docile now. Jerek put a hand on the top of his head so it wouldn't hit the door. He stepped back, wiping his hand on his pants. The young patrolman made sure the door was securely closed. "Yes sir," he said, his first words. Jerek rubbed his hands together as if one were stained.

The patrol car pulled away and Jerek started running again, looking for the nearest phone. It was in the security office. The guard let him in and stood there as Jerek dialed. Jerek didn't send him away. It wasn't secret any more.

First he called Cleveland Information, because he didn't have the numbers memorized. He got a recording at the federal marshal's office. Jerek looked at his watch and was amazed to see it was after seven. After six in Cleveland.

He dialed the second number, Karen's home phone number.

Why had Galvan given him that satisfied smile? Jerek knew the answer now. It was the same reason Galvan would have been displaying himself in public all day today, as he'd said. Jerek believed him. Galvan had been establishing an alibi.

Karen's number rang and rang.

CHAPTER TWENTY-SIX

* Earlier that day, Karen

*T*he creepy feeling had gotten worse. Her imagination was going to kill her. For the last two days she had felt watched every minute, every second of the day. She woke with the feeling, went to the bathroom with it, got no work done at the office because of it. She would have been all right if Jerek hadn't called; she'd have been better if he'd call again. As it was she was in the worst possible position: she knew something bad might be happening, but she didn't know what was being done about it and there was nothing she could do herself.

She had thought about taking the Truetts and just running. Cross the country in a haphazard pattern no one could trace. She didn't have much money but they could live off American Express for days. How long could it last 'till they cut off her credit? Could someone follow a trail of credit slips?

Besides, she couldn't go near the Truetts. Worry for John and Elizabeth was what frayed her nerves worse than anything, but she couldn't check on them. The only way to get to them was through her, so she had to stay away. She could see them already dead or running for their lives while she sat here. That was the one good thing about the creepy feeling, it was reassuring in that sense; as long as she was being watched, they hadn't found John and Elizabeth yet. If the feeling of being watched went away, then she'd really have to worry.

She would have felt much better if she just could have spoken to them for a minute. A dozen times an hour she reached for the phone and drew back. Whenever she drove, eyes constantly on the rearview mirror, her hands twitched with the desire to turn sharply at every corner and roar off toward Chagrin Falls, leaving any pursuit far behind. She tried to figure out how she could borrow a police car and tear down the highway in it, siren blaring and lights flashing, cars pulling to the side of the road and Karen blazing a trail no one could follow.

She went again and stood at the window in the hall, looking out at the row of government cars and beyond them the civilian vehicles, including her own. She could see her own ghostly reflection in the window, superimposed over that wide outside world full of hiding places, until it seemed she was the most conspicuous figure in the world. She drew back, then turned and walked quickly away.

*T*he truth was, no one was watching Karen. They were waiting for her at home.

Danny had gotten in this morning. Galvan had told him to grab her right away, but when Danny had driven by her office building and seen the array of witnesses, half of them different kinds of cops with bulges on their hips, he'd decided to wait. He had driven to her house and liked that much better. Quiet house on a quiet street, the house standing all by itself. He was glad she didn't live in an apartment with paper walls and a thousand people in screaming distance. Her house looked very substantial.

It would have made Galvan very nervous to know Danny was waiting, not snatching her the second his feet hit Cleveland dirt. Galvan was going to be putting himself on the line back in Baltimore; it would make him furious to know Danny didn't even have the girl yet. That made Danny smile.

Danny couldn't believe Galvan was really going to do it, but he'd been thinking about it all the way on the flight here and the inexorable sense of it pressed in on him. Galvan had to have an alibi for this one, a good alibi, not that cock-and-bull restaurant story he'd arranged for the first murder.

Being arrested that way might help Galvan's other case. "What was this supposedly frightened fugitive doing when you arrested him, Captain Jerek?" "Strolling through the Fisherman's Market, sucking on an egg roll." It would also make Galvan's story that he'd been out of town, not even knowing he was wanted, look better. Put all the elements together—

Galvan's restaurant alibi for the first murder, the only witness against him dead and no way to connect him to her murder, the innocence with which he let himself be arrested—and Galvan would walk away from this one like he'd walked from all the others.

There was also an unspoken reason Galvan and Danny knew between them. The police hunt for Galvan now was so ferocious he'd be captured soon anyway unless he fled at least the state and maybe the country. If he did that he'd no longer be able to direct things and he'd never be able to come back. Danny would see to that. Galvan knew it. Even from jail Galvan could run things, and he'd get out on bail anyway as soon as the witness was dead. They'd have no case without her.

So it all hinged on Danny, both the reason for the plan and the success of it. The thought of Galvan in police custody made Danny smile again, and he wished he knew how to prolong it indefinitely, but again Galvan was protected by his logic. Danny couldn't afford to have the witness alive any more than Galvan could. She could place him at the scene of Cook's murder too. And once Danny was arrested for anything Jerek would recognize him as Dennison's killer. So getting to Elizabeth Truett was as vital to Danny as to Galvan. And now was the only time to do it, because once Galvan was arrested they'd bring their witness back to Baltimore and keep her under such heavy guard no one would be able to get to her. Galvan liked irony. He liked making sure it was Bill Jerek himself who arrested him and therefore provided his alibi. He liked sending Danny, with his divided loyalties, off to do the killing that would free Galvan, knowing Danny had no choice but to do it.

But he hadn't sent Danny alone. He hadn't gone quite that far, Danny looked over at the passenger seat of the car, at Rick. Danny's lip curled. They send this goon with me, he thought. A young goon, not some ham-handed old thug, but still a goon. It was probably another condescending little joke of Galvan's, like Danny needed the help or to be watched over, and this is what he sends to do it. While Danny was sitting here thinking Rick was chewing on his thumbnail and staring vacantly out the window, not even at the right house. Goon. Rick was young, only two or three years older than Danny; he had a wide nose, white teeth, and black curly hair. He liked to wear light-colored jackets with flowered shirts underneath, the lapels of the shirt covering the lapels of the jacket. His fashion ideal was Ricky Ricardo, for Christ's sake. Rick's grandest ambition, the secret cherished dream he knew he'd never achieve, was to guest star on *All My Children*. A TV-age goon.

"I been thinkin'," Rick said suddenly, turning toward him. He either ignored or didn't hear Danny's groan. "Whyn't we wait for her inside? Don't you think we're kinda conspicious out here on the street all day?"

"Listen to him, the burglar," Danny said sarcastically, because burglary was a skilled profession and Rick was just a goon. He couldn't have gotten inside the house without breaking something. Danny couldn't have either, but that was because he left lesser jobs to lesser men. "For one thing, she's a cop, okay?, and a woman cop who's worried about getting raped and killed probably has alarms, don't you imagine? We don't wanta go breakin' in and have the cops come before we even see her, do we? For another thing, what if we're inside all cozy and she doesn't come home alone, huh? What if she comes home with her boyfriend, or the whole gang from the office for a drink after work. And they're all cops with guns? You wanta be hiding in the closet while that's going on? No thanks. I'd rather be out here where we can see what's happening first. Don't worry, we'll get in as soon as she gets here. And do me a favor, okay Rick? Don't try to think around me, okay? It's insulting. Don't start thinking you're the brains of the operation."

"You got a real way with people, you know that, Danno? You should be a personnel director."

Danny snorted. As if he'd ever need Rick's help or good will. "And don't call me Danno."

"You got it, Danno." Rick stared sullenly out the window. Danny kept watch out his own. It was hot in the car. Once in a while he'd turn it on to run the air conditioner.

Danny was a little worried about how long it might take to get the information. He didn't plan to try anything subtle or psychological, just scare the hell out of her and be as brutal as necessary, or maybe a little more. But sometimes people's resistance could fool you. No telling about this federal marshal. Danny was confident she would tell him what he wanted to know, but it might take time.

Then he remembered that wasn't a problem. They knew from Fred Tyler that this Karen Boone was the only person in the world who knew where Elizabeth Truett was. Once Danny snatched Karen the link to Jerek would be broken. And Jerek wouldn't even know it. The Truetts would be all alone, just waiting for Danny to finish with Karen and then come calling on them. Danny would be able to take his time with the woman cop. He might even enjoy himself.

The afternoon wore on, the car was hot, Danny and Rick snapped at each other. They sat in the car getting madder and madder, waiting for her to come home.

*K*aren drove home late in the afternoon, still with that watched feeling, but it was diminishing. She made a few sharp turns, once crossing three lanes of traffic to do so, she circled one lonely block completely, and she never saw any other car staying with her. If someone was following her, he must be using a helicopter. She felt better by the time she reached her own neighborhood.

Karen was young to have a house of her own. On her salary it would have taken her ten years to save a down payment. But the house she lived in had been her grandmother's. Karen had been the only grandchild and her grandmother had wanted her to have it. Karen had planned to sell it and maybe use the money to go back to school, but the first time she had walked into the house after her grandmother's funeral the house seemed—relieved, as if the house had been expecting some stranger to walk in and was glad instead to see a member of the family. Karen had spent a few nights in the house, waiting to sell it, and it had been so much better than an apartment, where even if your neighbors were nice you still lived with their stereos and their fights and their lovemaking. The house slowly turned into her house. In the two years since she had managed to make it her own, though once in a while, usually at midnight when she turned off the lights to go to bed, she still felt her grandmother's presence. But that was a friendly haunting; a blessing.

Now, though, she felt least safe when she got close to home, because that meant she had to get out of the car and go into the house, and she had begun to feel safe in the car.

Danny was in the shadows next to the garage, behind a screen of bushes. Rick had signaled from across the street when her car was coming and Danny had crouched down out of sight. He stood now at the front corner of the garage, only five running steps from the front door. As soon as she got that door unlocked he'd be right behind her, pushing his way inside with her. If she screamed it would only be a short one. He didn't expect it to bring anyone, and Rick would still be outside if it did. So Danny would be alone with her inside the house. He could do his work there or put her in the car and take her somewhere, out into the countryside.

Karen sat in the parked car in the driveway. Twilight came early to this old neighborhood with its full-grown trees. It was already gloomy in the shadows near her front door. Today she had remembered to leave a light burning inside, but in a way that was worse than coming home to a dark house. It looked like someone was waiting for her.

She was glad again that her father the safety fanatic had installed the automatic garage door opener. She pressed her remote control and the door slid up. Her headlights illuminated the interior of the garage like a stage. Boxes, the workbench, her bicycle she hadn't ridden in months. It was cluttered but the slot for the car remained empty. She pulled in, looking in both the rearview mirror and the side mirror to see that no one slipped in with her. The garage door clanked down behind her, cutting off the view and the light. When it was down she turned off the engine and then the headlights and it was very dark inside the garage. She felt the clutter pressing in toward her. The door to the house was in front of her and to the left. Karen tried to picture the obstacles between her and the door. She reached for the handle of the car door.

But she stopped before she opened it, and her hand found the button and locked it instead. Then she leaned across the front seat and locked the other door too. She lay there stretched out on the seat under the windshield, staring up through it at nothing. She imagined a face suddenly pressed against the glass, or the window next to her. She jerked her head to look at it but still saw nothing.

She had seen something, though. Just as she was reaching for the door handle there had been a flash of movement in the side mirror. Like someone crouched down, coming from the back of the car to her door. It hadn't been a face or anything recognizable, just motion where there should have been nothing moving.

It could be that just before the garage door came all the way down a man had rolled under it and was now in the garage with her. It was too dark to see anything around her. The door into the house might as well have been a hundred yards away. Karen's hands were twisting on the steering wheel. Adrenaline was coursing through her, telling her to run, run, but she had nowhere to run and no way to use this extra energy except in imagination. She sat there in the dark getting more scared and realizing she had nowhere to go. The fact that she saw no more movement made it worse, not better. The darkness grew more palpable until it seemed someone was right there in the car with her. She jerked her head around, saw nothing, and was not relieved.

It was probably her imagination, or a neighborhood cat that had darted inside the garage, but Karen decided not to risk it. She could afford to indulge herself. She didn't have to stay here. Maybe she shouldn't have come in the first place. The moment she realized she could leave, her fears subsided and the garage seemed empty again. She pressed the remote control button and the clanky old garage door gave the little jerk it always did, like it had been startled awake, and then started slowly up. Karen reached for the ignition key, breathing a long sigh of relief.

And the garage door stopped, made a sound of metallic protest, and started down again. Karen looked into the rearview mirror, startled, and watched as the door went down, once again shutting out the dim twilight outside.

Karen's hand was frozen on the car key. She hadn't turned on the engine. She stared in the mirror at the closed garage door. A ghost in the machinery. Maybe it was an electrical ghost, a short circuit. She pressed the remote control again, aiming it back over her shoulder and keeping her eyes on the rearview mirror. The garage door started obediently up again.

And stopped, three feet off the ground. And came down again.

Karen pressed the button again, and again. The door quivered for moment, then stopped before it even started up. Karen stopped trying and dropped the remote control on the seat beside her. The mechanism was jammed, she'd have to get out of the car to open the garage door. She wondered how many steps it would take her to reach it. As soon as she got it open to the light outside and the view and hearing of her neighbors she would feel safe again. She could feel her heart beating.

And then she remembered that the garage door could be controlled by another switch inside the garage. It was a wall switch beside the door into the house, just like a light switch, so you could open or close the door from there. It would override the remote control. She did what she should have thought of right away—turned on her headlights.

The garage was suddenly flooded with light, and the man was standing there in front of her, his hand still on the switch that controlled the door. Karen screamed a scream that was very loud inside the confines of her car, less loud in the garage. Outside the garage it was a tiny, thin sound like the squeak of a bat.

The headlights did Danny a favor. He could see what he had to work with. An axe was standing close to him, leaning against the wall. He picked it up before she screamed again, advanced slowly on the car, and slammed the ax down on the windshield. It felt good to feel his muscles strain and swell with blood after the long, cramped afternoon in the car. He put his back into it and the when the axe hit the windshield cracked and a root system of cracks spread all through it. It didn't shatter but he could tell it would after one or two more blows.

Karen was still screaming. She ducked and put her hand up in front of her face and scooted to the other side of the seat as the axe came down. As soon as she heard the crack she reached for the key and tried to get the car started again. Her attacker wasn't standing in front of the car—she couldn't crush him against the front wall—but she could get away. He was no longer standing at the switch. Karen hit her remote control and heard the reassuring clanking of the door as it opened behind her.

Danny heard it too. He checked the swing of the axe toward the windshield. He looked back toward the switch on the wall, but the door was almost high enough and she had gotten the car started again. Danny looked up over his head at the wiring and the ropes and pulleys that controlled the door. He swung the axe high, reaching like a child trying to break a piñata. Danny's first stroke cut deeply into the wiring and the garage door jerked to a halt. Sparks showered down but the axe handle was made of wood, insulating him. Danny pulled the axe free and swung it again. The car was moving now, but this time he cut the rope, and the door crashed down like a medieval draw-bridge.

Danny grinned through the window at her. He took his time and swung the axe again, sideways like a baseball bat, hitting the window beside Karen. It cracked too, but didn't give. Karen ducked away from it and put the car in reverse. She slammed it back into the garage door. The door shivered but held.

Danny ran around to the front of the car to put a stop to that. He swung the axe at the radiator to cripple the car. The blade crushed the grille and opened a slice in the radiator. Hot water gushed out onto him like blood. Danny grinned and pulled the axe free to swing again.

Before he could swing it Karen put the car in drive and hit the gas. As the car surged forward she turned toward the man with the axe, trying desperately to crush him against the back wall of the garage. Her teeth were gritted. She had stopped screaming.

Danny leaped aside, dropping the axe, falling. He landed on some boxes, bruising his ribs and stunning himself for a moment. But the car had missed him. When he rose to his feet he was furious. He had gone completely cold, he was no longer grinning. The woman had run into the wall and seemed as stunned as Danny had been. Both the windshield and the side window were studded with cracks. One good blow would shatter either of them and he could reach inside for her. It was almost like the first stage of undressing her. Just peel this car away and there she was. The thought warmed him. He picked up the axe again and advanced on the car.

Karen saw him coming, and she could read his thoughts. She wasn't thinking of the Truetts any more. She was the victim. She fumbled at the gearshift and got it into reverse again. But she had broken through the garage wall and the car was stuck. And the car was pumping water through the broken radiator. The needle was swinging into the overheated zone. The car sputtered when she hit the gas.

Danny heard it and his grin returned. He got a good grip on the axe, still trying to decide between the window and the windshield. He didn't want to mark her, yet. He wanted to take her intact from the car.

Karen let off the gas for an instant, then hit it hard. The car roared again. It jerked free of the wall and raced back the few feet to the closed garage door. This time the door shattered when she hit it. She went flying out into the driveway.

Karen saw the man emerging from the dark blue car parked across the street. She swung out into the street, just missing him, and took off down the block. In moments they were out of sight, she had lost them both.

But of course she didn't get far, not with that broken

radiator. When she came to a stop in a cloud of steam she was looking in the rearview mirror. She didn't see them, but she was still afraid to get out of the car. Night had fallen almost completely. She leaned on the horn, hoping help would come, but stopped immediately, terrified of the noise. She didn't want it to bring him again, the man in the garage.

Karen knew she had to keep moving, not sit there and wait for him to find her. She didn't know where to go. When she reached for the door handle she discovered she was still afraid to open it, like when she was a child and knew the monster under the bed would grab her feet as soon as she swung them to the floor. She shook her head to clear it of that image, opened the door, and stepped hastily away from the car.

Headlights came toward her. She stood frozen in them and then they passed over her and the car went by, the teenage driver glancing at her disabled car. Karen almost raised her hands to flag him down, but she'd be crazy to accept a ride from a stranger. Running from a kidnapper, get into a car with a rapist. She started walking fast. In the darkness it turned into running.

At the corner, under a streetlight, she stopped and looked back. The suburban street was full of shadows, quiet. Bushes, trees, cars parked in driveways. She looked intently for movement and saw none. Far down the block, a car turned and came in her direction. The streetlight no longer felt protective. It pinpointed her. She left it, running up the lawn to the nearest house. There was a light or two burning inside, but no sounds. A porch light over the front door kept her at bay. She didn't want to be standing there futilely ringing the doorbell when that car glided by. Instead she eased along the side of the house and without hesitation clambered over the wooden fence into the unknown back yard. It was comfortingly dark. She hurried through it toward the back fence, feeling safer now where no car could follow.

But in the middle of the yard she stopped, suddenly feeling no longer alone in the yard. She looked back, imagining a huge dog shadowing her noiselessly, padding closer until his teeth were within a lunge of her throat. The big back yard was shaded by two tall old trees that made it even darker, but there was enough light for her to see there was nothing moving close to her. The feeling persisted, though. She ran to the back fence and swung herself over.

She made it without incident to a strip shopping center and

felt relatively safer there. But she didn't know what to do. She had no allies in town. Bill Jerek couldn't help her out of her immediate danger, but she wanted to hear his voice on the phone. She'd feel safer just telling him what was happening.

But a hasty call to Jerek might reveal the link between them to Galvan. Maybe that hadn't been Galvan's man in the garage, maybe it had been just an unrelated robber or rapist. But the call itself would tip off Galvan, give away her own position and Elizabeth and John's. She couldn't go to Jerek yet. She was still entirely on her own.

For the same reason she didn't want to call the police just yet. She didn't know whom she could trust or what was related to what. She didn't want to explain to the police why the man might have been after her, didn't want to tell anyone about Elizabeth Truett. Jerek had driven the urgency of secrecy into her. She didn't know how far Marco Galvan's contacts might reach. Maybe into the Cleveland police department.

Karen needed a phone and a car. The only place she could find both was back at the office. And there were often people there working late, she wouldn't be alone. She'd imagined the safety of that familiar, drab place.

From a drugstore in the shopping center she called a cab and when it arrived, nosing slowly through the parking lot, she ran out to meet it. She spent the entire ride twisted around in her seat staring out the back window. She saw no dark blue sedan following her like the one that had been parked across the street from her house. She began to calm down.

Her building was more deserted than she'd hoped. A note told her the security guard was in the other federal building across the parking lot. She tore the note off the door and used her own key to let herself in. "Back in five minutes," the guard's note said, but she didn't put much faith in it. The guard could be napping over there in the other building.

The elevator doors opened on her completely deserted floor. The corridors were dim and her heels loud. The lights were out in her own office. She reached a hand inside to turn them on before she stepped inside. The fluorescent lights flickered and crackled before growing steady. The room was empty and lifeless, not entirely reassuring. Karen settled at her desk, got out her address book and called the Baltimore police department. She asked the switchboard operator for Bill Jerek, got the detectives' squadroom and was told Jerek wasn't there. Could someone else help? Karen hesitated and decided no one else could. She knew Jerek's suspicions of his own men. The one she was talking to could be in the employ of Marco Galvan. Karen hastily hung up without leaving a message. She looked at the clock on the wall and wondered if Jerek was at home. It was an hour later in Baltimore. She was reaching for the phone again when it rang.

Karen's hand jerked back as if the phone had shocked it. She scrambled up from her chair and stepped back from the desk, exactly as if someone had just walked into the office. No one could know she was here except someone who had followed her. The man in the garage. Or if he hadn't followed he might be guessing she'd come here, and was calling to make sure. Waiting for her to give herself away by picking up the phone. She yanked open the drawer where she kept her gun, feeling somewhat comforted when she found it.

The phone rang again and she itched to answer it. It wasn't her private phone, it was a phone in a federal office. It could be anyone calling. It might even be help. Bill Jerek calling to tell her something had broken.

She picked up the phone and a moment later forgot her other concerns. She didn't recognize the voice when it said, "Karen?" but then he went on hurriedly: "This is John, John Truett."

"John! What are you doing calling here? Is there something wrong?" She forgot about her safety and remembered she was supposed to be guarding the Truetts.

"I think so." His voice was low and a little shaky but she knew it for John's voice now. "I just got home and Elizabeth's not here. She's gone."

Karen stood at her desk and put a hand on it for support. "Maybe she's just gone for a walk?" she said hopefully, trying to think of a better answer. "Or to the store?" For a walk in the dark? No.

John echoed that: "She wouldn't have gone out without me, she's too nervous. And she would have left a note, but I can't find one."

"I'll be there," Karen said shortly, and hung up. She was running before the phone landed in its cradle.

It had been a coordinated attack, she saw now. Someone to take her out while someone else went after Elizabeth. The only reason for trying to take or kill Karen was so she wouldn't check on the Truetts, so her killers would have longer before anyone knew Elizabeth was gone. Somehow they had gotten past Karen to the Truetts. Somehow she had given them away. But how?

She had a wild ride through the night to Chagrin Falls. There was a wind and the trees tossed their branches, reaching into her headlights. She had come to the office to get a car, but it turned out everyone took their government cars home at night, one of the privileges of a high GS number. The only one left in the parking lot was one with a transmission problem. Karen took it anyway. It was drivable. It jerked and trembled when she first put it in drive, but it did better on the highway. Once in a while it would shift on its own accord into a grinding neutral and she'd find she was gliding along without power, but it did that less and less often as it warmed up. She flew through the night.

She kept a watch in her rearview mirror, but that seemed useless now. They were already ahead of her, they'd already gotten Elizabeth. She didn't see the dark blue sedan and that was all she watched for. She went faster and faster, hoping at least to get there before they came back for John. Karen discovered there were tears running down her face. Elizabeth must already be dead.

It was Elizabeth who answered the door when Karen knocked frantically on it. Karen could feel someone looking at her through the peephole, then the door was flung wide and Elizabeth stood there. Karen stared.

"Thank God."

"What?" Elizabeth said, and Karen heard John call, "Who is it?" from the living room. His tone was humorous, he knew they only had one visitor ever.

Karen came hastily inside and closed the door. "You're back," she said.

Elizabeth was looking at her politely but without understanding. "From where?"

"John said—" Karen began, but stopped. Her skin prickled. John came ambling into the foyer, smiling in greeting. "You called me," Karen said. "You told me Elizabeth was missing."

John glanced at his wife, looked back at Karen, and shook his head. "I never called."

Karen was freezing suddenly, so cold she had gone stiff. She turned and stepped to the dining room window. The scene outside looked normal. No car went gliding past, no one stood on the sidewalk. But there was her own car, white, government-issue, parked in the driveway like a beacon.

"Damn," she said.

CHAPTER TWENTY-SEVEN

Gathering

*K*aren stood at the window waiting for a car to glide into sight and park, but none did, for the moment. Fool, she thought to herself. How could she let them do this, panic her into giving away the Truetts? She had been sure it was John's voice on the phone. In her own defense she thought, how could she have ignored that call, even if she had been suspicious? Calling John back to verify it would have left her as nervous as she was now. *That* could have been what they wanted, there could have been a tap on her phone.

Her instinct now was to take John and Elizabeth and run, but she forced herself to slow down this time. She tried to think of an edge she could give herself.

She turned away from the dining room window and asked John to keep watch there. "But stay out of sight," she added sharply. Karen walked into the kitchen, past the useless phone. The only one who knew her problem was Jerek, and he was too far away to help. She fleetingly considered calling the local police, wondering if they could stay safe here in the house until they arrived. She didn't want to bet on it. And she didn't want to spend minutes on the phone describing the situation to a police dispatcher she didn't know.

She felt Elizabeth's stare on her. At the dining room window John was looking back at her too. Karen was the professional; they were waiting for instructions.

She looked out the back window, into the yard. They could go out that way and try to lose themselves in the back yards of the neighborhood. That might be a good idea, *if* someone were on the way to rescue them. But without back-up she didn't want to go floundering out into the dark, dragging two vulnerable, inexperienced people with her.

And maybe her pursuers were already out there, moving into position.

Karen had the gun she had picked up at the office, but one gun wouldn't be enough. There were at least two of the men, she had seen that many. They wouldn't lay siege to the house, they'd come in fast. They would separate and come in from different sides. She couldn't possibly keep them out. It would turn into a running gun battle inside the house, with Elizabeth and John in the crossfire.

"We're leaving," she said. Her gun was in her hand. "I'll go first. When I get to the car and see it's safe I'll wave you out. Hurry when you come."

She paused at the door and almost gave the gun to John. If she was the first one out and got shot the gun would be no use to anyone. But it was her responsibility, and she was probably a better shot than John. She thought about who was out there and for a moment it turned purely personal. She wanted one good shot at that bastard who'd been in her garage.

She slipped out the front door into the cool night. The porch light was off but there was a streetlight in front of the house next door. Her white government car seemed spotlighted in it. Karen walked softly to the corner of the house that jutted out into the front yard. Her back was to the garage. That's where he had hidden the last time, around that corner. But she didn't think he'd be hiding now. He wouldn't have time for that, he would have come charging in. Unless both of them were circling the house, looking for the best way in. Karen looked around the corner and saw no one. Far down the block a car was coming slowly, but it was too dark to see what it looked like or who it was carrying.

She ran to her car and opened the front door. The dome light came on inside and she glanced into the interior of the car. Then she looked at the house and urgently waved them out, her hand revolving in small circles.

Nothing happened. Karen stared. She had only left them alone for a moment, no one had had time—she took a step away from the car and the front door opened. John came out, his shoulders hunched. He came out three steps, looking around, before he motioned for Elizabeth to follow. "*Hurry,*"

Karen whispered. She had already checked the scene, that wasn't John's job. But she could understand why they might not fully trust her.

John waited for Elizabeth to catch up to him and put his arm around her, covering as much of her as possible. They finally hurried then, across the yard, into the glare of the streetlight toward the door Karen held open for them.

She got behind the wheel and started the car. It started without a problem and roared as she held the gas. John and Elizabeth hurried past her open door and got in the back. They closed their doors and felt safe for a moment, but the feeling quickly evaporated. Karen put the car in reverse and pressed the gas. The engine raced but nothing happened. She looked to make sure the parking brake was released and the car was really in reverse. She pressed the accelerator. The engine roared, the transmission slipped, the car didn't move.

Danny was coming slowly down the block, looking intently at the houses on both sides. Some of them had garages and that bothered him. If she had parked in a garage she was gone. He had followed Karen all the way from Cleveland but he had been hanging way back so she wouldn't see him. There had been enough traffic to hide in. Once they got to Chagrin Falls he had fallen even farther back, staying just close enough to see what turns she made. He had seen her turn down this street but now she had run to earth.

Rick was sitting beside him, a gun in one hand and both hands resting on his knees. He was bouncing his feet up and down on his toes like a damn pom-pom girl at a football game. "Maybe she turned down one of these side streets."

"Shut up," Danny said. He had just been thinking the same thing. But he'd find her. He passed more than one parked white car on the block, but the white car he was looking for had a U.S. Government seal painted on the side. It would stand out a mile.

He saw it. It was in the driveway a few houses ahead, under a streetlight, and he counted three heads inside it. There was exhaust coming from the tailpipe but the car wasn't moving. "See?" Danny said contemptuously to Rick. He grinned and speeded up.

John was the first to see the dark blue sedan. His quick intake of breath made Karen turn and look. She saw it too. She saw the man driving it. She pushed down hard on the accelerator and the engine only raced louder.

"Don't gun it," John said, leaning over from the back seat. "Coax it. And move the gearshift lever a little. Sometimes it's moved to a different spot and you can find it if you—"

Karen looked in the rearview mirror and saw the blue car glide to a stop in the street, blocking the end of the driveway. The driver's door opened but no one emerged immediately. The rider had jumped out on the other side and was running around the car. He was going wide around the passenger side of Karen's car to get position.

Karen stopped jiggling the gearshift and picked up her pistol again. She didn't have a good shot at the guy circling, but as soon as the driver came out from behind his door she was going to kill him. If nothing else she would do that. She wondered if she should open her door or just roll down the window.

Her car started moving. At first she thought it was just rolling down the shallow incline of the driveway, but when she pressed the gas it went faster.

"Get down!" she yelled to the Truetts. The blue car was looming in the rearview mirror. If she rammed it she might shake up the guy inside, but she might also weld the two cars together. She twisted the wheel and went careening across the front yard.

The other guy had been running in a crouched position. He stopped, stood up straight and stared stupidly at the departing car. Karen kept backing, across the yard next door. Her back bumper rammed a newly planted tree, little more than a stick. She felt it scrape the undercarriage as she went over it. Her back wheels went over the curb with a bump. She turned to point the car in the opposite direction. She was afraid to shift it into drive and her fear justified itself when the engine just raced again.

"Coax it," John repeated from the floorboard in the back. Karen eased off the gas and the car jerked ahead.

Behind her the dark blue sedan was pointed in the wrong direction. The passenger was running back toward it. The driver had stood up briefly but now jumped back behind the wheel and backed it in as tight a circle as he could manage. He went into the yard across the street. The other guy caught up to him there and dived into the passenger side, and the blue car came after her, a lot faster than Karen's white government car. She managed to stay ahead of him, even lengthened her lead when she went through a yellow, reddening traffic light and cars started across the street behind her, blocking the blue car.

But her lead wasn't big enough to turn off. Traffic was thin in the small town. Of course she saw no police cars. Her best bet was the highway. If she was lucky she'd find a highway patrol car. Her engine roared, caught, jerked her ahead. She made her way out of town.

Danny was close behind, hunched over the wheel, glaring ahead. "Hey!" Rick said as Danny almost sideswiped a big dumb station wagon on Rick's side. Danny ignored him. His eyes were fastened on the rear end of the little white car and on the back of its driver's head. He imagined her frightened eyes in the rearview mirror. He never had yet gotten a good look at the girl, but he would soon. He hoped she looked good. Danny was personally involved with her. The other two, the witness and the guy with her, they were dead already. But Danny was going to take his time with the female cop. His thoughts warmed him. He was smiling. They were heading away from town now, out into the country. That was all to the good. Like she was meeting him for a secret rendezvous. So far the bitch had been more trouble than she was worth, but she'd be worth it soon.

The car's transmission had settled down a little. It was better on the highway when she didn't have to stop and start again. Karen nursed it like John had told her. "Needs transmission fluid. I've had this problem with more than one car. That's why I never buy automatics any more," he said, as if he were having a chat in his hardware store. But it wasn't a normal conversation because he was still down on the floorboard behind Karen's seat. He raised his head to look out the back window, blocking Karen's view. "Get down," she said harshly.

John did, but he said, "They're not shooting at us."

Karen's shoulders stiffened, because if this had been a movie that's when the first shot would have come. It didn't, but her car did shift briefly into neutral and the blue car edged closer.

There was some traffic on the two-lane road, but little enough that the two cars were sometimes isolated. Karen went around a bend in the road, the blue car came around it immediately afterward, and they were alone in the deep black night. That's when someone back there did fire a shot. Karen wasn't sure at first. She saw the flash in the mirror but didn't hear the bullet hit. The next bullet, though, scored the side of the car, making a sizzling sound as it passed right by her. It sounded like a small, vicious animal trying to burrow its way in. The gunman was shooting low and outside. Trying to hit her tires, she realized suddenly. She veered back and forth and was grateful when another bend in the road appeared. She raced around it, momentarily losing them.

The two-lane road seemed very narrow in the night. It was black, and seemed to vanish a few feet beyond her headlights. The trees were tossing on either side, sometimes coming very close to the edge of the road, sometimes retreating behind fences that marked private property. There were places where the road had been built up high above the surrounding ground. There wasn't much shoulder in those places, just slippery gravel that fell to steep ditches. Once when Karen was paying more attention to her balky transmission than to the road she slipped off into that gravel and had to fight the car back onto the highway.

She pulled out into the other lane to pass a Volkswagen in hers. Danny also passed it immediately and it quickly fell out of sight behind them. There was no traffic in either direction for a moment.

The shots stopped. The blue car came creeping closer and there was nothing Karen could do about it. The transmission had slipped again, she was just gliding, slowing down. The blue car pulled out and began to come abreast. Karen reached for her gun.

There was a thud and her car veered wildly. The blue car fell back slightly. Karen saw it in flashes in the rearview mirror as her car swerved from one edge of the road to the other. One tire went into the gravel and she felt the right side of the car dip as the wheel tried to drag the rest of the car in after it. They were going over, and the ditch was so black she couldn't see the bottom of it.

Her transmission caught again and she fought the car back onto the road. She stomped her foot down on the accelerator, oblivious of the car's problems, and it responded for once. She raced up the road. Traffic appeared from the opposite direction and the blue car stayed back behind her, though coming closer in the mirror.

"They're trying to knock us off into the ditch," she said unnecessarily. The traffic would thin out again in a minute and he'd try again. There was nothing she could do about it. Karen thought about handing her gun to John so he could fire if the blue car came abreast of them again. Karen couldn't drive and shoot at the same time. But John would have to raise his head to fire. She couldn't risk him.

The blue car came very close to her back bumper, and the oncoming traffic swept by them and away, gone. Karen speeded up to the white car's limit, which wasn't enough. She was hoping for the sound of a siren. They were going fast enough to draw the attention of any highway patrolmen they might swoop past. But there in the black night with no other car in sight except the one trying to kill her, it seemed unlikely she could rely on such luck. Even if one of the drivers they passed was sufficiently alarmed to call in a report about their reckless driving, she and the Truetts would be dead by the time the police finally came looking for them.

As if to emphasize their aloneness the blue car pulled out and started slowly creeping up alongside her, drawing close like a lover. Karen edged over closer to the center of the road, away from the shoulder, as she rolled down her window. She held the steering wheel left-handed and fired back over her shoulder out the window. She barely had time to glance back and aim, but the windshield was a broad target. She hit it, but with no result except that the blue car fell back slightly. It began creeping up again almost immediately, though, and the passenger was leaning out his window, gun in hand. He had a good shot at her rear tire now but the blue car kept coming. They were going to fire into the passenger compartment. The white car decided to cooperate with them, and slipped out of gear. Karen lost speed immediately. The blue car seemed to jump forward, almost level with them.

John's head was coming up. "Stay down!" Karen screamed. Still holding the wheel, she leaned out her own window. She and the passenger in the blue car were facing each other for a frozen moment. Karen fired and he ducked back inside. But his hand holding the gun came out again. He was protected inside the car; all she could see was the gun, and the flash as it fired.

Karen pointed her own gun at the front tire of the blue car. The car fell back slightly and in that moment her own transmission caught again. She accelerated hard and the driver of the other car was caught off-guard. Karen raced ahead, traffic appeared from the opposite direction, and the blue car was forced back behind her.

But as soon as the road turned lonely again, she knew they'd be dead. The oncoming traffic dwindled, died, and the blue car pulled out again. It had to veer back as one more car came around the bend toward them. Karen pushed her car as hard as she could and gained a little distance on them. But nothing was going to be enough. The blue car came on relentlessly.

The road straightened out again, which frif,htened her so much that when salvation appeared in the highway ahead of her she took it only for a nuisance. There was an old Plymouth Valiant ahead of her in her lane, creeping along. The car was ancient, paint peeling off, and from its speed you would think the driver had just had a fatal heart attack. But the car was moving steadily, not slowing down. When the blue car came around the bend behind her it could push Karen's car right into the Valiant, killing everyone. Even the oncoming traffic wouldn't protect her.

There was a quite a bit of oncoming traffic suddenly, just when she needed most desperately to pass, and the Valiant wouldn't pull over to let her. There was no place for it to pull over, the shoulder was too narrow.

Behind her the blue car had appeared and slowed down too, but it was still gaining on her. The line of oncoming cars was steady, like a funeral procession.

Karen looked behind her and saw the blue car coming, slow with arrogance. Suddenly she was furious, glaring at it. She hated the car and everyone in it. Rage made her do something stupid. She floorboarded the accelerator.

The car leaped ahead, screaming toward the slow-moving Valiant, almost on top of it in a moment. The blue sedan was left in her wake, and Karen laughed triumphantly, maniacally. Down on the floorboard in the back seat John and Elizabeth stared at each other.

A tiny gap appeared in the oncoming traffic, too narrow to be used. Karen swung into it anyway, because the alternative was going over the Valiant. She was headlight to headlight with an oncoming car, so close she could see the driver's horrified, enraged expression. He threw up his arms in front of his face.

And Karen was past the Valiant. She pulled back into her own lane. More, cars were coming. She raced past them, getting snapshot impressions of faces staring.

The traffic in the other lane had slowed some. Cars coming up to join it bunched up more thickly than they had been. The Valiant dwindled rapidly in her rearview mirror. It had never changed position in the lane. Behind it was the blue sedan, trapped by the snail-paced Valiant and the thick stream of oncoming traffic. Karen gunned out of sight.

But she had no time for triumph. She was still less than halfway to Cleveland. The oncoming traffic would thin out again in a minute and it wouldn't take the blue car long to catch her. Even without Karen's transmission problems the blue car was much faster. And heavier. It wouldn't need subtlety to kill her. It could ram straight into her as they went around one of these bends, pushing her straight out over the edge or into an oncoming car.

As if she needed reminding, her car slipped out of gear and dropped her into a powerless glide. She looked in the rearview mirror. No car was coming behind her yet. Two twists in the road had left her alone, but that would only be momentary. This would be a wonderful time for police to arrive, like cavalry, but she had given up on that completely. The dark road seemed endless, and deserted. There were no houses nearby, no one to be disturbed by the chase rushing recklessly by.

Karen suddenly realized where she was. She knew this road better than the other driver possibly could. She had driven it a hundred times even before depositing the Truetts out here. She had an idea. It seemed like a desperately stupid thing to do, but her choices were painfully limited. She was coming up to the farm lane she always used to turn into to hide. She hadn't done that on this trip out, the other driver wouldn't know about it. But it panicked her, the idea of turning into that narrow lane, that led back to nothing but an abandoned farmhouse. It would be just the kind of spot a killer would choose.

Her car decided for her. That crippled car that was hobbling them. They couldn't be any worse off out of the car than they were in it. On foot in the dark woods they'd have a good chance of escaping their pursuers.

She was still undecided when she saw the dark mouth of the lane. It still scared her. Her hands wouldn't turn to steer her into it. In that moment her car slipped out of gear again. It was slowing already. Like a rabbit diving into its burrow Karen dived into the old country lane. Her heart hammered. If the blue car came around the bend now it would have them. She slapped at the button and turned off her headlights. Everything looked pitch black then but she didn't slow down. She was desperate to get out of sight of the road.

When she did let the car glide to a stop she said, "Shh," and the three of them sat there huddled in the dark, ears cocked like small frightened animals.

The silence was underlaid with the swish of tires on the

highway, out of sight but close at hand. Was the blue car past
yet, or had it slowed? How far would it go past this dark lane
without seeing them before it turned around and came back?
Karen drove slowly, slowly down the rutted track until she was
in the farmyard, where she turned the car around until it was
pointed back toward the highway. She put it in park, still
listening. Her gun was still gripped tightly in her hand. She
turned it, held it by the barrel, and reached up and smashed the
dome light of the car with the butt. Pieces of plastic fell down
on her passengers. They raised their heads curiously.

"Get out," Karen said. "Hurry."

This could be another stupid move, but she had settled on it.
If the blue car came down the lane they'd be trapped. If they
stayed in the car. But she could spare the Truetts that.

"Don't go into the farmhouse, that's where they'll look. Go
into the woods behind it. You'll be safe there."

That didn't even sound strange to her. She didn't reflect on
how the last hour had changed the values her parents had
taught her. Being alone in the woods at night was the stuff of
horror stories, but now it seemed harmless. There was nothing
in the woods as dangerous as the men chasing them.

"Hurry," she said. "Get out of sight before they come. I'll
come find you in a few minutes."

The broken dome light didn't come on when John opened
the door. Neither of them said anything, but Elizabeth put her
hand on Karen's shoulder as she climbed out, and gripped it
hard. Karen touched her hand and said again, "Hurry."

They got out and closed the door behind them. Karen didn't
watch them go. She was staring straight down that dark lane
back to the highway. Her motor was still running. When the
blue car came down the lane she was going to hit her headlights
and gas simultaneously, and if her damned car cooperated
she'd go roaring straight at the other car. There was barely
room in the lane for two cars to pass, right next to each other. If
she startled the other driver she could get past him. And when
he looked at her he'd see what he had seen all along, a woman
apparently alone in a car. With luck he'd assume the Truetts
were still hiding on the floorboard in back. He'd have to come
after her, and she'd lead him a good chase.

On the other hand, she might just shoot the bastard. Wait in
the car and shoot him in the face when he came for her. Karen
knew she had a good chance of getting killed. It hadn't come to
her as a complete thought, just as knowledge that settled

around her like a cloak: she could be a few minutes from dying. She wasn't resigned to the idea. It made her furious. It made her capable of killing.

She sat there in the dark, holding her gun, staring into that dark lane.

*B*ut Tripwire didn't come down the lane. He came through the trees, walking easily, feeling safe again in their shelter. He was at home in the woods. He sensed Karen's car before seeing it, because it was an intrusion here. Its mechanical heat and the metallic heart of its engine flavored the night for half a mile around it. Tripwire stopped behind a tree and watched the car. His eyes were used to the darkness. There was half a moon, its light sifting down through the trees. He saw John and Elizabeth climb out of the car and hurry off into the woods alone. That surprised him, because it was just what he wanted. He stood watching the dark car for a long minute before following them.

His bare face was sensitive to the gentle wind. He passed a hand over his cheeks. He had first shaved shortly after leaving Bill Jerek's house, because Jerek would have his men looking for a bearded soldier. He'd finally changed out of his fatigues, too, into jeans and a soft shirt, long-sleeved. He looked very young now. No cop seeing him in a mall or a record store would have given him a second glance.

He had John and Elizabeth in sight again, but knew they had no inkling of his presence. They paused and looked back in the general direction of the car. It seemed they didn't want to stray far from it, but after a brief, quiet conversation they moved on. They might have already been lost in the trackless woods. He followed with no trouble.

He had waited all day for Karen to bring him here. He had followed her one day when she had seemed to be leading him to the Truetts, but that was the day she had stopped at this hidden lane and then gone back. Tripwire was sure she hadn't seen him, but it seemed clear too that she wouldn't lead him to the Truetts without a push. Today, while Danny had been waiting at Karen's house, Tripwire had been near her office, trying to call her, to pretend to be John Truett and send her racing to them. But Karen would never answer the phone. She kept leaving her office on restless errands, and even when she stayed put she let others do all the phone answering. Tripwire had finally given up and decided he'd call her at home. When she'd left the office for the day he had followed, staying well

behind her. When she got close to home and it was clear that
was where she was going he had turned off to find a phone. So
he had missed the scene in Karen's garage. Her phone was
ringing while Karen's car was smashing through the garage
door. By the time Tripwire came back looking for her Karen
was on foot, he didn't know why. But he followed her cab back
to her office and that's when he finally got his chance. It
worked as neatly as he'd hoped. Karen had raced out of town
straight to the Truetts, seldom looking in her rearview mirror.

He didn't know it had worked for Danny as well.

Tripwire had dropped far back behind her when they got to
Chagrin Falls. He knew he was close then, he didn't want to be
spotted. Danny, less cautious, had passed him then and stayed
close to Karen.

Tripwire had been driving around the neighborhood still,
looking for the white government car, when it almost met him
at an intersection. He had seen John's head come up out of the
back seat, then duck down again quickly. Karen had already
had time to pick them up and was going back. She was waiting
at a red light when he saw her. Tripwire's light had been green.
If he had stopped there, waiting for her to pull out in front of
him, she would have looked at him suspiciously. So he had
turned in front of her, guessing she was heading back to
Cleveland. And he had been right. He had stayed ahead of her
all the way. He had allowed a couple of cars to get between
them, in fact, so he hadn't seen Danny's car bumping Karen's.
He hadn't seen anything unusual until she'd fallen far back
behind the slow-moving Valiant. Tripwire had had to slow way
down then. Karen's car had just been catching up to him when
it had turned off into the dark lane. That didn't make any sense
to him now, unless she was meeting other cops there, but he
had pulled off the highway and followed her in. On foot,
because he knew she'd been watching for a car. From there it
seemed his plan had worked perfectly. Without his intervention
the Truetts and Karen had separated, so he could come upon
Elizabeth and John alone. With the marshal back there waiting
in her car, it was as if the three of them were alone in the
woods.

*E*lizabeth stopped again. "Hurry," John whispered. Karen
had told them to avoid the old farmhouse, but John was still
guiding them toward it because it was a landmark, seen
vaguely through the trees. They would skirt it and then hide in

the woods behind the house. John was anxious to find a hiding place and wait, but Elizabeth kept pausing to look back in the direction of the car. She seemed reluctant to leave Karen behind.

"She'll be all right," John said insincerely. In fact he expected Karen to draw any danger that might be coming. But that had been her choice. He didn't want it to be a useless sacrifice.

Elizabeth said his name softly and he stopped with her. She was looking back but he didn't know at what. They were already out of sight of the car.

"There's someone—" she began. John pulled her behind a tree and looked back himself. There were barely-heard sounds, but they came from all directions. "No," he told Elizabeth, hoping it was just the life of the forest he heard.

But then he saw it too, a dim shape flitting from one tree to another. A shape too big to be any creature that lived in these tame woods.

John turned and pulled Elizabeth with him. She was resisting, and he couldn't understand why. Worry for Karen? But whoever it was had already bypassed Karen and was coming after them. "Hurry," John said again. Twigs scratched his face and shoulders. The night was so dark that thin young trees would suddenly appear directly in front of him, and he had to swerve aside to avoid being blinded. He knew they were making too much noise but was willing for the moment to trade stealth for speed.

When they had gone fifty yards Elizabeth stopped him again. "Shh," she said. They waited behind a thick tree and looked back the way they had come. There was a small clearing into which dim moonlight fell. The moon was far from full, but compared to the dark woods that clearing was an illuminated stage.

A man crossed the edge of it, briefly, moving fast toward them. John turned to run again, but this time Elizabeth wouldn't be moved. "It's Bryan," she said abruptly.

John stared at her. She was losing her mind. He had caught glimpses of the two men chasing them and neither of them even resembled Bryan. In the spooky moonlight Elizabeth was seeing a phantasm, her son brought back to life. Her eyes scared John worse than he had been scared a moment before.

"Elizabeth," he said.

She turned to look at him with that familiar expression, as if she were reading his mind. "It's *Bryan*," she said more emphatically.

John looked back, compressing his lips. He didn't see anyone now. "We can't stop," he started to say, but didn't. Elizabeth was still looking at him, and he knew what she was thinking. His guilt resurfaced. He had pushed their son out of the house, into the army, into his grave. Now he was abandoning Bryan again. "Are you sure?" he said instead. He couldn't believe he was stopping to be killed by a murderer who vaguely resembled his dead son.

"I saw him," Elizabeth said ambiguously. They looked back. This time they could both see a young man making his way slowly through the trees. His face was shadowed, but Elizabeth breathed, "Bryan," and started toward him.

"Wait," John said. "Wait. Let me go look." Elizabeth didn't stop, but he caught up to her. "Bryan," she said more loudly, almost running. And the man following them was beginning to run too, to meet her.

Elizabeth forgot everything else in the glimpse she caught of her son. She let the tree branches scrape her as she ran to meet him. She barely heard John's voice. He was running too, no longer trying to hold her back, just trying to get ahead of her. Trying to protect her. But she was past protection now.

John managed to catch up and started to overtake her. Just as he did he stumbled. It was only then that Elizabeth heard the shot. It sounded like an explosion, made louder by the crash of her husband's body. John slammed into her. He gave a groan as the breath left his body. He was still trying to cover Elizabeth as he fell, and his blood stained her. He fell heavily to the ground. There was another shot. Elizabeth screamed at the sight of John's feebly twitching hand. She reached for him.

In the next moment she was borne to the ground under a terrible weight.

CHAPTER TWENTY-EIGHT

Death

*K*aren turned off the car. That scared her for a moment. She had gotten used to the hum and vibration of the engine; the sudden silence sounded like helplessness. It had been ten or fifteen minutes; she thought they were safe now. The blue car must be long past, racing to try to catch up to them. Karen wondered what she should do next, after finding the Truetts: drive sedately into Cleveland or turn around and head back to Chagrin Falls? She'd rather be in the city, but she didn't want to meet the blue car coming back if its driver got frustrated and came back looking for them. Chagrin Falls should be just as safe, she could go to the police there, find a phone.

She opened her door cautiously and stood there, taking the car keys. The night didn't seem so impenetrable now. The half moon provided as much illumination as a false dawn. But the light was ghostly, and cold. It made the underbrush look like fog. There was a chill in the air that made her rub her arms. At night the summer was over. The silence and the chill seemed connected, as if one carried the other on its wavelength. Someone raised in the country would have known the night wasn't silent at all. There were just no mechanical sounds. But to Karen's city ears that was silence. She turned toward the trees, hoping the Truetts hadn't gone too far. She started walking, not wanting to call out.

She heard a shot. It was a thin, abrupt sound that vanished immediately. But to Karen the sound had been almost expected; it rang in her mind like an echo. She couldn't tell where it had come from. She started running.

*E*lizabeth was being dragged through the woods, her feet barely skimming the ground. She resisted, slapping at her abductor and trying to dig her feet into the dirt.

Tripwire effortlessly overcame her resistance. He hustled her through a stand of trees and as they came out momentarily into the open he stopped suddenly and turned aside. A bullet cracked through the air he had turned away from. Tripwire was grinning without knowing it. His instincts sang through his body. He felt an inch shorter and pounds lighter, condensed to his essential strength. He heard everything: Elizabeth's ragged breathing, the huge noise the killer made coming toward them through the underbrush, the hush of listening birds. He knew exactly what to do.

He dragged Elizabeth through the brush and trees with him. They were making too much noise. He slipped into another thick stand of trees so that they were momentarily lost again and clamped a hand over her mouth. They stood face to face, inches apart. "Mother," he said.

Elizabeth looked at him for the first time since John had been shot. Bryan. He was changed but he was her son. For a moment it seemed to her that she had willed this tragic exchange. She touched his hand and it slid away from her mouth. "Your father—" she began.

"First we stay alive ourselves. Understand?"

He didn't wait for an answer from her, but when he took her hand and moved on she was no longer resisting. She wanted to throw her arms around him but there was no time. There might be no time left in the world.

Danny was standing stock still a few yards away, listening. He had seen the old guy go down and wasted no more attention on him. It was the woman he was primarily after, and the one he'd been aiming at. Danny stood there in the woods in his business suit feeling like a fool. He had botched the first easy shot and now he was going to have to chase them all over this damned forest.

Rick stood still as well, his pose echoing Danny's. Danny heard people moving and pointed off to the right. Rick nodded and went. Danny started circling around the other way.

Danny's best piece of luck tonight had been spotting the kid. He'd been unlucky enough to lose the woman cop when she escaped from her garage, but he'd guessed—hoped—she'd go back to her office. He'd gotten there just in time to see her flying out of the parking lot in the white government car. And he'd also seen the kid following her. He'd guessed he was the soldier Galvan had told him about, and that for some crazy reason the woman was leading him straight to the witness. That meant she'd lead Danny too. When they hit the small town Danny had closed in, losing track of the soldier, but his luck held when the woman cop had almost lost him again on the highway behind that damned Valiant. Danny would have roared right past the dark country lane if he hadn't seen the soldier's car parked on the side of the road. He followed him again, into the woods, straight to the witness again. And that's when Danny had blown the first easy shot, when the woman's idiot husband got in the way. He cursed again and plunged into the trees, moving deliberately. Stalking. He wasn't going to make any more dumb shots.

Karen was in the woods now too, her own gun in hand. She was running blindly, almost bouncing off trees, branches tearing at her clothes, and she was afraid she had already overrun the area where the shot had come from when she came into a small clearing and skidded to a stop at John's body. She knelt beside him, wincing at the sight of his opened flesh.

But then she looked up rather than down. Someone was coming. Her gun didn't keep her from feeling exposed. There was no time to look at John. She ran off to the side, into the trees, and waited to see who emerged, friend or foe.

Tripwire stepped softly from tree to tree. He was alone, and no longer armed. He could smell other people nearby, but he heard noises from too many directions. He needed to give himself an advantage.

Danny had come to a stop. He still held his gun high, pointing straight up, close to his cheek. It was a reassuring weight in the dimness. He didn't like this underbrush that clung sinuously to your legs, these trees that loomed up like someone suddenly coming at you. A few minutes earlier, when he'd lost sight of the witness and the soldier, his heart had hammered at the strangeness of the place. But he was calm again now. The place was not so strange; he was growing used to it. He realized that when he stood still he could hear very well. No other sounds overshadowed the noises human beings made as they crept through the dark woods. And no one else was more accustomed to the place than he was. Danny's confidence was returning. If he just stayed quiet he would win. It would be over in a few minutes.

Karen heard the sounds in the woods moving away from her. No one had returned to the clearing. She was staring at John's unmoving body, the sign of her grimly failed responsibility. She didn't know who or how many people moved through the forest, but she assumed the men in the blue car had somehow caught up to her, bypassed her as she sat like a fool in her car, and gotten to John and Elizabeth. The only good news was that Elizabeth's body wasn't lying there as well, but the pursuit was obviously continuing. Karen expected any moment to hear another shot. She walked quickly into the thickness of the trees, anxious to catch up. She was Elizabeth's last chance.

Tripwire was moving through the grass, his limbs joyful. The pain from a cut on his face where a branch had whipped him assured him he was alive. He slithered up a tree and looked back along his own trail. His night vision was good and the two thugs coming after him were wearing light jackets and shirts, while Tripwire's clothing was dark. On the other hand, they had guns and he didn't. He had left his mother and it was his job to save her. His grin was savage. The threat of death had settled over him like a protective shawl.

Rick was discovering that he could read a trail. It was a happy discovery for him. He had looked down and seen that the grass was crushed down almost flat. Here in front of him it was rising again, but off to his left it was still stomped down. Clearly someone had passed that way. Rick was delighted with himself. He had hardly been out of the city in his life, and here he was taking to the woods like Davy Crockett. It was even better than the city, where no one left trails on sidewalk. Rick started to call to Danny but then stayed quiet. He didn't want to alert whoever was at the end of this trail. And he wanted to do the job himself. Maybe that would spare him more of Danny's smart mouth. In fact, once the woman was dead and the job done, Rick wouldn't be surprised if Danny had an accident in these dangerous woods.

The trail led him into a more thickly wooded area. Branches hung low enough he had to duck in some places, but he wasn't looking up at them, he was looking down at the ground, following the trail. He was so intent on it he barely heard the light thump behind him. But he stopped and raised his head.

Bryan had dropped out of the tree right behind him. It had worked just as he'd planned, but then for an instant he froze.

As Rick was turning back to him Bryan had no idea what to do. He had reverted to little Bryan Truett, alone in the woods, facing a man with a gun who was about to turn and blow his head off. And he couldn't think how to stop him.

The moment passed before Rick turned all the way around. It had barely been a shadow crossing Tripwire's mind, but for a moment it had frozen him solid. That moment was long enough for Rick to become aware of him and turn. Just as he did Tripwire hit him hard in the throat. It hurt, but the pain wasn't as important as the fact that he had lost his breath and couldn't get it back. Rick still held his gun but it was forgotten in his frantic effort to breathe.

When Tripwire hit him again, in the face, breaking his nose, the gun went flying. Rick didn't even know it. He went down in pain, still trying to breathe, still failing, dwindling away to nothing.

Tripwire moved off in the direction of the gun. He couldn't find it in the dense underbrush and he didn't have time to spare on it. He went back the way he'd come, his senses stretching to find the other armed man. His moment of helplessness was forgotten.

His reunion with his parents had been responsible for that moment. John going down before they could even touch, as if it were the sight of Bryan that had felled him. His mother crying and trying to scratch him, then clinging to him helplessly. He wanted just to hold her in return for long minutes. His identities were hopelessly confused. The continuing danger destroyed his homecoming. But now, moving quietly through the dangerous woods, he felt himself again, the self with whom he felt most at home: Tripwire. That was his real homecoming.

The idiotic heels Karen had been wearing had kept digging into the soft earth, almost throwing her down, so she had stepped out of them and walked on in her stocking feet. Not a good idea in the woods perhaps, but neither was it a good idea to be hobbled by your own shoes. She stood behind a tree, listening. She had a feeling the whole pursuit was moving away from her. She could no longer hear anyone. The reason for that, which she didn't know, was simply that after the initial rush for positions everyone had grown quiet and cautious, listening just as she was. Karen took two more steps to the shelter of another tree and winced as she stepped on the sharp end of a broken twig. She inhaled sharply.

The sound carried in the quiet night. Danny heard it, and turned back. Tripwire, watching him from a tree, cursed silently. Danny had just been on the verge of walking under the tree where Tripwire waited. Danny was more alert than Rick had been, but Tripwire had had position. Now he didn't. Now Danny was turning back and Tripwire had to follow on the ground. He was afraid he wouldn't get the chance to arrange such a good ambush again.

Karen had found a small clearing and was staring into it. She thought a clearing would appeal to men who weren't at home in the woods. She was waiting for someone to walk into it. Standing behind a tree had made her feel like a target, so now she was crouched down, hidden, less likely to be seen. Her left hand was on the tree to steady her, but her balance was still awkward. She touched her other hand, the one holding the gun, lightly to the ground.

And a hard sole came down on her hand, mashing it to the ground, crushing her hand against the gun.

"I'll break your fingers," Danny said. He picked up her gun and put it in his pocket. He was standing above her holding his own gun. Karen thought she was keeping her face expressionless but Danny saw fear. He reached out with his foot and pushed. She lost her balance and fell backward.

A shame, Danny thought. She lay sprawled there on the ground just the way he'd pictured her. It was a shame he didn't have time to do anything but shoot her. He swung the pistol toward her.

There was a noise. Danny crouched and spun to his left, holding the pistol outthrust with both hands. Nothing showed itself; the noise wasn't repeated. Danny relaxed slightly and turned back to the woman cop.

In the moment he had been distracted Karen had moved. Too large a movement would have brought his attention and his gun back to her. She moved only her hands. In fact, it seemed that the hands moved without conscious instruction from her. While Danny had thought he was reading her expression Karen had been reading his very accurately. When he turned away her hands began pulling her skirt up her legs.

Danny turned back to her and stopped.

"I just want you to see I don't have another gun," Karen said. "See? Nothing." Her skirt inched higher.

Danny stood frozen, struck by the terrible dilemma. His problem was that he was not a necrophiliac. His brain raced with the puzzle of how to leave her alive but immobile for the few minutes it would take him to take care of his main business. He would deserve a treat when that was over, and she was the one he had already promised himself.

Danny smiled. It was simple. He stepped forward to hit the girl—lightly, ever so lightly—on the head. She cowered back from him. He smiled more broadly to show her the benevolence of his intentions.

Dark motion burst from the undergrowth behind him. Danny had hesitated too long. Tripwire was on him.

Danny turned quickly when he heard the rushing movement. For an instant the gun was in the air between them. Then Tripwire had slapped it aside and smashed the top of his head into Danny's face. The gun fell into the underbrush, Danny stepped back to remove some of the force of Tripwire's attack, and Tripwire hesitated before rushing him, wondering if he should go for the gun instead.

Karen didn't hesitate. She was already scrambling toward the place where the gun had fallen. It was hidden there, but if she could reach it while the men were distracted—

Danny stepped back from Tripwire, turned, and kicked Karen hard in the side of the head as she tried to get past him. She fell against a tree, stunned.

Then he turned back and Tripwire closed on him again. It was clumsy, inelegant fighting, the kind that results from clear threat of death. There was no time for strategy, clever holds, or the slow motion grace of martial arts. There was only, for both men, an explosion of physical energy, nothing held in reserve because in moments one of them would be dead.

Tripwire leaped at Danny, driving a fist into the pit of his stomach. Trying to end it quickly, he drove his knee upward, but Danny had the presence of mind to close his legs, trapping Tripwire's leg between them.

That gave Danny time to regain his breath. He straightened and slammed an elbow against the side of Tripwire's head. Tripwire bent to the side, taking the impact, shunting off some of it. He wrenched his leg free, throwing Danny momentarily off-balance. Tripwire bunched both fists and swung them into Danny's ribs. It caused Danny to spin a little. Danny used that momentum to lift his leg and kick Tripwire in the knee.

The pain was intense. Tripwire couldn't keep from bending forward, reaching for his damaged knee. He was in perfect position then for Danny to knee him in the face.

Karen wasn't unconscious, but her body didn't know it. She lay with her back pressed against the tree, her eyes open, seeing the fight but unable to move. Her mind was very dim, doing nothing to interpret. She didn't know who Tripwire was. But she knew who Danny was, and that he was not on her side. When she saw him about to violently end the struggle she tried to move, but she seemed to be completely disconnected from her body. Her hands twitched but that was all, and she didn't even feel that.

But the fight didn't quite end as Danny moved in to knee the bending Tripwire. Because Tripwire had overcome the instincts of his pain. He didn't pause when his hands gripped his pained knee. He kept moving his head forward, using the leverage of his arms on his knee to give the movement added force. As Danny came in close, Tripwire drove his head into the killer's stomach.

The breath rushed out of Danny's lungs. He was bending forward as Tripwire straightened, and the back of Tripwire's skull hit Danny's nose with all the force of both their movements.

Danny fell back on the ground, arms sprawling open. His nose felt broken.

That should have been the end of the fight, but Tripwire didn't press his advantage fast enough. The crack on the back of his head had left him momentarily disoriented. The pain in Danny's nose worked to Danny's advantage, keeping him from passing out. He lay there on the ground, but his opponent wasn't coming, and Danny remembered he had Karen's gun in his pocket.

Tripwire started toward him as Danny reached into his pocket, but Tripwire was too slow. Danny's hand touched the smooth metal and he pulled it out. He was grinning through the blood streaming down from his nose, grinning with relief that he was going to be the one to live.

The sound of the shot startled all three of them. Danny looked at the pistol he was holding. It must have misfired when he pulled it out of his pocket, because he didn't think he had pulled the trigger yet. But he was the only one with a gun, so it must have been his that fired.

There was another shot, and Danny was no longer staring stupidly at his pistol. Because he felt the bullet this time. It smashed into his chest and it must have done some damage there but Danny didn't feel it yet. He could still pull the trigger of his own gun and end all this, he thought dimly. And he was trying to do that, pointing the gun at Tripwire who wasn't even looking at him, when the next bullet hit Danny's chest again and the next bullet hit his head, closing his eyes, and there was no more strength in his trigger finger or anywhere else and the world was leaving him behind. Danny wondered vaguely—his last thought—who was doing all the shooting, but it hardly seemed important any more.

Karen was staring upward. She thought maybe she could sit up now and she did, leaning up on her elbows. Tripwire was staring too. They were both watching Elizabeth, standing on the edge of the clearing holding her son's gun with both hands. He had left it with her for protection but instead she had come out of hiding to protect him. Elizabeth had fired all the bullets in the gun now, but she still stood there like a statue, staring at Danny as if he would come alive again. She had an expression on her face that made Karen turn away, not from fear but because she wouldn't want Elizabeth ever to know she had seen that look. It was a mixture of fear and rage and longing that was painful even to look at. When Karen turned her head she saw the same expression on Tripwire's face as he looked at Elizabeth. Karen saw that he was her son. It was very clear in that moment. And it was very clear that Elizabeth had just killed the man who had shot her husband and was about to shoot her son. It seemed perfectly natural to Karen.

The tableau broke apart. When Bryan moved, ever so slightly, toward his mother, Elizabeth dropped her gun and put a hand to her face. "John," she said clearly, and turned and ran. Tripwire shot one fast glance at Karen and ran after his mother.

CHAPTER TWENTY-NINE

*T*wo days later Jerek was looking at a thin sheaf of pages on his desk, almost smiling, thinking how like Karen it was to file a *report* with him. She had taken on a completely informal asssignment, no more than a favor for a friend, really, with no routine and no chain of command, but she didn't feel her job was over until she'd tied up the loose ends for him

Karen had been on his mind even before he received her report. Neither of them had been a model of efficiency, but they had accomplished their main tasks: keeping Elizabeth alive and finding Galvan. They deserved a celebration, some time. He was reaching for the phone when there was a quick knock on his office door and Fred Tyler came in.

Most of their conversation was unspoken.

That was Fred's impression, though from a transcript of what the two men said you wouldn't have guessed anything was different about them except that they were busy men, too rushed to make the little jokes that used to pass between them. But Fred knew things were very different. He could tell it from the way Jerek took his hand off the phone and put some pages on his desk into a drawer while nodding at Fred. In the old days Jerek would have leaned back in his chair and stretched his arms, looking forward to the diversion the FBI agent always provided. Now Jerek remained stiff. So things had changed even though he said, "Hello, Fred," pleasantly enough.

Fred wondered how much things had changed. He knew Galvan hadn't talked about their connection. But he also knew that Jerek suspected anyway. Fred had been the one who called to arrange the meeting at the Fisherman's Market then hadn't shown up. Instead Galvan had been there, waiting to be arrested as planned. After it was all over Fred had told Jerek that he'd heard Galvan was going to be meeting his traitor that day, an assistant d.a. who had worked on the previous Galvan investigation. Fred had been following the d.a. at the time he was supposed to meet Jerek, and didn't have a chance to call. But the d.a. had never gone anywhere. Apparently that had been a false lead, just to see that Fred got Jerek into place where Galvan wanted him. That's the story Fred had told Jerek. It was a good story and Jerek had nodded when he heard it. But not, Fred thought, like a man who believed it implicitly; more like a man who was too busy or too unconcerned to check it out.

And now there was this coolness. Fred didn't climb onto the corner of Jerek's desk the way he used to and sit there reading all the papers. He stood rather nervously, like a job applicant.

"Everything going smooth?" Fred asked.

"Yeah," Jerek growled. "Now."

He sounded gruff, but he always had. Fred would have really felt on the outside if Jerek had been polite to him. Fred experienced what he and every other cop in the world had seen and made use of a billion times: an urge to confess. If he could explain the circumstances he thought he could make Jerek see that he wasn't really a traitor. He'd just been given an opportunity, at a time when every other door had been closed to him, so he was being led down a tunnel. There'd been no question of choice. Galvan had paid for his brother's funeral. How could you fault a guy for taking money like that, at a desperate time when he had nowhere else to turn?

But Fred kept the confession to himself. He knew that Jerek might appear sympathetic, might make understanding noises the way you did to encourage some sniveling child molestor to continue with his confession, but Jerek would never understand how a cop who was worthy anything could do what Fred Tyler had done.

Fred went a little stiff himself. He dropped his hat-in-his-hands pose and took a few steps around the desk in imitation of the jaunty way he used to come into this office.

"Still got your witness all sewed up?" he asked.

Jerek glanced at him sharply and Fred regretted the question.

I don't care where you've got her now, he wanted to say. That was part of the unspoken conversation between Jerek and him.

"Yeah, she's safe. Back home, but not alone."

Fred nodded carelessly as if he hadn't even heard. "And the soldier was really her son."

"He really was," Jerek said. He did loosen up a little then, dropping his pen, leaning back. "I made a mistake there, you know? I just tried to ignore the kid. Galvan tried to use him. He thought maybe the son could lead him to the mother. And it looks like he was right."

The last sentence was said with no more force than the rest, but it sounded louder in Fred's ears. He forced himself to continue looking at a picture on the wall, then turned casually. "You think that's how he found her?"

"I don't see any other way," Jerek was looking penetratingly at the FBI agent. More silent dialogue between them. Fred wondered if that was going to be the official line. Perhaps there wouldn't be any investigation, no dogged pursuit of the traitor who'd been working for Galvan. Fred's punishment was going to be more subtle. It was going to be in the way Jerek and others looked at him, in the way Jerek was talking to him now, as to a reporter rather than to a fellow law enforcement officer. Fred wasn't going to be a part of the fraternity any more. Once in a while a cop would meet him and turn away from Fred's outstretched hand. He'd seen it happen to other guys. It didn't take long before they inspired pity rather than anger. Most of them ended up quitting their jobs, even quitting their lives. Fred thought suddenly of requesting a transfer, but he knew it wouldn't do any good. He knew the way rumors follow a man.

"Well, it didn't do Galvan any good, did it?" Fred said quietly.

"It sure as hell didn't do his own soldiers any good," Jerek said with satisfaction.

Fred remembered the last time he'd had to talk to Danny, how it had made his fists clench. They clenched again now, but he kept personal interest out of his face.

"You know what Galvan's angling for now, I guess," Jerek said.

"Yeah."

"A deal," Jerek said bitterly.

"Well, he is well-connected. I imagine he knows a lot about guys who are a lot more organized than he is, you know."

"I've got an airtight murder case against him," Jerek said, "and they're talking deals."

"Well, it wasn't much of a murder, was it?"

Jerek looked at him coldly. "Probably not his best one, no. But it's the one I caught him at."

Fred shrugged and Jerek softened a little. "It's like the old days around her. Assistant d.a.'s and Justice Department tightasses in and out of here all day long, looking smug like they all know more about what's going on than I do. And talking deals with that— You know, he's probably going to come out of this all right, no matter what? Even if I force him through and get him sent to prison, he'll be the boss of the place in a week. A guy like Galvan, with his money and his sources—"

"I know," Fred said. Jerek looked at him almost apologetically.

"Makes me wish I'd arrested him some place less public," Jerek went on after a moment. "And he'd had a gun, and reached for it. Or maybe I just *thought* he had a gun—"

"Why do you think he picked a crowded place like the Market?" Fred said.

After another pause Fred grinned. "Maybe making a deal will be the best thing for Galvan. You know? Let him testify against some of the really big boys, the ones who hold a long grudge. Can't you see Galvan in a witness relocation program, with a new name on his driver's license, looking over his shoulder all the time, hearing footsteps in the dark every night?"

Jerek smiled. "Try to give that elephant a new identity. Put a blonde wig on him and say, 'Oh it's *you*, Marco. No one'll ever spot you in that.' Him weighing three fifty if he's an ounce. It might not be bad at that. I'd like to be the one guarding him."

"Got him in the basement?" Fred asked, and the unspoken conversation resumed. Jerek looked at him flatly and Fred looked back innocently. The air was heavy with speculation. "I gotta talk to him myself one of these days. He claims to be in touch with two or three guys we'd like to find."

Jerek wasn't doing a good job of trying to look at him neutrally. "Yeah, he's down there. All by himself, when he's not chatting with various lawyers. We didn't want to take him to the county, we don't want anyone near him for a while."

"I understand that," Fred said. He stayed in Jerek's office for a few more minutes but it was all make-believe after that,

Jerek hardly looked at him. When Fred walked out, into the squadroom, he thought he saw already one or two flat stares coming his way, though most of the detectives greeted him as easily as ever. Still Fred walked out feeling depressed, isolated.

Fred seemed a little edgy, Jerek thought, but didn't think much of it. This case had made him suspicious of everyone, but that feeling was dissolving now that Galvan was in custody.

Fred made his way down to the basement. The police station was a solid old building built at the tail-end of the last century when they expected things to last forever. Upstairs the walls were plaster, but down in the basement you could see the stones the building was made of. They were grey now, and smooth. Fred wondered what they had looked like when they were young. Now they had a hunched look as if they had collapsed down on each other, growing stronger and tighter until they looked like something growing out of the earth rather then built by men.

Galvan was in a cell alone with empty cells on both sides. When Fred walked slowly toward him a couple of kids in grey suits were walking away, just finished with an interview. In their sober way they looked excited, and they looked at Fred jealously, like children who didn't want anyone else playing with their new toys. But they walked on out, leaving Fred to approach the cell.

Galvan looked up. Even his casual glances had force, and he was staring at Fred. Fred knew Galvan hadn't talked about him. But he might, later on when he got desperate and was offering anything he could think of. If he was still in custody then.

"Another one," Galvan said. He was a suspicious man, he believed in microphones. But he looked at Fred familiarly. He knew who he was and he was glad to see him. This was the first time they'd ever been alone together, and only the second time Fred had seem Galvan in the flesh. On other occasions he'd just gotten messages, from messengers like Danny or voices on the phone. "The boss would like a favor." And anonymous cash in Fred's mailbox. That was one way you could fool yourself into thinking it wasn't so bad, when the money seemed just to appear out of air, in return for nothing.

But here in Galvan's presence Fred felt his skin crawl. The terribleness of his betrayal struck him for the first time. His betrayal of himself most of all. That he had let this man turn him into something he'd never wanted made Fred almost physically sick now.

He could see how it happened, though, and he could feel it happening again. Galvan's power was palpable. This close to him, in person, you could feel it, like a black-light sunlamp. It wasn't that hard a trick. Galvan's secret was just his absolute confidence in himself and his goals. He never questioned himself. If for a moment your own confidence slipped, like any sane man's would, he'd have you.

Galvan wasn't wearing one of his eternal dark suits. He was in prison grey, a shirt open at the throat showing some pasty skin with black hairs crawling thickly on it. For a moment Fred got a disgusting image of what Galvan's flabby, toneless body must look like and he thought, the way to execute this man would be to strip off his clothes and leave him on the hot sidewalk to shrivel up in the sun like a slug. Maybe pour a little salt on him to speed up the process.

"I suppose you have questions like everyone else," Galvan said, play-acting. He was smiling very slightly at Fred. Fred hadn't said anything to signal him, but Galvan looked at him and knew Fred had gotten the phone call.

It had come just that morning. Mr. Galvan wants one last favor. Fred had listened to that oily voice on the phone offering him more money than his house was worth, enough money to live off for the rest of his life. Galvan didn't like jail. He wouldn't like prison even if he could run it, and he definitely didn't like the idea of testifying against men as ruthless as and more powerful than he was. He had decided he'd rather leave the country after all. It would be better for everyone.

Fred stood there looking at him and began rationalizing. Who would it hurt? Certainly not Fred. Not anyone else, either. Bill Jerek wouldn't like it, but he didn't like Galvan being offered deals, either. Jerek didn't even expect any more to get the kind of justice he wanted.

Fred's line of thought snapped and he saw Galvan looking at him, smiling more broadly. It was happening; standing here with Galvan, feeling that enormous confidence, Fred was wavering. "I suppose you'll want to take me to your office where we can talk more privately," Galvan said.

It was that smile more than anything that made Fred pull the gun out of his belt. The silencer was already screwed in place. Fred thought of things to say like, "I'm getting good at this,"

Or, "History repeats itself," but he didn't say them, he just stood there and let Galvan look at the gun.

"But this is silly," Galvan finally said. "Don't they realize I'm not really going to talk? Didn't anyone tell them that was just a delaying action?"

For a moment Fred didn't know who Galvan meant by "they," but then he realized. Galvan was staring at the gun, apparently talking to it, not even seeing Fred. Even when he looked up into Fred's face he wasn't really talking to him. Galvan didn't even know him.

"I can't outbid the guys you're working for," Galvan said. "No one could. But there's no reason for this. I can pay you on top of what they did and they won't even care, once I've disappeared. That'll be as good as dead to them. Why should anyone suffer?"

Fred marvelled at the question coming from him. And if Galvan had known what he was talking about Fred might have been persuaded by his logic. But Galvan had finally made a mistake. It was the uncertainty more than the hint of fear in Galvan's voice that strengthened Fred's resolve. Galvan finally looked at him, looked at *Fred Tyler* rather than trying to see through him to who was behind him, and saw that resolve. He stood up and stepped close to the bars, putting his hands on them. Fred was very close on the other side.

"Just tell me who's paying you," Galvan said. "Who are you working for?"

"Me," Fred said, but Galvan didn't even hear him. He was lunging through the bars. Galvan was very, very quick. Not just for a big fat man, quick for anybody. It was that confidence in himself, that steady belief that he was always in control. When he moved he had no hesitation. His hand was on the gun before Fred even knew he was moving.

Fred fired, and Galvan's grip on the gun tightened. Fred fired again. The shots made almost no noise with the silencer, and shooting into Galvan's body was like firing into a mattress. The bastard's too padded to die, Fred thought. Now Galvan had the gun.

Fred jerked it upward, ripping it out of Galvan's grip, thrust the gun between the bars and fired right into his face. Galvan finally fell back then. His look of surprise was what Fred savored. He lowered the gun and fired until it was empty. He even clicked the trigger a couple of times after that. Fred's teeth were clenched so hard they might have become welded together permanently. His hand was shaking. Fred dropped the gun inside the cell. If the cops worked really hard and got very lucky they might be able to trace the gun to an arms dealer Fred had arrested three years earlier, but the weapon was supposed to be untraceable and Fred didn't think anyone would work that hard at it. He stared down. The gun had fallen right next to Galvan's hand. Maybe the coroner would take the easy way out and rule it suicide.

No one was coming yet. Fred turned and walked quickly away. He didn't feel any better yet. He felt like crying. But he'd be okay in a while. He'd be okay. The next time he saw Bill Jerek they'd hold another unspoken conversation and that would probably be the end of the legal consequences.

What Fred regretted most was that he'd made another mess in Jerek's jail.

*E*lizabeth tumbled scrambled eggs from the skillet onto the plates. Yellow and white eggs onto the white plates with yellow trim. The colors of sunshine. She set the skillet back on the stove and without looking reached for the pepper, shook some onto the eggs, and set the pepper shaker back in its place. She reached into a cabinet and, again without looking, brought out two juice glasses. Being back in her own kitchen was a pleasure. For the last month she had been reaching for things that weren't there, looking up distractedly to see everything out of the order she expected. Now everything was back in place again.

She carried the plates into the dining room, set them down on the table, and went back for the juice. When she returned Bryan was at the table already eating. Elizabeth smiled at him. She was no longer surprised by his appearances. One morning she had seen him standing at the bus stop across the street, had seen the bus stop and then pull away leaving no one standing there, and five minutes later Elizabeth had gasped at the sight of Bryan standing in the kitchen. But he didn't do it to startle her, she had realized. He just had a powerful aversion to letting anyone know where he was.

"Hi, Mom," he said now, and she touched his shoulder lightly before she sat down.

The remarkable thing was how little Bryan had changed in appearance. His face was still boyish, his hair falling tousled onto his forehead. He was thin as a whip, but she was going to see about that.

There were moments of the day when nothing seemed changed at all. You could maintain that illusion until you looked outside and saw the plainclothes police constantly in attendance.

"Did you ever have real eggs in Vietnam, or just that powdered kind you father used to complain about when he was in the service?"

Bryan smiled. That was the only kind of question Elizabeth asked about his experience, trying to pin down some specific, homey detail as if she could build up the big picture out of such bits.

There were footsteps behind him that drew no reaction from Tripwire, and John walked in. He wore khaki pants and had a fishing cap set jauntily on the back of his head. A cast and sling held his right arm bent and tight against his chest. John had already had his coffee, and that was all he wanted at home these mornings. He had taken to having breakfast at the diner next door to the hardware store, where he was turning into a local celebrity. The sling gave him authenticity and the police officer who stayed near him didn't hurt his credibility either. John was smiling. He was happy to be home, happy to be working. He hadn't lost his new perspective yet, so tiny, simple things like walking out his front door made him happy.

He bent and kissed Elizabeth lightly and she held his free hand for a moment. "Call you later," he said. "Bryan, you taking care of things here?"

Elizabeth had heard them talking late into the night the night before after she had gone to bed. She knew John knew things about Bryan's life the last two years that she didn't want to know. But knowing, or being told, seemed to have pleased John. He too gripped Bryan's shoulder for a minute as he walked past him. Bryan nodded in answer to John's question.

"I might come down to the store later this afternoon," Bryan said casually. John stopped in the doorway and they looked at each other for a short pause.

"If you do I'll put you to work."

Bryan just laughed, and it wasn't until later Elizabeth realized it was the first time he'd laughed since he'd come back; she didn't realize it when it happened because it was as natural and unforced as spontaneous time travel.

Elizabeth did a lot of that lately—traveling in time. Back and forth in memory to the time before Bryan had left, before she'd seen the murder, and ahead to when she would have to testify against Marco Galvan. Now that she was back home with her husband and son it didn't seem believable that that one night had changed their lives.

She was still in danger. She had thought it might end when Galvan was arrested, but apparently it hadn't. He still had a long reach. Captain Jerek insisted on keeping her guarded. There were always at least two plainclothes police, sitting in their car at the curb or prowling around the yard. The first day Elizabeth had invited them in for coffee but it had made them uncomfortable. They weren't like Karen—they didn't want to make friends, they wanted to keep it clear they were working.

The sense of danger worked on Bryan, she knew. He had been to the police station, asking Captain Jerek where Galvan was being held. Bryan could find him if he wanted, he had told the policeman, and Bill Jerek had believed he probably could. But he had steered him gently out and asked him just to take care of his mother. Sometimes Elizabeth had seen Bryan standing stock still, torn, she knew, between staying close to her and slipping out to go on some mission of his own.

She saw him that way late in the morning. She looked out the big kitchen window and Bryan was standing in the middle of the back yard. Looking at him you could have thought he was standing easily, lost in thought, but Elizabeth knew he was coiled and tense. He looked like he could leap straight over the fence in one bound. Elizabeth glanced aside and saw Lois Daniels in her own yard next door. She was slipping into her house, looking back at Bryan almost fearfully. Lois didn't come over the way she used to, and Elizabeth thought it was because of Bryan. Elizabeth was afraid other people too would look at him like something out of place in the neighborhood.

But a minute later she was in the den with her back to the patio door when it slid open and he said, "It's only me." She turned around, straightening, and Bryan was smiling at her.

"All clear," he said, mocking his own sense of mission.

Elizabeth put a hand over her heart to indicate her peace of mind. She was smiling too, but she didn't want to make too big a thing of the easy moment so she didn't go hug him. Bryan flopped down onto the couch in that boneless way that looked so familiar to her. When she could see only the top of his head and his body stretched out he could have been fifteen again, spending a lazy summer day at home.

Bryan would be okay, she thought. They would all be, when this was finally over. If it ever was. Elizabeth was starting to worry about her testimony. For the first time she had begun to doubt she could do it. She would say what she'd seen, certainly, but she didn't know any more if she could be convincing enough. In the rush of subsequent events the night of the murder had receded deep into her memory, its details indistinct. And she was afraid. She kept picturing Marco Galvan watching her with his hard stare while she testified. It seemed wrong, after all this time of hiding from him, that she should have to sit in the same courtroom with him, almost within his reach. He would believe her testimony even if a jury didn't. That would be the worst that could happen, for her to testify against him and have him go free anyway. Even if he went to prison he might harbor a grudge, he might want to demonstrate what happened to people who tried to hurt him.

She knew that was the way Bryan was thinking. It was her own danger that kept him on edge, kept him from settling back into normal life. As long as he had that sense of mission he wouldn't be free of the terrible events of his immediate past.

She made them sandwiches for lunch. It was about that time that Marco Galvan was dying on the floor of his cell, but no one told Elizabeth, or even the cops guarding her. Jerek tried to keep a tight lid on it at first while he investigated. But a reporter for the *Sun* had been the first to see the body. He had made sure Galvan was dead and then had run for the phone without telling anyone, so by the time a policeman discovered the body the story was already being set in type.

Bryan did go off to the hardware store in the afternoon. Elizabeth thought he wanted to talk to John. Elizabeth and John's positions had reversed since Bryan's return, now it was John he could talk to and Elizabeth who produced awkward silences from him. But she didn't mind. She would be happy to see him growing closer to his father, closing a gap of years.

"Don't worry," Bryan said at the doorway, and they smiled at how silly that was. Through the window she saw him stop at the unmarked car and talk to the two plainclothes policemen before walking away. They nodded at him and looked at the house.

Late in the afternoon she made herself a cup of tea. When she was alone the story began to unroll in her mind all over again. Now that she had leisure she couldn't stop herself from thinking how easily she could have kept it all from happening. If she had never taken the books from the office. If she had never gone back that night to return them. If she had just been able to foresee the terrifying results they would have all stayed safe and happy. But Elizabeth was no psychic.

She was wrong about that. She heard a thump at the front door and went to open it. The newspaper was lying there on the step. One of the cops was just getting back into his car. The newspaper boy had thrown the paper onto the lawn and the plainclothes policeman had gotten out and thrown it where it was in easy reach when she opened the door. Elizabeth gave him a wave of thanks. Inside the house, the phone started ringing. She walked toward it, carrying the rolled newspaper that was still warm from the press. It warmed her hands, making her feel strangely comforted. As Elizabeth walked toward the ringing phone and began to pull the string off the newspaper, she had the only psychic moment of her life.

She knew it was going to be good news.

ACKNOWLEDGMENTS

I'm grateful to the people whose hard work has seen this book to publication: Alison Acker, Ginger Barber, Pat Coleman, Patricia Jozifek, Phil Smith; and to Yolanda, who made a home for me while I made this.